THE
GIRL
IN THE
PINK
RAINCOAT

ALRENE HUGHES grew up in Belfast and has lived in Manchester for most of her adult life. She worked for British Telecom and the BBC before training as an English teacher. After teaching for twenty years, she retired and now writes full-time.

THE
GIRL
IN THE
PINK
RAINCOAT

Alrene Hughes

First published in the UK in 2018 by Head of Zeus Ltd

9 7 5 3 1 2 4 6 8

A catalogue record for this book is available from
the British Library.

ISBN (HB): 9781788543965
ISBN (E): 9781788543958

Typeset by Adrian McLaughlin

Printed and bound in Great Britain by
CPI Group (UK) Ltd, Croydon CRO 4YY

Head of Zeus Ltd
First Floor East
5–8 Hardwick Street
London ECIR 4RG

WWW.HEADOFZEUS.COM

For Jeff

1

Everyone hated the heat and the deafening noise, but for Gracie the worst thing was the smell of chemicals that turned her stomach every morning when she arrived at the Rosenberg Raincoats factory. She put on her green wrap-round overall and covered her dark hair with a headscarf tied in a turban and stood looking out at the blackened perimeter wall and high tower of Strangeways prison not a hundred yards away.

'Late again, Miss Earnshaw, and in no hurry to get to your workbench, I see. I'll dock you half an hour for that.'

'But, Mr Rosenberg, it wasn't my fault, honestly. There was this woman – very well dressed, lovely hat with a peacock feather – stepped off a bus, missed her footing, practically fell at my feet—'

'I'm in no mood for your stories this morning.' He put his thumbs under his braces and stretched them. 'Now, get to work. We've had a big order from Kendal Milne for the new-season raincoats and it's all hands to the pump to deliver them before the Manchester rain beats us to it.'

Gracie went straight to her sewing machine, and Maria at the bench next to hers shouted over the noise, 'Did he catch you?'

Gracie rolled her eyes and snapped her imaginary braces, making Maria laugh. Then she started on her first raincoat of the day and was soon singing along with all the other girls. At mid-morning, when the blazing sun was streaming through the skylights, Jacob Rosenberg, the boss's nephew, arrived in the machine room to check production. He was always immaculately dressed in a hand-tailored suit, but this morning he had removed the jacket, and in his pristine white shirt, open at the neck, he drew admiring glances, causing a sudden drop in the work rate.

Every now and again Gracie, towards the back of the room, slowed her machine so she could watch him. He had a ready smile, knew everyone by name and had a quick chat with them as he recorded the number of garments completed. By the time he reached her row she had her head down, stitching at a furious pace.

'Ah, Gracie, making up for lost time, I see.' There was always a smile in his voice, and the hint of a foreign accent set him apart.

She stopped sewing and gave him her innocent look. 'Wouldn't want to let Rosenberg Raincoats down, would I, Mr Jacob?'

He checked her total and winked. 'Knew I could rely on you,' he said.

At midday the workers sat out in the yard, eating: the men who welded the waterproof seams sat in the shade, while the women enjoyed the warmth of the late-August sun. Gracie unwrapped the newspaper from her dinner and passed a bloater-paste butty to Maria who, in return, gave her a roll filled with Italian sausage.

'What are you doing this weekend?' asked Gracie.

'Same as I do every weekend – selling ice cream and sarsaparilla.'

'I thought I might go up to Heaton Park. There's a brass-band concert. Do you want to come?'

'I don't think I can. If this good weather holds, we'll be really busy in the shop.'

'I were up at park last week,' Charlie Nuttall shouted across to them. 'There's a bloody big anti-aircraft-gun placement and a searchlight right in the middle of it. Talk about wasting brass. And have you seen all them shelters they've built round the town? Don't they read the papers at the council?'

'Happen they know summat we don't,' said his mate Ernie.

'Nah, peace in our time, Mr Chamberlain said, and that's good enough for me.'

'Charlie, give over with all the war talk,' said Hilda, who folded and packed the raincoats. 'Hey, Gracie, you haven't told us about the book you're reading this week. Is it a love story?'

'I've only just started it, but I don't think it is. It's about a lad called Pip and so far he's met a prisoner on the run—'

'What, out a Strangeways?' asked Hilda.

'No, this prison's not round here, it's near the sea. Any road, after he meets the prisoner the lad gets taken to a big house and he's there in a strange room...' Gracie paused, all eyes on her. 'It's lit by candles and his eyes pick out a lady at a dressing table in front of a mirror. The strangest woman he'd ever seen. She was dressed all in white, like a bride – satins and silks and a long veil – jewels too.' Gracie mimed the necklace and earrings. 'But Pip looked closer, something wasn't right. The clothes might have been white once, but now they were yellow as parchment. The bride was a withered old woman, just skin and bone.'

'Oh my goodness, what's gone on there?' said Hilda.

'I could guess.' said Maria. 'It reminds me of one of my aunts. She were jilted at the altar, but she kept the wedding dress for her shroud.'

Gracie looked up and caught sight of Mr Jacob standing just inside the door watching her and she turned to the workers.

'Anyway, that's as far as I've got. I'll have to tell you the rest next week.

On cue, Jacob Rosenberg stepped into the yard. 'She's right, time to get back to work.'

Charlie fell into step beside her as they went inside. She could guess why – he was always asking her to go out with him. 'I could meet you at the park on Sunday if you want some company,' he said.

'Nah, you're all right, Charlie.' She laughed. 'I'd sooner spend day at council tip.'

Of all the bedrooms in the Midland Hotel, this one was Sarah's favourite. She went straight to the windows and opened them wide to gaze down at the vast, circular Central Library and across to the buses and cars in St Peter's Square. Then she got to work stripping the bed, leaving the eiderdown, bedspread and blankets to one side and putting the used sheets and pillowcases in the cart. Fresh white sheets, lightly starched, were definitely one of her favourite things. She stood at the end of the bed, tossed the sheet into the air and inhaled the smell of clean linen as it billowed and descended.

Bed made, she moved on to the bathroom. She had never seen one before she came to work at the Midland. In Belfast, where she had grown up, they had had a privy in the yard and a tin bath hanging on the wall, which they brought inside on a Saturday night and filled with hot water. When she'd come to Manchester, it was no different.

The bathroom gleaming, she set out the fluffy towels – so soft, she held them to her face – then placed a tiny Yardley soap in each dish. She ran the Ewbank over the carpet and polished the furniture, checking the writing desk had a good supply of Midland Hotel-headed notepaper and wondering what the guests might write about. Finally, she looked in every drawer and wardrobe and under the bed. The guests left things behind sometimes: a button, a handkerchief, a business card, the faint scent of French perfume... Once, she had found a beautiful silk scarf behind a dressing-table.

At the door she paused. She would never sleep in a room like this, but she made it new again every morning and allowed herself to think that one day her Gracie might rise in the world and enjoy such luxury.

When Sarah had finished her shift, she hurried home. She had left some sheets steeping in bleach that morning and she hoped that the few hours of sunshine left in the day would be enough to dry them. She turned into Pearson Street and the little girls gathered round the rope swing hanging from the lamppost called, 'Mrs Earnshaw, do you want a go?'

She waved at them, 'Not today, girls,' and hurried on.

As usual, the boys were playing football on the croft at the far end of the street, but she was surprised to see a group of women standing close to her house, having a serious chinwag.

'What's up?' she said, then noticed that Doris, her next-door neighbour, was sniffing and wiping her eyes with her sleeve. A few of the others looked close to tears.

'The kids are being evacuated.' Doris waved a letter in her hand. 'They came home today with this and they're going in a week's time. They're taking our kids.'

Another mother shouted, 'We're not even at war!'

'Now, hold on a wee minute.' Sarah's voice was calm. 'Nobody will take your children if you don't want them to go. But just think about it. The people who know what's really going on are making plans to keep them safe. Did you read the article in the *Evening News* last week?' It was clear from their faces that they hadn't. Sarah went on, 'It's very well organised. They'll be evacuated out in the country with decent people who'll look after them. Even their teachers are going. Think of it as a holiday for them. They'll have a great time and if there's no war, well, there'll be no harm done and they'll be back home before you know it.'

Sarah could see them weighing up her words. 'Did they tell you where they're being sent?'

'Ramsbottom – wherever that is,' said Lily, who had four children under ten.

'Well, there you are – there's a train from Manchester to Bury and I think Ramsbottom is near there. You could go and see them easy enough. You know, some children are being sent to Wales – a different country. At least yours'll be in the same county.'

The women looked thoughtful and she hoped they would mull it over and, while they were all together, she decided it would be a good time to mention something else. 'I've been thinking about shelters,' she said. 'Not many of us have the room for an Anderson in the yard and the nearest public shelter's on Oldham Road. I thought I'd ask the landlord at the Foresters Arms if we could use his cellar. It'll need a good clean, of course. What do you think?'

There were nods of approval, and Lily joked, 'That'll suit my Wilf down to the ground. He spends his days down the pub, might as well sleep there too!'

But Doris was crying again. 'It's really going to happen, in't it? We'll get bombed.'

Sarah put her arm round Doris's shoulders. 'Don't worry, sure it'll be fine. Look on the bright side – without the kids you'll have half the washing, cooking and cleaning to do and a nice cosy cellar to shelter in if the bombs start falling.'

2

Sunday afternoon was warm and sunny, and after dinner Sarah announced that she was going to whitewash the outside privy. 'If there's going to be a war, I want to make sure all my affairs are in order.'

Gracie looked at her mother, shook her head in disbelief and convulsed with laughter. 'What? What?' was all she could say.

'You know what I mean,' said Sarah. 'I wouldn't want anybody to talk about me if we're bombed.' By now Sarah knew how ridiculous she sounded and started laughing as well. 'Anyway, do you want to help me?'

'No, Mam. The last thing I want is to spend a lovely day in a lavatory. I think I'll change my clothes and go out for a bit. I'll be back for my tea.'

It was a fair walk from Oldham Road to Heaton Park, but Gracie didn't mind. It was good to be out in the fresh air, to leave behind the streets of two-up-two-down terraces and find herself in the leafy suburbs. She wore her Sunday best – blue floral cotton frock and cardigan with a matching ribbon in her dark hair. She strolled under the colonnade that marked the entrance to the park and joined the crowds of people enjoy-ing the warm sun and a holiday atmosphere. If anyone was concerned about the threat of war they certainly didn't show it.

The lake was crowded with rowing boats and she stopped to watch the antics of four lads who couldn't work out how to stop the boat going round in circles. Then she set off up the long drive towards Heaton Hall, a large and impressive Georgian house. To the right of it was a high vantage point topped by a little temple. She climbed the hill and looked out over the park from where she could see the anti-aircraft gun and searchlight that Charlie had described. The encampment was well dug in and surrounded by a wooden fence. Two soldiers stood on guard. The gun was much bigger than she had imagined and the thought of it in action made her shudder.

In the distance to the north and east were the mills of Bury, Rochdale and Oldham. To the south, as far as the eye could see, were the factories and canals of Manchester and Salford, and to the west, on this clearest of days, Gracie fancied she could see the port of Liverpool. Above her the sky seemed huge and for a moment she imagined it full of enemy planes.

'It's an impressive weapon, isn't it?'

She turned. Jacob Rosenberg was at her side. 'I suppose so, but I hope to God they never have to fire it.'

'I'm afraid they probably will, Gracie, and sooner than we think.' He went on, 'The news is bad today. The papers are saying we'll be at war this time next week. Just think, we could be enjoying the last Sunday of peace for a long time.'

'Well, that's put a dampener on the day, hasn't it?' said Gracie.

'Oh, I'm sorry, forgive me.' There was the lovely smile that brightened her working days. 'Let me make it up to you,' he said. 'How about an ice cream?'

They walked down the hill together, and Gracie couldn't help wondering why he was in the park and, of all the people there, he had ended up standing next to her. 'It seems a bit of a coincidence that you're here today,' she said.

'Not really. I often have a walk here on Sunday afternoon. I only live up the road.'

'So you didn't hear me say I was coming here?'

He pretended to be surprised. 'Why would you think that?'

She had the feeling he was teasing her, but she wouldn't let him get away with it. 'I know you watch me at work when you think I'm not looking,' she said.

'Ah, but that's because you watch me when you're supposed to be stitching raincoats.'

She opened her mouth to protest, but he was already laughing. 'Let's just say we keep an eye on each other. But today's different, isn't it?'

'Is it?' she said.

'Of course it is. We're not in the factory. It's just you and me out for a walk in the sunshine. So, how do you want to spend our time together on the last Sunday of peace?'

They went to look at the Hall, walking around the outside and peering through the tall windows at grand fireplaces, huge dark paintings of people long dead, an elegant table that would seat half of Gracie's street. 'It would have been such a bustling place at one time,' said Jacob, 'with carriages sweeping up the drive bringing the cotton barons to dine.'

Gracie's eyes lit up. 'Yes, and the lady of the house, in an Empire-line gown, embroidered with pearls, and long white evening gloves, would have stood at the foot of the sweeping staircase waiting to greet them.' She ran up the steps outside a French window and struck a pose. Jacob followed her, playing along, bowing low.

'Welcome, Mr Rosenberg,' she said, in her poshest voice, 'and how is the raincoat business?'

'Thriving, ma'am, thriving.'

'And, tell me, do you treat your workers kindly?'

'Indeed I do, ma'am, especially the pretty ones.'

She frowned. 'So, you have an eye for the ladies, have you?'

'I wouldn't say that.' He took her hand and brought it to his lips.

Gracie pretended to be shocked and looked up at him under her eyelashes.

'I shouldn't have done that, should I?' he said.

She laughed. 'Don't be daft, Mr Jacob, I'm just play-acting.' But she was surprised to feel her heart racing.

'Oh, you can't call me Mr Jacob when we're not in the factory.'

'No?'

'I'm just Jacob.'

She put her head to one side, pretending to study him. 'Just Jacob, I like that.'

They wandered through the rose garden, heady with scent, and into a shaded woodland walk. 'Do you like working at the factory?' he asked.

'Not really. Some days I think there's not much difference between us and them down the road in Strangeways.'

'Come on! My uncle's not that hard a taskmaster, is he?'

Gracie pulled a severe face and mimicked her boss: 'Miss Earnshaw, I don't pay you good wages for clowning around when there's raincoats to be stitched.'

Jacob threw back his head and laughed. 'You should be on the stage, Gracie.'

Back on the main path, Jacob bought them ice-cream cornets and they went to sit on a bench under a chestnut tree.

She studied him closely: his dark hair a little longer than most men's, strong nose and chin and, when he turned to look her, the darkest of brown eyes. 'I've not seen you wearing the little cap before,' she said.

'The kippah... Jewish men cover their heads to honour God. I don't usually wear it, but I've just been to shul, that's my church, for a meeting and, well, it's expected.'

'And the way you speak, is that Jewish too?'

'My accent, you mean?'

Gracie nodded.

'In a way... I grew up in Germany, but I've been back and forward to England every few years, sometimes London then Manchester, learning the family business. I was supposed to go back to Germany a while ago, but...' He looked away.

'But what?' asked Gracie. She saw his jaw tighten and it was a moment before he answered.

'I wanted to go back, but my parents thought I should stay here. Now is not the time to be a Jew in Germany. As we speak, thousands are fleeing the country, frightened for their lives.' He shook his head. 'It's a bad business.'

Gracie would have asked him to explain, but he looked so sad. After a minute, he checked his watch and his voice was brighter when he said, 'Come on. It's almost time for the concert.'

The bandstand was lower down the hill, set in an amphitheatre of grassy banks where people were sitting around, waiting for the music to begin. Jacob took off his sports jacket and spread it on the ground. 'There you are,' he said, and they sat down so close together their arms touched.

Besses o' th' Barn brass band, resplendent in their uniforms trimmed with gold and red, were straightening their music stands and playing random notes by way of a prelude.

The conductor stepped up, raised his baton, and the band members put their instruments to their lips. The baton fell, and the air was instantly full of the rich sound of brass. The programme of patriotic music lifted everyone's spirits, and at the end of the concert the conductor invited the audience to sing along to 'There'll Always Be An England'.

'Oh, you won't know the words,' said Gracie.

'It doesn't matter,' said Jacob. 'I'm happy just to close my eyes and listen to you.'

The day had turned chilly by the time they left the park and they stood together under the colonnade before they went their separate ways.

'I'm glad I came out for a walk today,' said Jacob.

'So am I,' said Gracie, and she thought he might kiss her, but then he frowned.

'Gracie, when we're back at work tomorrow...'

Instinctively, she knew. 'I understand,' she said. 'I won't say anything.'

'It's just that...'

Gracie touched his arm. 'It's all right, don't worry.'

Jacob took her hand and held it. 'Thank you. I'll see you tomorrow,' he said, and she watched him go.

On the long walk home, her thoughts were full of Jacob. He was nothing like other lads she knew: he was funny and sad, confident and shy and so very, very handsome.

At the bottom of Cheetham Hill, not far from the raincoat factory, she was surprised to see a ragged procession of people walking towards her up the road. Men with long black coats and high-brimmed hats, women in dark clothes with their hair covered, several with a baby tied in a shawl across their bodies. Closer they came, too weary to look about them, carrying bundles or battered suitcases. But it was the sad-eyed children

13

trailing in their parents' wake that touched her: a little girl in what was once a pretty party dress now ripped and stained; a boy with ringlets hanging in front of his ears and a little round cap on his head.

Gracie's heart went out to them for she knew at once that they were Jews and they had travelled a very long way to get to Manchester.

3

Gracie awoke to the sound of crying, and it was a moment before she realised it was coming through the paper-thin walls of the house next door. Then she remembered it was Friday morning and still Doris had not come to terms with her children being evacuated. She lay for a while, watching a shaft of sunlight coming through the gap in the curtains, and when the crying was replaced by the squeals and laughter of excited children, she got up.

By the time the children were ready to walk to school, a crowd had gathered in the street to see them off. Gracie and Sarah stood next to Doris as she held back her tears, hugged her two little girls and told them to be good and to write every week. An older boy, John Harris, took charge and it was clear that the evacuees had been drilled for this moment. At his command they left their mothers and lined up like little soldiers, with their gas masks and belongings, each with a brown luggage label fastened to their coat. Gracie scanned their faces: some were filled with excitement, others apprehensive;

and little Gladys Clark, with no mother to see her off, was sobbing her heart out.

John raised his hand and all eyes turned to him. 'One... two... three!' he shouted, and what happened next made the hair stand up on the back of Gracie's neck – the children began to sing.

'Farewell to Manchester we're leaving today,
We need a safe place where we can stay,
Away from the bombs that fall on our heads,
Where we'll sleep soundly and safe in our beds.'

Off they went, filling the street with the sweet sound of their voices, and all the composure that the mothers had struggled to maintain dissolved in an instant. 'Heaven's above,' said Gracie. 'I never expected that.'

'I tell you,' said Doris, 'every school in the city has been practising that for the last week. Mine have been singing it every night. Is it any wonder I'm in this state?'

The women waved until the children turned the corner at the end of the street.

'I can't believe they've gone,' said Doris. 'What will I do without them? I could cry me eyes out.'

'You can't mope,' Sarah told her. 'The best thing is to keep occupied.'

'Hah, like stitching those bloody blackout curtains, you mean.'

'Have you not done them yet?' said Sarah. 'You know it's tonight?'

'I do, but it won't matter if I haven't finished them, will it?'

'Of course it will. Sure you don't want to be the only house in Manchester showing light when the blackout begins, do you?'

'Right, I'm off,' said Gracie. 'If I run all the way I should get to work before the hooter goes. If I don't, the boss'll likely give me my marching orders.'

Gracie had kept her word by not telling anyone about meeting Jacob – she had even told an outright lie when Maria asked if she had gone to Heaton Park on Sunday. But as the week went by she had felt distinctly slighted by him. There was no friendly smile when he checked her raincoats and she never once caught him watching her. Then, late on Friday afternoon, she spotted him going into the haberdashery storeroom. She quickly checked that Mr Rosenberg was not on the factory floor, then left her machine. Jacob was up a stepladder at full stretch hauling a box off the top shelf. He had no idea she was there. She couldn't resist it – a couple of strides to the ladder, and she gave it a shake. It rocked from side to side, Jacob let go of the box to save himself and jumped down. Seconds later they were both showered with horn buttons as big as pennies.

'Gracie! What did you do that for? I could have broken my neck.'

She laughed. 'That'll teach you to ignore me.'

'Shush.' He lowered his voice. 'Nobody must know about us.'

'Us? Even I don't know about us,' she said.

Just then, Mr Rosenberg appeared in the doorway. 'What's going on in here?'

'Sorry, Uncle, bit of an accident. I was getting something from the top shelf and I overbalanced.' There was a stifled laugh from Gracie.

Mr Rosenberg glared at her. 'And what are you doing here, Miss Earnshaw?'

'Well, you'll never believe it but—'

Jacob intervened: 'Miss Earnshaw was walking past and she came in to help me pick everything up.'

It was then Mr Rosenberg noticed the buttons all over the floor. 'A farthing apiece, those best horn buttons – gather them up this instant.'

When he had gone Gracie and Jacob looked at each other and laughed. 'You're incorrigible,' he said.

Gracie wrinkled her nose. 'Is that good?'

'No!' Then he shrugged his shoulders. 'Well, maybe in your case, yes.'

'So, you like me, then?'

'I didn't say that.'

Gracie pouted and blinked, as if she was going to cry.

'Oh, Gracie, I'm sorry. Look, I probably shouldn't say this, but I haven't stopped thinking about you since Heaton Park. What if I asked you to meet me again?'

Gracie's smile said it all.

'Can you meet me on Sunday at seven outside Lewis's?' he asked.

'Where are we going?'

He tapped the side of his nose. 'It's a surprise.'

'All right, I'll see you then.' She turned to leave.

He called after her, 'Where are you going? You have to help me pick up the buttons.'

'Oh, I think not.' She laughed. 'People might talk.'

The raincoat factory closed early on Fridays for the Jewish Sabbath, and because Gracie was the first home, it was her job to make the tea every Friday – always the same meal: meat and potato pie with red cabbage. While the pie cooked she sat on the back doorstep in the sunshine reading a copy of *Tit-Bits*. She liked the letters page, the stories and the film reviews best. Maybe Jacob would take her to the pictures on Sunday.

'All right for some who can sit and read, while the rest of us have to slog.' Sarah stood in the doorway.

'Never mind, Mam. You'll get your reward in Heaven and a nice potato pie for your tea.'

Sarah dumped the string shopping bag of library books on the table. 'I'm jiggered. We'll have to start reading thinner books.'

'If you're tired go and have a lie-down. I'll shout you when your tea's ready.'

Upstairs Sarah took off her shoes and rubbed her aching feet. She felt drained, but that was more to do with the worry of the letter in her handbag than a hard day's graft. The postman had given it to her that morning when she'd met him in the street. One look at the handwriting and she'd almost thrown it away unopened, but something had stopped her. After all, she told herself, Jean had been a good friend to her all those years ago when they were growing up in Belfast. They had kept in touch for a while after she had left Ireland and moved to Manchester, but then the letters, Christmas cards and, eventually, the friendship had petered out.

She lay on the bed and tried to clear her mind, but she kept seeing Jean's face in front of her, looking just as it did all those years ago when they were girls together. 'Oh, for goodness' sake, just read it!' said Sarah, out loud. She took the letter from her bag and tore it open. Typical of Jean, the letter was short and straight to the point. As she read it, she could hear her friend's voice in that long-forgotten Belfast accent. 'Your da is dying and he's asking for you.'

Sarah went to the window and looked out over the roof-tops and chimney pots. This was where she had built her life, surrounded by good friends and neighbours. The girl who had left Belfast all those years ago didn't exist anymore and, in her mind, neither did the people she had left behind.

Just then Gracie called from the bottom of the stairs that the tea was nearly ready, and she shoved the letter back into her handbag.

'When are we putting up the blackout curtains?' asked Gracie, as she dished up the pie.

'Well, the streetlights will come on at the same time as last night, just before nine o'clock,' Sarah explained. 'So the sooner we get them up the better. Then we'll switch on the lights in the house and go outside to wait for the blackout so we can check there's no light showing.'

'I heard everybody in the street'll be outside waiting for the moment when the lights go out. It's so exciting,' said Gracie. 'They say you won't be able to see your hand in front of your face.'

'I don't know why you're making such a drama out of it,' said Sarah. 'We're going to be without any streetlights for God knows how long, and by the end of next week you'll wish you'd never heard of the blackout.'

Just before nine the neighbours were outside. After a few minutes the lights came on and everyone cheered. It was a balmy evening and they stood around chatting while they waited for the practice blackout. There was plenty of banter about what might happen in a blackout, and Billy from the tripe shop on the corner was telling the sort of music-hall jokes that weren't suitable for mixed company.

It was nearly ten o'clock before Doris appeared. 'Did you get your curtains sorted?' asked Sarah.

'Did I 'eck as like!' Doris's voice was strained. 'And that Lily Roper says anybody showin' a light'll be put in jail.'

'Not on the first night they won't. They're just trying to get us used to it. Anyway, if your curtains aren't right I'll—'

Suddenly they were plunged into darkness: Doris screamed; some people laughed; others cheered. But within half a minute all sound had ceased and the people of Pearson Street looked upwards to a sky as black as a coal shed. Slowly, their eyes adjusted to the darkness and they began to distinguish shapes. It was then that a reedy voice, instantly recognisable as that of Albert, Sarah's next-door neighbour, began to sing, '"Pack up your troubles in your old kit bag..."' and everyone joined in. At first, they didn't see the thin beam of light at the bottom of the street, but the piercing whistle drew their attention. They could discern only the dark outline of a man carrying a torch, shaded so the light fell downwards. 'What's all this noise?' he shouted.

'Is that you, Ted?' said Billy.

'Aye, it is and I'm here to tell you there's lights showing at the back of three houses in this street. The ginnel looks like a landing strip. You'd better get them seen to or I'll have to report you to the peelers.'

'For Christ's sake, why would you do that?'

'Because it's my responsibility as ARP warden to make sure you lot observe the blackout regulations.'

'Trust you to be first in the queue to throw your weight around,' said Billy.

'And trust you to talk tripe like you sell in your shop!' Ted stalked off, taking the light with him.

Billy laughed. 'Anyone fancy a pint down the Foresters, if it hasn't been commandeered for Ted's headquarters? Come on, Sarah, I'll treat you to a port and lemon in the snug.'

'Not tonight, Billy, but can you do me a favour and remind the landlord that the women will be there early in the morning to clean out his mucky cellar.'

'I will, that's if I can find my way there in the dark.'

'I'm sure you'll manage it,' said Sarah. 'Just follow the smell of beer.'

Sunday morning dawned bright and clear, but Sarah's spirits were low with the thought that the country could be at war by the end of the day, not to mention the ache in her back from all her efforts yesterday at the pub, clearing out rubbish and scrubbing away the dirt and grime of decades.

She had just finished her wash at the sink when there was a knock at the door. It was Albert, looking shaved and well-scrubbed, wearing a collarless shirt and his funeral suit all shiny at the elbows. 'Just been to the paper shop for me *News of the World* and they told me the prime minister is to speak on the wireless at quarter past eleven this morning.' He sucked on his few remaining teeth. 'It doesn't bode well, if you ask me. Thought I'd let you know that the pub will be open if you want to hear what he's got to say?'

Sarah sighed. 'What's to become of us, Albert?'

'Chin up, lass. We gave the Hun a bloody nose last time and we can do it again. I'll see you down there.'

The smell of breakfast cooking was enough to get Gracie out of bed. 'Ah, you can't beat bacon and egg on a Sunday. Who was that at the door? They woke me up.'

Sarah handed her the breakfast, then set the teapot on the table and covered it with a cosy. 'Albert,' she said, and cracked another egg into the pan. 'Letting us know there's going to be an announcement on the wireless about the war. So, when you've had your breakfast, get ready and we'll go to the pub and hear what Mr Chamberlain has to say.'

'Do I have to?' Gracie moaned. 'I want to wash my hair. I'm going out tonight.'

'Oh? And where are you going?'

Gracie giggled. 'Guess.'

Sarah was busy with the egg and the spitting fat. 'Gracie, just tell me, will you?'

'I'm meeting Jacob Rosenberg.'

Sarah took the frying pan off the gas and turned to face her daughter. 'Is that wise?' she said.

'What do you mean?'

'Well, you know… different religions and all that.'

'For goodness' sake, Mam, it's just a date.'

'Hmm. Well, don't say I didn't warn you.' She slid the egg on to her plate. 'Anyway, you can wash your hair later, so you can. It's important to hear what the prime minister has to say this morning because it'll change our lives and I want you to know why. So, no arguments, you're going.'

The Foresters Arms was a red-brick building on a corner plot. Inside there was the vault where the men drank, no women allowed, and a snug where women and men could drink together. The wireless sat on the bar between the two. The snug was chilly, despite the sunny day outside, and the smell of stale tobacco hung in the air. Sarah and Gracie nodded to the few women already there and sat down at a table. Mary, the land-lady, made them welcome with a spread of sandwiches and cups of tea from a large tin pot. 'It's the least I can do after all your hard work in the cellar yesterday,' she said.

As the minutes ticked away towards the announcement, the

pub began to fill. As usual there was plenty of noise from the vault, but the few women in the snug talked quietly among themselves, or listened with half an ear to a talk, 'Making the Most of Tinned Food', on the wireless. At eleven fifteen the pub fell silent, and moments later the prime minister, his voice tired and sad, began: 'I am speaking to you from the Cabinet Office...The British ambassador in Berlin handed the German government a final note... I have to tell you now that no such answer has been received and that consequently this country is at war with Germany...'

In the vault someone swore and in the snug someone sobbed. Then the National Anthem blared out, too loud after Chamberlain's sombre tone, and startled some of the listeners. Next to Sarah a woman stood up, then another and another, and from the vault came the sound of singing. Soon everyone was on their feet and joining in. As the last note died away there was a sudden ear-splitting noise and everyone froze. Billy was the first to realise what was happening. 'It's the air-raid siren! We're being bombed. Get into the cellar quickly!' Everyone found their wits and their voices, running and pushing to get downstairs to the safety of the pitch-black shelter.

4

'Mam, are you sure there's enough hot water to rinse my hair?' Gracie asked for the third time, as she sat in the tin bath in front of the fire.

'Aye, of course there is. I've told you already.'

'But I want it to be really shiny.'

'You've used enough of that coal tar soap, but we'll give it a final rinse with vinegar. That's as much as we can do.' Sarah took the pan of water off the stove and tested the temperature with her elbow. 'Right, cover your eyes.' She poured it over Gracie's head. 'How's that?'

'In my eyes!' cried Gracie.

'Ach, well, the next one'll wash it out.'

When Gracie's dark hair was squeaky clean she stepped out of the bath and her mother handed her the warm towel from the fireguard. Then there was the painful ritual of teasing out the knots and tangles. Finally Gracie, in her candlewick dressing-gown, took her book and sat in front of the fire to dry her hair.

It took her nearly as long to decide what to wear on her

25

first proper date with Jacob because she had no idea where he would take her. On a Sunday night not everywhere was open and it was quite likely plenty of places would be shut because of war being declared. She hoped they might go dancing and kept imagining what it would be like when he held her in his arms. Or they might go to one of the better pubs where they could spend the evening getting to know each other better. In the end, she decided that her navy dress with the peter-pan collar would look smart wherever they ended up.

She stood in the kitchen doorway and asked, 'How do I look?'

Sarah put down the book she was reading and smiled. 'Lovely, and your hair's so shiny.'

'Ah,' said Gracie, 'I think we overdid the vinegar – I keep getting a whiff of it.'

'Never mind,' said Sarah. 'Once you're out in the fresh air it'll go.'

Gracie caught the bus to Piccadilly and went to stand outside Lewis's department store. There were several people on their own, just like her, and she watched each one as their date arrived, imagining their stories: the accountant with the shorthand typist who hadn't known each other long; the factory worker and the shop girl who had saved up almost enough to get married; the couple in their thirties, married, but not to each other.

The minutes ticked by and she began to wonder if he was waiting at one of the other entrances. She was about to walk round the corner to see if he was there when she spotted him running across the road. He was frowning as he dodged a bus. His tie had blown over his shoulder and his hair had fallen forward. In one graceful movement he pushed it back. Then he saw her and his smile made her catch her breath.

'Thank goodness you're still here,' he said. 'I'm sorry I'm late. I had to help my uncle—'

'It's all right. I knew you'd come.'

He nodded and looked pleased. 'Come on then, it's not far.'

She hoped he might take her hand or, at the very least, offer his arm, but he did neither. He was more concerned about the outbreak of war and talked non-stop all the way to Shudehill. 'We'll be bombed for sure,' he told her. 'Next to London, Manchester is one of the biggest industrial cities, with its aircraft factories, engineering works, food-processing plants, you name it – everything needed to supply the armed forces. And, as if that wasn't enough, my uncle's worried about his business.'

Gracie looked at him. 'But he makes raincoats.'

'Yes, but the factory is owned by a German family.'

'You mean—'

'If we're lucky we'll get some abuse, maybe a brick or two through the factory windows, but who knows what'll happen when the fighting starts?'

Gracie was shocked. 'But your family's been in the city for such a long time, nobody could think they supported Hitler, especially when Jewish people are fleeing Germany because of the way they've been treated.'

'Ah, Gracie, not everybody has a heart as kind as yours.' His mood seemed to lift. 'You look lovely,' he said, and took her hand. 'I like your hair.'

At the top end of Shudehill they stopped outside a narrow four-storey building with a façade of brown glazed tiles. 'Here we are,' he said, and Gracie had just enough time to look up at the pub sign – the fearsome, swarthy face of a man with a jewel in his ear, wearing a huge turban and, below it, 'Turk's

Head' painted in gold. It was packed inside with the sort of rough-and-ready types her mother wouldn't have approved of, and Jacob read the disappointment on her face. 'Don't worry, it might look a bit seedy but I'll get us some drinks and then we'll go upstairs.' He left her to go to the bar.

With the smell of drink, the swearing and raucous laughter, Gracie began to feel uncomfortable. A man in the corner, puffing his pipe, caught her eye and beckoned her over. She quickly looked away. Jacob had seemed so respectable, why would he bring her to a place like this? She noticed a sign on the wall 'Rooms upstairs', glanced at the door and thought about leaving, but then he appeared at her side and handed her a glass. 'I got us some lemonade; I hope that's all right. Let's go upstairs.' He took her arm, but she pulled back. 'What's the matter? I promise you'll enjoy it.' Then he saw the look on her face and understood. 'Oh, Gracie.' He laughed. 'You didn't think...'

'What's upstairs, Jacob?'

His face lit up. 'Just the most wonderful music you'll ever hear and some dancing, if you like, but I have to say I'm not much of a dancer.'

The room was dimly lit by candles stuck in green bottles on each small table. At one end there was a raised stage with an upright piano, a snare drum and a microphone. In front of it was a small dance-floor. Several people were already seated, and Gracie was pleased to see that, in contrast to the bar below, they were chatting quietly. She was reassured to see some well-dressed women among them. A few men acknowledged Jacob as he led her to a table near the stage.

'You've been here before?' asked Gracie.

'I'm here most Sunday nights. It's one of the few places where you can listen to jazz in Manchester.'

At that moment a spotlight lit the stage and the pianist and drummer took their places. They were followed by a thick-set black man, carrying a trumpet, who drew enthusiastic applause. Jacob leaned towards Gracie and whispered, 'Leroy Skinner – he's the nearest thing you'll get to Duke Ellington this side of the Atlantic.' Gracie had never heard of Leroy Skinner and had no idea who Duke Ellington was, so she said nothing.

The applause died down, the piano played an introduction and the snare joined in. Leroy moved to the beat, with one hand tapping the trumpet against his leg, the other softly clicking his fingers. He licked his lips, brought the trumpet to his mouth and blew. It was a sound such as Gracie had never heard. It reverberated inside her, and each note that followed was so unexpected that at first she couldn't discern a tune. But still she was drawn to it. Jacob leaned towards her, his breath on her ear. 'Just relax and let the music take you.' Slowly what had seemed like discord emerged into discernible patterns, changing like a kaleidoscope in her brain. The tunes came and went, and she wondered how she had lived twenty years without ever hearing music like this.

In the interval Jacob left to get them some more lemonade while Gracie went to powder her nose. She studied her face in the cracked mirror on the windowsill: her skin was flushed, her eyes were bright, and she couldn't help smiling. There would be dancing after the interval.

Jacob was talking to some lads around his age when she came back. She would have joined him, but as soon as he saw her he left them.

'You didn't have to leave your friends,' she said.

'I know, but I just want to be with you.' He moved his chair closer to hers. 'Tell me, did you really like the music?'

'I did.'

'And would you come here with me again?'

'Of course.' Gracie saw the tenderness in his eyes. 'I'd go anywhere if you asked me.'

At that moment the performers returned to the stage and this time they were accompanied by a woman in a tight-fitting black dress and black evening gloves who went straight to the microphone. Leroy counted them in and, on cue, she began to sing, in a husky voice, 'Dream A Little Dream Of Me'.

'Will you dance?' asked Jacob.

Gracie had been to the Ritz and other ballrooms plenty of times with her friends. She liked the lively dances; the foxtrot and the quickstep were best. If a lad liked you he would choose a slow dance, but you had to be careful because some of them just wanted to touch you in a way they shouldn't.

'Yes, I will,' said Gracie, and gave him her hand.

He held her close, but there was gentleness in his touch. She rested her head against his shoulder and they moved together to the slow rhythm of the song. Her fingers were on his neck and she wanted to stroke it. She felt his hand on her back and longed for him to caress her. He stepped away a little and she looked up to see him smiling down at her. 'How am I doing?' he said.

'Fine, so far, but I'll have to make sure you get more practice.'

He laughed and swung her around just as the music ended, then pulled her close to him and held her for a moment.

The light was fading when they left the Turk's Head. 'Where do you live?' he asked.

'About twenty minutes up Oldham Road. I could run it in fifteen minutes and get there before it's completely dark.'

'Or I could walk you home and we'd have another twenty minutes together.'

'But you'll be in the dark then.'

'Not at all.' He patted his pocket. 'I've a torch to light my way and the memory of dancing with you to keep me company.' He took her hand and they set off. 'So, what do you really think about jazz?'

'I love it,' said Gracie. 'I'll never forget tonight.'

'I remember when I first went to a jazz club,' he said. 'It was when I lived in Berlin, and my father took me. I must have been about sixteen. That sort of music was very popular in Germany, but the clubs are probably all gone now. I don't know…'

They walked a while in silence, and Gracie thought about Jacob coming to live in England. 'Can I ask you something?' she said.

'Of course.'

'What was it like to leave your home and come to a strange country?'

'It wasn't easy,' he said. 'People are wary of you. You might look different, sound different, and all you want to do is to fade into the background. You keep your head down, try to become invisible.'

'And do you forget the place you left behind?'

His voice was strong. 'Never. You carry it with you. You'll always be different, but you wouldn't have it any other way.'

When they reached Pearson Street Gracie stopped. 'I live just down here. You don't need to see me to the door. There's still a bit of light.'

Jacob looked about him and pulled her into a nearby shop doorway. She felt his arms around her, sensed the dip of his head as he bent towards her. His kiss was warm and gentle on her lips. His hands caressed her, then suddenly his kiss was urgent and Gracie felt her stomach tighten with the pleasure of his body against hers.

'Eh-up! What've we here?' They quickly pulled apart. 'Well, if it ain't our Gracie with a fella in m'shop doorway.'

Gracie grabbed Jacob's hand and pulled him out into the street. 'Sorry, Billy, we were just—'

'Aye, lass, I know what you was doin'.' He put his key in the door. 'Watch out your mam doesn't catch you.' They could still hear him laughing when the door was locked and bolted.

'I'd better go now,' said Jacob, and stepped back from her. 'I really enjoyed the evening.'

'So did I.' Gracie desperately wanted to be kissed again, but she knew it would be wrong to reach out to him.

'I'll see you tomorrow,' he said.

'Yes, and thank you for tonight.' But Jacob had already turned away and she didn't catch the words he called over his shoulder. The whole evening had been wonderful... the music, his kiss... She had thought he liked her, but it was as though he couldn't get away from her quickly enough.

She ran all the way to her front door and let herself in. The light was on in her mother's bedroom and she went in to say goodnight.

Sarah put aside her book. 'Did you have a nice time?' she said.

Gracie told her about the jazz club and the music.

Sarah pulled a face. 'Doesn't sound like a respectable place to me.'

'Oh, but it was. The people there weren't rough at all and Jacob knew some of them.'

'And what about Jacob?'

'What do you mean?'

'A Jewish lad whose family owns a factory, he sounds well-to-do. I'd have thought he'd be going out with girls, you know, like himself.'

'Mam, I've been out with him once. We're not getting married or anything.'

'Well, that's all right, then. Just don't let yourself down. You know what I mean?'

Gracie rolled her eyes. She knew quite well what her mother meant. 'Yes, Mam.'

5

The more Gracie thought about it, the more annoyed she became. The evening with Jacob had been lovely, but at the end he had spoiled it by rushing off, just because Billy made one of his silly jokes – and that was exactly what she would say to him when she got the chance.

She clocked in on time on Monday morning and went to change into her overall. She had just come into the cloakroom when someone was saying, 'Bloody nuisance having to carry it everywhere with you.'

'But handy to keep your lipstick in,' said someone else. It was then Gracie noticed that on every peg around the room there hung a cardboard box.

'Oh, Hell's bells,' she shouted. 'I've forgotten my gas mask.'

'You'd better go home and get it,' they told her.

'What – and lose an hour's pay? I don't think so.'

When they went through to the factory floor, Maria didn't waste any time in questioning Gracie as they set up their machines. 'So how was your date with, em… What was his name again?'

Gracie smiled. 'You'll not catch me out like that.' She began to thread her machine.

'Well, tell me all about it – the whole story.'

Gracie pulled the thread through the needle and, without looking up, she said, 'It was nice. We went to a jazz club, had some lemonade and a couple of dances. That's all.'

'That's all? But what about after that? Did he walk you home? Did he kiss you?' Maria pouted and made a kissing sound.

Gracie took an unstitched sleeve from the pile and lined up the seam. 'Yes and yes.'

Maria's eyes opened wide. 'And how was it?'

'It was nice,' said Gracie, matter-of-factly.

'Is that it? Nice? I thought you'd have lots to tell me.'

Gracie shrugged her shoulders, pressed the pedal on her machine and it roared into life.

As the morning wore on she kept a lookout for Jacob, but he didn't appear and neither did Mr Rosenberg. 'Why are there no bosses around this morning?' she asked Maria, at tea break.

'I heard they're out drumming up business,' said Maria. 'There's talk of clothes rationing and there'll probably be a rush to buy before it's introduced. They'll want to step up production to sell as many as they can before then. The commercial traveller is going all over Lancashire and Cheshire. Mr Rosenberg is down at the cloth wholesaler's placing an order.'

'And what about Mr Jacob, where's he?' asked Gracie.

Maria looked around before leaning over to her. 'He was supposed to be in charge, but then he had to go to London. I heard Ma Rosenberg say it was family business.'

Gracie was so disappointed that Jacob had gone away. At Heaton Park he'd said he had worked in London. What if he'd gone back there to work? She might never see him again.

'Are you all right?' said Maria.

Despite the turmoil in her head she gave her brightest smile and kept her voice light. 'Of course I am. Why wouldn't I be?'

The morning wore on and, without any supervision, the production slowed. There was a fair amount of chatting, coming and going to the lavatory and nipping into the yard for a crafty fag, but nobody took more advantage of all three than Charlie and his mate Ernie. At dinnertime in the yard Gracie told the story of the evacuees leaving home, describing how, when they'd lined up, they'd sung 'the saddest song you've ever heard' as they marched away.

'Aw, bless them,' said Hilda. 'I tell you, if I could get my hands on that Hitler fella, I'd give him what for!'

'Good on ye, Hilda,' shouted Charlie. 'You'd only have to sit on him and he'd surrender.'

For a large woman, Hilda was quick on her feet and she crossed the yard before he had stopped laughing at the extent of his wit. However, the punishment she would have meted out to him instead of Hitler never happened because at that moment one of the welders appeared with a gas mask box in one hand and a large pair of pink knickers in the other.

'Who the 'ell's been at my gas mask? I had five Park Drive in it! All they've left me is a pair of bloomers.'

Hilda's face turned the colour of her knickers. 'Them's mine!' She moved even quicker to retrieve them than she had to threaten Charlie moments before.

'Not so fast,' said the welder, and he held the knickers up in the air.

Hilda attempted a few jumps to retrieve them but he was too tall for her. 'What you doin' with my gas mask?' she demanded.

'It isn't yours. It's mine. I left me fags in it.'

'No, it's not, it's mine and I left me spare knickers in it. See, there's my name on the bottom.'

There were shouts from some of the men: 'Go on, Hilda, show him your bottom!'

The welder glared at them and turned on Hilda. 'It were on my peg.'

'No, it weren't, it were on mine!'

By this time, everyone was laughing, none more so than Charlie and Ernie, and then the penny dropped.

'You buggers!' shouted Hilda. 'All that sloping off this morning when you were supposed to be working. How many other gas masks have you switched?'

'Stop moaning, woman,' said Charlie. 'It'll take at least half an hour to sort them all and that's half an hour we don't have to work.'

As the week passed, there was still no sign of Jacob. Gracie went from longing to see him to wanting never to set eyes on him again. One minute she completely understood that he had gone to London on family business, the next she was certain he had left Manchester in a hurry because he didn't want to see her. It was just the same as when he had rushed away from her on Sunday night, only now he'd gone all the way to London!

In the early hours of Friday morning the good weather broke. Thunder and lightning rolled in and rain rattled the windowpanes. By the time Gracie got up for work, her mother had lit the gas oven to warm the kitchen while they got washed.

'The tea's brewed and there's bread and the last of the bramble jam you can have,' said Sarah.

'It's coming down in stair rods – I'll get soaked,' said Gracie.

'What did you expect? It was bound to break sooner or later,' said Sarah.

When Gracie arrived at the factory, looking like a drowned rat, she was surprised to see the workers standing around in the machine room. Not just machinists, but welders, cutters, Hoffman pressers, packers... even the office staff.

'There's a meeting called. Mr Rosenberg wants to speak to everyone,' Maria told her.

'Are we in trouble?' asked Gracie.

'I don't think so. I saw him come in earlier and he looked a bit puffed up, you know, like when he's managed to get thirteen raincoats out of a bolt of cloth meant for twelve.'

There was a bit of a stir at the far end of the room near the offices and Mr Rosenberg appeared with his wife beside him. He held up his hand and the room fell silent. 'I want to speak to you today about some changes to the business. Over the past week we have managed to secure some important contracts and as a result Rosenberg Raincoats will be expanding. We will be manufacturing a new design that will be in shops not just in Lancashire but in London too.' He paused, a smug look on his face, as if he expected a round of applause, but there was none. He hurried on: 'But that's not all. The big news is that, alongside the fashion wear, we have been commissioned to supply heavy-duty waterproof clothing to the military. Mr Jacob has been in London working hard to secure this government contract and I'll ask him now to explain what it will mean for all of us.'

Gracie couldn't believe it. Jacob was back. She hadn't noticed him standing with the cutters, and now he was about to address them all. How smart he looked, every inch a businessman, one who went all the way to London to meet with the government. How clever he was. And she longed to tell them that he had held her in his arms and kissed her.

He began by saying he had assured the Ministry of War that his employees were both hard-working and skilled. 'I told them that Manchester has been the home of raincoat manufacturing for at least fifty years. Our designs and production levels are second to none. We have already acquired the empty premises next door, and over the next few weeks it will be fitted out with new machines to deal with the heavy garments for the military. We will also be taking on extra staff.'

Someone called, 'Happen the company will do right well out of this war work.' It was Charlie. 'What about the workers?' he said. 'What's in it for them?'

Before Jacob could answer, Mr Rosenberg intervened: 'We've always looked after our employees. You will continue to be paid a decent wage and I'm sure there will be plenty of overtime for those who want it.'

Charlie tried to come back at him, but Mr Rosenberg held up his hand. 'It's early days. Our priority is to get production up and running and that's expensive. Now, let's get back to work, everyone.'

At the tea break, there was plenty of talk about the new contracts. A few like Charlie complained that it would mean working harder for no more money, but most were proud to do something for the war effort. Hilda summed it up when she said, 'There's plenty of them at Trafford Park building tanks and the like, but now we're part of this war effort and, to my way of thinking, keeping soldiers dry is just as important.'

Gracie listened with only half an ear to the talk and concentrated on looking out for Jacob. He had gone straight to the office after the meeting, and as time went on she became desperate to speak to him. Just before dinnertime he emerged and walked the length of the machine room, his face blank, and, although she willed him to look at her, he never once glanced in her direction. He didn't normally leave by the back door and, for a moment, she wondered if he meant her to follow him. It would be risky, they might be seen, but how else could he get the chance to speak to her?

'Are you all right?' said Maria.

'What?'

'You look like you've downed tools, but there's another ten minutes till dinner.'

Gracie wasn't listening. 'I'll be back in a minute.' There was no one in the corridor outside the machine room. The door to the cloakrooms was open, but no one was inside. Out into the yard she went, just in time to see Jacob leave by the back gate. She was about to run after him, but the memory of how he had turned away from her on Sunday night stopped her. It was clear he had no intention of speaking to her and her hopes of another date with him were dashed.

'Are you going out with your mystery boyfriend again this weekend?' asked Maria, as they left work.

'I don't think so. I haven't heard from him.'

'Never mind. Plenty more fish in the sea.'

'Maybe there are, but they're all slimy sprats,' said Gracie, and turned to go. 'Ta-rah, see you Monday.'

'Hang on,' Maria called after her. 'There's something caught in your gas mask. It looks like it's been opened. Did you have something in it?'

'Not likely after Charlie's antics,' said Gracie, She pulled out the piece of paper. 'It's a note. It says "Meet me outside Victoria station at eleven o'clock Sunday morning."'

'Who's it from?'

Gracie turned the paper over. 'It doesn't say.'

'It'll be Charlie playing tricks again,' said Maria.

'I wouldn't put it past him. He's always asking me out.' Gracie managed a smile. 'Any road, it doesn't matter who it's from. I don't expect to be summoned like that by a fella who can't even be bothered to put his name to it. It could be Charlie or anyone else. Either way, I won't be there.'

That evening after they had washed the pots, Gracie and Sarah sat in the back kitchen reading their library books as usual when Gracie suddenly remembered there had been a letter for her mother on the mat when she arrived home. 'I forgot all about it. I just put it behind the clock.'

Sarah's heart sank at the sight of Jean's handwriting.

'Who's it from, Mam?'

Sarah didn't answer, just opened the envelope and removed the single sheet of writing paper. She scanned it, returned it to the envelope and, with a flick of her wrist, threw it into the fire.

Gracie jumped up. 'What did you do that for?' Instinctively she tried to rescue it from the flames.

'Leave it!' shouted Sarah.

'But who's it from?'

'It doesn't matter.'

'It does! Look at you, you're shaking. Is it bad news?'

Sarah covered her face with her hands and tried to push away the feelings of hurt and resentment that threatened to overwhelm her after all these years.

Gracie knelt beside her. 'Will you not tell me?'

Sarah removed her hands. There were no tears, just anger in her eyes. 'It's from someone I knew years ago in Belfast – a neighbour. We wrote to each other for a while after I left Ireland, but then we lost touch. She's only writing now because she thought she had to share some bad news, but she needn't have bothered.'

'Bad news?' said Gracie. 'What's happened?'

'My father died.'

'Oh, Mam, I'm so sorry,' said Gracie.

'Don't be. I haven't seen him or heard from him in twenty years. Sure, you know that.'

'But he's your dad and my granddad.'

Sarah looked away.

'You've never talked about him, have you?' said Gracie. 'Not even when I was small and asked you what he was like.'

Sarah felt the old hatred rise, like bile, in her throat as she remembered her father dragging her by the hair and throwing her out into the street with just the clothes she stood up in, yelling names after her that wounded like knives. She would never tell anyone about that, least of all her daughter. But, on the other hand, she wouldn't pretend that her father was a good man. Maybe it was time Gracie knew something about her grandfather.

'You want to know what he was like? Well, I'll tell you. He was a hard man, so he was. No compassion at all, ruled the house with a rod of iron and drove my mother to an early grave. By the time I was your age I was desperate to leave. One Friday I collected my pay after work and, instead of going home, I went to the docks and bought a boat ticket to England. I've never been back.'

'I thought you came to England because you couldn't find work, then met Dad and fell in love with him. That was why you never went back, wasn't it?'

Sarah gazed into her daughter's concerned face and the anger seeped away. 'Yes, that was it and then, best of all, I had you. My little Lancashire lass, your dad used to call you.'

'Will you not go over for the funeral?'

'There's no point. The man's dead and, anyway, I can't afford to lose two or three days' pay.'

6

Gracie slept late on Sunday morning. She had been tossing and turning in the night, thinking about the grandfather she had never met and now never would. She had always known he existed and that, besides Mam, he was her only relative, yet she knew nothing about him beyond his name and that he lived across the Irish Sea... until now... Now she knew Mam hated him, which made her realise how little she knew about her own father. She had been five when he'd died and had only a vague memory of him tossing her up in the air and catching her, making her squeal in delight. There was also the photograph of him in uniform that Mam kept beside her bed. When she was growing up she would sometimes ask to hold it. Then she would search his serious face, looking for something she recognised.

She yawned and sat up in bed. No need to rush: Sunday was a lazy day – a bit of ironing, some reading, a nice roast dinner with apple pie. Then she caught sight of the scrap of paper on her dressing-table mirror – the mysterious note in the gas mask. Curious, she stepped out of bed on to the cold lino and ran on tiptoe to retrieve it.

The words still grated – summoning her without any of the niceties of an invitation. What a cheek! She turned it over and saw that it was a scrap of a blank invoice, but no clue there. She read the message again and was about to put it aside, when she saw it…

She jumped out of bed and shouted downstairs, 'What time is it, Mam?'

'Just after ten.'

'Will you boil me a kettle for a wash? I'm going out.'

It was five past eleven by the station clock when she arrived at Victoria, but rather than walk under its iron and glass canopy she crossed the road so she could observe from a distance the people waiting on the pavement outside. To her disappointment there was no one she recognised – it must have been a joke, after all. She was about to turn away when she saw him come out of the station, very smart in a blazer and grey flannels. She saw him smile and wave and went to meet him. 'Hello, Jacob,' she said.

He kissed her cheek. 'I'm so glad you've come. I owe you an apology for not letting you know I was going to London. I'd sent a tender to the War Office hoping to win the contract for military waterproofs. I never thought we'd get it, but out of the blue they asked me to go to London to discuss it. I was in meetings for four days.'

'It's all right,' said Gracie. 'It's good that you went and got the contract for us.'

He took her hand. 'But never mind all that, I'm so glad you're here. I thought we could have the whole day together, maybe go to Blackpool. What do you think?'

For a moment, Gracie hesitated. She hadn't told her mother she would be out all day, but she didn't care. To spend a day with Jacob was all she wanted in the world. 'That would be lovely,' she said.

Together they queued for tickets. 'I love trains,' Gracie told him. 'They're so exciting. I love the noise, the steam and the slamming doors, being locked in.'

Jacob looked down at her animated face. 'You're such a romantic,' he said.

'Am I? Is that good?'

'I think so.' He squeezed her hand. 'Have you been to Blackpool before?'

'A long time ago when I was seven or eight, I think. Mam took us out for the day. I remember it was Whit week and we went on a chara.'

'A what?'

'A chara – charabanc, you know, a coach.'

'Was it good?'

'Rained all day, but it didn't stop us going on the sands.'

The train was already in the station and the platform was crowded with people. Some were boarding, others wandering along, looking in each carriage for window seats or seats together. Several were rushing the length of the train to be near the engine. Jacob took her elbow. 'Quickly, there are seats in here.' He helped her into a carriage. Within minutes the doors were shut, the stationmaster blew his whistle, dropped his flag and the train, wreathed in smoke, chugged out of the station.

Jacob leaned towards her. 'Bit of a rush. Are you all right?' Gracie nodded. Then he lowered his voice. 'I'm so glad you're here. I was worried you wouldn't see my note.'

'I saw it, but I wasn't sure it was from you.'

Jacob looked surprised. 'Do you get lots of notes from men asking you out?'

Gracie giggled. 'No, but you didn't sign it. It could have been from anybody.'

'I didn't want to risk putting my name on it. Anyway, why did you come if you didn't know who it was from?'

'I read the note again this morning and I noticed the clue you left in the corner.'

Jacob laughed. 'Ah, you recognised my tiny drawing.'

'I thought it was just a scribble, but when I looked closely I could see it was the little Jewish cap you wore when we met in Heaton Park. Even then I wasn't sure. That's why I was standing back, waiting to see who would turn up. If it hadn't been you, I'd have slipped away.'

'Would you really?'

'Oh, yes,' said Gracie, 'but I so wanted it to be you.'

At Blackpool station the crowds swarmed off the train and they followed them to the promenade. The day was bright, with a blustery breeze off the sea, but there were plenty of people on the beach in deckchairs, children riding on the donkeys and a few hardy souls swimming in the sea. They wandered on to the North Pier – a cast-iron structure with little hexagonal shops selling souvenirs and Blackpool rock. Close to the entrance there was a kiosk with velvet curtains at the windows and photographs outside of famous people, all of them with the same woman.

'It's a fortune-teller,' said Gracie, and peeped through the open doorway. It was dimly lit, but she glimpsed a little room towards the back where a dark-haired woman sat at a lace-covered table.

'Do you want to have your fortune told?' asked Jacob.

'I can think of nothing worse!' said Gracie. 'Where's the fun in knowing what's going to happen to you?'

'Ah, but she might warn you to stay away from a tall, dark, handsome man.'

'Oh, I think I'll take my chances,' said Gracie, and put her arm through his.

Further down the pier they stopped to look back at the town to get a good view of Blackpool's famous landmark. 'It's a bit like the Eiffel Tower,' said Jacob. 'I'm impressed.'

'Have you seen the Eiffel Tower?' asked Gracie.

He shook his head. 'Only in pictures, but one day I'd like to go to Paris.'

'Me too,' said Gracie.

'We could go together.' Jacob laughed. 'But today, it's Blackpool and, if I'm not mistaken, that's a carousel near the end of the pier.'

There was room for the two of them on the brightly coloured horse and, as he climbed up behind her, Gracie was aware of how close his body was to hers. Lively music blared out, and it began to move, slowly at first, but soon they were whirling around. Faster and faster it went, and now the horses moved up and down. The sea… the beach… the Tower… the people… They flashed again and again before her eyes.

'Do you like it?' Jacob shouted, above the music.

She looked back over her shoulder. 'I love it!'

They left the carousel and went to look at the Pavilion Theatre at the end of the pier. 'There might be a matinee,' he said, 'but that would mean we'd get back to Manchester quite late.'

'And we wouldn't see as much of Blackpool,' said Gracie, but what she really meant was that she wanted to be with him to enjoy his company, not stuck in a dark theatre.

'You're right, another time maybe. Do you like the theatre?' he asked.

'I don't know. I've never been.'

'You've never been to the theatre?'

'No, but I've been to the pictures hundreds of times.'

'But that's not the same thing at all. Seeing a play on the stage is wonderful. You get drawn into the drama, and the people aren't on a screen – they're right in front of you, living and breathing every moment. I've been to plays so intense that I've forgotten where I was. It's as though I'm inside the story. I'm part of it.'

Gracie looked at him in wonder. He was so different from any other lad she'd met, the things he said and the way he would suddenly be excited about something, like the jazz and the plays. 'You really love it, don't you?' she said.

His eyes were bright. 'Gracie, you would love it too, the way words can make you weep or laugh, make you angry or fearful. I wish I could...' He stopped himself.

'Tell me,' she said. 'What do you wish?'

He looked a little embarrassed. 'It's nothing, just a dream, really.'

'Tell me,' she said again.

He looked out over the sea, as though he was recalling a desire buried deep and never before spoken aloud. 'One day I'd like to write a play.'

Gracie stared at him in awe. 'You could do that?'

He gave a nervous laugh. 'I don't know. Maybe, if I found the right story... full of drama, tragedy... love.'

Gracie was struck by how little she knew about him. His good looks and friendly manner in the factory had attracted her, but every time they had been alone together, she had glimpsed another side to his nature that was sensitive and passionate. 'I think you could do it,' she said.

All at once he was confident and outgoing again. 'Well, who am I to argue with that? Now, it's time we had some fun. What do you want to do next?'

She pointed into the distance at the far end of the promenade. 'I think that's the Pleasure Beach – you can just see some of the rides. Can we go there?'

They strolled along the packed promenade from the North to the South Pier, and with each step Gracie felt she and Jacob were getting to know each other. The more he talked, the more she liked him. They stopped on the way to look in a souvenir shop and bought some rock. Then Jacob made her wait outside. 'I want to buy you something,' he said, and when he came back he handed her a small box wrapped in brown paper. 'Put it in your bag. You're not allowed to look at it until you get home.'

'What is it?'

'I'm not telling you. It's a present to remind you of the day we went to Blackpool.'

At the Pleasure Beach, he asked, 'What do you want to go on?'

'The Big Dipper,' said Gracie.

He looked up at the rollercoaster towering above them. 'I might have known. I don't suppose I could wait here while you risk life and limb?'

'Of course not! There's no point riding a rollercoaster if you haven't got someone to be frightened with.'

Up close, the structure looked decidedly rickety, with criss-crossing iron beams and struts bolted together. Jacob seemed worried, but Gracie pulled him on to the carriage and they waited, fastened in and squashed together, until everyone was on board. The steep climb was slow as the carriages strained towards the summit with a steady clack-clack. There was time to look out across the bay, glistening in the sun, and the concrete blocks scattered over the beach to repel invaders. When it seemed they could go no higher, they crested the slope and for a split second were suspended… then plunged head first in a rush of wind and deafening noise, unable to draw breath, but finding a scream ripped out of them. Seconds seemed like minutes, and all they wanted was for the terror to end. A brief respite on the level, then they were whipped round tight bends to face another climb – only this time they knew what to expect and their panic was unbearable. Twice more they completed the circuit before the carriage glided to a stop and, with pounding hearts, they were released. Back on the ground, their legs unsteady, they clung to each other, laughing.

'I can't believe you made me do that!' Jacob exclaimed.

'Now you've done it, it'll be easier next time.'

He looked at her, aghast. 'Gracie, I am never doing that again.'

But there were plenty of other rides to go on and, when they tired of spinning round, they headed for the Fun House to put pennies in the slot machines. At the door a crowd was gathered in front of a glass box with a life-sized dummy inside – a large, jolly man in an ill-fitting suit wearing a bowler hat. Suddenly he jerked, his mouth opened wide and he began to rock from side to side laughing fit to burst, and the crowd laughed, too, until they were howling. Gracie laughed so much she cried. At first Jacob managed a smile, but when he looked at her he couldn't stop himself and joined in. Then, as quickly as it started, the mechanical laughter ceased and the man was still.

It was a moment or two before Gracie could speak. 'My sides are sore – I've never laughed so much.'

Jacob was smiling. 'Oh, Gracie, watching you laugh like that… you're so beautiful.' He pulled her towards him and kissed her – right there on the street. 'What do you think about that?' he said.

Gracie pulled a cross face. 'It was about time you kissed me. I was seriously thinking I'd have to buy a kiss-me-quick hat!'

'No need for that,' he said, and kissed her again.

Gracie wondered if this might be the moment to ask him about their last date. 'Jacob... the night we went to the jazz club and you were kissing me, why did you suddenly rush off?'

The laughter left him, and he stared at the ground. Her heart sank. She shouldn't have asked, and now she'd spoiled the whole day.

When he raised his head, she saw only kindness in his eyes. 'It was a lovely evening at the jazz club,' he said. 'I really enjoyed your company and I thought that kissing you was the right thing to do.' He paused as though choosing his words carefully. Gracie waited. 'Our first kiss was sweet, and I had to kiss you again... Then, forgive me, Gracie... I'd never felt such passion before and it wasn't fair on you...'

Gracie wondered if she should be shocked, but the gentle words had no harm in them, and it was clear that he really did like her. In her modesty, she didn't know how to tell him that she had felt that rush of passion too. So she stood on tiptoe, closed her eyes and kissed his cheek.

Later, they found a little café and had fish and chips with mushy peas, a pot of tea and bread and butter, sitting by the window watching the world go by.

'There are a lot of men in uniform about the town,' said Gracie.

'They'll be from the air-force base near here,' said Jacob. 'I noticed the control tower from the train and what looked like a new hangar. There'll be a camp too, probably camouflaged, and a lot of intense training going on.'

Gracie noticed that the man on the next table was staring at Jacob, listening intently.

'We're not far from the Liverpool docks either, so the navy—'

Gracie interrupted him: 'Maybe it's time we got going,' she said, but the man was already on his feet and moving towards Jacob.

'And who are you,' the man demanded, 'sittin' here discussin' an air-force base and where it is and what they're doin' there?' His breath smelt of drink.

Jacob shrugged his shoulders. 'I'm just someone visiting Blackpool.'

'You're not English, though, are you?'

'You don't have to be English to come to the seaside.'

'No, but a German might come here to spy on us.' The man looked around him at the other customers, making sure they had heard him. 'I think we should report you to the police.'

Gracie was horrified, but Jacob stood up and faced his accuser. 'That would be a mistake,' he said. 'Let me explain. I'm not a German. I come from Switzerland, a neutral country, and I've been living in Manchester for quite a while. I'm a businessman, and my company has just signed a contract with the British government to provide supplies for the armed forces.'

The man narrowed his eyes. 'Why would I believe that?'

Before Jacob could answer, Gracie began to cry. 'He's not a German, honestly, I can vouch for him.' Her face anguished, she turned to the other customers. 'We only got married yesterday, and we're on our honeymoon,' she sobbed.

A woman with bleached hair and bright red lipstick shouted, 'Eh, love, don't fret yerself. This daft apeth wouldn't know a German if he fell over one.' There were murmurs of agreement from the other customers.

'He doesn't look like a German, does he?' said another woman.

Gracie tugged at Jacob's arm and begged. 'Can we leave, please?'

'Of course,' said Jacob, and squared up to the man. 'Report me to the police if you like. We'll be in the Tower ballroom if they want to speak to us.'

Outside Jacob took her hand and they walked quickly away. When they were sure no one had come after them, they crossed the road and sat in a shelter at a tram stop. 'Gracie, are you all right?'

'Yes,' she said.

'You were pretending?'

She raised an eyebrow. 'Well, we're certainly not on our honeymoon, are we?'

'I'm so sorry you had to experience all that.'

'It's happened to you before, hasn't it?'

'A couple of times, but that was the worst. The man would really have called the police if you hadn't done what you did.'

'So you tell them you're Swiss?'

'It's easier than trying to explain that not all Germans are Nazis.'

How sad he looks, thought Gracie. His shoulders seemed less broad; his face was drawn; his eyes were closed. She reached out and pushed back the lock of hair that had fallen over his forehead.

He turned to her. 'I wanted this to be a lovely day when we would get to know each other better.'

'It has been a lovely day,' said Gracie. 'I don't care about that stupid man.'

'Oh, it could have been worse, believe me. Sometimes they don't bother calling the police.' He gave a half-hearted laugh. 'Thank God I'm a fast runner.'

'That's terrible,' said Gracie. 'You should be reporting them.'

He put his arm around her and drew her close. 'Gracie, I hope you know how I feel about you, but I'll understand if you don't want to see me again.'

Gracie pulled away from him, shocked. How could he think she would be so shallow? 'I don't care where you were born. I know you'd never do anything bad. All I care about is that we like each other.'

Jacob nodded. 'You're right. That's all that matters.' He gave a deep sigh. 'Would you like to go to the Tower now? I can promise you there won't be any police there.'

But the warmth had gone from the sun and grey clouds were scudding across the sky.

'No, let's go home,' she said. 'All this fresh air has made me tired.'

Back in Manchester they made plans to meet again. Jacob told her he would be away in London for a week or two. 'There's a lot to sort out with the contract,' he told her, 'but I'll write to you as soon as I get there, and again when I know I'm coming home. I wish I didn't have to go.'

'So do I, but you'll be back soon and we'll be together again, won't we?'

'Yes, Gracie.' He kissed her tenderly, but when he drew back she reached up and pulled him towards her again. His kisses thrilled her and she wanted to stay in his arms for ever. She had never felt like that before.

'Gracie, I have to go now,'

'Not yet... please.'

He held her tight and kissed her again. Eventually he took her arms from around his neck. 'I have to go, my darling, *mein*

Liebling.' Gracie's eyes glistened with tears; she couldn't trust herself to speak. Jacob traced her lips with his finger. 'I'll soon be back,' he said, and then he was gone.

7

The weather grew colder as September slipped by, and every morning when Gracie left for work she hoped a letter from Jacob would be waiting for her when she got home. Jacob had written to her a week after he'd left for London – a letter so full of love that she cried. He called her his *Liebling*, wrote that he longed to hold her in his arms and kiss her, and couldn't wait to see her again. She kept the letter hidden at the back of her dressing-table drawer along with the snow globe of Blackpool Tower, the souvenir he had bought for her.

October brought misty mornings, the first frosts and the slow withering of leaves but no word from Jacob. One day when she arrived at the factory a lorry was parked outside the new premises and a group of men were standing around smoking. One shouted, 'Y'all right, sweetheart?' Gracie ignored him and there were a few wolf whistles – she ignored them, too, and slipped through the gate into the yard.

Maria was in the cloakroom, putting on some lipstick. 'Did you see them fellas out there?' she said.

'I didn't take much notice. What's going on anyway?'

'It's the new machinery for the army contract. I was chatting to one of them, Tommy, the tall one with blond hair, did you see him?'

Gracie wasn't interested. 'Can't say I did.'

'He's got the foreman's job next door in Rosenberg Waterproofs.'

'What?'

'Rosenberg Waterproofs, that's what they're calling the new factory. Tommy told me all about it, says he'll have it up and running in a week. He's in charge of everything and you'll never guess…' Maria giggled '… he asked me if I'd like to transfer to work under him!'

Gracie was sceptical. 'He won't be in charge. Mr Jacob's the one who got the contract and he'll be managing everything.'

'So why isn't he here, then?' Gracie had been asking herself the same question for weeks. 'If you ask me,' said Maria, 'I don't think he'll come back from London.'

Gracie turned on her friend. 'Why are you saying that?'

Maria lowered her voice. 'Because I overheard Ma Rosenberg talking to that miserable typist in the office. "You can't beat a good matchmaker. I'll warrant Jacob will be engaged before Hanukkah." That's what she said – heard it with my own ears.'

The words were like a knife in Gracie's heart. She opened her mouth to deny Maria's gossip, to yell in her face that it couldn't be true because she knew Jacob was longing to come home to her. He'd said so in his letter. But she swallowed the words and turned away to hang up her coat and blink back her tears. 'Good luck to him,' she said, and busied herself tying her turban.

At the workbench she went through the motions of setting up her machine in a fog of despair. She might never see Jacob again and, even if she did, it wouldn't be the same, knowing that he loved someone else. The voice of reason in her head told her to pull herself together: she hardly knew Jacob, for goodness' sake. She'd only been out with him three times. But, really, that was irrelevant because, from that first kiss in the shop doorway, she'd known she would fall in love with him and had dared to hope that he felt the same.

Gracie stitched collars all morning and at tea break she didn't join in with the usual banter between the machinists, most of it concerning the men who would be working next door. At dinnertime, Maria put on some more lipstick and announced that she was going outside for a breath of fresh air. 'Are you coming with me?' she asked.

'Why would I do that? It's freezing out there.'

Maria just laughed.

'Oh, I see,' said Gracie. 'It's the blond fella, in charge of everything, isn't it? Well, you won't catch me standing out there like a very cold gooseberry.'

By the end of the week the new premises had been cleared out, given a coat of distemper and a connecting door to the main factory. By the end of the following week, thanks to an advert in the *Manchester Evening News*, it was fully staffed. Charlie was made senior cutter, Maria machine supervisor, and she had talked Gracie into transferring too.

The new sewing machines were heavy-duty and the thick material was difficult to handle. Every night during that first week Gracie went to bed exhausted, with aching arms. On the Friday when they left work Maria seemed overexcited. 'Isn't it great that Tommy persuaded Mr Rosenberg to keep the new premises open all day on Fridays? You'll have another five shillings in your pay packet this week for working till five o'clock tonight.'

Gracie managed a nod. She was growing a little tired of hearing how wonderful Tommy Holt was, but there was no escaping it. Maria linked her arm. 'I've something to tell you.' Her voice was bubbling with excitement. 'You know I've been having a lot to do with Tommy these last two weeks, getting the machinists up to speed and the like? Well,' her voice quickened, 'he's asked me to go out with him.'

'There's a surprise,' said Gracie.

'He wants to take me dancing at the Ritz ballroom tomorrow night.'

'I'm sure you'll have a great time.'

'Hmm,' said Maria. 'The only problem is, I don't think Papa will let me go. You know what he's like when it comes to lads.'

'You don't have to tell him. Just go.'

'I was thinking, Gracie, that you could come with me. It's ages since we were last out together. My father likes you, he thinks you're sensible, and he doesn't mind when I go dancing with you.'

'I don't feel like going out. To tell you the truth I'm so tired, I just want to sleep all weekend. Can you not ask somebody else?'

'I thought you'd like to come. It might cheer you up, you've been so miserable lately.'

'No, I haven't!'

Maria gave her a hard stare. 'You're as miserable as sin and I can guess why. You haven't mentioned that lad you went out with a few times. The one you were so secretive about. It's time you went out and had fun. Please come, Gracie. You could stay the night at my house – we haven't done that for ages. And Tommy's mates will be there too. You might meet a nice lad.'

'I'm not interested in lads,' said Gracie, 'and I don't want to go dancing.'

Maria looked close to tears. 'Please come, Gracie. Otherwise I won't be able to go. Will you not do it, just for me?'

'I'm sorry, Maria. Don't upset yourself.' Gracie felt really mean. She knew she hadn't been good company since Jacob had left for London, and she had been even worse since she'd heard he was getting engaged. Maria was her best friend and the least she could do was help her have a bit of romance in her life. 'All right, then,' she said. 'I'll go with you.'

Maria threw her arms around her. 'Thank you!'

Gracie couldn't help smiling. 'Just don't expect me to pair off with one of Tommy's mates.'

On Saturday night Gracie was glad of the full moon and clear skies: they made it easier to find her way in the blackout through the packed streets of Ancoats to Mancini's ice-cream parlour. She came in out of the cold night to the sound of the shop bell ringing and the wonderful smell of vanilla ice cream and coffee. People were sitting in the booths that ran along one wall, and Luigi Mancini stood behind the long counter, wearing a spotless white apron and a huge smile. 'Ah, Gracie, have you your dancing shoes on?'

'I have, Mr Mancini.'

'I tell you, Gracie, if I were thirty years younger I would come with you – my foxtrot, it was a legend in Rimini.'

Gracie laughed. 'I'd like to see it one day.'

'Come here to me.' He beckoned. 'I hava something to show you.' He took a spoon and went to the fridge. 'Now I want you to tell me what you think.' He handed her a spoonful of speckled ice cream.

Gracie put it into her mouth and let it melt on her tongue. She closed her eyes and crunched… 'Mmm, are there bits of chocolate in the ice cream?' She opened her eyes to see Mr Mancini beaming.

'You like?'

Gracie nodded. 'It's delicious. I've never tasted ice cream like that before.'

He bowed his head in acknowledgement of the compliment. 'I hava been working on this so many years and only now I hava perfected it.'

'Gracie, is that you?' Maria called from upstairs. 'Come on up.'

'Time to get a ready for the dancing, I think,' Mr Mancini said, and did a little soft-shoe shuffle.

Gracie laughed. 'You still have it, Mr Mancini.'

The living room upstairs was warm, cosy and filled with the sound of dance music on the wireless. There was a picture of the pope on one wall and one of Jesus on another. Gracie loved visiting the Mancini family and they always made her welcome. She had taught Maria, a shy fourteen year old, to sew when she joined Rosenberg's and they'd been friends ever since. The youngest children, two boys, were on the floor playing with some tin cars and they paused a moment to wave at her. Tony, the eldest of the Mancini offspring, was slouched in an armchair next to them. He looked up from his newspaper. 'How do, Gracie?'

'I'm all right, Tony. Have you been working today?'

He pulled a face. 'Took the cart over to Platt Fields, but there wasn't much doing. I told Papa it's time to quit for the winter. Nobody's buying ice cream now the weather's turned so cold.'

'Ignore him, Gracie. He's always moaning,' Maria called from her bedroom. 'Come in here!'

Maria was sitting at her dressing-table, arranging her dark curls to frame her face. She was wearing a lavender dress with a sweetheart neckline, a tiny gold cross at her throat. Gracie had always thought her friend was pretty, but tonight she seemed more sophisticated and certainly older than eighteen. 'You look lovely,' she said.

'So do you. I like your makeup.' She lowered her voice. 'I'll have to put mine on when I get to the Ritz. Papa won't let me out of the house with it on.' Maria folded a silk headscarf into a triangle and draped it over her shoulders, then put on a navy nap coat lined with tartan. It looked so warm and stylish that Gracie felt a pang of envy: her coat seemed thin and cheap by comparison.

Maria's mother had come out of the kitchen to see them off. 'You brought your things to stay the night, Gracie?'

'Yes, thank you.'

'Now don't be late, will you, girls? I'll send Tony into town for ten o'clock and he'll walk you home.'

'There's no need, we'll be fine,' said Maria, and smirked at her brother. 'Anyway, Tony's far too tired after working all day.'

'Well, make sure you look after each other,' said her mother.

It was crowded in the Ritz foyer. 'Just look at everyone, all dressed up – and such style,' said Maria. 'I told Tommy I'd meet him in the ballroom. He'll be looking out for us.' They paid their one and six admission and thruppence to leave their coats in the cloakroom. Then Maria wanted to do her makeup before they went to look for Tommy.

The Ladies was packed and they couldn't get anywhere near the mirrors. 'Never mind,' said Gracie. 'I'll do it for you. You'll be just like those posh ladies being made up in Lewis's.'

She set to work using the powder in Maria's compact, then added a little of her own Bourjois rouge. 'You don't need much of this and the same with your lipstick, just a light covering will do. Then I'll do your eyebrows.' After a few minutes, Gracie stepped back. 'That's it… Lovely. You look just like Hedy Lamarr.'

'Let me see. Let me see!' Gracie gave her the compact and Maria turned her head from side to side in the little mirror. 'I like it,' she said.

'Come on, then,' said Gracie. 'Let's find Tommy and have a few dances.'

The ballroom was one of the biggest in Manchester and the only one with a sprung floor. The dancing was in full swing and the orchestra's playing enveloped them.

'He's there!' shouted Maria. 'Over by that pillar.' She grabbed Gracie's hand. 'Isn't he gorgeous?' she whispered, when they were only feet away from him, and Gracie had no doubt that he was, but she hoped that Maria would want more than a handsome face.

'Thought maybe you wouldn't be able to get away,' said Tommy.

Maria was blushing under the rouge. 'It was all right because Gracie came with me.'

Tommy looked beyond her and noticed Gracie for the first time. He nodded, then turned to the three lads behind him. 'Well, girls, you know Charlie from work, don't you, and Alan and Brian are mates from school.'

Gracie's heart sank. If she'd known that Charlie was going to be there she wouldn't have come. For a split second she wondered if Maria hadn't told her deliberately, but she dismissed the thought. Maria would never do that.

'I'll get a round in,' said Tommy. 'There's a table behind us. Why don't you girls sit down and I'll bring you some drinks?'

Being that bit further back from the dance-floor, the table was in shadow and it was a moment before Gracie realised that Charlie had sat next to her. On her other side was Maria, then an empty seat presumably for Tommy. Maria leaned towards her and whispered, 'We'll get plenty of dances tonight.'

Gracie, hearing the excitement in her friend's voice, was determined not to spoil the evening by being awkward. 'It'll be smashing,' she said.

The lads were good company and there was plenty of laughter around the table at their jokes and antics. The girls were never without a dancing partner either. Gracie soon realised that Alan was the best dancer, able to go way beyond the basic steps and so confident in guiding her round the floor that it was a joy to dance with him. They were waltzing when he said, 'I like dancing with you – you've good, natural rhythm.'

Gracie looked up at him. 'I was just thinking the same about you.'

He stepped back from her, still holding her hand, and instinctively Gracie spun away from him. Seconds later he swept her back into his arms. 'I was wondering if you'd like to come dancing with me next Saturday,' he said. 'I usually go to the Plaza on Oxford Street – the music's better there.'

'I'm sorry, I can't,' she said.

'Got a boyfriend, have you?'

She had only to say, 'No,' and that would be the end of her and Jacob. After all, a few dates with him, then finding out that he was getting engaged to someone else certainly didn't make him a boyfriend. But she couldn't bring herself to deny him, not yet. 'Yes, I have, sorry.'

Alan gave a rueful smile. 'If you were my girl, I wouldn't let you out dancing with other men on a Saturday night.'

When the music ended, they went back to the table, but before Gracie could sit down, Charlie was on his feet, holding out his hand. She didn't want to dance again: Alan's comment had somehow made her feel cheap for being in a dancehall at all, but that was ridiculous. She was only there so that Maria could go on a date, and as for Jacob, he wouldn't care what she did. She took Charlie's hand and, even though he had two left feet and too much beer in him, she tried to look as if she was enjoying herself.

Throughout the evening Gracie had kept an eye on Maria and Tommy. He was certainly very attentive and sat close to her, watching her face as she spoke. Later she noticed he was holding her hand and whispering in her ear. Towards the end of the evening when the music was slower and the lights dimmed, she caught sight of them clinging to each other as they danced. The evening was almost over when Alan and Brian left to get to the pub before last orders, leaving her and Charlie alone. The last waltz was announced and the lights dimmed.

'Do you want to dance?' asked Charlie.

That was the last thing she wanted to do. 'No, thanks,' she said, and turned her back on him to watch the dancers. She had always thought of ballrooms as romantic places where hopes and dreams hovered just above the heads of lovers, where the touch of a hand could make the heart soar – a prelude to the walk home and the goodnight kiss. But something had changed inside her. She had been a foolish romantic, but now she knew that for every romance that flourished many more ended in heartbreak.

After 'God Save the King' they stood around in the foyer, Tommy with his arm around Maria and Charlie looking awkward, his eyes flitting towards her.

'We'll walk you girls home,' said Tommy. 'You never know who's lurking out there in the blackout.'

Gracie was about to protest, but Maria got in first. 'That would be lovely, thank you.' Gracie shot her a look, hoping she'd get the message that she didn't want to go anywhere with Charlie, but it was too late. Tommy had his arm round Maria and was already leading her out into the night. Gracie had no choice but to follow them and Charlie walked alongside her.

'Great night,' he said.

'Hmm,' said Gracie, in no mood to speak at all. She had tried all evening to put on a brave face, being part of the company, dancing and laughing, but away from the warmth and glamour of the ballroom, she was overcome with sadness at the loss of Jacob.

The further away they walked from the Ritz, the more deserted the streets became, and by the time they arrived in Ancoats there were just the four of them on the road. Tommy and Maria had kept up a conversation the whole time, but their companions had been silent. Sometimes Gracie could detect the subtle changes in Maria's voice from giggly or coy to soft and appealing. At other times there was the whispering of intimacy and Gracie could hardly bear it.

In the warren of streets off the main road, Tommy called to Charlie, 'We're just stopping here for a bit, mate. You walk on with Gracie – she knows the way. We'll catch you up.'

'It's not far,' said Gracie. 'We need to follow this road. Her street's up here on the left.'

They set off walking. 'What do you think they're doing back there?' asked Charlie.

'None of our business,' said Gracie.

'It's a cold night. Maybe he's giving her a hug... or summat...'

Gracie heard the snigger in his voice. 'Why don't you just go now? I'll find my own way.' She quickened her pace.

He caught her arm. 'What's the matter with you?'

'Nothing.'

He put his other arm around her waist and pulled her towards him. 'Come on, Gracie, one kiss isn't going to hurt you.'

She tried to keep calm. 'Charlie, let me go.'

He laughed. 'All right, but you have to give me a kiss first.'

'I'm not kissing you. Now, let me go.'

'No, not till you kiss me.' He touched his cheek. 'Just here.'

She could feel his strength as he held her and knew he wouldn't let her go until she obeyed him. She leaned towards him and brushed her lips against his cheek, but when she tried to pull away, his grip tightened. 'Charlie!' she cried. Then his lips were on hers. A kiss to let her go, he'd said, but now his hand had slipped across her back and up under her jumper to her breast. 'Charlie, stop it!' she cried. He lifted her inches off the ground and carried her the few steps into a ginnel. She kicked at him, but he rammed her against a wall cracking her head. He held her tight, pinned there with an arm across her throat. 'Let me go! Let me go!' she cried. He was pulling at her skirt. 'Charlie, stop it! Stop it!' she begged. Now his cold hand was on her bare thigh... and seconds later he found what he wanted. She screamed.

'Hey, what's goin' on here?' The woman's voice was followed by a beam of light sweeping over them.

Gracie blinked and cried out, 'Help me!'

Charlie stepped quickly out of the light and Gracie slumped to the ground.

'Dear God!' In seconds the woman was on her knees next to Gracie. 'What's happened? Are you hurt?'

Gracie was shaking. 'Where's he gone?'

'He scarpered soon as he seen me. What did he do to you, love?'

Gracie looked around confused. 'What?'

'He was attacking you. Do you know him?'

'Yes.'

'Come on, let's get you inside. My house is just here. I'll get you a cup of tea, calm you down.' She helped Gracie across the yard and into the kitchen. 'Goodness me, you're shakin'. What's your name, love?'

'Gracie.'

'I'm Annie. Now, sit there next to the fire. Good job I was out at the privy when I heard you scream. If you'd been five minutes later, I'd have been in my bed at the front of the house. Never would've heard you.'

Annie busied herself filling the kettle, lighting the gas and keeping an eye on Gracie. The shaking grew worse and she began to sob. Annie knelt in front of her. 'There, there, love. Just let it come out of you. You've had an awful shock. It looked vicious what that fella was doin'. I wish I'd thought to pick up the shovel from the yard. I'd have beat him round the head with it!' When Gracie was calmer, Annie spoke again: 'Listen to me, Gracie. I'm sorry to ask you this, but what did that lad do to you out there before I arrived?'

Gracie's eyes widened again with fright. 'He said if I gave him a kiss he'd let me go, but then he dragged me up the ginnel and started touching me. It was horrible. I tried to stop him, but he was too strong. I know what he was going to do,' Gracie shut her eyes tight, 'what he would have done to me, if you hadn't been there,' and the tears came again. Then, suddenly, she was on her feet. 'I need to get home,' she cried, and rushed to the door, but almost immediately she swayed and would have fallen had Annie not supported her and led her back to the sofa.

'You're as white as a sheet, girl. Sit down and put your head between your knees. There now, take deep breaths.' Then Annie gasped. 'Oh dear! I think you've cut your head. 'Let me have a look.' She parted Gracie's blood-soaked hair. 'It's not deep, thank goodness, but there's quite a bump. Did he do that to you?'

'I think he pushed me against the wall. I don't know...'

'I'll bathe it in warm water for you.'

Eventually, with a cup of tea inside her, a blanket round her shoulders and her head bathed with warm water and TCP, Gracie felt a bit better. 'I suppose I should go now and let you get to bed,' she said.

But Annie shook her head. 'I'd be loath to let you go out in the blackout again. Where do you live?'

'Oh, no.' Gracie groaned and put her head in her hands. 'I'd forgotten I was supposed to stay at my friend's house – do you know the Mancinis?'

'Yes, I do. Were you out with Maria?'

Gracie nodded. 'We got separated on the way back from the dancehall. She'll probably be home by now.'

'Yes, and the house locked up for the night,' said Annie. 'Look, love, it's up to you, but maybe it would be better if you stayed here tonight. You can sleep on the sofa and go home to your own house in the morning. What do you think?'

Gracie saw the sense in that. She could hardly turn up at Maria's now when they were supposed to have come home together. Besides, she couldn't face the Mancinis, or walking all the way home in the dark and waking up her mother. She would certainly realise something was wrong, and the last thing she wanted was to explain what Charlie had done to her. 'Can I stay with you, please?'

'Of course you can, love.'

8

When Gracie arrived for work on Monday morning Maria was waiting for her in the cloakroom. 'Where did you get to on Saturday night? I waited for you outside my house for ages.'

Gracie hung up her coat. 'I don't want to talk about it.' She turned away to put on her overall.

Maria looked around – there were just a few women sharing a cigarette on the other side of the room. She lowered her voice. 'I had to lie to my mother. I told her you didn't feel well when we were walking home and wanted to sleep in your own bed. Your bag with your things in it is on my peg.'

'Thank you,' said Gracie.

'Is that all you can say?'

Gracie didn't meet her eye.

'You went off with Charlie, didn't you?'

'You're the one who went off!'

'That's not fair,' said Maria. 'Yes, we did stop to... well, you know, but we said we'd catch you up. It was only about fifteen minutes Tommy and I had together.'

The smokers finished their cigarette and Gracie waited until they left. 'It was long enough,' she said, and even though she was determined to be strong, all the horror came rushing back. She pressed her fingertips against her eyes to hold back the tears.

'What do you mean "long enough"? Gracie, are you crying?' Maria gently pulled Gracie's hands away. 'Long enough for what?'

'Swear you won't tell anyone.' Gracie sobbed.

Maria put her arms round her. 'Shush, Gracie, don't cry. Just tell me what happened – I won't tell a soul.'

Gracie shook her head in agitation. 'No, we have to start work now or we'll get into trouble.'

'Never mind that. I'm not leaving here until you tell me.'

Gracie wiped her eyes. 'We were walking to your house, Charlie and me. I was so stupid, so stupid.' Her breath was shallow and her words broken, punctuated with sobs. 'I... should never... ever... have got myself into that situation, being on my own with him. He lifted me up... carried me up a back entry.'

'Holy Mother of God,' said Maria. 'What did he do to you?'

'I kicked him and screamed – he was inside my clothes,' Gracie shuddered, 'touching me. I begged him—'

'Gracie, did he... you know?'

She shook her head. 'A woman heard me screaming and came out of her yard into the ginnel. Charlie ran away. I must have banged my head. I couldn't think straight but Annie, that's the woman, took me into her house and she let me stay there till the morning.'

'Gracie, you have to tell somebody about this. He can't get away with doing that.'

'There's no point. It's his word against mine.'

But Maria wasn't listening. 'If you won't do it I will. I'm the supervisor and it's my job to look after you. I'll tell Mr Rosenberg. It's not right that you have to work with him after what he's done.'

'No!' cried Gracie. 'I don't want Mr Rosenberg to know what happened – I'd die of shame. I'm not telling anyone. I shouldn't have told you. Now just forget about it.'

'I'll speak to Tommy,' said Maria. 'He'll know what to do.'

'You'll do no such thing! I'll not have people talking about me behind my back. It was a dirty thing that Charlie did to me and I don't want anyone to know about it. I'd be so ashamed.' She wiped her eyes and tucked a loose strand of her hair under her turban. 'I think it's time we did some work, don't you?'

Gracie kept her eyes lowered as she came into the workshop. The last thing she wanted was to face Charlie. She had told herself over and over again that he was the one in the wrong, not her. He should be ashamed, not her, but that didn't stop her heart pounding. She had almost made it to her machine when there was an outburst of laughter. She looked up and there at the back of the room stood Charlie, laughing with Tommy. Both were staring at her. She wanted to run as far away from the factory as she could, but the anger was rising inside her. How dare they? she thought. She stood a little taller and met their gaze. But a moment later her courage failed her... Jacob was coming through the door. She turned away and focused on reaching her workbench. Her mind was in turmoil. Seeing Jacob again after all this time, she felt a surge of the love that she had tried so hard to deny. She longed to feel his arms around her, and the thought of his mouth on hers threatened to overpower her.

'Are you all right?' asked Maria.

Gracie couldn't trust herself to speak.

'Look, go and sit in the cloakroom for a while.'

Gracie shook her head and started up her machine, thinking it best to focus on the repetitive work, but try as she might she couldn't clear the horrible thoughts from her mind. Jacob's intended engagement had knocked her sideways, and Charlie's attack had disgusted and frightened her, but she had never for one moment thought that she would come to work and face such humiliation. She was convinced that Charlie had been telling people what he had done to her – no, what she had let him do: she had seen it in his face and Tommy's when they stared at her and laughed. But the final blow was when she glanced up to see that Jacob had joined them.

Gracie worked all day and tried not to speak to or make eye contact with anyone. She didn't even stop for her dinner. Towards the end of the day, her head was aching and her eyes were so strained she could hardly see the stitches on the fabric.

'Maria, I don't feel very well. Do you think I could leave a bit early?'

'Of course you can. You look washed out. Would you like me to come with you?'

'No, no... I'll be fine. Tommy won't mind, will he?'

'Of course not. I'm responsible for the machinists, not him.'

'I'll make up the time tomorrow, I promise.'

'Don't worry about that, Gracie. In fact, if you don't feel like coming in tomorrow, I'll understand.'

Sarah was peeling potatoes when Gracie arrived home. 'Goodness me, you look weary today.'

Gracie slumped into the chair. 'It's those waterproofs we're stitching. They're twice as heavy as the fashion raincoats and sewing them makes your arms ache.'

'Well, the tea won't be ready for a while, so you can have a wee snooze, can't you?'

The room was warm, and the tension that had built up in her throughout the day began to ebb away. She must have fallen asleep, because she felt a touch on her arm and opened her eyes to see her mother looking down at her. 'Wake up, Gracie.' Her voice was hushed, but urgent. 'There's somebody here to see you.'

'What? Somebody's here?' She looked around the room.

'Not in here, he's in the parlour.'

'Who is it?'

'Mr Rosenberg.'

Gracie jumped up. What was Mr Rosenberg doing in their parlour? Then she realised: Maria must have told him about Charlie. How could her friend do that, when she had begged her not to say anything to anybody?

'He's waiting for you, hurry up.'

Gracie rubbed her eyes, smoothed her clothes and at the parlour door she took a deep breath.

He was standing in front of the empty grate looking at the picture above the fireplace. He turned to face her. 'Hello, Gracie.'

She caught her breath. 'Jacob?'

There was no warmth in his voice and no smile on his face. 'You left early,' he said. It felt like an accusation.

Gracie nodded. 'I didn't feel well. Maria gave me permission.' He stared at her, as though weighing her up. She could think of absolutely nothing to say. Heavy seconds ticked by, and she wondered whether she should invite him to sit down, but from his stern look it was clear that this was no tea-in-the-parlour matter.

His next words confirmed it. 'I need to speak to you...' He bit his lip. 'About a delicate matter.'

Oh, God, thought Gracie, he knows about Charlie. Her face burned and she bowed her head. 'Please don't say anything, I can't bear it. I... I think you should go.'

'No, please hear me out. Let me explain what happened.'

She looked up and saw the anguish in his face. 'Explain? Explain what?'

'Why I didn't write to you after that first letter I sent from London. I'm so sorry.'

Gracie couldn't believe it: he thought she was angry because he hadn't written but, more importantly, she realised he didn't know about Charlie. She held up her hand. 'I know why you didn't write,' she said. 'It's because you're engaged, isn't it?'

Anger blazed in Jacob's eyes. 'Who told you that?'

She kept her voice calm, as though she didn't care. She didn't even look at him as she spoke. 'Doesn't matter who told me, doesn't matter that you didn't write either. It's not as though we were walking out together. In fact, we hardly know each other.'

'But it's not true! I'm not engaged.'

'Well, I've heard you soon will be so I don't know what you're doing coming round here to *explain*.' She spat out the word.

The speed at which Jacob moved took Gracie by surprise. His arms were around her like a vice, his lips crushing hers. Gracie gasped for breath as fear overtook her. 'Don't do that to me!' she shouted. 'Do you hear? Don't do it!' But the panic was rising in her chest and, even though she wanted him, she pushed him away. All the time he had been gone, even when she knew she could never have him, she had dreamed of such an embrace when he returned, but not now.

Jacob's face was a picture of misery. 'Don't you know that I've come here to tell you that I'm in love with you?'

Suddenly the door to the kitchen was flung open and Sarah stood in front of them, hands on hips. 'What's all the noise in here?'

Gracie didn't answer. Jacob's words had lodged in her brain and in that moment she heard nothing else, saw no one else. And when her mother spoke again it was as though she was surprised to find her in the room.

'Gracie, what's the matter?'

'Nothing, Mam, don't worry.' Her voice was calm. 'Jacob and I just need to sort something out.'

'Are you sure? Because I'd sooner he went and didn't come back.'

'Everything's fine, Mam. We'll just sit in here and talk things through.'

Sarah gave them a hard stare and closed the door, but they could still hear her chunnering away to herself in the kitchen.

'You'd better sit down,' said Gracie. 'If you want to explain, I'll listen.'

They sat opposite each other and Gracie watched every fleeting expression on his face as he spoke. 'My family have been saying for a while that it's time I got married. There's a Jewish girl in London they thought would suit me. Her father is in partnership with my cousin and they asked me to advise them on how to secure a government contract for their factory. I agreed to go to London to help them with the business but, I'll be honest with you, I knew that I'd be meeting the girl.' He sighed deeply. 'Then, just before I left, you and I spent the day together in Blackpool, which changed everything.'

'Why did you ask me out in the first place when you knew your family wanted you to marry the girl?'

'Because I liked you – you always seemed such good fun. Oh, I know they want me to marry a Jewish girl. That's the way it is and, if it wasn't for you, I'd probably be engaged to her by now.'

'In time for Hanukkah. That was the plan, wasn't it? And you never said a word to me.' She shook her head in disbelief. 'You must have known how I felt about you yet you went to London to meet this girl, and the first thing you do is send me a letter so full of love that I—'

'Oh, Gracie, I meant every word I wrote. But you've got to understand that you and I had only gone out together a few times and there was a lot of pressure on me at least to see the girl. I know now that I wasn't thinking straight and, honestly, I wasn't sure if you were... well, if you felt the same as I did.'

'And then there were no more letters,' said Gracie. 'Not a word.'

'I wanted to do the right thing – to see if I could accept my family's choice of a wife – and I couldn't do that if I was deceiving them and her by writing love letters to you, pouring out my feelings. But in truth I knew that I couldn't marry her...' For the first time since he had arrived, he smiled.

Could it be true? She searched his face. There was only one way to be sure. 'Why couldn't you marry her?' she asked.

He stood and held out his arms to her. 'Because it's you I love.' Gracie went to him and he kissed her so tenderly. 'Now it's your turn,' he said.

'I don't know what you mean.' But there was mischief in her face.

'Ah, Gracie, it's not like you to fluff your lines.' He kissed her again. 'I think you understand.'

Gracie opened her eyes and looked up at his handsome face. 'I love you, Jacob.'

They sat together in the cold parlour, wrapped in each other's arms, talking about the future, until her mother knocked on the door and shouted, 'Your tea's on the table.'

'I'd better go,' he said. 'I'll see you tomorrow.' He kissed her again, but still he lingered. 'Have you told anyone at work about us?'

'No, of course not.'

'Not even Maria?'

'No, but can I tell her soon?'

'We'll just leave it a while longer. My uncle knows I haven't proposed to the girl, but I need a bit more time to talk to him about us. Then you can tell anyone you want.'

'When can we be together again?'

'I thought we might go out on Saturday night and have dinner in one of the hotels. Would you like that?'

'Yes, I would.'

'That's settled, then. I'll call for you at seven on Saturday.' He stroked her hair and kissed her forehead. 'Don't worry, Gracie. Everything will be fine. You'll see.'

Sarah was waiting for her in the kitchen with a face like thunder. The tea was put on the table and they ate the neck-end stew in silence. When Gracie went to wash the pots, her mother poured the last dregs of tea into her cup and sat back. 'So that's your Mr Rosenberg, is it?'

Gracie, her back turned to her mother, rolled her eyes and scrubbed the plates furiously with the dish mop. 'Yes, Mam.'

'Well, are you going to tell me what he wanted?'

Gracie left the pots in the sink and dried her hands. 'He's asked me to go out to dinner with him… in a hotel.'

'What? A hotel? For dinner? I never heard the like! I'm

forty years old and I've never been "to dinner" anywhere, let alone a hotel. I'm telling you, girl, this fella Rosenberg is from another world. Jazz clubs, hotel dinners – that's not for the likes of us.'

'Why are you saying all this? He's nice and kind and he likes me. Why shouldn't I go out with him? You're the one who always said I should try to better myself, and here's a chance to see there's a world beyond Pearson Street.'

Sarah shook her head. 'Gracie, I would love you to make your way in the world. If I were to see you come through the doors of the Midland Hotel in fine clothes and jewellery I would be so proud of my lovely daughter. But this young man is different. His religion sets him apart, and because of that I'm certain his family wouldn't want him to be courting you.'

'That's it, isn't it? It's because he's Jewish! I can't understand why you're like this. You've always taught me to treat every-one fairly. You told me tales about when you came to England and some people looked down on you because you were Irish. You said we're all the same inside. And now you've the nerve to sit there telling me I shouldn't go out with a Jewish lad because he's different!'

'I'm only thinking of you. If you fall for him… You know how much I worry. A girl's reputation is a fragile thing.'

'Do you think I don't know that?'

Sarah pursed her lips, but she didn't keep the words inside. 'I'll tell you something for nothing – he won't marry you.'

'You don't know that!' screamed Gracie. She ran out of the kitchen, up to her bedroom and slammed the door behind her.

Sarah went to the foot of the stairs and shouted, 'I know this much – whatever happens, it'll end in heartache. Just don't say I didn't warn you!'

9

Sarah couldn't sleep. She and Gracie didn't have rows very often, which made it even more difficult for her to accept her daughter's angry outburst. Even worse was her own reaction to it: she cringed at the memory of standing at the foot of the stairs screaming like some deranged harridan. You had to speak out to nip it in the bud, she told herself. Lord knows, you've seen enough mixed marriages tear families apart back home in Belfast. Then, as if in answer, she chastised herself: No, a girl and a boy falling in love is a beautiful thing. It's all those bigoted killjoys who spoil it. She got out of bed, put on her dressing-gown and slippers and crossed the landing.

'Are you awake, Gracie?'

'Yes.' A little word, full of sadness.

Sarah went into her daughter's room and sat on the bed. 'I'm sorry, love. I shouldn't have said those things. Mothers worry. They think it's their job to keep a child safe and easily forget that the child is grown. Tell me, do you really like this lad?'

'Oh, yes, Mam. I've never met anyone like him.'

'And how does he feel about you?'

Gracie didn't meet her mother's gaze. 'I think... no, I'm sure he likes me a lot.'

'Well, I suppose if you like each other, there's no harm in seeing where this romance is going. Just be careful about other people, who might not like the two of you being together. You know what I'm saying?'

Gracie nodded. 'So, I can go to dinner with him?'

'Of course you can, love, and I'll tell you what I'll do. I'll see if I can alter that green woollen dress of yours to make it look more modern, maybe add some lace or ribbons. Sarah Earnshaw knows a thing or two about style. I see enough of it at the Midland.'

When Jacob arrived in a taxi to pick up Gracie on Saturday evening, Sarah opened the door to him and ushered him into the parlour. He was carrying a large box – the sort a posh department store would use to pack a purchase. 'Gracie'll be down in a minute,' she told him. He was dressed in a dinner suit and bow tie, and his shoes were highly polished. Unlike his first visit, he was relaxed with a ready smile. They exchanged pleasantries and Sarah realised she had been wrong to think of him as a lad: he wasn't much older than Gracie, but he had the manners and self-assurance of a successful man, not to mention that he was very good-looking. As Gracie came into the room, Sarah watched her face light up at the sight of him. She had never seen Gracie so beautiful. A quick glance at Jacob, and Sarah knew there was something special between them. He gave Gracie the box and she opened it to find, wrapped in tissue paper, a beautiful coat. 'My, my,' said Sarah. 'Did you ever see...?'

'It's a Parisian design,' said Jacob. 'What we call a model – only one was made. We didn't put it into production because… well, not many women could carry it off.'

Gracie slipped into the coat and hugged it to her, a full-length raincoat, cut on the bias to swing outwards, but it was the dusky pink colour that made it so striking, Sarah thought it could have been made for Gracie.

After they had gone, she went back to the kitchen to make herself a cup of tea. She was pleased that she had done the right thing in allowing the romance to grow but, truth be told, Gracie was headstrong enough to have defied her anyway. She could only hope that others would be so tolerant. While the kettle boiled she went up to her bedroom to fetch the parcel she had hidden in the wardrobe that morning. Luckily Gracie had been in bed when the postman had delivered it so there had been no awkward questions to answer. She put it on the kitchen table and let it sit there while the tea brewed, while she drank it, while she washed and dried the cup and put it back in the cupboard. She sat at the table and scrutinised it – brown paper, rough string, lumps of sealing wax like splodges of blood – full of its own importance. She unwrapped it carefully, neatly folding the paper, rolling up the string. Inside there was a shoebox and a letter.

Dear Sarah
I know you said you wanted nothing from your father's house, but when I cleared it out, I couldn't bear to throw these things away. I'm sure you'll want to have them.
Jean

She removed the lid from the box and, one by one, she took out each item, examined it, wept over it and set it on the table.

Her mother's rings: the wedding band, paper thin where it met her palm and the engagement ring with four diamond chips, the fifth missing from the gaping claw. The little Bible she remembered from Sunday school, with her own name on the gilded page inside the cover, 'Awarded for Best Bible Study'. A well-thumbed copy of *Wuthering Heights*, which she had read so many times as a teenager, thrilled by the tragic love between Catherine and Heathcliff.

Until, at last, she came to the photographs. There was her mother as a young woman, sitting on an elaborate chair in a studio in Belfast wearing a Victorian blouse with rows of pin-tucking and a pie-crust collar, a long skirt in a heavy material and buttoned boots. Sarah turned it towards the light to study it more closely and was amazed to see Gracie's face looking at her: the same almond-shaped eyes, the full lips and an expression she recognised as annoyance.

Underneath that was a black-edged photograph of a soldier, her brother Peter, in the uniform of the Ulster Division. Only twenty when he died on the Somme. Her mother had died a year later. Her heart was weak, they said, but Sarah knew it was broken. There were a few more family photographs, which she glanced at, before she reached the bottom of the shoebox where she found an envelope. Inside was a photograph of a draper's shop with the staff standing outside. She gasped. There she was in shop-girl black and smiling, not at the camera but at the handsome young man standing next to her with his hand on her shoulder. She could feel it there now across the years. Martin Quigley, the boy she'd loved.

Sarah was fast asleep in bed when Gracie came into her room, flushed and excited.

'Are you awake, Mam?'

Sarah rubbed her eyes and yawned. 'Is it late?'

Gracie sat on the bed. 'Let's just say the coach didn't turn into a pumpkin.'

'Did you have a nice time?'

'Oh, Mam, it was wonderful. We went to the Grosvenor Hotel. It was all decorated for Christmas with a huge tree, lights and baubles, and there were boughs of holly tied up with ribbons. There were musicians called a string quartet playing carols. The tables were beautiful with sprays of flowers… and the crystal glasses and silver cutlery. I hardly knew what to do with them all, but Jacob helped me. And so much to eat – I'm full to bursting.' She shook her head at the wonder of it all.

'Were lots of people there?'

'Yes, every table taken and such stylish clothes… I've never seen such beautiful dresses.' She sighed. 'It was like I'd slipped into another world.'

'And did Jacob have a good time?'

'I think so. He said being with me and seeing things through my eyes was… What were his words? Oh, yes – "like a breeze that quickens the air".'

'Well, I've not heard that one before,' said Sarah. 'Did he say anything about going out with him again?'

'Yes, he did. Next Saturday he's taking me to the Palace Theatre to see *Romeo and Juliet*. Can you believe it? I just wish I had a new dress to wear.'

'You know we've no money for new clothes. Anyway, you'll have your new coat and if he really likes you he won't care what you're wearing.'

'I suppose you're right,' said Gracie.

'Of course I am. Now get off to bed,' said Sarah.

In her room Gracie took off her coat and hung it up. It was

the most beautiful thing she'd ever owned. As she waited for sleep to come, she recalled Jacob's words when they had said goodnight. 'I'll try to speak to my uncle about us this week.' He added, 'I want everyone to know how much you mean to me.'

10

Gracie's worry about a suitable dress for the theatre was solved by a passing conversation between her mother and Doris. It turned out Doris knew that the landlady of the Foresters had bought a second-hand cocktail dress to wear at the Manchester publicans' annual dinner dance some months before. Gracie was dubious when her mother suggested she should ask to borrow it. 'Ach, if you never ask, you never get,' she said.

It turned out to be a beautiful off-the-shoulder style in emerald taffeta. 'I bought it in a jumble sale at the Freemasons' Hall on Bridge Street,' the landlady told her. 'But it wasn't quite me – mutton dressed as lamb, you might say – so you're welcome to borrow it. All it needs is a damp press.'

Gracie brought it home and modelled it for her mother. 'The colour is just right for you, and the shape's lovely too,' said Sarah. 'You could put your hair up for a change.' Gracie, in front of the mirror, turned this way and that and smiled. She had never felt so glamorous.

★

On the night of the play, Gracie was at the parlour window looking out for Jacob when she heard the roar of an engine down the street. Seconds later a sports car pulled up sharply at her door. She called out to her mother to say she was going, as Jacob held open the car door for her.

She settled into the leather seat. 'I didn't expect this.'

'I've borrowed it from a friend,' said Jacob. 'It's nice to arrive at the theatre in style.' He leaned across and kissed her cheek. 'You look so lovely, Gracie.'

On the main road he put his foot down and the car roared away. Gracie was thrilled by the speed and laughed out loud. 'I could get used to this.'

'You might have to, I'm thinking of buying one.'

The foyer of the Palace Theatre thronged with people. They checked in their coats and Jacob bought her a programme. 'To remember your first visit to the theatre,' he said. 'We don't need to take our seats yet. We'll just enjoy the atmosphere.' Gracie tried to take in the scene: from deep maroon walls and gilded pillars to sparkling chandeliers, from modest outfits to evening dress. She ought to pinch herself, but she wouldn't take the risk of waking up.

'What do you think?' asked Jacob.

'I thought it would be like the pictures, queuing outside in the cold to get in.'

Jacob chuckled. 'Gracie, you say the funniest things. I ought to write them down.'

'Don't laugh. How was I to know it would be like this?'

'I'm not laughing, really. It's just that I love taking you to places you've never been. It makes me see things in a completely different light. I can't wait for you to watch the play.'

Their seats were in the dress circle near the front with a good view of the stage, but Gracie kept turning round as people took their seats. 'Who are you looking for?' asked Jacob.

'No one. I'm just looking at all the dresses. Aren't they beautiful? Is that why it's called the dress circle?'

'Maybe it is,' said Jacob. 'And as for the dresses, the only one I noticed was yours.' He stroked her bare shoulder. 'You look stunning.'

Their eyes met and Gracie felt a rush of excitement at the love in his eyes.

'Jacob! Jacob Rosenberg! Haven't seen you for ages.' A young man was shouting from the aisle.

'Will you excuse me a moment?' said Jacob, and made his way along the row. Gracie watched them talk. Every now and again the man would look over at her. There was a handshake and Jacob returned. 'I'm sorry about that,' he said. 'He's an old friend.'

'He kept looking at me,' said Gracie.

'Yes. He wanted to know who you were. I didn't tell him.'

'Oh,' was all she could say, but she remembered that this wasn't the first time he had avoided introducing her to his friends. She couldn't help but wonder whether he was ashamed of her.

'Gracie, he's one of those men who never misses an opportunity to flirt with a beautiful woman.' Jacob's tone was curt. 'That's why I don't want him to meet you. Besides, he thought you were Jewish, and if he met you he'd know in an instant that you are not.'

Gracie was confused. Jacob thinking she was beautiful and wanting to protect her made her feel wanted and loved, but she didn't understand his remark about being Jewish... or not. She ought to ask him what he meant, but he was staring straight ahead and she didn't want to upset him. All week she had been dreaming of seeing *Romeo and Juliet* with him: she knew how much he loved the theatre and felt certain she would love it too. She leaned towards him and whispered, 'I love you, Jacob,' and his smile was enough for her to know that nothing would spoil their evening.

The lights dimmed, the theatre was hushed and, with a swish of the curtain, Gracie was transported to the streets of fair Verona. At first she leaned forward in her seat trying to catch the gist of what was being said: two families, enemies fighting in the street, followed by clashes of swords and the shouts of the young men intent on killing each other that shook her to her core. The masked ball filled the stage with colour, music and dancing. But there was danger too, for Romeo was in the house of his enemies. Juliet looked so fresh and young, and when Romeo spoke to her, Gracie just knew they would fall in love. They married in secret and she couldn't help but cry, softly of course, because it was so romantic. Mercutio was her favourite character, so headstrong and funny. How could he be so reckless, challenging horrible Tybalt to a sword fight? She held her breath for they were both as strong as each other... She gasped as Mercutio fell and Tybalt, without a scratch, ran away. Romeo was wild for revenge, and Gracie wanted to scream at him, 'Get away from there!' Too late – Tybalt returned. They fought and Romeo killed Tybalt – Juliet's cousin. The Prince banishes him from the city and his Juliet. The curtain fell but Gracie didn't move, didn't speak, even when Jacob touched her arm. She had forgotten he was there, forgotten she was not in Verona but in a theatre in Manchester. 'Come on, Gracie. It's the interval, time to stretch our legs.'

Neither of them spoke until they were in the circle bar, drinks in hand. 'Are you enjoying the play?' he said.

'Oh, yes! I can't wait to see how it ends.'

Jacob smiled. 'And what do you think of the theatre?'

It was a moment before Gracie answered. 'I feel like I belong here. Like the theatre's been waiting for me all my life and now I've found it.'

'What did you think about the actors?'

'It's funny, but you completely forget they're acting. I believed they were Romeo and Juliet, and I could see they loved each other. What must it feel like to become another person and speak the lines as though you'd just thought of them? I wish I could do that.'

Jacob tilted his head and looked at her. 'I think you could… if you wanted to.'

Just then the bell rang for the start of the second half and they took their seats.

On the way home Gracie couldn't stop talking about the play, flitting from one scene to another, reliving her favourite moments. 'They fell in love so quickly, didn't they? It was so romantic when he climbed up to her balcony. And later when they spent the night together before he had to leave the city, they thought they would be together in the end, but it wasn't to be.' She turned to Jacob. 'Why couldn't their family just accept they were in love?'

'Because families are like that. Scratch the surface and you'll find prejudice in the nicest of people. At least the lovers don't die, these days, but lives can be ruined. You know what I'm talking about?'

'Yes,' said Gracie. 'You're talking about us.'

'It won't be easy.'

'Is that why you still haven't told your family?'

'That's not fair, Gracie. I have to find the right moment.'

She could feel the tears welling in her eyes and didn't dare speak. Instead she stared into the darkness and they drove for a while in silence, except for the sound of the wipers on the windscreen. When they reached her house, Jacob turned off the engine and took her in his arms. 'Over Christmas when the factory is closed I'll still be there working with my uncle. That's when I'll tell him about us, I promise. I know he won't like it, but by the time the factory opens again he'll have come round, I'm sure.'

'But what if he doesn't?'

'It won't change a thing, *Liebling*. Trust me, whatever happens we'll be together.' His kiss was gentle on her lips and the touch of his hands on her waist and back thrilled her. He kissed her neck and sent a shiver through her. 'You like that?' he whispered.

'Oh, yes,' she breathed.

He lowered his head and kissed the line of her breasts where they swelled above the taffeta gown and she sighed with pleasure.

Alone in her room, Gracie put the theatre programme into the drawer next to the snow globe and Jacob's love letter. It was as though every moment she spent with him was precious and the little keepsakes were a comfort when they were apart.

She stepped out of the taffeta gown, ran her fingers over the low-cut neckline and smiled before hanging it on the wardrobe door. How she wished she could keep that as well.

She couldn't sleep – images of the play fluttered through her mind: the rich costumes, the scenery, the words. She tried to remember how Juliet spoke of her love, but she could only manage a line or two. She put on her dressing-gown, crept downstairs to the parlour and went straight to the bookcase. It was here somewhere... an old leather-bound book... Ah, there it was: *Shakespeare's Dramatic Works*. She blew off the dust and took it upstairs.

11

In the week before Christmas everyone in the factory was working flat out to fulfil the first government order. They were tired but determined to do a good job, and in good humour because they had been promised a bonus for completing the order before the holiday. At mid-morning on the Friday, Jacob came on to the factory floor. To the sound of cheers and whistles, he announced that the deadline had been met. He had also ordered mince pies for everyone to have in their tea break, and when the trolley came round the workers downed tools. Some of the women sang carols while the men lounged about, and none of the foremen bothered about getting them back to work.

Gracie and Maria were sitting at their workbenches chatting. 'Will you be out with Tommy over the holiday?' asked Gracie.

'Probably, but since I told my parents about him they keep asking me to bring him home and, to be honest, I'm a bit worried about it.'

'Oh, they're bound to like him when they see how happy he makes you.'

'I hope so. Anyway, what about you? You've seemed far happier these last few weeks.' In reply Gracie raised her eyebrows and grinned.

'No!' said Maria. 'Don't tell me the mystery boyfriend is back on the scene.'

'He might be...'

'He is! I know he is!' Maria laughed. 'Tell me.'

'Well, we've been out a few times recently,' Gracie lowered her voice, 'and I have to say... I'm head over heels.'

'I can't believe it,' said Maria. 'Why didn't you say something? Does he feel the same about you?' Gracie nodded. 'But who is he, someone I'd know?'

'I can't tell you, not yet, maybe after Christmas.'

'Why can't you tell me now? I won't breathe a word, I promise.'

But before Gracie had time to answer, the women, who had stopped singing and were casting around for some other way to extend the tea break, called on her to entertain them.

'We haven't had a story since we started on this government work,' shouted one.

'Give us something romantic, Gracie,' said another.

And Gracie, her heart full of romance and her head full of *Romeo and Juliet*, climbed on to the cutting table and faced her audience. The room fell silent.

Gracie announced, 'Tonight at the Palace Theatre the audience in their finery will pay their guinea to see the most famous love story in the world. But in Rosenberg's factory, the workers will get a taste of it for free in their tea break.' At the sound of clapping, Gracie bowed, and when she raised her head, all eyes were on her and she began.

'In a town far away and long, long ago there lived two families who hated each other. One family had a daughter, Juliet, the other a son, Romeo. They met at a masked ball in Juliet's house. Of course, Romeo should never have gone there – he could have been killed if anyone had recognised him. Picture the scene: tall pillars of gold, and red velvet curtains, tiny gilded chairs for those who didn't dance, and long tables covered with wonderful food you wouldn't even recognise. There were servants passing through the ballroom with drinks, and a group of musicians played in the gallery above.' She extended her arm. 'And here is Juliet, so young and beautiful in a dress of palest pink encrusted with diamonds. Romeo catches sight of her as she dances, and he's smitten. "Did my heart love till now?" he says.'

Gracie sensed the stillness in the room and, slowly, she brought Romeo and Juliet together for their first kiss. Somewhere to the side of her, she heard a door swing open, but the eyes of the audience never wavered from her face.

'Now Romeo is in the orchard, standing below Juliet's balcony, and he listens while she speaks about her feelings for him.' Gracie looked around the dingy factory walls and felt again the excitement of those first meetings with Jacob. How light her heart had been when they'd walked together in Heaton Park and, later, when she'd recognised the desire in those first kisses. She understood completely that people would disapprove of their love, but that didn't matter as long as they loved each other. She raised her head and spoke Juliet's words into the dark night. '"O Romeo, Romeo, wherefore art thou, Romeo?"' So absorbed was she that, when she finished the speech, she was still for a moment. Then she was aware of the workers turning towards the door and the sound of raucous laughter.

Somebody was shouting, 'You what? You didn't know she were a slut?'

'You're lying, lying!' came the reply – Jacob's voice, and she saw him grappling with someone. 'Take it back!' Jacob shouted, and threw the man against the wall. She froze.

It was Charlie and he wasn't laughing now: he was staring straight at her, his face twisted in anger. 'Look at her!' He pointed, and the workers turned to where she stood on the cutting table. He shook himself free of Jacob and sneered, 'She looks like butter wouldn't melt, but there's nothing our Gracie likes better than a quick one up a back alley!'

Like a statue on a plinth, Gracie stood alone – every eye in the room watching her. Instinctively, she looked across at Jacob. He was stony-faced, and when their eyes met he turned away.

Charlie's laugh broke the silence and Jacob looked as if he was going to hit him again. Then he seemed to regain some control, and when he spoke his voice was low and threatening. 'Get out,' he told Charlie. 'You're sacked, do you hear? If you come anywhere near my factory again I'll – I'll...'

'You can't sack me.'

'Oh, but I can,' said Jacob. 'And if you don't leave right now I'll call the police.'

Gracie could stand no more. She climbed off the table and, tears running down her face, she walked through the silent crowd that parted to let her through.

Alone in the cloakroom she slumped on a bench while her whole body shook with sobbing. She didn't hear the door open and it wasn't until she felt a touch on her shoulder that she opened her eyes. It was Maria. They clung to each other and Maria, through her tears, told her that Charlie had gone and Mr Jacob had ordered everyone back to work. 'I don't know how it all started,' she said. 'Charlie was standing next to Mr Jacob and they were watching you, but it seems Charlie said something he didn't like and suddenly there was shouting. Oh, Gracie, those awful things he said… and after what he did to you. I've a good mind to go out there and tell everybody what really happened between you and Charlie.'

'No, you can't do that! They'll think you're saying it because you're my friend. I told you, it's his word against mine. Oh, Maria, people think that I'm—'

'Maria, get back to work.' Jacob stood in the doorway, his eyes blazing.

'But, Mr Jacob, I'm just trying to help Gracie.'

'Get back to work,' he snapped, and all the time he was staring at Gracie. 'I'll deal with her.'

Maria hesitated, looked from Gracie's tear-stained face to Jacob's anguished look. It was then she realised. 'Oh, I see… It's you, isn't it? You're the boyfriend. The one she couldn't tell me about, the one she's in love with.'

'Just leave us, will you?'

'Mr Jacob, please don't listen to what Charlie says, it's all lies,' Maria pleaded. 'I know what happened, believe me – he's lying.'

'This has nothing to do with you. Now get out.'

Maria tried again to protest, but Gracie spoke up: 'It's all right, Maria. Just leave us alone, please.'

When she had gone, Gracie sat crying softly, unable to look at Jacob for fear of his anger. He paced the room… stopped… then came to stand in front of her. 'Look at me,' he said. She raised her eyes.

'I was standing next to Charlie when you were giving your little performance and he said to me, "You like her, don't you? I've seen how you look at her." When I didn't react, he thought he'd show off. "You could get in there... you know what I mean?" he said. I could have walked away but, to be honest, I'm glad I asked to him to explain. He told me he'd met you in a dancehall a few weeks ago – I assume that was when I was in London. He walked you home and you kissed him. You kissed him. Then he said—' Jacob struggled to frame the words. 'He said, "I've had her... up against a wall... putty in my hands."'

'It's not true!' Gracie was on her feet pleading. 'That didn't happen. Please believe me. I wouldn't let anyone—'

'But you danced with him and let him walk you home, you kissed him, you were in that alleyway. Yes or no?'

Gracie's cry was piercing 'Yes, yes, but...'

'That's enough, I can't hear any more.' Gracie saw the tears in his eyes and the slump of his shoulders. 'I thought you were the one for me – my beautiful, funny girl. I even thought you were naïve.' He shook his head. 'How could I have been so wrong?' He searched her face. 'Ah... now I see it. Of course! You were playing a part, acting the perfect love of my life. To think I was going to...'

Gracie went to him. 'I was always myself with you, Jacob.' She touched his arm. 'I love you.'

He shrugged her off and breathed deeply, as if summoning his courage. 'Don't touch me. Get out of my sight. I never want to see you again.' He crossed to the door and, in that space of time, he had hardened into an employer sacking a dishonest worker. 'Collect your wages on the way out and don't ever come back!'

When Sarah arrived home from work, she was surprised that there was no smell of the potato pie cooking, and when she went through to the kitchen there was no fire in the grate and no sign of Gracie. Maybe she'd gone out with some friends after work for a Christmas drink. She put the kettle on and went upstairs to get a warm cardigan. On the off-chance she peeped into Gracie's room. The curtains were closed and there was something on the bed. She switched on the light and there was Gracie curled up like a ball.

'What on earth…' said Sarah, and Gracie woke up with a start. One look at her daughter's face and she was horrified. Gracie's eyes, blinking in the light, were red and puffy. She was shivering and seemed disoriented. 'What's the matter with you?' asked Sarah.

'I don't feel well. I came home from work early.' Gracie was close to tears.

Sarah touched her forehead. It was cold and so were her hands. 'Have you a pain? Do you feel sick?' Gracie shook her head. 'Right, then, we have to get you warmed up. The kettle's on so I'll fill the hot-water bottle and bring you up a cup of tea and something to eat. That'll do to be going on with.'

Downstairs, Sarah was uneasy. She knew of no illness whose only symptoms were crying and being cold. It was too late to start making a pie so she made some cheese on toast and took it up to Gracie.

'I don't want anything to eat,' she said.

'I'll not waste good food. You have to eat something so sit up and get it down you.'

Sarah sat on the bed while Gracie ate the toast. 'Are you going to tell me what's the matter?' she asked.

Gracie handed her the empty plate. 'I'm ill.'

'No, you're not, you're upset.' Gracie couldn't look her in the eye, but Sarah pressed on. 'Something's happened at work, hasn't it?' Gracie's eyes were brimming with tears; another word and they would fall. It could only be one thing. 'Oh, dear God, this is about Jacob, isn't it?'

Gracie blinked and the tears ran down her face.

'I knew it!' cried Sarah. 'What did I tell you? A Jewish lad isn't going to get tied up with someone like you. His family wouldn't let him...' By now Gracie was taking great gulps of air as she cried uncontrollably. Sarah realised she had gone too far, there was no point in recriminations. Besides, she well understood the anguish Gracie was going through. She tried to soothe her. 'I know you're fond of him, love, but it's not meant to be. You'll get over him – you will – I promise you.'

Gracie lay back on the bed and pulled the bedclothes over her. 'Go away, Mam. I don't want to talk about it any more, except to say I'm not fond of him... I love him.'

Sarah sighed. This would be a Christmas of tears and heart-break and there was nothing she could do but comfort her daughter and endure it.

The following morning, Christmas Eve, Sarah left early for work, having put a ten-shilling note with a message on the kitchen table, asking Gracie to buy vegetables, a chicken – not too big – and anything else she could get with the change for their Christmas dinner. Gracie didn't want to think about Christmas but, with her mother working all day, she'd have to make an effort or it would be a poor Christmas for them both.

The streets were icy underfoot and an Arctic wind blew at her back all the way down Oldham Road to Smithfield market. The red-brick and wrought-iron Victorian building was packed with people. Just inside the door there was a stall with a few turkeys hanging on rails. They were far too big for the two of them, but on the counter there were chickens, capons and other small fowl. Two stout men with ruddy faces stood at the counter calling out their wares. Gracie joined the queue.

'Now, then, lass, what'll it be?'

Gracie dithered. 'Ah… a chicken… not too big.'

He held one up. 'There you are, darlin' – Lancashire's best.' He threw it on the scales. 'Five shillin' – a bargain.'

'That's quite a lot,' she said.

'Not at Christmas, it isn't, but I'll throw in a bit of ham as well.' He wrapped it all in newspaper and she put it into her bag. Then she walked round to Church Street to the barrow boys and got half a stone of potatoes and vegetables. Now all she had to do was buy a present for Mam, and Affleck & Brown's was just across the road. She was glad to be out of the bitter cold in the warmth, with the festive atmosphere. She was in no rush to go home to an empty house, so she wandered through the shop looking at everything. She lingered at the costume jewellery – such beautiful things. A delicate silver chain caught her eye.

'It's nice, isn't it?' said the assistant, a middle-aged woman in a white blouse, her grey hair pulled back in a bun. 'It's lost the little pendant, I'm afraid, but I could let you have it for half-price.'

Gracie thought about it. Her mother had a little cameo, no bigger than a farthing, set in silver. She kept it in a lozenge tin on her dressing-table with other odds and ends. There had never been a chain to it as far as she could remember. She ought to be practical and buy something useful, like a pair of gloves, but the chain for the cameo would be so much nicer.

Shopping for Christmas dinner and wandering around Affleck & Brown's had kept her sadness and distress in check, but once she was at home, Gracie relived the awful events of the previous day. Jacob's searing anger, his cutting words and the contempt in his eyes overwhelmed her, and she wept again until her eyes were sore. Still there was no respite because her mind switched to the scene in the factory and she saw herself from afar, standing alone on the cutting table, dirty words condemning her, eyes judging her, and she howled at the shame. At least she would never have to face the factory workers again because not only had she lost Jacob and her reputation she had lost her job as well. And she hadn't told her mother. And it was Christmas!

On Christmas morning Gracie and Sarah were up early, and after breakfast they exchanged gifts. Sarah gave her daughter *A Christmas Carol*. 'I know you've borrowed it from the library a few times, but now you have your own copy.'

'I'll start reading it tonight,' said Gracie.

Her second present was a hand-knitted pale blue jumper with three-quarter-length sleeves and pink crocheted roses across the yoke.

'When did you make this?'

Sarah laughed. 'Every time I told you I was going to bed early.'

'They're lovely presents, Mam, thank you. Now open yours.'

Gracie had found the little cameo, polished the blackened silver setting until it gleamed, and put it on the chain. Sarah unwrapped the tiny package and held up the necklace.

'Is it...'

'Yes, it's your cameo. I bought the silver chain so you could wear it.'

'Thank you,' said Sarah. 'It's lovely.'

'Here, give it to me,' said Gracie, and she fastened it round her mother's neck.

Sarah touched the cameo where it rested on her throat and seemed moved by the gift. 'It's so lovely,' she whispered, 'it was a gift from a friend. I never thought I'd be wearing it again,' then shook her head as if to clear it. 'Well, this won't get the baby a new bonnet. Let's have a look at the chicken you've bought.'

Gracie fetched it from the pantry, still in the newspaper, and unwrapped it.

'Good grief, it's big enough,' said Sarah. 'We'll be eating this till New Year! You know what I'm thinking? Maybe we should invite Albert round to share it with us.'

'Will he not be making his own dinner?'

'Aye, a pan of soup. That's all he ever makes. Nip next door and ask him if he wants to come round about three o'clock.'

Albert arrived at ten to three, smelling of Lifebuoy soap. 'Called at the outdoor,' he said, and he handed Sarah a brown-paper bag. 'There's a present for each for you. I know you ladies like your Mackies – stout's good for you, full of iron.'

The chicken, roast potatoes and vegetables were delicious, and there was plenty left over. There was a plum pudding, too, with custard, thanks to the Midland Hotel's management, who gave all their staff a pudding and a bottle of sweet sherry at Christmas. After they'd washed the pots, they sat talking and sipping the sherry. Albert got out his baccy pouch and carefully packed his pipe, pressing down the tobacco before putting it to his mouth and concentrating on getting it going, puffing and checking it until he was satisfied and the room was fragrant with the smell of Old Holborn. The whole ritual took a while, but all through it he told the story of the first Christmas in the trenches during the Great War. 'I were in't Lancashire Fusiliers, and we was dug in near Wipers. Christmas morning, I remember it were brass monkeys. Me and me mate

Harry were up the line on guard duty. It were quiet, like, no guns or shellin'. We heard voices driftin' 'cross no man's land. It were Fritz. We could even smell their bacon cookin'. Next thing there's a shout. "Hey, Tommy, merry Christmas." It were a German. We sneaked a look. He were holding up his rifle with his helmet balanced on top. Next thing we know he's climbin' out the trench, no rifle, just wavin' a handkerchief and shoutin', "Merry Christmas." Then Harry's out of the trench too and walkin' towards him. They met in the middle of no man's land and shook hands. Before you know it, we was all standin' out there – us and the Germans together, talkin' and swappin' Woodbines and chocolate what we had from the Queen's Christmas tin. We even had a game of football.' He paused, as if marvelling still, all these years later, at the strangeness of it all.

'What did you think of the Germans?' asked Gracie.

Albert shrugged his shoulders. 'They was just boys, same as us. Happen it'll be the same this time too.' He puffed on his pipe and stared into the fire. 'They said it would be over by Christmas. This one's got to Christmas and it hasn't even started.'

'Maybe it won't get going at all,' said Gracie.

'Oh, it will and, mark my words, it won't just be Tommies dyin' in a foreign field. It'll be ordinary folk like you and me in our beds.'

'Well, let's not think about it, especially not at Christmas,' said Sarah. 'Now, what about a few hands of whist and a bit more sherry, Albert?'

'Ah, no,' he said. 'I think I'll go home now and have a sleep. It were kind of you to invite me. Best dinner I've had in years, Sarah.'

'You're very welcome, Albert. Thanks for your company.'

'Will you be goin' to the pub tonight?' he asked. 'There'll be a good crowd in.'

'Ah... maybe.' Sarah glanced at Gracie, who looked away. 'We'll see how we feel.'

When Albert had gone, they sat at the table playing cards. 'It might be good to go to the pub – take your mind off things,' said Sarah.

'It'd take more than a couple of drinks and a singsong to do that.'

'I hate seeing you so sad, Gracie. What can I do to help you?'

'Mam, it's time you understood that you can't fix everything. I love Jacob, but he doesn't love me and I'll never see him again...'

Sarah patted her hand. 'Course you will. You'll see him at work, won't you? He might change his mind.'

Gracie panicked at her mother's question. Should she tell her that she'd been sacked by Jacob himself? No, she couldn't, not now. She didn't have the courage to explain why he would do such a thing. 'Mam, why don't you go to the pub tonight? I'm not much company.'

'No, I'm not going,' said Sarah. 'It's not fair on you, leaving you alone at Christmas like this.'

'The truth is, Mam, I can't face the pub. I'd rather be on my own, read A Christmas Carol and drink my Mackie. You go and have a good time. I'll be fine, honest.'

12

Gracie was awake when her mother came home. She must have had a few more drinks on top of the sherry and the Mackie because it took her a while to get the key into the lock. She climbed the stairs slowly and stopped on the landing. Gracie hoped she wouldn't come in to say goodnight, then heard her yawn, go into her own room and shut the door behind her. Ten minutes later she was snoring.

Gracie lay in the darkness going over and over the mess she was in – no job, no wages and no idea how to get away with not telling her mother that Jacob had shunned and sacked her for being a slut. In the end she could see no way out of it and resolved to break the news to her first thing in the morning. But still there was no sleep. She had lost Jacob for ever and crying into her pillow brought no comfort.

A sudden crash startled her. She sat up in bed almost certain it was the sound of the bath falling off the wall in the yard below her window. Then silence. A minute later there was a sharp cracking, like hailstones, on the window. She got out of bed and parted the blackout curtains just as something hit the glass. She couldn't make out anything in the blackout, but she was certain it wasn't hail. She pushed up the sash window and leaned out into the bitter wind. 'Is anyone there?' Her voice was low.

'Yes,' came the soft reply, then the sound of someone scrabbling about. She heard the rattle of tiles on the coal-shed roof, then saw a dark figure just below her window. 'Gracie?'

She gasped. 'Jacob?'

'I need to talk to you.' He stepped towards her, only to slip on the tiles, grabbing the drainpipe to steady himself.

'What are you doing here? You'll break your neck!'

'There are things I have to say to you.'

'Go away. I had enough of your hateful words on Friday and I'm not standing here freezing to death in the middle of the night to take any more of it. Anyway, it's ridiculous climbing on to a coal shed.' She reached up to close the window.

'Wait!' Jacob shouted. She hesitated, and the next words Jacob spoke shocked her. '"With love's light wings did I o'erperch these walls. For stony limits cannot hold love out…"'

Gracie let out a cry at Romeo's words of love and called his name. At that moment a window opened nearby: 'What's all the bloody noise?'

Gracie grabbed Jacob's arm and pulled him towards the open window. He lurched, slipped, grabbed the window frame with both hands and thrust himself head first into her bedroom, knocking her over. They lay on the floor in a heap. 'Shush,' whispered Gracie, worried that her mother might have woken. She crept to the door and listened, but there was only the sound of snoring. She felt her way back across the room to close the window and the curtains, then switched on the light.

Her heart missed a beat as she saw Jacob standing there, so handsome, his eyes drinking her in. Then he looked away awkwardly and, with a shock, she remembered she was wearing only her nightdress. She snatched her dressing-gown from the bed and put it on. 'What do you want to talk about, Jacob?' she whispered.

'I was wrong.' He too spoke softly. 'I'm ashamed of what I did to you.' His eyes searched her face. 'Can you forgive me?'

'It's not about forgiveness, is it? You believed what Charlie said about me and that's the end of it.'

'What if I said it's you I believe?'

'We both know it's his word against mine,' said Gracie. 'Oh, you might want to believe me, think you believe me, but it'll always be there between us, like a broken bone that heals but aches on a cold night.'

He came to her then, stood close and took her hand. '*Liebling*, I believe you because I know exactly what happened.'

'How could you know?'

'Because you have a friend who would not give up, even when I was at my most stubborn and stupid.'

'Maria?'

'She knew I would be working in the factory today, and when she was supposed to be at mass, she found me and made me listen.'

Gracie was sceptical. 'But, as you say, she's a good friend. Why would you listen to her today when you wouldn't before?'

'Because I knew I'd acted out of hand, not giving you a chance to explain, and the decent thing to do was to listen to her. To begin with she said that you only went to the dancehall as some sort of chaperone so that she could meet Tommy. Then she told me there was a witness to what happened – a lady called Annie. We went together to speak to her. Oh, Gracie, she told me that—'

'No... no... please...' Gracie held up her hands to stop

him because to hear Jacob speak the shameful words would somehow make the awful attack a memory they shared, when she had sworn to bury it deep and never speak of it again.

Jacob put his arms around her. 'It's all right. I understand.' His next words mirrored her thoughts. 'We will never speak of it again, I promise you, and it's not the reason I'm here in the middle of the night.' Gracie looked up and saw him frowning. 'Tell me, Gracie, do you still love me after all the awful things I said?'

'I do,' she said, and his smile warmed her heart.

'Then I think I know how we can be together. Sit down, and I'll explain.' They sat on the bed and he held her hand. 'I told my aunt and uncle tonight that I am in love with you. They were very angry and made it clear they wouldn't accept you into the family. I think they thought I'd give you up because I was so committed to the business. They've always said that it would come to me in the end, but tonight they threatened to disinherit me and give it to a second cousin who knows nothing about manufacturing. But that doesn't matter, Gracie, because you mean more to me than any business. I went to bed but couldn't sleep with everything going on in my mind. In the end I knew there was only one solution, and the sooner I got on with it, the better. That's why I'm here.'

'What is it? What will you do?'

'I'm going to London on the first train from Manchester in the morning. I've plenty of connections with factories there and, with my experience and contacts, I'd be a valuable asset to any business. Can you see, Gracie? It's a new life.' His eyes were bright with excitement.

'You're going away?' She couldn't hide her sadness.

'I have to. It's the only way.'

'And what about me? When will I see you again?'

'As soon as I find a job I'll come back for you, I promise. Oh, Gracie, I want to marry you so that we can be together always. Please say yes – say you'll marry me.'

It was what she had longed for, and she had only to say one word for the dream to come true. She wanted to say it so much… but all she could think of was her mother. It had always been just the two of them – could she leave her on her own?

Jacob let go of her hand. 'You don't want to marry me?'

She smiled. How could she refuse him? 'Yes, Jacob, I will marry you.'

He took her in his arms and kissed her, then gently lowered her on to the bed. She trembled as he lay beside her and sighed with pleasure as he pulled her against him. Their kiss lasted and lasted, and his hands caressed her until he raised his head to look at her, to stroke her face. '*Liebling*, I am so tempted and desperate to make love to you… but I must not. Soon we'll be married and then we'll have the rest of our lives to be together… but now I have to go.'

She clung to him. 'Stay a bit longer, please.'

'I wish I could, Gracie, but I need to be ready for that train in the morning.'

One last lingering kiss and a promise that he would soon be back, then he climbed out of the window and disappeared into the darkness.

Gracie was up early in the morning, even though she hadn't slept a wink all night thinking about Jacob. She lit the fire and had some breakfast, then waited for her mother to get up so that she could tell her the news. By ten o'clock she could wait no longer so she brewed a pot of tea and took a cup up to her mother. Sarah was bleary-eyed when Gracie pulled back the curtains. 'Oh, my poor head.' She groaned.

'Good night was it, Mam?'

'It was – what I remember of it. We had a right good sing-song and I think I might have done a bit of dancing at one point. Billy was on good form but, come to think of it, that whisky he bought me must've been a double.' She closed her eyes as if to sleep again.

'Mam, you'll never guess what...'

Sarah didn't open her eyes. 'With a thumping head like I've got, Gracie, I'd have no chance of guessing. So why don't you just tell me?'

'Jacob's asked me to marry him.'

'What?' Sarah bolted upright in bed and groaned again. 'When did that happen?'

Gracie didn't hesitate, she laughed. 'When you were out singing and dancing and supping whisky.'

'But I thought it was all over between you. Have his family changed their minds?'

'No,' said Gracie. 'But he doesn't care what they think – he loves me and we're getting married.'

Gracie watched her mother's face, hoping for some excitement or sign that she was pleased, but there was nothing. 'Are you not happy for me, Mam?'

'I don't know what to say, love. I'm happy for you, I really am, but you know my worries.'

Gracie was sharp. 'Then stop worrying. We love each other and that's all that matters.'

'When are you planning to get married?'

'As soon as we can.'

Sarah looked uneasy. 'Gracie, I have to ask you... you're not...'

'No, Mam, I'm not expecting, and I can't believe you'd think I was.'

Sarah's face flushed. 'I'm sorry, I shouldn't have—'

'No, you shouldn't!' Gracie turned her back on her and went to the window, trying not to be annoyed. This wasn't how she'd imagined her news would be received. She'd thought there would be excitement and congratulations. She watched the grey clouds cross the sky, calmed down a little, then went back to sit on her mother's bed.

'Look, Mam, he can't work at the raincoat factory anymore and neither can I. So he's gone to London this morning on the train to find work. He knows lots of people down there and he's sure he'll get a new job with all his experience running a factory. Then he'll come back for me and we'll get married.'

'You'll be leaving Manchester?'

And Gracie, who had been so excited by the prospect of marrying and living in London, was struck by the sadness in her mother's face. How she seemed suddenly older, smaller.

'Yes,' said Gracie and, without thinking, words were on her tongue and she spoke them. 'I'm going to ask him if you can come too.'

It was a moment or two before her mother said anything and Gracie watched her anxiously.

'You can't expect your husband to take in his mother-in-law, Gracie. That's not a good start to a marriage. Besides, I can't up sticks and go to London. I have my work and my friends. Manchester's my home.'

'Do you not want me to marry him?'

'I didn't say that. If you love each other, you should get married. Don't worry about me, I'll be fine.' But Gracie could hear in her voice and see in her face that she wasn't fine at all.

★

In the afternoon Gracie walked to Maria's house and, as usual, the welcome from the Mancini family was warm. She had coffee with cream and almond cake with them, then she and Maria went into her bedroom to talk.

As soon as the door was closed Maria couldn't contain her excitement. 'Have you heard anything from Jacob?'

Gracie's face was sad. 'Nothing.'

'What? I thought—'

Gracie interrupted her. 'What did you think?'

'I just thought he would, you know, come to his senses and maybe apologise to you.'

'And why would he do that?'

Maria shook her head. 'I'm so sorry. I felt sure he'd make it up with you.'

'Well, that wasn't going to happen, not unless somebody persuaded him that there was a witness to what happened with me and Charlie and marched him round to Annie's house to hear the truth!'

Maria looked puzzled, and then it dawned on her. 'You've seen him, haven't you?' She jumped up and down, giddy with laughing. 'Oh, you had me going there for a bit!' Then they were hugging each other. 'So, you're together again? Did he go to your house? Tell me, tell me!'

'You'll never believe it,' said Gracie, and she told the story of Jacob climbing on to the coal-shed roof and into her bedroom.

Maria gasped. 'He never did?'

Gracie nodded. 'And that's not all. He's asked me to marry him and we're going to live in London.'

'Oh, Gracie, it's so romantic. I think I'm going to cry.'

'And it's all because of you, Maria. I don't know how to thank you.'

'Well, you could start by telling me the whole story of you and Jacob from the very beginning and don't you dare leave anything out.'

Days passed, and Sarah could only watch as Gracie, like an actor standing in the wings, went from confident one minute to a bundle of nerves the next. It didn't help that Sarah herself was balancing her worries against her desire to see Gracie happy. She didn't like the idea of a quick marriage – they hardly knew each other. 'Marry in haste, repent at leisure' was a well-known adage because it was often true. Then there was the move to London – that was the worst of it. Life without Gracie would be lonely. But time and time again her thoughts turned to long ago when she had been Gracie's age. What would she have done if she had received such a sudden proposal? She knew the answer to that – if he'd asked her, she'd have married Martin Quigley like a shot.

Time went by, and Gracie became even more restless. The fact that she had no work to go to made it worse. Sarah suggested she should clean the house and make all their meals. 'It'll get you used to running your own home for when you go to London,' she told her. Soon the house was shining like a new pin and, apart from walking to the Co-op for groceries, Gracie spent her days alone and bored. The weather had turned bitterly cold and, with only enough coal for a fire in the evening, she spent her mornings in bed with a hot-water bottle and a book – her ear cocked for the sound of the postman. Jacob had written two or three times a week, his words full of love and plans for their future, but he still hadn't found a new position.

Then just as she was about to give up hope, the letter she had longed for arrived. Jacob's opening words made her laugh in delight. He had a job, thanks to friends at the synagogue he had attended in London. A factory owner had died suddenly, and the family needed someone with experience to take charge. He even had the offer of a flat. He told her to go to the register office immediately and arrange for a special licence so that they could marry the following week. He gave his date and place of birth, which she would need to complete the forms and he had enclosed a ten-pound postal order to pay for the licence and to buy herself a wedding outfit. He would bring the ring. Gracie hugged herself and read the ending of the letter.

When you have the licence, let me know the time and the place. I will be late arriving in Manchester so I'll spend the night in a hotel and then I'll meet with my uncle the next morning. He owes me a hefty bonus for the government contract and I mean to have it. Then I'll meet you at the register office. I long to see you again, I've missed you so much, but next week we will be married, and we'll never be parted again, I promise you.

You are my life, Liebling.

13

The register office on Jackson's Row was a dismal place, cold and musty. Gracie followed the sign to the special-licence counter and was surprised to see a bit of a queue. A girl in front of her, about her own age, asked her whether her sweetheart had been called up too. Gracie was immediately wary. 'Em, no... he's been working in London. He's coming back next week for us to get married.'

'Good idea,' said the girl. 'He could get his call-up papers any time.'

At the counter the clerk went through the form with her, filling in the details. When she told him Jacob had been born in Berlin, he gave her a hard stare. She held her breath, thinking he would not approve the licence, but he signed it, stamped it and booked the wedding for the following Wednesday at noon. Outside she was elated that her wedding was a step closer, but she would never forget the look of disgust on the clerk's face.

Kendal Milne on Deansgate was the best department store

in the city. Gracie had never been inside before because she couldn't possibly have afforded their prices. Besides, she would have felt out of place mingling with well-dressed wives from Altrincham and Didsbury. But today was different: today she had money in her pocket to buy something stylish. She came in from the cold street to a rush of warm air and stopped to take it all in: counters of perfume and makeup, scarves and gloves, hats and umbrellas. She was offered a spray of Elizabeth Arden perfume and, in a cloud of tea-rose scent, she followed a sign up the wide staircase to Ladies' Gowns. She wandered around looking at dresses, feeling the material and noting the price tags. She could afford some of them with the money Jacob had given her, but she couldn't bring herself to spend so much on a dress that wouldn't get much wear.

'Are you looking for something in particular, madam?' Gracie turned to see a blonde girl, beautifully made up.

'I'm not really sure. Everything is so nice.'

'Is it for a special occasion?'

'Ah…' Gracie hesitated '… I'm getting married, but it's in a register office so I'm not sure what would be suitable.'

'How lovely.' The girl smiled broadly. 'Well, lately we've had a few ladies in exactly the same situation as you and they've gone for costumes, two-piece suits. Would you like me to show you?'

Gracie knew a well-tailored garment when she saw one and the designs were so modern. She tried on half a dozen and the shop assistant stayed with her, giving advice on the cut and colour. In the end Gracie settled on a maroon fine wool, double-breasted costume, with a nipped-in waist on the jacket and an A-line skirt with a vent at the back.

'The design is very similar to one worn by the Duchess of Windsor,' the girl told her.

Gracie didn't know about that, but she did know that the suit might have been made for her.

The night before the wedding Gracie had her bath, washed and dried her hair, then sat on the rug in front of the roaring fire while Sarah made her favourite supper – bread and warm milk with a sprinkle of nutmeg.

'Can you believe I'm getting married tomorrow, Mam?'

'No, Gracie, I can't. It's all happened so fast. I knew you'd meet someone some day, but I wasn't expecting it so soon.'

Gracie laughed. 'Maybe I should've warned you, because after our first date I knew I loved Jacob. Was it like that with you and Dad?'

'Not really. It was more that I got to know him first as a friend.' Sarah handed her the bowl of bread and milk.

Gracie raised the spoon to her mouth and stopped. 'I've never seen your wedding photograph. Did you not have one?'

'No. There weren't many ordinary people who owned cameras back then. You had to go to a studio and we didn't have the money. That's why I'm glad you borrowed Albert's box Brownie so we'd have photos of you and Jacob.'

They sat quietly awhile, Gracie eating and Sarah staring at the flickering flames. 'You'll be all right in the hotel tomorrow night, will you?' said Sarah, without looking up.

Gracie didn't answer.

'I mean, you could have come back here.'

The unspoken thoughts of the wedding night lay awkwardly between them.

'I'll be fine, Mam, don't worry. Jacob loves me, and I love him.'

Sarah looked up and Gracie met her gaze. They exchanged a nod and a soft smile, and the moment passed.

The next morning Gracie woke up shivering with cold. She listened for the sound of her mother in the kitchen, hoping she was downstairs getting the fire going. She listened for the comings and goings outside too, but everything was eerily silent. She got out of bed and pulled back the curtains. The world was white. It must have snowed all night for every surface was thick with it: every sharp angle and corner was rounded and smooth. The coal-shed roof was a glittering eiderdown and a two-foot drift blocked the privy door, but it was a beautiful day.

She thought of Jacob waking up in his hotel room. Was he as excited and nervous as she was? In a few hours they would be man and wife – till death us do part – and by this time tomorrow she would be on her way to a new home in a new city.

There was a knock on the door and her mother came in. 'Ah, you're awake,' she said, and kissed her cheek. 'Happy wedding day, love. What do you think of the snow? It'll be a white wedding after all.'

'At least we haven't the Manchester rain.'

'Sure we'll have a lovely day. I know it,' said Sarah. 'Now, I'll go and make you some breakfast.' She got as far as the door and stopped. 'Oh, I nearly forgot.' She took a paper bag from the pocket of her pinny. 'Doris brought this round for you.'

'What is it?'

'Just a bit of fun.'

Gracie pulled out a blue frilly garter and laughed. 'It's my something blue, isn't it? I forgot about all that. So, I've got the blue, now all I need is something old, something new, something borrowed. My costume is new, and I've borrowed Albert's camera, which just leaves something old.'

'Hold on a minute,' said Sarah, and left the room, returning moments later with the cameo necklace. 'You should wear this. It's older than you are.'

'But don't you want to wear it?'

'No, love. It's only right that you should have it today.'

Doris, dressed in a tweed coat and a brown felt hat, arrived excited and not a little nervous about being a witness, but a glass of sherry settled her. Sarah, in her bottle-green coat with a paisley scarf at her neck, checked her hair in the mirror and poured herself a glass.

A few minutes later Gracie appeared in the kitchen, and the sight of her took Sarah's breath away. The rich colour of the costume was perfect for her, her dark hair shone, and her smile was pure joy. How proud her father would have been to see his daughter. Sarah felt the tears prick her eyes. 'Oh, Gracie...'

Doris was less restrained, with tears running down her cheeks. 'Eh, lass, you're a sight for sore eyes and no mistake.'

They caught the tram into town and walked through St Ann's Square where an old woman was sitting outside the church selling little violet posies. Gracie bought one for each of them to wear. They arrived early at the registry office, but a clerk directed them to the waiting room and they sat on the wooden benches with another wedding party. Within minutes a newly married couple with their guests, all smiling and laughing, emerged from the chamber where the weddings were conducted. The registrar then invited the waiting bride and groom and guests into the chamber. Gracie took off her pink coat and wandered round the room looking at old photographs of Manchester on the walls.

From where Sarah sat she could see out of the window towards the town-hall clock and noted the time – a quarter to twelve. It was the same view she'd had twenty years before when she was the bride and she felt again the relief of being married, mixed with the shame of having given birth to a daughter just a fortnight before.

The door opened and the happy couple came out, pausing only for the bride to throw her bouquet. It was almost noon. The registrar looked over his glasses at them and returned to his chamber.

'Where is he, Mam?'

'Don't worry, he'll be here.'

The door to the waiting room opened – another couple had arrived with their friends and family, the man in an RAF uniform, the girl in a flimsy wedding gown and veil. The registrar returned and spoke to Gracie. 'I see the groom has not yet arrived and it is now past noon.' He cleared his throat. 'In such circumstances I usually suggest that I proceed with the next couple, if they are agreeable, thus leaving time for your groom to appear.'

Gracie just stared at him. Sarah could see how fragile she was, so she answered him: 'Yes, that's fine. Thank you very much.'

When they were alone again Gracie said, 'He's not coming, is he?'

Sarah patted her hand. 'Of course he is. He's only five minutes late.'

Gracie paced the floor, Sarah prayed, and poor Doris didn't know what to say.

The RAF man and his new wife left the building, and by the time two other couples had tied the knot and filled the room with their happiness, Sarah knew she had to bring an end to their waiting.

'Gracie, I think we should go home now. Jacob must have been delayed somehow. He wouldn't expect you to wait this long.' Gracie's face was pale and expressionless as if she had withdrawn into herself. Sarah picked up her coat and held it out for her. She put it on and Sarah buttoned it and, with a nod to Doris, they left the building. Outside the day had turned bleak and sleet blew into their faces until their eyes watered.

Back in Pearson Street they said goodbye to Doris and, once inside, Sarah made a brew while Gracie sat staring into space. She hadn't spoken since they'd left the register office and Sarah felt it best to let her come round in her own time. They had hardly finished the tea when Gracie stood up and announced that she was going to look for Jacob. 'I'll start at the factory. That's where he was going first thing this morning.'

'I wouldn't do that if I were you,' said Sarah.

'Well, you're not me, are you? Something must have happened to him. He would never leave me like that.' She headed for the door.

Sarah ran after her and managed to get there first. 'Please, Gracie, don't go out in this freezing weather. Stay here and wait for him. He probably missed his train yesterday or something happened this morning... I beg you, love, stay here.'

'But I want to see him so much,' sobbed Gracie.

'I know you do,' said Sarah, and put her arms round her. 'Don't fret yourself, love, you've had a bad shock. There must be a good reason he wasn't there and I'm sure he'll want to explain. That's why you have to be here, waiting for him.'

'Do you really think that?'

'Yes, I do. Now why don't you lie down for a while?' And Gracie let herself be guided up the stairs. 'Try and have a sleep, love. I promise I'll wake you as soon as he comes.' Sarah covered her with the eiderdown. 'I could sit with you if you like.'

'Just leave me, Mam.'

In the kitchen Sarah could finally shed her own tears for the awful shock and hurt Gracie had suffered. She prayed that Jacob would soon arrive to explain himself, one way or another. The day grew dark and there was still no sign of him. She closed the blackout curtains and put on the light, then went to check on Gracie. She was sound asleep, so she crept away. No sooner was she back in the kitchen than there was a pounding on the front door and she rushed to open it. It was Maria.

'Mrs Earnshaw, I have to see Gracie straight away. I'd have come sooner but I had to finish my shift. Where is she?'

'Upstairs. Come in, I'll fetch her.'

'I'm here.' Gracie was standing at the foot of the stairs.

Maria ran to her. 'Oh, Gracie, I'm so sorry. It's about Jacob.'

'What? What? Tell me!'

'The police came for him this morning at the factory. They said they were arresting him because he was an enemy alien and they took him away.'

14

No matter what her mother said, Gracie couldn't sit in the house any longer waiting for news of Jacob. After a wretched weekend she decided there was nothing else for it but to speak to Mr Rosenberg: he would know what was going on. The only trouble was, she would have to face the workers who had witnessed Charlie's humiliation of her. But what did that matter? Jacob loved her, and they would be married once this misunderstanding was sorted out.

She went through the back gate to the factory and crossed the yard. Once inside, she walked quickly along the corridor, paused in front of the machine-room door and took a deep breath, but before she could open it, someone behind her called, 'Well, look what the cat dragged in.'

Gracie froze. That was the last thing she had expected. She turned to face Charlie, leering at her. She fought to keep her voice calm even though she was shaking. 'What are you doing here?'

'Working, what do you think?'

'But you were sacked.'

'Only by somebody who's locked up for bein' a Nazi.' He laughed. 'Rosenberg gave me my job back 'cause he couldn't find another cutter as good as me.' He moved closer to her. 'I've been thinkin' about you a lot since... well, you know... that night at the Ritz. Thing is, I rushed you a bit, didn't I?... You weren't quite ready. If you like we could go out again for a few dates... and take it slowly, you know what I mean.' He winked at her. 'What do you think?'

Gracie felt her stomach turn and she swallowed the bile in her mouth. 'I think you're disgusting. You make my flesh creep, and I wish I'd gone to the police when you attacked me.'

'Come on, love. I were just chancin' me arm.' He went to touch her.

Now she had no choice: better to face the whole factory than to spend another second with Charlie. She pushed open the door and stepped inside to the familiar sound of sewing machines and women singing. She had walked the length of the factory floor a thousand times, but never had it taken so long to reach the office. As she walked, one by one the machines fell silent, the women stopped singing and Mr Rosenberg came out to see what was happening. At last she stood in front of him. 'I'm here to talk about Jacob,' she said.

He ushered her into the office and closed the door. 'I didn't expect to see you back here, after all that's gone on,' he said.

'I need to know what's happened to Jacob. Where is he?'

Rosenberg gave an exaggerated shrug. 'He might be at a police station or Strangeways. Who knows?'

'But surely you've tried to find him.'

'It's not that simple. They're rounding up German and Austrian citizens, even some Jews who have fled Germany. We have to be careful. We do not know who will be next. Our rabbi is speaking to the authorities, but it is chaos.'

'What did they say when they arrested him?'

'Only that he was a German citizen who had been back and forth to Germany several times over the years and they were taking him into custody under the Emergency Powers Act.'

'How did they know about him?'

Rosenberg shrugged again. 'German citizens have always been registered with the police, but since war broke out the authorities have been looking into our backgrounds. There are three categories and it seems Jacob was found to be category A – a threat to the country. That's why he was arrested.'

'But they didn't take you or any of the Jewish people who work for you?'

'No, but they could come back for us at any time. We have to keep our heads down.'

'So, you're going to do nothing?'

He didn't answer, and she knew it was hopeless. She would have to find Jacob herself.

Outside, snowflakes the size of pennies were falling and sticking to the pavements, but Gracie put her head down and set off down the road. Strangeways Prison was a forbidding sight, with its high walls and a tower as tall as a factory chimney. It was one thing to walk past it, as she had done many times, but quite another to stand in front of its iron gates and ring the bell. A peep-hole at eye height opened and she found herself looking through a grille at a prison officer. 'There's no visiting today,' he said.

'I don't want to visit. I just need to know if somebody is here. His name's Jacob Rosenberg and he was arrested on Wednesday morning. I don't know where he is.'

'Look, love, there's over a thousand men in here. I wouldn't know who's been brought in and I wouldn't tell you if I did.'

'He's not a criminal. They say he's an enemy alien, but he isn't, honestly.'

His tone changed. 'Enemy alien, you say. In that case he'll be banged up for the duration. Now, why don't you go home and forget about your Nazi fella? Do the decent thing and get yourself an Englishman.' And he slammed the grille shut. She didn't believe for one moment that Jacob would spend the war in prison. He hadn't committed any crime, he knew people in the government, for goodness' sake, and he was going to marry an English woman. No, they would have to let him go. The snow grew thicker, sticking to her coat, and she could hardly feel her feet, they were so cold, but she was determined to keep searching. There was a police station close to Piccadilly Gardens: maybe they'd taken him there.

The sergeant on the desk listened carefully when she explained her fiancé had been taken from the factory and she was trying to find out where he was. She didn't mention enemy aliens this time, but when she gave his name the sergeant asked whether he was German. She could only nod and wait for the abuse, but he told her to take a seat and he'd get someone to speak to her. Gracie had never been in a police station before, and watching what went on was an eye-opener: a man held between two policemen thrashing around and swearing at the top of his voice; an old woman crying about her stolen purse; a lost child...

A young woman in uniform appeared at her side. 'I understand you've been asking about your fiancé. All I can tell you is that a lot of people have been taken into custody, mostly German citizens. We don't know where they've gone, or how long they'll be held. There's no point in trying to find him. Just go home and wait.'

'But he's not—'

'I'm sorry, there's nothing more I can do.' She turned and walked away.

By the time her mother came home from work, Gracie had a plan of action. 'I think they'll soon realise that Jacob is no threat to the country and they'll let him go but, just in case, I'll go out every day and do the rounds of the police stations. I'm sure somebody knows something about the German citizens being arrested. Sooner or later they'll either tell me where he is to get rid of me or they'll let something slip. I'll go to the town hall, too, and the *Manchester Evening News*, then back to Strangeways.'

'You'll run yourself ragged, Gracie. They did the same thing in the Great War, you know, put them in camps miles from anywhere. Why don't you just keep in touch with his family? They'll be the first to know any news. They might even give you your job back.'

'Mam, you know they don't want me there.' And she told herself, even if they did, she would never work in the same building as Charlie again.

'I'm only thinking we've been struggling with just my wage. I can do overtime but...'

'Mam, I have to find him, don't you see that? His family might have abandoned him, but I never will.'

In the coldest weather for more than twenty years, Gracie walked the streets searching for news of arrested German citizens, but everywhere she was met with indifference or, worse, suspicion.

A week later, Sarah came in from work with a copy of the

Manchester Evening News. 'You'd best take a look at this,' she said.

Gracie's eyes widened at the headline: 'German Nationals Arrested'.

'At last something's happening,' she said. 'I told you about the reporter I spoke to at the paper, didn't I? He didn't know anything about it then, but he must've thought it was a story worth chasing.' She quickly scanned the report. 'A few hundred Germans and Austrians rounded up… being held in camps… whereabouts unknown… wholesale internment. What does that mean, Mam?'

'Internment? It means they're not being charged with any crime, but they'll be put in a camp and, I hate to say this, Gracie, but you have to face the fact that Jacob will probably be held there till the end of the war.'

'But he hasn't done anything wrong! They'll have to let him go.'

'They won't, love, but maybe he'll be allowed to send you a letter and there might even be a chance to visit him. That would be something, wouldn't it?'

Gracie gave her mother a hard stare. 'No, Mam, it's not enough. Can't you see? He should be free, and we should be married.'

At that moment there was a knock at the door and Sarah went to answer it. It was Maria. Gracie jumped up as soon as she saw her. 'Has something happened? Have they found Jacob?'

Maria shook her head. 'Not as far as I know, but the rabbi came to see Mr Rosenberg today. He was there quite a while so at least they're still trying to find him.'

Gracie sighed. 'Surely somebody must know where Jacob and all the other people are. They can't have disappeared into thin air.'

Maria looked uncomfortable. 'I'm sorry, Gracie.'

'Would you take a cup of tea, Maria?' said Sarah.

'No, thanks, I'm not stopping,' said Maria. 'Actually, I came over with some good news. Gracie, do you remember Alan, that friend of Tommy's? You met him at the Ritz.'

Gracie flashed her a look at the mention of that night, but Maria hurried on: 'Tommy was out for a pint with him the other night and he happened to mention that they're looking for people to work at Metrovicks out at Trafford Park. Tommy told him you might be interested, and Alan said if you went to the factory and mentioned his name you might get taken on. It's war work so the wages are good.'

'That's just what you need,' said Sarah. 'It's really kind of you to let us know, Tommy too. Isn't it, Gracie?'

'Hmm,' she said. 'Thanks, Maria, I'll think about it.'

'Gracie!' her mother shouted.

'It's all right, Mrs Earnshaw, I know Gracie's going through a hard time. I just thought… Anyway, I'd better be going.'

'I'll come to the door with you,' said Gracie. Outside she explained, 'I have to keep looking for him, Maria. I can't let him think I've abandoned him.'

When Gracie returned Sarah spoke bluntly. 'Are you going to try for that job?'

'I don't know, maybe.'

'Never mind "maybe". Get off to Trafford Park in the morning to see if they'll take you on.'

'But what about Jacob?'

Sarah sighed. 'Look, love, I understand how you're feeling, but you have to think about the practicalities. You've done all you can to find him, but my guess is it'll be a while before you know where he is and even longer before he's released. If you want my opinion, you'd be better off getting back into work.'

'But I don't want your opinion,' snapped Gracie. 'And I don't see how you could understand what I'm feeling – you've never lost the man you loved on the day you were meant to be married, have you?'

'I'm just saying you could get a job while you wait to see if Jacob is released and, as I said, we could do with the money.'

After tea of bread and dripping, for the second time in a week, Gracie went to bed without saying goodnight to her mother. She lay on her bed rereading the letters Jacob had sent her when he was in London, and in each one he had written of his longing to be with her. Was he thinking of her right now? Was he missing her?

Of course she knew Mam was right: he could be anywhere and she could walk the streets for weeks and never find him. Her only hope was that someone would realise that Jacob's arrest was a mistake and let him go. She took the snow globe from the drawer, shook it and watched the snow fall over Blackpool Tower. Even on that day at the seaside while they were falling in love, the shadow of war had hung over their future, and she recalled how deeply Jacob had been affected by the man who had threatened him with the police.

That night she dreamed that Jacob climbed through her bedroom window to lie with her again. His kisses were full of passion and his gentle hands made her cry out for him, but this time she didn't let him go. 'Please… please…' she whispered. Her breath quickened, and she moaned with pleasure… Then, suddenly, she was awake and calling his name. 'Jacob! Jacob, where are you?' She cursed herself for waking up, then wept to feel the weight of him again.

15

The following day Sarah went to work with a heavy heart. The last thing she had wanted to do was to upset Gracie, but she had to make her understand that life goes on and the best remedy for heartbreak is to grit your teeth and carry on. Thanks to Maria, there was a chance she could get a new job, a well-paid one at that, and she couldn't bear the thought that Gracie would pass up the opportunity.

She clocked in early at the Midland and went straight to the housekeeper's office. 'Excuse me, Mrs Jones, could I have a word, please?'

The housekeeper, a woman seemingly born without the ability to smile, looked up from the laundry ledger and put down her pen. 'What do you want, Mrs Earnshaw?'

'I was wondering if there might be any shifts you need covering. I'd be happy to do more hours.'

'Would you, now?' she said. 'Well, as it happens, the head waiter has a few big functions coming up and he may need waitresses or kitchen staff at short notice. You'd be working late, sometimes after midnight, and I'd expect you to be back here for normal chambermaid duties the next morning.'

'Oh, I could do that, all right, Mrs Jones.'

'In that case I'll pass on your name.' She picked up her pen and went back to her ledger.

Sarah loaded her cart with fresh linen and towels and set to work in better spirits now that she had a chance to earn a bit more money. If Gracie could get a job, well, they'd soon be living in clover.

Towards dinnertime she was cleaning one of the single rooms on the second floor when she noticed on the writing desk what looked like a postcard tucked into the corner of the blotting pad. She pulled it out and was about to throw it away when her eye caught the letters 'RAF' in the corner and below that the words 'Embarkation Card'. A split second later she caught her breath... The name... How could it be? She sat on the bed, her mind racing, and scanned the card. It was some sort of authorised travel schedule. 'Port of Embarkation: Belfast, Destination: Liverpool, Returning from leave', and the name: Martin Quigley. She stared at it in wonder. Could it be her Martin Quigley? It wasn't a common name and the man had spent his leave in Belfast. She was being silly: there could be other Martin Quigleys in the city. Besides, her Martin would be forty-two: was that not too old to be serving in the RAF? But still she sat there, holding his name in her hand, remembering the boy from the draper's shop she had loved all those years ago.

Her mind slipped back to Belfast, and the memories crowded in. Their relationship had been so innocent at first – she had liked his smile and his easy manner. He'd talked nineteen to the dozen, made her laugh – made her blush too, calling her the prettiest girl in the city. They would meet a good distance from where they lived: in quiet bars, to sit and talk, in empty moonlit parks, and under the railway bridge where she had learned how to please him.

But a Catholic boy and a Protestant girl falling in love was the road to heartache. Maybe it could have worked, if they had faced their families together. In the end it wasn't to be: he had stayed in Belfast and she had been cast out.

She stood up, dismissing her romantic notions. Martin Quigley meant nothing to her. If he was to walk into the room right now, she wouldn't give him the time of day. Anyway, she was done daydreaming and went straight to her cart, intending to throw the card in with the rubbish. She paused and, for no reason she could think of, put it into her pocket instead.

Sarah got off the tram just as Doris came out of the corner shop. 'Are you hitting the beer and fags, then, Doris?' she said, nodding at the bottle of Boddingtons and packet of Player's in her hand.

'I should be so lucky. No, his nibs came home with a thirst on him and no smokes, so I've to use the housekeeping to pay for them. I saw Gracie go out again today. She's looking a bit better. Has there been news of Jacob?'

'Not a word,' said Sarah, 'but we think he's been sent to some sort of internment camp. God knows when he'll get out of that.'

'It's terrible, poor Gracie. I can't imagine what it must be like for her to have her man snatched away on the very day they were to be married.'

Doris looked close to tears and Sarah changed the subject. 'What about your girls?'

'They're doing fine. I'm going to Ramsbottom to see them on Sunday. You're welcome to come with me, if you fancy it.'

'I would, but I don't like to leave Gracie at the moment.'

They parted at Doris's door. 'I'll see you in the week then, ta-rah.'

Sarah came into the house to the unexpected smell of meat cooking. In the kitchen the table was set and Gracie at the stove turned to smile at her.

'That smells good,' said Sarah, and she could have added that Gracie looked a lot happier than she'd seen her in weeks.

'I thought I'd make stew and potatoes, and there's rice pudding in the oven.'

'Where did you get the money for all that?'

'I borrowed it from Billy.' Gracie laughed at the look on her mother's face. 'Don't worry I'll pay him back... when I get my wages.'

'What wages would they be?'

'The wages I'll get now that I'm working at Metrovicks in Trafford Park.'

Sarah could hardly believe it. Last night Gracie had been so angry about going for the job. 'What made you change your mind?'

'I kept thinking about Jacob. He'd expect me to be strong and I should be. It wasn't as if he jilted me. He loves me and we will get married. In the meantime, I can do something useful for the war effort. No point in sitting here moping, eating bread and dripping for tea.'

'That's my girl,' said Sarah.

16

It was still dark when Gracie boarded one of the works buses at Piccadilly for the trip to Trafford Park and the Metrovicks factory. It was standing room only and she spent the journey pressed against oily boiler suits, hacking coughs, and breathing the smog of cigarette smoke. At the end of the line she emerged into the half-light and stood a moment to get her bearings. Everything looked so different from the day before when she had come to ask about a job. The scene in front of her was devoid of colour: workers, like smudges of charcoal, hurried down the road towards the grey buildings in the distance; a huge metal tower, dark and menacing, pierced the smoky sky—

'Flippin' 'eck, get a bloody move on, will ye!' A man pushed her forward into the flow of workers and she quickened her step to keep pace with them.

She was one of ten new workers joining Metrovicks that day. They were taken to a canteen where they filled in forms and had a lecture on 'Careless Talk Costs Lives'. She sat with Trixie, a plump girl with a bonny face, and, as luck would have it, they were both assigned to the anti-aircraft-gun factory.

'At least we know each other,' said Trixie.

'We'll pal up together,' said Gracie, and they shook hands on it.

They were taken to the stores where the foreman, Mr Greaves, an older man with wire-rimmed spectacles and a pencil behind his ear, was waiting for them. 'I weren't expectin' women,' he said, looking them up and down. 'Ye can't work in stores dressed like that. Ye look like you're going to a dance. Follow me.' He set off at a quick pace past rows of tall racks and crates. 'Here we are,' he said, and went quickly up a ladder, a good fifteen feet in the air, and came down with two boiler suits. 'Get them on,' he said. Gracie and Trixie looked at each other. 'Is there somewhere we could—'

'Don't be stupid, just put them over your clothes.'

They did as they were told and stood there like sacks of potatoes. The arms and legs were far too long and everything else was baggy. 'They don't fit us,' said Gracie.

Mr Greaves gave her a hard stare. 'Like I said, I weren't expectin' women.'

Gracie and Trixie spent their first day learning how to log items in and out of the stores and, when the hooter went for clocking off, Mr Greaves told them, 'At least your writing's a lot neater than some of these fellas workin' here. Mind you, that's not sayin' much. You'll be trained on the ladders tomorrow and we'll see how strong you are when it comes to liftin' and layin'. I lost two strappin' lads from here when they got their call-up papers and you'll be expected to replace them. And I'll tell you this for nothing – you've got till the end of the week, and if you don't shape up, you'll be out on your ear!' He walked away, shaking his head and tutting.

'Gracie, I don't think I could climb these ladders,' said Trixie.

'But we'll have to if we want to keep our jobs. Look, we'll help each other. If those fellas can do it, then so can we.'

'Do you think so?'

'I do,' said Gracie. 'Now, let's get out of these boiler suits. I'll take them home and see if I can alter them tonight.'

It was almost dark when they headed towards the factory gates. They hadn't gone more than a few yards when Gracie thought she heard someone call her name. She turned to see Alan coming towards her, pushing a bicycle. 'How was your first day?' he asked.

'Oh, it was all right. I'm working in the anti-aircraft-gun stores.'

'Yes, I know.'

'This is Trixie. She started today too.'

Alan gave her a nod and turned back to Gracie. 'I usually go for a drink after work, just the one, you know. Do you fancy coming?'

'Thanks, Alan, but to tell you the truth, I'm dead on my feet. It's been such a long day.'

'Fine. Just thought you might like to catch up.' He got on his bike. 'Maybe another time.' He cycled away.

'Who's he?' said Trixie.

'A friend of a friend. I don't really know him, but it was through him that I heard there was a job going here.'

'He seems nice enough,' said Trixie. 'Anyway, I'll see you tomorrow.'

'You don't get a bus?'

'No, I'm only ten minutes away. I'll see you in the morning.'

At home that evening Gracie set to work on the oversized boiler suits. She asked her mother to help by unpicking the seams and one by one Gracie laid each section, body, legs, sleeves, on the kitchen table to trim the excess material.

'I'll do mine first to get it right, then Trixie's. She's a bit bigger in the body and shorter in the arms and legs than me.' Gracie had a good eye for size and shape and was soon passing the pieces back to her mother to pin them ready for stitching. Then she threaded up the treadle machine and started sewing while her mother worked on Trixie's suit. It was nearly midnight before they finished.

'Thanks, Mam. If it wasn't for your help I'd never have got them done.'

'Oh, don't thank me, love. I'm just pleased you've got a job. Now get yourself to bed – you've an early start in the morning.'

By the end of the week the two girls could manage most of their duties by working together. Gracie would climb the high ladders, while Trixie would deal with the heavier boxes to be shifted. If Mr Greaves realised what was going on, he didn't say anything, and that was because the girls kept the stores much tidier and the invoices correctly filed.

Gracie hadn't seen anything of Alan since that first night when he'd asked her to go for a drink. He had been very kind in getting her the job and she felt bad that she hadn't thanked him properly. Then on that Friday dinnertime, when she and Trixie were in the canteen, she spotted him sitting on his own and went over to speak to him. 'Hello. Is it all right if I join you?' she said.

He looked up and smiled. 'Of course. How are you getting on with Mr Greaves?'

'Oh, his bark's worse than his bite.' She sat down opposite him. 'I didn't get a chance to thank you properly for getting me this job. I'm really grateful to you.'

'You're welcome. It was the least I could do when Tommy told me what had happened to you.'

Gracie was immediately wary. What exactly had Tommy told him? But Alan went on: 'A terrible thing to happen on your wedding day. He was interned, wasn't he?'

'Yes, but it was a mistake. I'm hoping he'll be released soon,' said Gracie.

'Is he the boyfriend who didn't mind that you were out dancing that night when we met at the Ritz?'

'Yes, he was away in London...' Gracie bowed her head at the familiar stab of shame she felt every time she thought of that night. Did Alan also know what Charlie had tried to do to her? She felt a touch on her hand and looked up.

Alan's face was full of compassion. 'I'm sorry, I shouldn't have mentioned him. I can see it upsets you.'

'It's just that I find it hard to talk about it.' She stood to go. 'Anyway, thanks for what you did in getting me the job.'

'Look, if there's anything else I can do to help you've only to ask. Tommy and Maria are good friends of mine. You can trust me.'

'I know.' She managed a smile. 'I'll see you around.'

'I think he fancies you,' said Trixie, when Gracie returned.

'He knows I'm not available.'

Trixie's eyes widened. 'You never said you had a boy-friend.'

'Well, he's not around at the moment. He's in a camp.'

'Oh, he's in the forces. Where's he stationed?'

'I don't know exactly.' Gracie knew she should have corrected Trixie's misunderstanding, but she couldn't face explaining the whole internment situation and that, although Jacob was born in Germany, he was no threat to anyone.

'Never mind. Think of all the love letters he'll send you.'

Gracie swallowed the lump in her throat. 'And what about you? Have you got a sweetheart?'

Trixie laughed. 'I wish I had...'

One evening a couple of weeks later Gracie noticed Alan was on the same bus as her going home from the factory. She said hello to him and went to sit at the front. When she got off at Piccadilly so did he.

'What's happened to your bike?' she asked.

'Somebody stole it.'

'That's awful. Have you far to go from here?'

'Not really,' he said. 'You're up Miles Platting way, aren't you?' And he took her arm while they crossed the road. They walked for a few minutes – Alan chatting about the goings-on in his workshop in the new aircraft factory. Then he said, 'Mr Greaves tells me you've settled in well, Grace.' She was surprised at him calling her that, but she didn't like to correct him. 'Anyway, this is where we part company,' he said. 'I'll see you tomorrow. Goodnight.'

The weeks went by and Gracie was glad to be going to work and coming home in daylight. She and Alan would often catch the same bus; she looked forward to his company and felt a little lonely when he worked late and she had to travel alone. She liked the way he tried to cheer her up when the strain of not knowing what had happened to Jacob became too much. He would listen to her fears and soothe her anxiety. 'Keep your chin up, Grace,' he'd say. 'It looks to me like you're in this for the long haul and you need to stay strong.'

And she tried, she really did. Then one evening, Maria called at the house with news that Mr Rosenberg had received a letter of sorts from Jacob that day. He told the workers that his nephew had sent a short, heavily censored note saying he was in a camp and in good health. Gracie was overcome with relief and went to bed to sleep soundly for the first time since Jacob had been taken. Yet she awoke with a sense of unease. He had sent a note to his uncle – a man who was prepared to disown him because he had chosen her for his wife.

She set off for work in a dark mood, trying to understand why Jacob, given the opportunity, had not contacted her. She needed to speak to Alan. Maybe he would know why Jacob hadn't written to her. But he must have caught an earlier bus, as he did sometimes when there was a deadline to meet. All day she found it hard to concentrate on her work, and by the time she clocked off, she was beginning to wonder whether his family meant more to him than her. She was relieved to see Alan waiting for her at the bus stop, but his smile was replaced by concern as she approached him.

'What's the matter, Grace? Is something wrong?'

It was all she could do to stop herself crying. He took her arm and got her on to the bus, found a seat for them, then said quietly, 'Take your time and tell me what's happened.'

She told him about Jacob's note and asked him the same question that she had struggled with all day.

'I don't know why he didn't write to you,' said Alan, 'but there must have been a good reason. He loves you, doesn't he?'

'I… I think he does.'

'Of course he does. He asked you to marry him. Remember, you need to be strong. Now, let's see if I can cheer you up. You'll never believe what happened this morning…'

Gracie listened in silence to some silly mishap by an apprentice that had had the men falling about laughing, but she hardly smiled at all, and when they arrived in the city centre she was no lighter in her heart than she had been all day. They came to the corner where they usually went their separate ways, but Gracie didn't say anything, just stood there, reluctant to be alone.

'Worrying won't bring him back any sooner, you know,' said Alan, and still Gracie didn't move. 'Look... maybe I shouldn't suggest this, but would you like to go somewhere quiet where we can talk?' he asked. 'There's a café in Stevenson's Square I go to sometimes.'

She was grateful to have someone who would listen. 'Yes,' she said.

They went upstairs to the little café with its bright gingham tablecloths, silver teapots and quiet chatter. Alan ordered a pot of tea for two and toasted teacakes. 'I'll bet you haven't eaten today, have you?' Gracie shook her head.

They ate the teacakes and drank the tea, and Gracie thought about Jacob. She longed to talk about him, but she held back, uncertain as to whether telling Alan would somehow be a betrayal.

'How did you meet Jacob?' His words opened her heart.

She told him about the raincoat factory and how she had been attracted to him. About Heaton Park where she realised how thoughtful and gentle he was. The jazz club and the trip to Blackpool, when she knew he was attracted to her. 'But then he went to London and I thought he'd forgotten me.' She paused. 'Strange, he didn't write to me then either. I thought I'd lost him.'

Alan's voice was soft. 'How could he not write to you? He must have known you'd be upset.'

'Oh, no,' she corrected him. 'He had good reason. I understood why it was difficult for him and when he came home...'

'You fell in love and he asked you to marry him.'

'It wasn't that straightforward. He went away again, and then something bad happened to me.' She caught the sob in her throat and tried to push away the horrible memories of what Charlie had done to her body and her mind.

'Oh, Grace, don't cry.' He squeezed her hand. 'I don't know what happened to you, but I wish I could have been there to help you.'

She managed a smile. 'Anyway, we made up and he asked me to marry him.' She drank the last of her tea and put an end to her story. 'I was in the register office waiting, but he didn't arrive. I found out that night he'd been arrested.'

'That's so cruel,' said Alan. 'You didn't have long together, did you?'

'No... To tell you the truth, sometimes when I try to bring his face to mind, it won't come, but now and again, when I sleep, I dream that he's with me...' She traced the pattern on the tablecloth and the silence stretched between them, until Gracie looked up and saw the troubled look on Alan's face. 'I'm sorry,' she said. 'I've sat here talking about myself all this time and I haven't once asked about you.'

'Oh, I'm fine. I'm a better listener than a talker. Do you feel any better now?'

'I think I do. Next time you'll have to tell me all your troubles.'

'Oh, I don't think so. Come on now, Grace, time you went home.'

Alan said very little as they walked back to the corner, and when it came to saying goodbye, Gracie sensed his hesitation. 'Is something the matter?' she asked.

'I was just thinking... No, it doesn't matter.'

'What is it? Tell me.'

He was clearly weighing something up. 'I was going to make a suggestion, but it might be seen in the wrong way.'

'You're going to have to tell me now, aren't you?' she said.

'I can see it's hard for you, coming to work, going home, worrying all the time about Jacob. You don't have much to brighten your life yet you always manage a smile. I was wondering if you might like to have a day out over Easter. I usually go to Belle Vue—'

Gracie held up her hand. 'I don't think I could—'

'Hear me out, Grace. I was going to say I always take my mother there on Easter Monday – it's a sort of family tradition.'

Gracie wished he'd never suggested it. He was just being kind, she knew that, but it wouldn't be right for her to spend the day with him. He seemed to read her thoughts. 'You could ask Trixie to come as well. My mother doesn't get out much and she'd enjoy the company of two young women. Anyway, why don't you speak to Trixie about it and let me know?'

That evening Gracie, feeling a touch of guilt and a bit embarrassed, told her mother about Alan's invitation.

'Listen, love, he's right. You've not been over the door for weeks, except to go to work. It would do you good to go out with some people and just do something normal. I could understand your worry if he was asking you out for a date, but his mother'll be there and your friend from the factory. You can't sit in the house every weekend.'

17

The Easter weekend began with blue skies and Sarah felt a sudden urge to give the house a spring clean. After breakfast she heated water on the stove and fetched floor-cloths, a scrubbing brush, rags to use as dusters, soap, disinfectant and furniture polish. She started at the top of the house and worked her way down. When Gracie arrived home, after working the Saturday half-day, her mother gave her instructions. 'Have something to eat, then get started out the front and wash the windows, sills and the door – don't forget to donkey-stone the step. Then you can clean the parlour, and make sure you pull out the furniture to wash every bit of the lino and skirting boards. While you're doing that, I'll wash all the curtains and get them out on the line. Then I'll do the kitchen and swill down the back yard.'

Gracie was standing on a chair, cleaning the upper part of the sash window, when Doris came up the street with her shopping. 'How do, Gracie? Any more word about Jacob?'

'Nothing. How are the girls?'

'Oh, they're all right, but I'm missing them more than ever, you know. They've been away since September and we haven't seen a single bomber. It peeves me that I could have had them with me all this time. Anyway, seeing as it's Easter I'm going to Ramsbottom on Monday to see them. Been thinking I might bring them back with me.'

'Is that wise?' said Gracie. 'You know what they say about this Phoney War – the real thing'll get going very soon.' Doris gave her a sceptical look, but Gracie went on: 'I'm telling you, they've started making all sorts of preparations at Trafford Park. They've been painting factory roofs green to make them look like fields from the air and they're dumping kerb stones in all the open spaces to stop enemy planes landing.'

'Maybe you're right,' said Doris. 'I couldn't live with myself if they came back and something happened to them – and I don't like to say it, but they're probably better off there. The woman's a bit strict, but that'll do them no harm, and they're well fed and clothed. Anyway, I'd better get on. Ta-rah, love.'

Gracie and her mother worked for the rest of the day, only pausing for a cup of tea and an arrowroot biscuit. It was almost dark by the time they stopped, once the clean curtains were ironed and hung. Then they sat down, exhausted, to eat a sandwich of Billy's best brawn.

'Now that's all done, we can have a nice restful Easter Sunday,' said Sarah. 'Then you're off to Belle Vue on Monday with your friend Alan, and I've got a bit of overtime waitressing at the hotel.'

Gracie shot her a look. 'It's not just Alan, it's his mother and Trixie too.'

'I know that,' said Sarah. 'It was very kind of him to invite you.'

★

Gracie arrived at the entrance to Belle Vue a few minutes after two o'clock, expecting to see the others waiting for her, but it seemed that hundreds of people had made similar arrangements. She wandered through the milling crowds, worried that they might have gone in without her, when she felt a touch on her arm. It was Alan, looking very smart in grey flannels and a white shirt with a pullover round his shoulders. 'Found you at last,' he said, with a beaming smile.

Gracie looked around. 'Where are the others?' she asked.

'My mother's at home in bed. She wasn't well in the night – something disagreed with her. She sends her apologies. She really wanted to meet you.'

Gracie was taken aback and felt a little awkward. Somehow his mother not being there made her feel uneasy, not to mention that Trixie hadn't appeared. 'What about Trixie?' she said.

'I've been here a while walking up and down, but I haven't seen her. Did she definitely say she was coming?'

'Yes, of course,' said Gracie, a little sharply.

He looked at his watch. 'Ten past two. Maybe she changed her mind.' He paused. 'What do you want to do?'

'We'll wait,' she said.

Alan kept up a conversation about all the things they could do once inside, but as the minutes dragged on, Gracie became more and more unsettled. She liked Alan, he was a good friend, but this felt wrong. What would Jacob think of her if he ever found out that she was out on a lovely sunny afternoon with another man? She knew the answer: it would be the same as he'd thought when he'd heard she had gone to the Ritz, and, of course, Alan had been one of those she'd danced with that awful night.

'Alan, I'm sorry but I—'

'I'm here!' Trixie emerged from the crowd waving and

shouting. 'I'm really sorry, the buses were packed. Thanks for waiting.'

'Don't worry, Trixie,' said Alan. 'We're glad you're here, aren't we, Grace?'

'Yes.' She managed a smile. At least it wouldn't look like she was on a date with him.

'Is your mam not here?' asked Trixie, and when Alan explained, she nudged him. 'So now you've got a girl on each arm and no mother to keep an eye on you!'

Gracie was surprised that Trixie was so forward, but Alan just laughed and offered an arm to each of them. She had to take it, of course, but she knew it wasn't right.

'Now, what do you want to do first?' Alan asked.

They started with the fun fair. Gracie and Trixie went on a few rides, while Alan watched and waved at them as they went past. They tried their hand at hoop-la without any success. 'Well, at least we don't have to carry a goldfish in its bowl for the rest of the day,' said Alan. Slowly, Gracie relaxed. Alan was just as he always was – friendly and kind – and her misgivings about spending the day with him disappeared. It helped that they were a threesome: the conversation and laughter never waned, and she was happy to see that Alan was just as nice to Trixie as he was to her. They bought ice cream and sat on a bench, watching people wander by, while they decided what to do next. 'How about the zoo?' said Alan.

'No, it'll be full of kids,' said Trixie. 'What about roller skating?'

'It's good fun,' said Gracie.

Alan was unsure. 'I can't roller skate.'

'It's so easy,' they told him. 'Anyone can do it! Come on.'

Between them they kept Alan on his feet, explaining what he had to do and guiding him round the rink. By the second circuit he was floundering. 'Push each foot along the floor,' Gracie told him.

'And let it glide,' said Trixie.

He tried so hard, but his skates ran away with him, he over-balanced and fell backwards taking the girls with him, all three landing in a heap, laughing uncontrollably while skaters whizzed past them. They got him to his feet and between them they manoeuvred him off the rink. 'That's me done,' he said. 'I know when I'm beaten.' At least he was still laughing. 'Good job my mother isn't here. She'd tell me not to play with rough girls!'

'Don't be such a mardy,' Trixie told him, and he pretended to chase her. She screamed in delight. Then she shouted, 'Come on, Gracie, let's show him how it's done,' and the two of them went round together.

'He's nice your Alan, isn't he?'

Gracie was shocked. 'He's not my Alan,' she said. 'I've got a boyfriend, you know that.'

'Yes, but I thought maybe you and Alan were… you know…'

'No, we're not! He's a good friend, that's all.'

'But you have to admit he's quite good-looking, isn't he?'

'I don't know… I suppose so.'

'Well, I wouldn't say no to him.' She giggled. 'He might not be tall, but his eyes are very blue, and I do like a man with a cleft in his chin. Why do you think he wanted me to come out today? He could just have asked you. It doesn't make sense.'

'He said his mother would enjoy our company. She doesn't get out much. Anyway, I'm glad you came, or I'd have been on my own with him.'

'Would that have been so bad?'

Gracie thought for a moment. 'No, it wouldn't, but it wouldn't have been right either.'

It was Alan's turn to choose what to do next. 'My mother and I always watch the speedway when we come to Belle Vue, but I don't suppose you girls would enjoy that.'

'Speedway?' asked Gracie.

'Motorbikes racing round a track,' said Alan. 'It's very exciting.' The girls looked unconvinced. 'All right, then. We could go to the ballroom, if you like. There's usually a band playing.'

Despite the lovely weather outside, there was a good crowd in the ballroom, most of them dancing. They found some seats and Alan bought them some Vimto to drink.

'Do you dance, Alan?' asked Trixie.

He smiled. 'It has been known.'

'He's an excellent dancer,' said Gracie. 'Why don't you two have a dance?'

Trixie listened a moment to the music. 'A quickstep and a fast one, too.'

Alan held out his hand to her. 'They're the best kind.'

Gracie watched them walk on to the dance-floor, saw Alan take Trixie in his arms and off they went, quick-stepping into the crowd. She couldn't help recalling how she had danced with him at the Ritz – he had such skill and grace that it had felt like gliding. They passed her again and she heard Trixie's laughter and caught sight of Alan's smile. At that moment she longed to dance with him again, but if he asked her, as he surely would, she would refuse him.

They returned to the table after a second dance. 'Your turn now, Gracie,' said Trixie, and she nodded towards Alan. Gracie opened her mouth to speak, but Alan seemed to sense her unease. 'I'm happy just sitting here,' he said. 'Why don't you two go and have a few dances?'

Gracie was taken aback. 'I don't think I—'

'Oh, come on,' coaxed Trixie. 'We'll have some fun.'

And before she knew it, Gracie was on the dance-floor doing the foxtrot with Trixie, her heart lighter than it had been for weeks.

They were having one last dance before rejoining Alan when Gracie felt a tap on her shoulder and turned to see a tall man, probably in his late twenties, wanting to dance with her. A quick glance showed her Trixie was in the same position, but while Trixie smiled and accepted her invitation, Gracie stepped back. 'No, thank you,' she said.

He reached out and took her hand. 'Aw, come on, it's only a dance.'

'I don't want to. Please let me go.' She tried to pull away from him, but his other hand slipped around her waist and he held her fast. 'Just one dance. Where's the harm in that?' he said. He had clearly had a few drinks and she tried to push him away. All at once he jerked backwards and it was a moment before Gracie realised that he had been pulled away from her. 'What the bloody hell—' he shouted.

Alan had him by the collar, but the man wrenched free and the two of them faced each other.

'Hey, mate, you keep out of this. She's dancin' with me,' said the man.

Gracie was shocked by the cold look in Alan's eye and the menace in his voice. 'She's here with me and she won't be dancing with other men.'

The man hesitated, glanced at Gracie then back at Alan. 'All right, don't get your knickers in a twist, easy mistake, thought she was here with her mate.'

Without another word Alan took Gracie in his arms and, as if the incident had never happened, he waltzed her around the ballroom and his eyes never left her face.

The music died away and still Alan held her. 'You enjoyed

that, didn't you?' he said. She lowered her eyes. 'Grace, there's no harm in dancing. It can lift your spirits like nothing else.'

'I know,' she said.

The music began again – a tango, this time – and Alan said, 'So, would you like another dance?'

She hesitated… Would it be so wrong to dance with a friend? By now, couples were moving around them, picking up speed. She looked up at him. 'Yes, I would,' she said.

After that they had two more dances, but when the music switched to a slow waltz they left the floor. 'It's good to see you smiling, Grace. Do you want another drink?'

'Ah, no, thanks. I think I'd like to go home now. Is Trixie still on the dance-floor?'

'Yes, I've just seen her go past. I'll tell her we're ready to go.' Gracie watched him disappear into the dancers. How thoughtful and sensitive he was.

He returned with a shrug of his shoulders. 'She's with that fella who asked her to dance – says she'll see you tomorrow at work. So it's just you and me on the bus again.'

They left the ballroom and went out into the sunshine, blinking at the light.

'I don't know about you, but I'm starving,' said Alan. 'Fancy something to eat?'

On the top deck of the bus they ate their chips, with lashings of vinegar, out of newspaper.

'I've enjoyed today,' said Gracie.

'Better than you thought you would?'

She gave a half-smile. 'Well, I did wonder. When I have time to myself I spend it worrying about Jacob. Things go round and round in my head.'

'And you thought it would be disloyal that, if you went out, you might forget about him for a while.'

'Yes… yes, that's it.'

'Oh, Grace, if I was Jacob I would be glad that the woman I loved was happy, if only for a little while.'

'Don't say that.' Her voice cracked. 'My heart's breaking, but he's suffering far more than I am and I'll never stop thinking about him.'

'I'm sorry. The last thing I wanted to do was upset you. We've had a lovely day and I don't want to spoil it now. Will you forgive me?'

'There's nothing to forgive, Alan. You help me so much, I'd be lost without you.'

When Gracie arrived home she was surprised to see Doris sitting with her mother. From the look on their faces something had gone on.

'You'll never guess!' Doris's face was flushed with excitement.

'Calm down,' said Sarah, then turned to Gracie. 'Doris has got something to tell you. You'd best sit down, love.'

Doris took a deep breath and sat for a moment, as if ordering her thoughts. 'You'll remember I told you I was going to see the kids today. Well, I were in the station this morning waiting to get on the train when there was all this commotion. Next thing I know there were soldiers with guns escorting a bunch of men – odd-looking, some of them – on to the platform and into one of the carriages. I asked the guard what were going on. You know what he told me?' Gracie shook her head. 'He said, "Them's German prisoners on the way to a camp. Seen a lot of them coming through lately."' Gracie's hand flew to her mouth. 'And, sure enough, when we got to Bury, the whole parade of them got off and the soldiers marched them away.'

'Oh, my God,' said Gracie. 'That's where he is! That's

where they've taken him, I'm sure of it. I need to go there. I'll go tomorrow and ask if I can see him.'

'Now, hold on a minute,' said Sarah. 'You can't go tomorrow. You have to go to work and, anyway, I don't want you going on your own.'

'But I have to see him!'

Then Doris spoke up: 'It strikes me that if he's in that camp he's not going anywhere, so you might as well wait till the weekend. That way you won't lose a day's pay.'

'And I'll come with you,' added Sarah.

Gracie could see the logic in what they were saying, but after all these weeks with no news she was desperate. 'All right, then, but if you have to do a shift at work, Mam, I'll ask Maria to come with me.'

'Very well,' said Sarah, 'but don't get your hopes up. He might not be there, and even if he is, I doubt they'll let you speak to him.'

'Oh, he's there all right, I know it, and I won't leave till they let me see him.'

18

The two girls stood alone on the platform at Bury station and looked around them.

'Where to now?' said Maria.

Gracie sighed. 'I thought somebody like a guard or the station master would be here, so we could ask them where the camp is.'

'Well, no point in standing here any longer. We'll ask in the town.'

But it was Sunday morning and the streets were empty. 'You'd have thought somebody would be around,' said Maria.

They walked on and arrived at a junction with a pub on one side, a statue in the middle and a fine church in front of them. Gracie stopped. 'Listen,' she said.

'What is it?' asked Maria, but then she, too, caught the sound of singing.

They slipped into the church and sat at the back. When the service was over they waited until the congregation had left before they approached the minister. Gracie explained that they were looking for the camp where enemy aliens were being held. He looked at her sternly. 'That's no place for young women,' he said.

'You don't understand. My fiancé was arrested two months ago and I haven't heard anything from him since. He's German but he has nothing to do with the Nazis.'

'Is he by any chance Jewish?'

'Yes, he is.'

The minister shook his head. 'It's an absolute disgrace. We've been trying to get into the camp to inspect the conditions, but no one will give us permission. I'm afraid it's unlikely they'll even confirm he's being held there, never mind let you see him.'

'I have to try,' said Gracie. 'Can you tell us where the camp is?'

'It's in a disused cotton mill about a mile and a half from here...' He gave them directions and added, 'My name is Reverend Baldwin. I'm the rector here. Please let me know if you find out anything about the conditions.'

Radcliffe Road seemed so ordinary: neat houses, a pub, a row of shops. Just beyond them, opposite a row of cottages, they got their first sight of Warth Mills: a sprawling, two-storey red-brick building with a tower and a tall chimney. It was protected by two high fences topped with barbed wire, one within the other, and armed soldiers patrolling the space between. At the heavy metal gates, the girls could see a wooden hut, outside which stood a soldier with a rifle over his shoulder, smoking a cigarette.

Gracie was convinced that Jacob was somewhere within those walls and her heart began to race.

'Are you all right?' asked Maria.

Gracie nodded, then called to the soldier, 'Can we talk to you?'

He came over to them straight away. 'Hello, girls, don't tell me you've come here thinkin' that these fellas might be wantin' some female company. You're not wrong, but you wouldn't want to have anything to do with them buggers. Now, if you fancy a bit of fun with a squaddie, I'm going off duty any minute now.'

Gracie ignored his leer. 'I'm trying to find my fiancé. He was arrested as an enemy alien, but it's all a mistake. He's called Jacob Rosenberg. Do you know if he's being held here?'

The soldier's face hardened. 'There's over a thousand men in here, and more arriving every day. I don't know any of their names. They're all Germans to me.'

'Is there anyone I could speak to, someone in charge?' asked Gracie.

'No, there isn't, so you'd best clear off.' He was shouting now. 'Bad enough we have to guard these bastards without having to deal with their whores!'

Gracie was about to yell back, but Maria caught her arm and pulled her away. 'Ignore it,' she whispered. 'You'll get nowhere with him, but if he's going off duty there'll be another soldier to replace him and you can ask again.'

They walked further along the road and came to a bridge over a fast-flowing river with a weir.

'What will you do if you don't find Jacob?' asked Maria.

'I'll keep coming back, keep asking. I can't explain it, I just have this feeling that he's close by. Anyway, what else would I do on my day off?'

'A little bird told me that you were at Belle Vue with Alan on Easter Monday.'

'It's not what you think,' said Gracie. 'He's a friend, and he looks out for me. I wouldn't have a job if it wasn't for him. He invited me and another girl from work to go there with him and his mother. He's really kind like that.'

'His mother? Sounds a bit odd to me.'

'She didn't come in the end – she was ill.'

Maria laughed. 'Well, there's a surprise.'

But Gracie didn't laugh. 'You don't know him like I do,' was all she said.

They walked back to the camp gates and were glad to see a different soldier on duty, younger and with less swagger than the previous one. 'My name's Gracie Earnshaw and I'm looking for my fiancé Jacob Rosenberg...' The soldier listened to her story, but he didn't know the names of the prisoners and, although a few people had come to the camp looking for their relatives and friends, no one had ever been allowed inside.

'What about letters?' asked Gracie.

'I think they were allowed to send a note to their family when they first arrived, but I don't think there's been anything since.'

'But if I sent a letter here, would he get it?'

The young soldier shrugged his shoulders. 'I doubt it,' he said.

Ever since Gracie had learned about the Bury camp, her expectations that she would find Jacob there had grown each day, but now, standing outside the forbidding mill with its high fence and barbed wire, she realised she was no closer to making contact with him.

'We might as well go home now, Maria.' She was about to thank the young soldier, but he looked quickly over his shoulder.

'I shouldn't tell you this, really,' he said, 'but you could go on the railway bridge at the back of the mill. There's usually a group of prisoners allowed in the yard for some fresh air and you can just about see them from there.'

Gracie could hardly believe her ears. 'How do we get to it?'

'Walk over the bridge and follow the river upstream. It's not far and you can't miss it – criss-cross metal girders.'

'Thank you,' said Gracie, as she grabbed Maria's arm and hurried away in the direction of the bridge.

'Watch out for the trains,' shouted the soldier.

From the bridge they could make out about fifty men in the yard, some walking around, others standing in groups talking. None of them near enough to identify.

'There's a tall man leaning against the wall, could be Jacob,' said Maria.

'Or that one walking with two other men, see? His hair is longer.' But they couldn't be certain.

'We could shout his name,' suggested Maria, but the wind was blowing in the wrong direction and not a single man lifted his head in acknowledgement.

'Oh, it's useless,' said Gracie. 'I can't believe we're so close and I still can't find him.'

'What else can we do?' asked Maria.

'It's getting cold,' said Gracie. 'Time to catch the train home.'

'You're not giving up, are you?'

Gracie looked at her as if she were mad. 'Never,' she said. 'I'll be back next Sunday with a plan.'

The next day, Gracie couldn't wait to tell Alan about her trip to the camp, and at the end, she said, 'Isn't it great news? The longer I was there, the more certain I was that he was in the camp. I couldn't be sure if he was one of the men in the yard, but there were definitely Jews there in their long coats and high hats.' Alan had listened without comment, and she asked, 'What do you think?'

'What do I think?' He shook his head as if in disbelief.

'I think you should never have gone there. Have you any idea the sort of rough characters who hang around places like that? Loose women, spivs – even the guards are the lowest of the low.'

Gracie remembered the first soldier and his lewd comment. 'But Maria was with me, and we were fine,' she protested.

'If I'd known you were going there, I'd have come with you to protect you.'

Gracie heard the anger creep into his voice. 'I don't need protection,' she said.

'Grace, you are so naïve. I worry about you. Please promise me, if you must go there again, you'll let me go with you.'

She didn't look at him, didn't answer. This was about her and Jacob, no one else. It wouldn't be right to have another man standing beside her on that railway bridge looking for him. What if Jacob were to see her with him?

'Grace, look at me.' She raised her head. 'Promise me.'

She looked him in the eye. 'I promise,' she said.

The following Sunday morning Gracie was up early, made her own breakfast and got dressed. Then she sat at the kitchen table with a writing pad, wondering what she should say. *My Darling Jacob...* That was a start, and the words flowed. How she missed him, loved him and longed to be in his arms again. She recalled the evening at the jazz club, their first kiss, and the night he had climbed on to the coal-shed roof. But most of all she told him about their future. How they would marry, have a family, and their life together would be blessed... She sealed the envelope, wrote his name across it in her best copperplate handwriting and put it into her bag.

Above her, she heard her mother yawn and the bed creak

as she rolled over. She had been waitressing at the Midland till after midnight and deserved a Sunday lie-in. I'll take her up a cup of tea before I leave, thought Gracie.

Her mother was sitting up in bed when she came in. 'Are you off now, love?'

Gracie nodded. 'I'm meeting Maria at Victoria we're catching an earlier train this time.'

'Why have you got your best coat on?'

Gracie gave a twirl showing off the pink Parisian coat Jacob had given her. 'You remember I said I could see the men in the yard, but I couldn't make out whether Jacob was there? Well, if he can't pick me out in this coat made in his own factory, I might as well give up.'

Sarah smiled. 'Ah, I see. At least he'll know you've found him. You're a clever girl, Gracie.'

At the station she bought her ticket and waited for Maria to arrive, but with the clock ticking towards the hour she went through to the platform, hoping at the last minute to see Maria come running towards her. The guard was walking up and down with his flag and whistle at the ready. ''Ere, love, time to get on board, if you're going.'

Gracie hesitated only a moment before rushing on to the train. She suddenly thought of Alan – he'd be so cross if he knew. But she didn't care because today she hoped to see Jacob and he would certainly see her.

She waited until the guard at the mill gate changed, as it had the previous week, and her hopes were raised when she saw the same young soldier arrive at his post. She looked around her, then went to speak to him.

'Hello,' she said. 'Do you remember me?'

The lad blushed. 'Of course I do. You're Gracie.'

'Last week we talked about letters and I thought maybe, just on the off chance that my Jacob is in the mill, I could give you this.' She took the envelope from her handbag.

'Put it away!' he hissed.

His sharpness threw her and she shoved the letter into her pocket. 'I'm sorry, I just thought—'

'Listen to me. There's a guard patrolling the perimeter fence. He knows I'm talking to someone outside the gate but I'm not sure if he can see you. In a minute he'll turn round and walk the other way. Then I'll step forward against the gate and that's when you'll give me the letter. Get ready.'

Gracie clutched the envelope in her pocket, her heart racing, but it was all over in a split second. Her letter was inside the camp. 'What's your name?' she asked.

'Arthur.'

'I don't know how to thank you,' she said.

'You don't need to. I'm not promising anything. Now, you've stood here long enough for me to have told you to go away, so look upset and walk on past.'

Gracie congratulated herself on succeeding with the first part of her plan – Jacob might soon be reading her letter – and the best was still to come. She walked along the open ground beside the river towards the railway bridge. The day was clear, and she was sure her striking pink coat would draw the eye of anyone who looked in her direction, but when she got there her heart sank at the sight of the empty yard. She walked down on to an overgrown path that ran close to the perimeter fence. She hadn't gone far when she was startled by the sound of someone's voice, '*Guten Morgen*,' and turned to see a woman sitting on a picnic blanket, half hidden in some bushes. '*Guten Morgen*,' she said again.

'Pardon.'

'You don't speak German, but you come to see prisoner, yes?' Her accent was thick.

'Yes, my fiancé.'

The woman patted the blanket. 'Come, sit. The men will be out soon, I think. They sometimes have a late roll-call on Sundays, when they line up in the yard.' She held out her hand. 'My name is Clara. My husband Kurt is in the mill.'

The woman was middle-aged and stout, with a toothy smile that lit up her face. Gracie shook her hand. 'I'm Gracie, and my fiancé is Jacob. Do you come here all the time?'

'Perhaps two times in a week. Sometimes I see my man, he sees me and we wave – from bridge, you know?'

'Yes, I was here last week, but only a few men were outside and I couldn't spot Jacob.'

'Today you may see him, and maybe he see you too. But we must be careful. Do not shout and make a fuss. If you do, they will send the guards to chase us away.'

'Has that happened before?' asked Gracie.

Clara rolled her eyes. 'There was a silly girl who kept screaming. She nearly spoiled it for the rest of us.'

Gracie was surprised. 'There are other women who come here?'

'Four of us, but the other three can't come as much – they have children. And now, Gracie, you are number five. I'll show you something else, if you like.'

They walked a little way along the river, the vegetation shielding them from sight of the perimeter guards. 'Don't come along here if it's wet. You could slip and fall in.' She stopped suddenly. 'And never go any further than this or they'll see you.' She hunkered down and gestured for Gracie to do the same. 'You see that bush outside the fence? Sometimes my husband stands at the inside fence, only a couple of yards between us then, and I talk to him.'

Gracie couldn't believe her ears. 'You talk to him?'

'Yes. He whistle and walk away when the guard comes close. We can't always do it, there are too many guards, but sometimes we get the chance when guards are called away for other duties. We take a big risk to do this. I could be arrested and something far worse would—' She stopped mid-sentence. 'Listen. It's the men coming out for roll-call. Let's get back to the bridge.'

Gracie couldn't believe her eyes when the prisoners poured out of the mill and sorted themselves into lines in the yard. They faced away from the bridge towards the mill, and guards with guns across their chests watched them.

'How will we recognise them all crowded together?' asked Gracie.

'Be patient,' said Clara. 'First you have to listen.'

The roll-call began with an officer barking out names in alphabetical order, followed by each prisoner's reply. Gracie could feel the tension building inside her. What if Jacob's name wasn't called? She'd be right back where she started, not knowing where he was. On the other hand, hearing his name would confirm he was locked up in this prison. Clara leaned towards her, smiling. 'That's my Kurt answering,' she said. 'To know that he's still here and he's not ill is the best we can hope for.'

Gracie wanted to contradict her: the best she was hoping for was that Jacob would be free and they could get married, but it was getting close to the letter R. She held her breath. His name, when it was called, felt like a kick in her stomach, but Jacob's answering voice made her cry out. She had found him.

'Watch now,' said Clara. 'You see the man swinging his

arms like he's exercising, walking around coming closer to the bridge?'

'Is that your husband?'

'It is. He'll stop in a moment.'

Gracie watched in amazement as Clara's husband came within thirty yards from where they stood, and there was no mistaking the smile on his face. She glanced at Clara and saw how their eyes were locked and the expression on their faces was pure joy.

Heartened by this, Gracie scanned the men in the yard, her eyes darting this way and that, but she couldn't find Jacob. Maybe he was at the far end, close to the mill, but she could hardly make out the faces at that distance. Concentrate, she told herself, focus on the taller, slimmer, younger men... men with longer hair... narrow it down.

Clara touched her arm. 'I'm going to see if I can speak to Kurt down on the path. Have you seen that man walking towards us?'

Gracie followed her gaze. A tall figure in a dark coat and fedora hat pulled low over his face walked deliberately through the men milling around and headed towards them. He stopped not twenty yards from the bridge. Gracie held her breath. He reached up and removed his hat, and she looked into the smiling face of Jacob Rosenberg. And Gracie couldn't help smiling too, as he touched his coat, then pointed at her and mimed his surprise. She was sure he was trying to tell her he had recognised her coat. They both knew that they couldn't stand like that for long or the guards would become suspicious. Jacob walked back into a group of men and she went to the far end of the bridge. They could still see each other and that was all that mattered. Then the command was given to line up and the men were marched back into the mill. Before he disappeared, Jacob lifted his hat above his head as though to say goodbye.

Clara returned breathless. 'I speak to Kurt for a couple of minutes. Told him about your Jacob. He'll look out for him. He says men are still arriving and conditions are getting worse. Did you make contact with Jacob?'

'Yes, and it was wonderful, but now...' Gracie shook her head. 'Now I feel worse than ever.'

'Don't think like that. You came here today not knowing where Jacob was, and you hadn't seen him for so long. How much better off are you now? You know he's safe, you've seen each other, and you can come here again. To me, that's something to be thankful for.'

'You're right, Clara.' Gracie smiled. 'Thank you for helping me today.'

'You don't have to thank me. We're in this together just the same as the men are, and we will all get through it, Gracie. I know we will.'

19

'You're very chirpy for a Monday morning,' said Trixie, as they queued for toast and tea in the canteen. 'Did that boyfriend of yours finally get some leave?'

Gracie couldn't keep the smile off her face. 'Let's just say we've seen each other.'

'Oooh, how romantic. I hope you sent him away happy.' She winked.

'I think so,' said Gracie. Just to see Jacob again was worth a thousand kisses.

'Talking about romance, did you know that *Gone with the Wind* is on at the Odeon in Oxford Street? It's supposed to be the most romantic film ever made, four hours long and in Technicolor.'

'I'd love to see it,' said Gracie. 'They say Vivien Leigh is so beautiful in it. Did you know they searched and searched for Scarlett O'Hara? All the big American film stars auditioned for the part, but in the end they chose an unknown English actress.'

Trixie linked Gracie's arm. 'Right, that's decided then. We'll go Saturday.'

'You're on,' said Gracie, and the two of them left the canteen laughing.

They hadn't gone far when Alan came up behind them. 'A little bit of sunshine and you two are full of the joys of spring.'

'Well, this one's got her head full of romance, that's for sure,' said Trixie.

Alan raised an eyebrow. 'Is that so?'

Gracie had only a split second to stop Trixie letting the cat out of the bag. 'What she means is we're going to see *Gone with the Wind* and I can't wait to see Clark Gable. He's so handsome.'

'Do you think so?' said Alan. 'I heard he had to have his ears pinned back with tape because they stick out so much.'

Trixie threw back her head and laughed. 'It's not his ears we're interested in.' Gracie couldn't help but laugh, especially when Alan looked embarrassed and muttered something about getting back to work.

When he had gone, Trixie looked hard at Gracie. 'You don't want Alan to know that you've seen Jacob this weekend, do you?'

'Eh, no, I don't.'

'Well, it's none of my business, but—'

'No, it isn't,' said Gracie, 'and it's none of his either.'

On Saturday Gracie and Trixie decided to go to the second house of *Gone with the Wind* at three o'clock. It was a long film and they didn't want to be walking home at eleven in the blackout. They met outside the library in St Peter's Square, and as soon as Trixie caught sight of Gracie she screamed with excitement. 'Oh, my! You look like a film star yourself.'

'I thought I'd try to do my hair and makeup like Scarlett. I saw it on the cover of *Picturegoer Magazine*.'

'You'll have to show me how to do it.' She linked Gracie's arm as the two of them crossed the square. 'I love it, and your coat. It's beautiful. I've never seen one like it.'

'It was a gift from Jacob.'

'I've never had a gift off a lad in my life. No, wait, Davey Brown bought me a fish supper one time. Is he well-to-do, your Jacob?'

'He... em... worked in his family's business – they make coats. I was a machinist there.'

'So you met, fell in love and he asked you to marry him?'

Gracie picked her words carefully, not wishing to give anything away. 'Yes, we were going to marry and move to London...'

'Is that when he got called up?'

Gracie hesitated. Should she tell Trixie the truth? But at that moment they caught sight of the queue outside the Odeon. There were so many people, including several groups of women chatting and laughing together as they waited to get into the cinema. They walked past them down Oxford Street and joined the end of the queue. As they waited a deep, rich sound filled the air – a saxophone – playing 'Tuxedo Junction'. A busker and a tap dancer were entertaining the crowd. They moved along the queue while everyone clapped, and now and again the dancer would pull out a girl and dance with her. The tune changed to 'Moonlight Serenade' just as they came alongside Gracie and Trixie. The dancer bowed in front of Gracie. 'My, my,' he said, in a fake American accent. 'What have we here? Would you care to dance, Miss Scarlett?' She stepped forward and he whisked her away in a waltz along the pavement and back again with so many twirls that her head was light. When the music ended, the handsome dancer kissed her hand, then set about passing his hat around. Gracie's face was flushed with delight not only because she had been chosen to dance but because she'd been compared to the famous actress, Vivien Leigh.

The first house ended and the people leaving the cinema flooded into the road.

'Is it good?' shouted someone in the queue.

'Smashing!' came the reply.

The queue shuffled forward. 'I hope we get in,' said Gracie. 'I don't want to wait till seven o'clock for the last house.'

'We should get in. The Odeon seats three thousand,' said Trixie. They edged closer and closer to the front and eventually they were within sight of the doors. A commissionaire in his maroon uniform, with enough gold braid to command a battalion, was counting people twenty at a time into the foyer to get their tickets. They were almost there... but Trixie was number twenty and Gracie would have to wait. 'But we're together,' Gracie told the commissionaire. 'Please let me in.' He looked at her sternly, then his expression changed. 'Ah, you're the lass who danced earlier... I enjoyed that. Go on then, Scarlett, in you go.'

Gracie usually went to the Playhouse on Oldham Road. It was a big picture house, but not a patch on the Odeon, which was vast and sumptuous: red carpet, red velvet seats, a Wurlitzer organ, and plenty of maroon-clad usherettes. They had good seats in the stalls, halfway back in the centre, and the atmosphere was charged with expectation, while the noise of excited women grew louder with each passing minute. At last the lights dimmed, the chattering ceased, and the curtain rose.

The familiar sight and sound of a cock crowing introduced the Pathé newsreel. The announcer, with a cut-glass accent, talked confidently about the British Expeditionary Force, who were doing 'a sterling job along the Belgium-France border digging field defences'. On the screen soldiers were taking a break, leaning on their shovels, smiling for the camera, smoking a fag and giving the thumbs-up. They looked like any lad you'd see from the factories and mills out on a Whit Sunday jaunt to Southport sands.

After the news they waited in the dark... Bells began to chime... and the huge screen was filled with rolling clouds and a white mansion surrounded by lawns. Then a camera shot of a mighty tree and the violins soared, making Gracie tingle as the title scrolled across the screen, *Gone with the Wind*. She had no idea what it meant, but she knew there would be romance and drama. The opening scene on the porch showed two young men talking to... the camera shifted position... and there she was, Scarlett O'Hara. A beautiful face, dark hair, and dressed in a wide crinoline of white flounces.

She was already entranced, carried away to a strange country of plantations, slaves and civil war, and she felt she was inside Scarlett's head – a wayward girl who flirted and pouted, a girl so spoilt and wilful that she thought of no one but herself.

The effects of the war moved Gracie so much more than the Pathé News – the dying men, the burning of Atlanta. Scarlett returns to the ruined Tara and, with her fist in the air, vows, 'As God is my witness, I'll never be hungry again.' The music soared and the camera pulled back and back until Scarlett was a tiny figure silhouetted against a red sky and the word 'Intermission' appeared on the screen. Gracie blinked as the lights came on and looked around her; she was back at the pictures in Manchester.

'Well, she's a right madam, isn't she?' said Trixie.

It was a moment before Gracie answered. 'I thought she was wonderful.'

'Scarlett?'

'No, Vivien Leigh. She was perfect. I've never seen such acting.'

By the time Gracie arrived home, her mother had already gone to the Midland to work an extra shift in the dining room, but she had left her a tea of herrings and potatoes on a low light in the oven. She had just finished eating when there was a knock at the door. It was Maria. 'I'm so glad you're in,' she said. 'Thought I'd come round. Haven't seen you for ages.'

They went through to the kitchen and Gracie made a fresh brew while Maria brought her up to date. 'Well, our Tony's gone. He's doing his basic training somewhere down south. I thought my mother was bad when he enlisted, but when he left she was even worse. My father has no sympathy for her. He says, "This country's been good to us and the boy wants to do his duty." But that's only the half of it. There's no money coming in from Tony's ice-cream cart and, to tell you the truth, the whole ice-cream business is dying on its feet with the rationing. I don't know how we'll keep going. I'm doing all the overtime I can get at the factory.'

Gracie poured the tea. 'And what about you and Tommy, still going strong?'

Maria looked away. 'All right, I suppose.'

'Oh, come on, I thought you were mad about each other.'

'Hmm... It's just that he wants more from me than I want to give.' She glanced up. 'You know what I mean?'

Gracie nodded.

'Then he talks about maybe getting married... but I'm not so sure that's what he wants... Sometimes I think I should just give in to him. I want to, but I know it's wrong. It's a sin in the eyes of the Church and I'd rather die than let my family down.'

Gracie could see she was close to tears. 'Aw, Maria, I know you love him, but don't ever do something you'll regret. If he loves you, he'll wait until you're married.'

'Have you ever... you know... with Jacob?'

Gracie thought of the first time Jacob took her in his arms, the passion in his kisses that had awoken such a longing in her. And at Christmas, the last time she'd seen him, when they'd lain together on her bed she could so easily have given herself to him, but Jacob had said they should wait until they were married. 'No,' she said. 'We never did.'

'Have you heard anything from Jacob?'

'I haven't heard from him, but I have seen him.'

Maria's eyes widened. 'Really? Tell me everything!'

When Maria had gone, Gracie went upstairs and made herself up like Scarlett again, arching her eyebrows a little higher and applying more lipstick to practise her pout. She stood up and flounced about the room, with a haughty look, trying out a few of Scarlett's lines to perfect her Southern drawl: 'Why, fiddle-de-dee, war, war, war. This war talk's spoiling all the fun.' She shook her head and narrowed her eyes. 'Tomorrow is another day.' She repeated the phrase until it seemed that Scarlett's words became hers. She would stay strong, just like Scarlett, and one day she and Jacob would have a life together. Tomorrow she would go again to the mill in the hope of seeing him, and if she did, it would be a good day. If not, there would surely be others.

★

In the canteen on Monday morning Trixie was telling the women about *Gone with the Wind.* 'It's the best film I've ever seen,' she said.

'What – better than *Dark Voyager* with Bette Davis?' someone asked.

'Knocks it into a cocked hat,' said Trixie.

'What's it about?'

'Oh, everything, love and war and…' Trixie shook her head, as though overwhelmed with the whole scope of the story, and turned to Gracie. 'Go on, Gracie, you can tell it better than me.'

Gracie looked at the expectant faces turned towards her and it seemed the most natural thing in the world to spin the story. 'Picture the scene,' she said. 'We're in America. There's a gleaming white mansion, surrounded by lawns, and beyond that the cotton fields where slaves pick cotton in the blazing sun.'

'Is that the cotton that comes to our mills?' asked Jeanie, a thin girl with wire-framed spectacles.

'Course it is,' said Trixie, as if everyone knew that. 'Go on, Gracie, tell them about Scarlett.'

'The daughter of the plantation owner is Miss Scarlett O'Hara. You'd never meet such a wilful, self-centred or more beautiful girl. Her clothes are expensive.' Gracie used gestures to show her dress and bonnet. 'She's going to a party where she'll see Ashley Wilkes, the lad she loves, but he's in love with Melanie.' Gracie's face changed to that of a spoilt child and when she spoke it was with the voice of Scarlett. '"Melanie Hamilton is a pale-faced, mealy-mouthed ninny, and I hate her!"' The girls around her in the canteen grew curious: they hadn't expected a performance. Gracie went on, 'As if that wasn't bad enough, word comes that war has been declared and that doesn't suit Scarlett either.' She stamped her foot.

'"War, war, war… it's positively ruined every party this spring! I'm so sick of all this talk about war I could scream!"'

Another girl called, 'I know how she feels!' and everyone laughed.

Something made Gracie glance across the canteen. Alan was getting to his feet, and before he turned away, she caught the sullen look on his face. She hesitated, but by then the girls were asking for more, so Gracie introduced them to the dashing Rhett Butler…

'Oooh,' they cooed.

When Gracie described him, Trixie chipped in: 'Hey, girls, I wouldn't mind some of that, would you?'

When the hooter sounded to go back to work, they were still talking about the story and looking forward to the next instalment.

After work Gracie caught the bus into Piccadilly with Alan. She thought he seemed preoccupied, and he didn't respond to her attempts at conversation. 'What's the matter with you?' she asked.

It was as though he had been waiting for her to say something for he came straight back at her. 'You've a bit of a gift for telling stories, have you?' But the words, which might have been a compliment, were, from the tone of his voice, an accusation.

'Oh, it's only a bit of fun. I like telling stories – there's no harm in it.'

He didn't look at her but spoke to the head of the man in the seat in front of him. 'I never had you down as a show-off.'

Gracie felt as if she'd been slapped in the face. 'It's not showing off, it's…'

He turned to look at her. 'It's what?'

'It's… sort of entertaining people. They enjoy it.'

'Ha! Is that what you think? Well, I didn't enjoy it and I wouldn't want to see you doing it again. It was embarrassing.'

They didn't speak for the rest of the journey, and when they got off the bus, Alan wished her goodnight, but Gracie was too upset to say anything.

20

It was clear to Gracie that Alan had fallen out with her. She didn't see him on the bus either going to work or coming home; nor did he come into the canteen. At first she wasn't that bothered. He had hurt her feelings with his blunt dismissal of her storytelling but, when the girls insisted they wanted to hear more about the film, she felt confident enough to do her best to please them. By the end of the week the story had been told and there was still no sign of Alan. She was worried about him, and she missed his company. The more she thought about it, the more she realised that the way he had spoken to her was not like him at all.

The Metrovicks' hooter sounded the beginning of the weekend and Gracie and Trixie left work together.

'You're very quiet, Gracie. Is something the matter?'

Gracie shook her head.

'I take it you still haven't heard from Jacob,' said Trixie.

'No.'

'Not much of a writer, is he?'

Gracie was about to make up some excuse, but she was tired of pretending. She had wanted to tell Trixie the truth about Jacob a few times and always stopped herself, but Trixie was a good friend and it would be a relief not having to lie any more. 'He doesn't write because they won't let him,' she said.

Trixie gave her a puzzled look. 'What do you mean?'

'He's not a soldier, he's being held in a prison camp because he's German.' There, she'd said it.

'A German?' Trixie stared at her in disbelief. 'Really, you were going to marry a German?'

'Yes, but he's not a Nazi. He's a Jew and he's lived in England on and off since he was a boy. He loves England. It's his home.'

'A Jew, Gracie? I don't know what to say.'

'You don't have to say anything, I'm just telling you. He's a lovely person, he wouldn't harm anyone, but they rounded up all the Germans and put them in camps and they'll have to stay there till the end of the war.' Gracie's voice cracked with emotion.

'Oh, Gracie, don't get upset.' Trixie put her arms around her friend. 'I'd no idea you were going through all that. I wish you'd told me sooner.'

'I wanted to, but...'

'Is there anything I can do to help you?'

Gracie wiped her eyes. 'No, not really, but I feel better now I've told you.'

'Can you visit him?'

'No, but I go to the camp every Sunday and sometimes we see each other from a distance.'

'That must be really hard for you. If he hasn't done anything wrong, maybe they'll let him go.'

Gracie shook her head. 'I know now that they won't.'

They walked in silence until they were outside the gates

where Gracie's bus was waiting. 'Trixie, you won't tell anyone, will you?'

'Of course not, don't worry. See you on Monday.'

But Gracie did worry. Trixie had said all the right things, yet there had been something in her reaction, not exactly disapproval, more a lack of understanding. Maybe she shouldn't have told her, but it was hard bottling everything up when all she wanted was someone to talk to. Mam was working so hard that she didn't want to burden her, and she rarely saw Maria, but it was Alan avoiding her that hurt most.

The bus had just set off when someone slipped into the seat beside her. 'Hello, Grace, how are you?'

She turned to see Alan smiling at her, but before she could answer he carried on. 'Had a bit of an up-and-down week – that's why I haven't been on the usual buses. My mother hasn't been well so I've had to change my hours, coming in later, going home early and working through my breaks. A neighbour's been keeping an eye on her when I'm not there.'

Gracie was surprised by his friendly tone – it was as though he had forgotten how they had parted. 'I'm sorry to hear your mother's ill again,' she said.

'She's feeling better now. In fact, she keeps asking me to bring you round to meet her. What would you say to that?'

It seemed odd to be invited to meet his mother, but he looked so eager that she thought it would be rude to refuse. 'Yes, I could come and see her.'

'Why don't you come now? She's at her best in the afternoon.'

'But I—'

'Oh, say yes, Grace, please. She really wants to meet you.'

★

The house was in a quiet cul-de-sac, semi-detached with a garden. The front door opened into a little square hall with stairs straight ahead. Alan called, 'I'm home, Ma,' and ushered her into the front room. Gracie was immediately struck by the musty smell and the heat from a fire lit on a warm May afternoon.

'Well, here she is, Ma. This is Grace.'

The woman by the fire was tiny, like a wraith, her hair barely covering her scalp. Gracie crossed the room and shook her hand. The skin was papery over little bones. 'It's lovely to meet you,' said Gracie.

'And you, love. I've been wanting to meet you for ages. Alan talks about you all the time, you know. He said you were lovely, but I wouldn't use that word. I'd say you were beautiful.' A smile lit her face.

Gracie blushed and, for a moment, she couldn't think of a response.

Alan laughed. 'Ma, don't be embarrassing me. Come on, Grace, sit down and chat to Ma.'

'Call me Hilda,' she said. 'Now tell me all about yourself, where you live, who you live with...'

Gracie told her story – how there was only her and her mother. 'Just like me and Alan,' said Hilda.

She told her about being a machinist in the raincoat factory, but something stopped her mentioning Jacob.

'And you met Alan at a dance hall, didn't you? He's a great dancer, our Alan, isn't he?'

'He certainly is.'

'And then he got you the job at Metrovicks and now you're here.' Gracie glanced at Alan, who sat smiling at them.

'Now then, Alan, put the kettle on and there's corned beef for sandwiches.'

'Oh, don't go to all that trouble,' said Gracie.

'It's no trouble,' said Hilda. 'Off you go, son, and don't forget to use the best china.'

Once Alan was out of earshot, she leaned towards Gracie. 'It'll give us a chance to have a private chat. I presume Alan's told you that I'm poorly.'

'Yes, I was sorry to hear that, but you're better now?'

'No, not really, I have... em... a woman's problem.' She patted her breast. 'Same thing carried off my mother and sister, so I know the course it takes. But I wanted to talk to you about Alan.' She put her hand over Gracie's. 'I'm ever so glad he's got you.' Gracie wasn't quite sure what she meant by that, but Hilda went on: 'Alan's a good lad, kindness itself, but I worry about him, you know, when I'm gone. There've been other girls, of course – he's a handsome lad with a good job and this is a decent house – but they come and go. I thought the last girl might have...' She sighed. 'I'll give him his due, he was good to her, looked after her so well. I couldn't believe it when she ended it. Never saw her again.'

All the time Hilda had been speaking, Gracie grew more and more uncomfortable. Was this wishful thinking from a worried mother or had Alan told her she was his girl? She wanted to say that they were friends, that was all, but then Hilda squeezed her hand. 'Thank God he's found you,' she said.

They had tea and sandwiches and Alan kept the conversation going. His mother was content to listen to the news from the factory and Gracie joined in a little, but all she could think of was the awkward situation she'd have to deal with when she and Alan were alone.

As soon as she could, without appearing impolite, Gracie said she had to be going. 'I'll walk you back into town,' said Alan.

'Why don't you take your bike, Alan?' suggested Hilda. 'Then you'll be back quicker.'

'I thought your bike was stolen?' said Gracie. 'Wasn't that why you started going on the bus to work?'

'It was, but I got it back. Anyway, I hardly use it now.'

For a moment Hilda seemed confused, but then she turned to Gracie and smiled. 'I'll see you again soon, love.'

'Yes,' said Gracie, 'and thank you for the tea and sandwiches.'

They walked to town in the afternoon sunshine. Alan was on good form, talking about his mother and how she seemed so much brighter. 'She really took to you, Grace. I've been so worried about her, but maybe she's turned a corner. You'll come again to see her, won't you?'

Gracie didn't answer. Instead she said, 'Her illness sounds really bad.'

'No, she's fine. I wouldn't be going back to work full time if she wasn't.'

Gracie took a deep breath. 'Alan, does your mother think that I'm your girlfriend?'

He stopped walking. 'Is that what she said to you?' His voice was sharp.

'Not exactly, but she implied it. She said she was glad you'd found me.'

'Oh, don't take any notice of that. I told her you're a good friend, but she gets confused sometimes.'

'Well, you need to tell her that I'm not your girlfriend.'

'I will, don't worry.'

'There's something else I want to tell you. I've been to the camp again—'

'I thought we agreed that you wouldn't go there on your own.'

'I'm not on my own. I've met a woman whose husband is in the camp. We're there together. It's perfectly safe and the great thing is that I can see Jacob in the yard. There's even a chance I could speak to him.'

Alan stared at her, then smiled and touched her shoulder. 'I'm really happy for you, Grace, but be careful not to get your hopes up.'

They parted on Chapel Street and Gracie walked on towards Deansgate. She was just passing the Opera House when a poster caught her eye, *Lancashire Hotpot – a Revue*, with garish pictures of people laughing. It looked like fun.

'The three o'clock matinee's about to start, I can recommend it.' A lad probably in his twenties, in shirt sleeves, hands in his pockets, was leaning against the wall. 'You look like you could do with a good laugh,' he said.

Gracie thought for a moment. She wasn't hungry after the corned-beef sandwiches at Alan's and she didn't fancy going home to an empty house. 'How much is it?' she asked.

He looked around, then lowered his voice. 'I'll get you a good seat for a shilling. Come on.' She followed him into the theatre.

21

Sarah didn't usually wear makeup, but when she started waitressing she decided that a bit of powder and rouge would brighten her up, not to mention Gracie's coral lipstick to add the finishing touch. She had to do something with her hair too. It was all very well for a chambermaid to have wild Irish red hair, but a waitress was expected to keep her curls under her cap. It was a while, though, before she could admit there was another reason she wanted to look her best. Ever since she had found that RAF embarkation card in the hotel room with Martin Quigley's name on it, she hadn't stopped thinking about him. The chances were it was some other Martin Quigley, but nevertheless it had set her wondering. Did he visit the Midland Hotel often? Maybe he dined there sometimes. But even if it was her Martin Quigley, she had no desire to speak to him – not after what had happened between them all those years ago. Then the voice in her head would ask her bluntly, 'So why are you getting dolled-up to wait at tables?'

Then everything changed. It was a Saturday night and as usual the waitresses were run off their feet. She had her own tables to see to, one of them a party of eight, who were very demanding, so it was a while before she noticed the four RAF officers at a table near the door. They had finished their meal and it was evident they'd had a few drinks because there was quite a bit of banter going on. She had cleared one of her tables, and on her way to the kitchen she made a detour past them. She could see two of them and was fairly certain, even after all these years, that neither was Martin. The other two had their backs to her: one a young officer, the other older, judging by his steel grey hair. She was so close that she could have reached out and touched him. At that moment he laughed at something the young officer said and shouted, 'Ach, you're such an eejit!' There was no mistaking his Belfast accent, but by the time she came out of the kitchen they had gone and she was shocked at how disappointed she felt. She was almost certain he had been her Martin and she told herself she had only wanted to see what he looked like after all these years. Yet the memories of that hot summer in 1919 crept into her mind and settled there as she went about her day, and at night he lingered on the edge of her dreams just out of reach. She volunteered for every Saturday shift, but weeks went by and she began to accept that she would never see him again. 'Get a grip,' she told herself. 'You've been acting like a slip of a girl.'

Then one morning, cleaning the hotel rooms as usual, she let herself into a room that should have been empty, went straight to the bed and began to strip it when someone spoke. 'Good morning.'

She jumped at the sound and swung round. A man was sitting at the desk behind her. The hotel rules for situations like this were that she should apologise and leave immediately, but all she could do was stare at him. His smile was unmistakable.

Now he was saying something about having decided to stay another night. That he'd arranged it at the desk late last evening. 'Anyway, I'll leave you to it,' he said, took his RAF tunic from the back of the chair and put it on.

Sarah found her voice, 'No, no, I'm sorry… I'll come back later,' but she was rooted to the spot.

He smiled. 'Are you from Belfast?'

'Yes.' Sarah's voice was no more than a whisper. Her eyes never left his face: the square jaw, the piercing blue eyes. Older, yes, but she would have recognised him anywhere as the boy in the photograph with his hand on her shoulder outside the draper's shop. She'd been angry with him her whole adult life, but seeing him again, she remembered only that she had loved him all those years ago.

His friendly smile faded. She saw his expression change as though he was solving a puzzle. 'What's your name?' he said.

For a split second she thought about lying, walking out of the door and carrying on with her life. 'Sarah.'

Martin stared at her and she watched him as realisation dawned and turned to wonder. 'Sarah, is it you?'

She nodded. 'Aye, it's me, Martin. How are you?'

He took a step forward, almost held out his arms, but dropped them again. 'I'm fine, so I am. What about you?'

'You're in the RAF, I see.'

He gave a wry smile. 'Sort of – I was in the RAF for quite a while, came out a few years ago. Then when this show started I was called up, reservist, you see. It's a desk job really, training new recruits. I'm based at…' His voice trailed away and there was the smile again. 'I can't believe it's you, Sarah. And how long have you been in Manchester?'

She could have said, 'Since I left Belfast,' or 'Since you put me on a boat to England,' but there was no point in recriminations: it was half a lifetime ago. She was suddenly embarrassed in her chambermaid's uniform while he looked so smart and saw no point in swapping life stories. 'I'll have to get on now. It was nice to see you, Martin.' She turned to go, but he moved quickly to block the door.

'Wait, Sarah. I – I can't just let you walk away. We're old friends, aren't we?'

'I have to go.' Her heart was racing. 'I'm not allowed to be in a room with guests. I could get the sack.'

But he didn't move. 'Please, Sarah, I really want to talk to you. When do you finish work? I could meet you.'

'What's the point?'

He shook his head in disbelief. 'How can you say that? My God, I can't let you walk away.' His face was stern and when he spoke again it was with the authority of a man used to giving orders. 'I'll be waiting for you in the lounge downstairs when you finish work.' Then he stepped aside.

Out in the corridor she leaned against the wall until she had stopped shaking. It was true she had longed to see him again, there was no harm in that, but did she really want to talk about what had happened between them all those years ago?

She went through the rest of the day barely aware of what she was doing, and with so many conflicting thoughts flashing through her brain that she could hardly pin them down. She swept the rooms, reliving the rejection she had suffered from those who should have supported her. Polished the furniture, and recalled her devastation on the boat to England. Made the beds, and felt again the despair of being alone in a strange country. All that and so much more while she was carrying Martin's child all those years ago.

At the end of her shift she clocked out and left by the staff entrance, but as she rounded the corner into the square she stopped. She could go home to Pearson Street and her dreary life, or she could steal a few hours of… what? Company? A chance to feel young again?

She walked through the revolving doors into the grand entrance hall, out of bounds to a chambermaid, and into the plush Octagon lounge where the handsome RAF group captain rose to meet her.

'You came,' he said, and she could see how pleased he was.

'Yes, but we can't stay here because—'

'Because you'll get the sack.' He smiled. 'Come on, then. Are you hungry? I know a place to eat just round the corner.'

For a split second she thought about Gracie waiting at home, but she'd assume there was an extra shift going in the dining room.

The restaurant was tiny and they were shown to a table tucked away in a little alcove. There was no menu, just a meal of the day. Martin ordered some wine too, not something she would ever drink, and she began to relax a little. He didn't ask her about her life in Manchester and she was glad of that. She remembered that he had always been good company – a storyteller – and he was soon making her laugh with tales of life in the RAF. She was content to be in his company. They talked about the draper's shop and the people they'd worked with, and she told him about the photograph.

He seemed so excited about it. 'I remember it being taken. I'd love to see us all together again. Next time I come to the Midland you'll have to show it to me.'

So he expected to see her again? 'Why do you stay at the Midland?' she asked.

'We have a joint North West Command meeting every month. It lasts an afternoon, then a few of us might have dinner, or sometimes I go to the Hallé at the Free Trade Hall.'

'And do you ever go back to Belfast?'

'I hadn't been back for years, but my mother's not so good now, so I've been over to see her a few times recently.'

The meal arrived – a peppery stew with dumplings – and Martin topped up their glasses. 'I should have recognised you straight away,' he said. 'You really haven't changed at all.'

Sarah couldn't help but smile. 'Ach, away on with you!' The Belfast sayings were coming back to her.

'Your hair is just the same.' He opened his eyes wide and she laughed. 'And that habit you have of glancing around as if you don't want to miss anything, and the way you raise an eyebrow as if to say, "Who are you trying to kid?" And that round your neck, is it...'

'Yes, it's the cameo you bought me.'

He reached across the table and touched her wedding ring. 'You're married.'

'I was – he died a long time ago. He was a good man.' And it seemed the most natural thing to ask, 'What about you?'

'Never married. I joined the RAF instead, then spent a lot of time overseas.' He tilted his head and smiled at her. 'But I always thought about you.'

Sarah could feel the blush cover her cheeks and hoped he would think it was the wine.

'I've wondered about our child as well.'

Sarah felt like she'd been punched in the stomach. She couldn't look at him – kept her eyes on the tablecloth.

'Will you not tell me?'

Still she didn't reply.

'Was it a boy or a girl? Did it live?'

Silence.

'For God's sake, Sarah...'

'A girl, she lived. She was adopted.'

'Did you name her?'

'Gracie.'

'Gracie, I like that. Tell me about her.'

'There's nothing to tell, Martin.'

They came out of the restaurant into the fading light, the sky streaked pink, then walked back to the square where they sat on a wooden bench under the portico of the library. 'Sarah, look at me,' he said, and something in his tone made her wary. He seemed to search for the words. 'I was... young and foolish beyond measure. I knew that even then, but I was sure you'd come back to Belfast after you'd had the baby.' There was sadness in his eyes. He took her hand. 'How could we have been so much in love and let it all slip through our fingers?'

Sarah sighed. 'Ah, Martin, you didn't know that my father beat me to tell him who had made me pregnant, and when I wouldn't say, he threw me out. Yes, you gave me the money to go to England... on my own. What was I to think? In the end, I decided I couldn't come home. There was nothing for me to come home to.'

'I let you down so badly, didn't I?'

She touched his face. 'It just wasn't meant to be.'

He leaned across and kissed her softly. 'And now?'

It had all been too much today. Her head was full of emotions she had never expected to feel again. She knew the kiss was a promise of much more, but she had no answer for him.

'I have to go,' she said, and stood up.

'Stay with me, please.'

She shook her head and walked away.

22

Gracie never missed a Sunday at Warth Mills and she usually saw Jacob from a distance – herself on the bridge, him in the yard. She was grateful, too, for the few short letters they had exchanged through Arthur, the young soldier, but what she really wanted was to speak to him, just as she had seen Clara do with Kurt, but the number of guards patrolling the perimeter fence had increased. Clara blamed one of the other women because she had been spotted on the riverbank trying to throw something into the yard.

It had rained throughout the night, and when she arrived in Bury, a low mist shrouded the hills. By the time she got to the mill the drizzle had soaked through her headscarf and her mascara was running. Clara was already there with Eva, another woman who had tracked down her husband to the camp.

'Not so many guards on the fence today,' said Clara, 'so there won't be a full roll-call, and a lot of men will stay inside out of the rain.'

'That's good,' said Gracie. 'Jacob always comes out to exercise so I might try to speak to him.'

'I will try too,' said Eva.

Clara pointed along the riverbank. 'That might not be such a good idea. The land slopes towards the river down there and the vegetation has spread along the bank. You can't see the edge of the path in places.'

The morning passed slowly and there was no sign of the prisoners. 'We should go home,' said Clara. 'Nothing is happening today.'

Eva pointed to the hills behind them. 'I think it's clearing up.' And she was proved right when, ten minutes later, the men emerged into the yard. There were about fifty, and Gracie quickly picked out Jacob in his overcoat and fedora, which he raised to show that he had seen her. There were only six guards on the perimeter fence and Gracie was hopeful that the gap between them would give her a chance to speak to him. It seemed that he had the same idea because, seconds later, she watched him meander towards the spot where Clara normally spoke to her husband.

'He's there, see?' Gracie said. 'I'm going to speak to him.'

'Don't go,' said Clara. 'It's not safe down there.'

But Gracie was already running and moments later she was picking her way down to the river's edge.

Meanwhile Eva had spotted her husband in the yard. 'I'm going as well. I'll never get a better chance.' She ran after Gracie.

The grass was thick and wet and Gracie found herself half running, half jumping to get through it. The river edge was completely overgrown but when she saw a huge boulder in her way she swerved sideways to avoid it, only to feel the ground slip away beneath her feet. She was on her knees scrambling to get a grip on the grass, when her hand touched something solid... a tree root. She grasped it and pulled herself up. She was only yards from the place where Jacob would be waiting for her—

There was a scream. She looked back and saw that Eva had also misjudged the river's edge, but she had tumbled into the water and was struggling. Gracie was horrified to see her go under, but almost immediately she bobbed up again, gasping for breath. The fast flow of the river was taking her towards the spot where Gracie stood. She had to help her. Gripping the tree root with one hand, she lowered herself into the water. Now Eva was only a yard or two away from her. Gracie waited, her hand outstretched to grab her. It could only have been seconds, but it seemed an age until Eva, trying to keep her head above water, came alongside her. Gracie grabbed her by the arm and struggled with all her might to pull her to the bank, but the woman was a dead weight. There was a crack as the root came away and Gracie fell backwards. In that split second she thought she heard Jacob call her name before the water closed over her head.

Her raincoat was like lead, pulling her under, and she wriggled and wriggled until it fell away and she surfaced momentarily, but the current pulled her down again and the water filled her lungs as she tumbled into the weir.

The wooden ceiling above her head was warped and stained, the smell of damp and boiled cabbage filling her nostrils. Her head was throbbing and she closed her eyes, waiting for the dream to fade. She dozed off, and when she awoke, the ceiling, the cabbage and the throbbing were still there. It was a moment before she realised that her clothes were soaking wet. Then she remembered she had been in the river. Jacob had called her name, and she had tried to reach Eva...

She sat up, her eyes darting around the room. She saw six hospital beds, none of them made up, and only one other person there with her. She could tell by her clothes that it was Eva. 'Oh, thank God.' She called out to her, but Eva didn't move. She must be asleep, thought Gracie, so she left her bed and went to speak to her. There was a gash across her forehead and her eyes were closed. Gracie shook her. 'Wake up.' No answer. Then she looked again at the pallid skin and the blueness of her lips and screamed.

Suddenly a nurse was at her side, pulling her away. 'Leave her. There's nothing we can do. I've just been to get a sheet to cover her.' She threw it over the body. 'Now, what's your name, love, and who's your friend here?'

'I'm Gracie Earnshaw and she's Eva. I don't know her other name.'

'Well, Gracie, you've had a lucky escape. My name's Sylvia and I'm a nurse at Bealey's Hospital.'

'I'm in hospital?' asked Gracie.

'No, my dear, you're in Warth Mills Camp.'

'In the camp?' Gracie gasped. She couldn't believe it. 'Oh, please, please, my fiancé, Jacob, is in here! Where is he? Can I see him?'

'One thing at a time. First you need to get out of these wet clothes. I've sent for some hot water for you to wash, that river's filthy, and brought some clean things for you.'

'And then can I see him?'

'That won't be up to me, I'm afraid. I have nothing to do with the camp. They just asked the hospital to send a nurse to attend to two women who had fallen into the river. But they did tell me that as soon as you're ready we've to see the CO, the officer in charge of the camp. If I get a chance, I'll speak up for you and suggest you're allowed to see your fiancé.'

'Thank you so much,' said Gracie. 'What about Eva's husband?'

'I'm told they're trying to find out who he is.'

When Gracie had washed and dressed, she and Sylvia left the sick bay to be escorted down a long corridor to the office of the CO. The smell there was even worse. The corridor walls were rough brick, everywhere was damp, and in places they were forced to walk through puddles. Gracie was aware of a muffled noise somewhere beyond the corridor that grew louder and louder. She stopped... listened... and the realisation struck her like a blow to the heart. It was the sound of human voices echoing, the hubbub of a hundred conversations. Jacob was just beyond the wall and, a few feet away, she could see a door.

She pushed past the soldier escorting them. The door wasn't locked. She threw it open and stopped dead in her tracks. Her eyes widened. She was in the heart of the mill, a vast derelict space stretching into the distance. The looms and machinery had gone and in their place were the prisoners, enemy aliens, hundreds of them. Men lying on rough mattresses, groups standing around talking, lines of washing strung between pillars, littered belongings over the floor. And the smells: rancid meat, urine, filthy clothes and more cabbage. Then, unbelievably, she heard the sweet sound of a violin soaring above the chaos.

Gracie plunged into the crowd, calling at the top of her voice, 'Jacob! Jacob! Where are you?' In and out of the men she ran and they turned in amazement to see a girl in their prison. Someone caught her arm and she pulled away. 'It's all right, Gracie, it's me! It's me, Jacob!' She turned to see him smiling at her, and she was in his arms, and they wept together, and he buried his face in her hair. 'Thank God, Gracie, thank God. I thought you'd drowned.' His voice cracked. But now someone was pulling at her and shouting, 'You're not allowed in here. Come with us!' Two soldiers were trying to pull her away from Jacob, but they clung to each other and the prisoners rushed to their aid, dragging the soldiers away.

A shot rang out and everyone froze.

The prisoners fell back and an officer stepped forward, still wielding his gun. He went straight to Gracie and Jacob. 'If you know what's good for you, you'll do as you're told.' His voice was menacing. Then he barked an order at the soldiers: 'Get these two out of here – at the double!'

They were manhandled down the corridor, closely followed by Sylvia, to the office of the CO. He sat behind his desk, a thick-set man with a bristling ginger moustache, and eyed Gracie with contempt.

'So, you're the one they fished out of the river alive. Do you realise you've committed a crime under the Emergency Powers Act and I could have you prosecuted?' Gracie opened her mouth to speak, but he held up his hand and turned to Jacob. 'As for you, if you think it's bad enough being interned, I could make it a whole lot worse.'

'I don't care what you do to me,' said Jacob, 'but you can't blame Gracie. All she wanted was to speak to me because, like every other man in this camp, I've been denied the right to send a letter to someone I love. Is it any wonder she was desperate?'

'You have no rights – you're a German! And as for you,' he glared at Gracie, 'my men will escort you to the camp gate, and if I see you or any other women in the vicinity again I will call the police and have you arrested. Take her away.'

'Excuse me.' Sylvia stepped forward. 'You can't do that.'

The officer looked her up and down. 'Who the hell are you?'

'I was sent for to tend the women who fell in the river. I work at Bealey's Hospital.'

'Who authorised that?' he shouted at the officer.

'I'm afraid I did, sir. I thought it best to have a woman look after them.'

'Oh, did you? And now she's telling me how to run my camp!' His face was flushed with anger.

Sylvia spoke calmly, as though to an unsettled patient. 'There has been a death here. I'm hoping the police have been informed and a doctor summoned. Gracie here is a witness to the event and I'm sure the police will want to interview her. Not only that but, in my professional opinion, she is in a state of high anxiety after her ordeal and is certainly not fit to travel.' Sylvia gave Gracie an almost imperceptible nod. Gracie threw her arms around Jacob and began to sob uncontrollably. The soldiers again tried to pull her off him, and her sobs became screams.

'I need to get her back to the sick bay quickly,' said Sylvia. 'It would be best if the prisoner could come with her. I think his presence might calm her down.'

The officer hesitated, but at that moment Gracie slumped to her knees and let out a piercing scream. 'Yes, yes, whatever. Just get her out of my office!'

Back in the sick bay, Sylvia explained, 'I'll be outside the door, but you haven't long. The police could be here at any moment.'

Jacob took her in his arms and kissed her, then held her face in his hands. 'You're even more beautiful than I remember. God, how I've missed you.' She could have cried to see him so thin and pale, but instead she felt such joy that she couldn't stop smiling, even when he scolded her for being so foolhardy as to end up in the river.

Her eyes were full of mischief. 'Well, it worked, didn't it?'

Now Jacob was smiling too. 'That first time I saw you on the bridge in your Parisian coat, I just thought, That's my Gracie!'

She suddenly remembered. 'I lost my coat in the river! I'll have to find it.'

'It'll be halfway to Manchester by now. Don't worry, I'll have another one made for you.' His face grew serious again. 'The notes you got Arthur to smuggle in kept me sane in this hellhole. Oh, *Liebling*, what would I do without you?' He kissed her tenderly. 'Now I must tell you the good news. There are rumours that we might be released. With any luck, I could be out of here soon.'

Now the tears welled in her eyes. 'And we'll be together again. We'll get married?'

'Yes, Gracie, and we'll never be apart again.'

There was a knock on the door and Sylvia popped her head in. 'The police have arrived and they'll be here any minute to interview you, Gracie. I think it's time you said your goodbyes.'

When she had gone, they clung to each other. Gracie couldn't bear to let him go, but at least there was hope that soon they would be together and nothing would ever separate them again.

'I love you so much, Jacob.'

'And I love you, Gracie—'

A soldier came in and took Jacob by the arm. 'I'll love you for as long as I live,' Jacob shouted, as he was led away. Gracie had hardly a moment to deal with her anguish before two policemen came in, followed by a doctor.

When the statements had been taken and the death certificate signed, Gracie and Sylvia left the mill together. 'Are you sure you'll be all right travelling back to Manchester? You've had a real shock.'

'I'll be fine, but I feel so sorry for all those men living in such awful conditions.'

'I feel the same. I've never seen such squalor. Those poor men, something should be done.'

'I've been thinking about that,' said Gracie. 'The first time I came to Bury I met the rector, Reverend Baldwin, at the parish church. He was desperate to find out about the conditions so he could contact the Red Cross, but they wouldn't let him inside. He said if I ever heard about what was going on in there I should tell him and, now that I've seen it, I'm going to call on him before I go home.'

'Maybe I'll come with you. I could comment on the physical state of the men from what I've seen. Who knows? Maybe something good might come from poor Eva's death.'

23

Gracie had never been so glad to see Pearson Street. If the rector hadn't offered to drive her home she would never have made it back under her own steam, she was so exhausted. She let herself into the house and shouted, 'Mam!' but there was no answer. Well, at least she didn't have to explain what had happened to her. The truth was she didn't feel at all well and she went up the stairs on all fours, crawled into bed and was asleep within minutes.

She awoke in the pitch black with searing cramps in her stomach and knew at once that she was going to be sick. Her first thought was to get the chamber pot from under the bed, but as soon as she stood up her legs went from under her, she fell on her knees and vomited all over the floor. There were spots before her eyes and she felt herself fading.

'Gracie! Gracie!' It was her mother calling from far away. Now she was being pulled upwards. 'Come on, Gracie, try to sit up for me, love. My goodness, you're so clammy. Are you going to be sick again?' Gracie shook her head. 'Then I think it's best to get you downstairs so I can clean up the mess in here.'

'Wait a minute, Mam, I've something to tell you. I saw Jacob and talked to him. He thinks there's a chance he could be released.'

'That's great news. Did he say when?'

'No, but I'm sure they'll let him go and then we'll get married.'

In the kitchen Sarah gave her a drink of water and put a bucket next to her just in case. That was when she noticed Gracie's clothes. 'What are you wearing?' she asked.

Gracie glanced down. 'Em… I had a bit of an accident at the camp today.'

'What kind of accident?'

'I fell in the river. Mam, don't look at me like that. It was nothing – just a slip.'

'It was enough to wet every stitch on you! Who gave you those clothes?'

'There was a nurse who looked after me and she gave me the clothes.'

Sarah's face changed as the thought hit her. 'Oh, dear God, did you swallow any of the water?'

'Maybe a bit.'

'Have you any idea of the muck in rivers? They're enough to give you the fever.'

'Give over, Mam. At least I didn't drown.'

'That's as maybe, but you look like death warmed up and you certainly won't be going to work in the morning.'

'I have to go or I'll be sacked,' cried Gracie, and promptly threw up into the bucket.

She slept right through to Monday afternoon, but when she woke up she felt worse than ever, and when she tried to get out of bed her legs could hardly carry her. Sarah came home from work early, and as soon as she walked into the room she opened the window to let in the fresh air, then felt Gracie's forehead. 'You're running a temperature. Do you want anything to eat?' Gracie shook her head. 'Just as well, really. They say you should feed a cold and starve a fever.'

Gracie dozed again and woke up at the sound of voices at the foot of the stairs. 'She's been very poorly, you know, but I'll see if she's awake.'

Gracie looked up as her mother opened the door. 'You've got a visitor, if you're well enough.'

'All right,' she said, expecting to see Maria or Trixie even, but it was Alan. Her mother left them and Alan greeted her with a shy smile and a soft 'Hello'.

Gracie tried to sit up and he was there helping her and rearranging the pillows. Then he sat on the edge of her bed. 'What's happened to you, Grace?' he said. 'Your mother's so worried about you.'

Gracie closed her eyes and breathed deeply. While she had been in the mill, the excitement of seeing Jacob had meant she'd hardly thought about her fall into the river, and once she was back home, she'd needed to hide from her mother the truth that she had almost died. But now she was ill and frightened by the thought that she could have died, like Eva, and she had to tell someone. The tears seeped through her eyelashes as she tried to find the words. Then she felt the lightest touch on her hand and opened her eyes to see Alan's face full of concern. 'Tell me what happened, Grace.'

By the time her mother returned she had told him everything: from the drowning to Jacob's good news, from the conditions in the camp to visiting the rector, and the threat of being arrested. 'And now I'm sick and I'm scared I'll lose my job,' she said. 'I'll try to come in tomorrow, but what if I'm not well enough?'

'Grace, I'll sort it out with your foreman. He's a friend of mine, so you mustn't worry. Come back when you're well and not before. Now go back to sleep and don't be frightened. You're safe now. I'll see you soon.' He stood up, hesitated a moment, then bent and kissed her forehead.

When Gracie returned to work two days later she was surprised at how everyone asked if she was feeling better. She felt a bit guilty telling them it was food poisoning and blamed it on a dented tin of mackerel. At the morning tea break in the canteen Trixie told her she was really glad to have her back: not only had she been run off her feet in the stores, but she was hoping Gracie would be well enough to go to the pictures with her on Friday night. 'It's the new Fred Astaire film – I read about it in *Picturegoer Magazine*. They said it's "a must for lovers of Hollywood glamour", and that's us, isn't it? Hey, we could have our tea at the Kardomah before the film. What do you think?'

'I'm up for that,' said Gracie. 'I could do with a good night out.'

'I can see that – you look terrible,' said Trixie. 'And I suppose you didn't get to see Jacob this weekend.'

Gracie couldn't lie, not to her friend. Anyway, she wanted to tell her the good news. 'I certainly did see him.' Her eyes lit up just thinking about it. 'And that's not all. I sat and talked to him, and there's a chance he might be released. Can you believe it?'

'That's wonderful, Gracie, but how on earth did it happen?'

She hadn't intended to explain how she'd come to be inside

the camp, but Trixie was waiting for an answer and she knew she could trust her. 'It came about because I fell in the river...'

Alan was on her bus after work and she thanked him for speaking to the foreman about her being ill. 'You don't need to thank me. Anyway, he's not a bad bloke. I've known him for years. But, Grace, I'm really worried about you. You look so tired and I'm afraid all this business with Jacob is really sapping your strength.'

'Don't fuss, Alan. I'm fine.' By the look on his face she could see he didn't like the sharpness of her tone so she changed the subject. 'What about your mother? Is she feeling better?'

'I don't know. She sleeps such a lot and she eats next to nothing.'

'Well, tell her I was asking for her, will you?'

'I will, yes, but I was thinking maybe you could come and see her again. She'd really enjoy that.'

Gracie had felt so uncomfortable the first time she'd met his mother, when she had confided in her that she was very ill and assumed she was Alan's girlfriend – but she didn't want to upset him. 'Maybe I will sometime,' she said.

'What about Friday night after work?'

'I'm really sorry I can't. I'm going to the pictures with Trixie. Another time, perhaps?'

He stared out of the window and said nothing. They were almost at Piccadilly before he spoke again. 'There's something else I want to say to you, Grace.' She was immediately on her guard. 'I don't want you to go back to that camp. I dread to think what might happen if you turn up there again. You can't defy the military. They'll get you in the end.'

Gracie gave him a hard stare. 'I won't be going back, but

that's not because they'll prosecute me. It's because Jacob will soon be free.'

'You can't pin your hopes on—'

'Alan, if I don't have hope, how can I go on?'

When Gracie arrived home her mother was sitting in the kitchen with Albert from next door. 'You mark my words.' He shook his finger. 'The Phoney War is over and we've already been caught on the hop.'

'What's to do?' asked Gracie.

'Ach, I don't understand it,' Sarah said. 'You explain it, Albert.'

Albert's face was grim. 'Nine months we've been living through this Phoney War. We've not been seriously threatened by the Nazis at all, but that's going to change. The British Expeditionary Force is across the Channel trying to hold back the German advance across the continent.' He shook his head in despair. 'But they're no match for the Germans. They're losing ground, forced to retreat, and now they find themselves with their backs against the wall or, more like it, with their feet in the English Channel. It's humiliating. But the worst of it is, our brave soldiers are dying on the beach at a place called Dunkirk and there's no way to save them.'

'Why can't they save them?' asked Gracie.

'The German planes are bombing the beaches and any ship that tries to get near them. Make no mistake, a lot of them will drown.'

For a brief moment Gracie felt again the rush of water in her mouth and nose on that awful day when she'd fallen into the river. She excused herself and went out into the yard to fill her lungs with air.

★

By the time they'd finished work on Friday, all the talk in the factory was of the huge rescue operation to evacuate the Dunkirk beaches. Every seaworthy craft capable of crossing the Channel was facing enemy fire to bring the soldiers home.

'I'm so angry!' said Trixie, as they sat in the Kardomah eating their tea. 'They say thousands of men have died on the beach and in the water. A lad from down our road, he's part of that force. His mother's in pieces waiting to hear if he's safe. Bloody Germans!'

By Sunday night the horror of Dunkirk was filtering through, and so, too, were the stories of sacrifice. Gracie and Sarah went to the pub to listen to the late-night news report, and although much was said about the bravery and the spirit of Dunkirk, it was clear that Britain had come up against Germany and been found wanting.

The next day at work, a sombre mood pervaded the factory and Gracie listened to the endless conversations about the defeat at Dunkirk. As the day wore on she began to notice that some of her workmates were avoiding her. There were snide remarks, too, about collaborators, and comments about Nazis. It all came to a head a few days later when the news spread around the stores that the foreman's son had been killed at Dunkirk. At tea break Gracie joined her friends in the canteen, but they immediately stood up and walked away to sit at another table. Trixie was the last to go. 'I'm sorry, Gracie. I'm going to have to sit with them. They're sending you to Coventry because they know you have a German boyfriend. They'll do the same to me if I stay with you. You understand, don't you?'

'No, I don't! He might have been born in Germany, but he hates the Nazis.' But Trixie had already turned her back on her.

When she told Alan what had happened he was angry. 'They've no right to treat you like that. I'll not stand for it!'

'But what can you do? The man I love is a German and I can't change that.'

His eyes blazed. 'How could they have known about Jacob? Did you tell anyone?'

'Only Trixie, but she's my friend.'

'So she's still talking to you, is she?'

The realisation hit Gracie hard. Trixie must have told them about Jacob and, with so much anti-German feeling, she knew her workmates would never speak to her again. She covered her face with her hands and tried hard not to cry.

'Don't upset yourself, Grace.' He put his hand on her shoulder. 'Everything will be all right. Look at me. Tomorrow when you come to work don't go to the anti-aircraft stores. Come to my workshop in the aircraft factory. I'm going to get you a transfer away from those people.'

She was amazed. 'Can you do that?'

He nodded. 'Oh, yes, and, I swear to you, no one in my workshop will say a word against you.'

24

Gracie was so grateful that he had arranged for her to be transferred permanently out the of anti-aircraft factory, but when he told her on her first day that she had also been re-graded to stores clerk on a higher wage, she was overwhelmed. 'It's just common sense, Grace,' he said. 'I'd have got you in here earlier, but there wasn't a vacancy. Come on, I'll introduce you to the stores foreman. He knows that you worked hard organising the paperwork in the anti-aircraft stores and he wants you to do the same for him.'

'What about the workers here? Will they not find out about Jacob through the people in my last job?' Gracie asked.

'They might, but I'll see that they don't blame you. Although it might be as well not to get over-friendly. We don't want another Trixie situation, do we?'

The other good news was that she received a letter from Reverend Baldwin, the rector in Bury, telling her that, thanks to the statements she and Sylvia had made about the conditions in Warth Mills, he had persuaded the Red Cross to inspect the camp. The result was that an immediate order had been issued for improvements to be made and for privileges, including letter-writing, to be extended to the internees.

When it came, Jacob's letter was both disappointing and wonderful. Disappointing because there were only twenty-four words on a form and six had been blacked out by the censor, but wonderful because he had written, *Feeling hopeful, things are happening, don't know what. I love you, don't worry, we'll soon be together again.*

Early June brought longer days and shorter blackouts, raising everyone's spirits. When Gracie left work for the weekend she thought about the extra money in her pocket and decided to make a detour into Quay Street to see what was playing at the Opera House. She'd been to a few Saturday matinees over the past few weeks and enjoyed the variety of shows. Today a poster outside advertised '*Much Ado About Nothing*, a comedy by William Shakespeare'.

'Oh, Jacob, I wish you were here.'

'Talking to yourself, are you? You know what they say about that.'

She turned to see a handsome lad on the theatre steps smiling at her. 'I know you, don't I?' she said.

'Only you can answer that.' There was a glint in his eye, and he turned his head from side to side, showing his profile. 'Do I look familiar?'

She pretended to study him. 'I never forget a face, but somehow yours escapes me.'

'Here's a clue,' he said. '*Lancashire Hotpot – a Revue*, belly laughs or your money back!'

Gracie's face lit up. 'Oh, you're the one who—'

'Persuaded you to see our show.' He made an elaborate bow.

She was surprised. 'You remember me?'

'I, unlike you, never forget an interesting face,' he said.

Gracie blushed. 'I'll take that as a compliment.'

'You're welcome, but I have to confess that I've seen you at a few of our Saturday matinees.'

Now Gracie was puzzled.

He laughed. 'Mostly from the wings, sometimes in the foyer, occasionally from the stage.' He held out his hand. 'I'm Sam Maguire, the stage manager.'

Gracie smiled and shook it. 'Gracie Earnshaw, how do you do?'

'So, how about a bit of Shakespeare on a Saturday – belly laughs or your money back?'

'Sold,' said Gracie.

He winked. 'Now I'd better get backstage, or the curtain won't come up. Enjoy the play, Gracie.'

Later, when she came out of the theatre, she was smiling. The play was so full of fun and joy, and she kept thinking about the clever lines and the banter between Benedick and Beatrice. Of course, they'd hated each other at first, but she'd known they would fall in love. Why, they were made for each other. Sam, the stage manager, had been right – she didn't want her money back.

On her way home she called at the chippie for meat pie and chips, then the paper shop for an *Evening News*. The front-page headline screamed, 'Italy Declares War!' and she wondered who they had declared war against. She would read about it after her tea but, as it happened, she got side-tracked by *Shakespeare's Dramatic Works*, and stayed up late to read *Much Ado About Nothing*.

Gracie and her mother usually had a lie-in on Sunday mornings, but for some reason Sarah was up early, even though she had come home very late, and was already well into her repertoire of the Irish songs she liked to sing when she was happy.

'You're full of the joys today, aren't you?' said Gracie, rubbing the sleep from her eyes.

Sarah laughed. 'Sure it's a lovely day, great for getting the washing done, and I might go out later.'

'Where to?'

'A wee walk, maybe. I've not decided.' She cocked her head. 'Was that somebody rapping the door? Away and see who it is.'

It was Doris, looking agitated.

'What's to do?' asked Gracie.

'Thought I'd best come and tell you, seeing you've that friend in Ancoats.'

'Maria, you mean?' asked Gracie. 'Why, what's happened?'

'I were over to me sister in Ancoats first thing. Her youngest has the whooping cough and I brought her some linctus and I...' She took a hanky from her sleeve and wiped her eyes.

'Don't get upset, Doris. Look, why don't you come in and tell us? Mam's just making some tea.'

When Doris had her hands round a strong brew, she began again. 'I went over to Ancoats. I knew summat were up with so many people on't streets. Women with kids were standin' around cryin'. Me sister were fair upset herself on account of her neighbours.'

'What happened?' asked Gracie.

'It were after midnight when it all started. Police bailing out of Black Marias, bangin' on doors and draggin' men out of their beds into the streets. It were Italians they took.' She paused to gather her thoughts and wiped her eyes again.

'I saw something in last night's paper,' said Gracie, and fetched it from next to the fireside chair. 'Here it is.' She scanned the front page. 'It's Mussolini. He's thrown in his lot with Hitler and now he's declared war on Britain as well!' She shook her head in disbelief. 'You know what this means? It's happening again. I'd better get dressed and go over to see Maria and her mother. They'll be out of their minds with worry.' She raced upstairs.

Sarah called after her, 'I don't understand.'

'The Italian men have been rounded up. Now they'll end up in camps just like Jacob did!'

Everything was quiet when Gracie arrived outside Mancini's ice-cream parlour. She knocked on the door, but there was no answer. She looked through the window and saw chairs overturned, boxes of wafers strewn about, and tubs of ice cream melting on the floor. She walked round to the back of the premises and looked up at Maria's bedroom. The curtains were closed, but Gracie took a deep breath and shouted, 'Maria! It's Gracie, let me in!' On the third shout, Maria's face appeared at the window. A minute later the back door opened and Maria pulled her inside.

'Oh, thank God you've come, Gracie. I'm at my wits' end. Did you hear what happened?'

'I heard some men have been arrested. Did they take your father?'

Maria nodded. She looked close to tears but she bit her lip and said, 'Mamma's upstairs with the boys. She's very upset. We'll go through to the shop – it'll be easier to talk there.' She fetched a jug and two glasses and they sat in one of the booths drinking sarsaparilla and staring at the mess around them. 'There was no reason for them to do this. Papa didn't put up any resistance.' Then Maria fell silent as though ordering her thoughts. When she spoke again there was no hiding her anger. 'It was after midnight and we were all asleep. The first thing I heard was the shouting and banging on doors out in the street. We watched from my parents' bedroom window. There were policemen everywhere. They didn't care about the blackout – they were carrying torches and the headlights lit up the street. We watched them dragging men out of their homes and pushing them into the vans, and the women and kids were crying and screaming. A few minutes later they were banging on our door. My father told us to stay in the bedroom and he would go down and speak to them. My mother begged him to hide somewhere, but he said it was all a misunderstanding. He would speak to the policemen and explain to them that he loved England and would never do it harm. To prove it, he would tell them that he had a son serving in the army protecting this country. Her fists clenched. 'I crept downstairs after him, but they were already in the shop throwing stuff around. Then they dragged him into the street. I could hear him shouting about England, but they just threw him into the van like a side of meat!'

For a moment Gracie felt Maria's anger. Was that how Jacob had been taken? 'Oh, Maria, they'd no right to treat your father like that. Were they all Italians who were arrested?'

'We think so. They say the government had it all planned and it was Churchill himself who gave the order. "Collar the lot," he said, as soon as Mussolini declared war. You know, they even took our priest, but the worst thing is the rumours...'

'What rumours?' asked Gracie.

'They say they'll all be shot.'

Gracie's eyes widened with fear. If they shot the Italians, they were certain to shoot the Germans too. 'They won't do that. I'm sure they won't,' she said. 'They'll intern them, like Jacob.'

'Do you think Papa might be at the same camp as Jacob? Maybe I should go there.'

'It's very hard now to get near the camp. I haven't been there for a while. You know they threatened me with prosecution? Anyway, the chances are your father will be able to write and tell you he's safe.'

Maria gave a half-smile. 'Somebody else said they'd be shipped out to Canada and I thought that wouldn't be so bad. At least Papa would have better food to eat, and the Germans wouldn't be dropping bombs on him.'

'What will you do about the shop? Open it again?'

'I don't think so. Even with Papa here, we wouldn't have been able to carry on much longer. So it'll just be my wage coming in... for now.' Maria lowered her eyes and Gracie wondered if something else was troubling her.

'Gracie, if I tell you something, promise me you won't think bad of me.'

'I would never think bad of you.'

Maria spoke in a whisper: 'I'm going to have a baby.'

Gracie couldn't believe her ears. Maria was the last person she would have expected to fall pregnant. 'Oh, my goodness, I don't know what to say. What will you do?'

'I'm hoping Tommy and I will get married. We were going to tell my parents, but I sort of put it off. I was so frightened because I knew they'd be angry, and now Papa's gone... I don't think Mamma could stand another shock. Oh, Gracie, I don't know what to do.'

'It's not for me to say, Maria, but maybe you should tell her the truth, and Tommy should be there with you. That way she'll know he's going to stand by you. You could get a special licence and be married within a week.'

Maria nodded. 'I know you're right, but I never thought

this would happen to me. I always said I would save myself for my wedding night, after a church service with bridesmaids and flowers and Papa walking me up the aisle… but it's done now, isn't it? I was so carried away with being in love and I wanted him so much that nothing else mattered.'

Gracie understood absolutely what Maria had felt in the moments before she had given herself to Tommy. She would have done the same that Christmas night when she and Jacob lay together on her bed, the only difference being that Jacob had been strong enough for both of them.

'Gracie, did you hear me? I said I'll speak to Tommy. I'm going to be so embarrassed telling Mamma that I've let her down, but maybe it'll be easier without Papa there.'

25

Sarah stood in front of the sandbags stacked ten feet tall round the town hall, feeling as nervous as a girl on a first date. She had vowed not to see Martin Quigley again, but the letter he had left for her at the hotel reception desk was such a gentle invitation to meet up that she saw no harm in it. He cut a striking figure crossing Albert Square: tall and upright in air-force blue, with ribbons on his chest, his serious expression befitting a group captain. Then he caught sight of her, and when he smiled, she felt a rush of pleasure just seeing him again. Was this the same effect he'd had on her when she was young? No, this was altogether different.

There was no formality this time: he took her hand and kissed her cheek. 'I'm so glad to see you. I was worried you wouldn't come.'

'Well, I'm here,' she said, 'but it was a bit risky leaving a letter for me at Reception. Good job the girl on duty is a friend or—'

'Or you could have got the sack!' He laughed. 'So you'll

have to give me your address. Then I can write and tell you when I'm in town.'

They left the square and walked up Cross Street. 'Where are we going?' asked Sarah.

'There's a pub just up here where they have a pan of Irish stew on the go and plenty of fresh bread. It's very good. Then I thought you might like to listen to the Hallé at the Free Trade Hall. What do you think?'

'I'd like that. I've never been to the Hallé.' She was glad she had changed into her black woollen dress with the lace collar, tidied her hair and freshened her makeup after her shift.

Mr Thomas's Chop House had been part of Manchester life since Victorian times, and was popular with the cotton merchants, who traded stock at the Royal Exchange in the mornings, then retired to eat a good lunch and discuss business in the afternoon.

'Is this all right for you?' said Martin.

She looked around at the elaborate mahogany bar and the green tiled walls. 'Of course. I've always wanted to see inside. It looks like something out of a Dickens novel.' Her eyes came back to Martin and the look on his face. 'What is it?' she said.

'I still can't get over meeting you here in Manchester after all these years. Who'd have guessed back then, in that draper's shop in Belfast, that we'd be sitting here?'

'That reminds me. I've brought the photograph of us all.' She took it from her handbag and, heads together, they pored over it. 'I look about twelve,' said Sarah.

Martin laughed. 'There's old man Jenkins. He used to shout at me about wasting brown paper. "Wrap parcels sparingly, Quigley, and use minimum string, or you might find your pay packet light at the end of the week!"'

'I don't remember that girl with the curly hair,' said Sarah.

'Of course you do. It's Jenny. She's the one who was always chasing after me.'

'I didn't know about that!'

'Oh, I could have gone off with her, all right,' Martin winked, 'but it was only you I ever wanted. Remember those trips on Sundays to Holywood on the train? Walking along the beach or up the woods behind the town where we could be alone?'

Sarah looked away as she felt a flush spread up her neck and across her face.

'Ah, Sarah, don't be embarrassed. Weren't they the loveliest days of our lives?' She nodded, but she still couldn't look at him. He took her hand to his lips and kissed it.

The barmaid brought them steaming bowls of stew, with coarse brown bread, and Sarah was grateful for the diversion. Martin talked about his life in the RAF and the places he had seen. 'I learned to fly and it gave me the confidence to command.'

'And do you think you've changed as a person?' asked Sarah. 'I don't mean just growing older, but have you changed in here?' She touched her heart. 'What I'm trying to say is, if we'd married as we planned to do all those years ago, would we be the same people we are today?'

She could see him struggle with his answer, rejecting his first thoughts, searching for something nearer the truth. 'When I lost you, I thought that one day I'd find another girl. She wouldn't be you, but I thought I could be happy. Trouble was I didn't look hard enough. I joined the RAF and that became my life. But I've always thought about you, Sarah, and as the years went by I realised you weren't the only thing I'd lost. There was something else – something precious...' Sarah could imagine what he was going to say by the sadness in his face. 'Just like you,' he said, 'I've thought of our child every day of my life.'

Later, they went to the Hallé as Martin had planned, but Sarah would sooner have stayed talking the evening away in Mr Thomas's Chop House. She sensed he felt the same. He took her hand as soon as the opening bars of Beethoven's Pastoral Symphony began, and now and again she felt him looking at her. They slipped away at the interval. 'I'll walk you home,' he said.

She didn't want him to see the poor area where she lived, but on the other hand she wasn't ready yet to say goodnight. In the gathering twilight they cut through the maze of narrow streets towards Market Street, heading for Oldham Road. Inevitably, their steps slowed and it seemed that they could do no other but to step into the shadows. Sarah was lost in his arms, a girl again with no sense, and she didn't care.

'Sarah, my darling, listen.' His warm breath was on her neck. 'We can't do this, not here, not like this.'

She knew she was hanging from a precipice and all she wanted was to let go, but his words were soothing. 'I have a room – not at the Midland this time, at the Victoria Hotel on Deansgate. We could go there, it's not far. Do you want to do that?'

The voice in her head screamed, 'You can't! Say no, say no,' but the words on her tongue said, 'Yes, I want to.'

26

Liebling, we're moving, destination unknown, but full of hope. Juliet said, 'The orchard walls are high.' But I will climb them for you. Jacob x

Gracie held his permitted twenty-four words to her heart and rocked back and forth, dripping tears. Somehow, knowing that Jacob was in Warth Mills and being able to picture him there had been a comfort to her. But this changed everything – no mention of release and, worse still, no idea where he had been sent.

She decided to walk over to Ancoats after her tea to see Maria and tell her the news. Maybe the family would have had a letter from her father by now. She also wondered if Maria and Tommy had told her mother about the baby.

Maria brought Gracie through the ice-cream parlour and up the stairs. 'I see you've got it all neat and tidy again,' said Gracie.

Her mother, hearing the voices, shouted, 'Is that you, Gracie?'

'It is. I've come to see how you are.' She was shocked by Mrs Mancini's appearance – she had lost weight and was pale and drawn.

'What news of Jacob?' she asked.

Gracie sighed. 'Only a short letter from him saying he's being moved, but he doesn't know where.'

'You are lucky to have that. We have heard nothing since my husband was taken. But what hope is there if even the Church cannot find our priest?'

'We have to keep hoping, Mrs Mancini, that's all we can do.'

'*Sì, sì*, you are right, but it does not take away our sadness.'

The two girls went into Maria's bedroom and closed the door so they could talk.

'Actually, I did hear something about the Italian prisoners,' said Maria. 'There's a friend of mine in the next street – Irish family, her father's a policeman – she heard him telling her mother that Italian prisoners were being sent to Canada.'

Gracie was puzzled. 'That rumour's been around for a while, but I still can't see why they'd send them there.'

'I don't know, but she seemed fairly certain. I'm not telling Mamma – I don't think she could cope if that happened.'

'Your friend, did she only mention Italians, nothing about Germans?'

Maria shook her head, and inwardly Gracie gave a sigh of relief. 'And what about you and Tommy? Have you spoken to your mother about the baby?'

Maria lowered her eyes and stroked her belly. 'He said he would come round one evening, but that was two weeks ago and every time I ask him he gets annoyed, says he'll do it when he's good and ready and I'd best not keep going on about it.' Maria lifted her head, her eyes full of despair. 'But I don't believe him,' she said. 'He's angry and it's like he blames me, but he was the one who…' Maria could say no more.

Gracie put an arm around her. 'It isn't your fault, it's his. He's got to be made to face up to his responsibilities.'

'How can I make him do that?'

Gracie thought for a moment. 'You know what? I'm going to speak to Alan about him. They're mates, aren't they? Maybe he'll listen to him.'

'Why would Alan upset his friend for me? I hardly know him.'

'He won't be doing it for you. He'll be doing it for me.'

The next day at work Gracie told Alan about Maria's pregnancy and Tommy's reluctance to face the music. 'She's going through an awful time at the moment with her father arrested and the loss of their business. She's so ashamed, Alan, and he promised he'd marry her but he's doing nothing about it and time's getting on.'

'I don't like interfering in other people's business, Grace.'

'Oh, Alan, it's not fair if he abandons her. She doesn't deserve that. Please will you talk to him, just for me?' Gracie begged.

'All right. I'll take him out for a pint, see what I can do.'

She squeezed his arm. 'You're the best pal ever!'

Alan was as good as his word, and a few days later he reported that his man-to-man talk with Tommy had gone well. He had agreed that telling Maria's mother about the baby was the right thing to do, and after his fourth pint, he'd agreed that marriage was a good idea as well. 'I think it's sorted,' Alan told her. 'So don't worry.'

When she didn't hear from Maria, Gracie assumed that Tommy had taken Alan's advice and she expected a wedding invitation any day. There was no word from Jacob either, but she told herself, 'No news is good news,' and felt sure that she would hear from him once he got to the new camp.

It was a sunny morning towards the end of June when Alan did not arrive at work. Gracie kept an eye open for him, but he didn't appear. By late afternoon the word went round that his mother had died suddenly in her sleep. As soon as the hooter went for the end of the day, Gracie clocked out and went straight to his house. He must have been watching out for her because he opened the door as she came up the garden path. 'I hoped you would come.' He took her coat and hung it in the hall, then ushered her into the parlour.

'I'm so sorry about your mother, Alan.' He seemed to struggle to find the right words, and it occurred to Gracie that she had never seen him so unsure of himself. 'Do you want to tell me what happened?'

He nodded. 'I always take her up a cup of tea before I go to work. She likes me to give her a kiss before I leave. Her eyes were closed and I thought she was sleeping. I said, "Here's your tea, Ma," but her cheek was cold and I knew she was gone.'

'It must have been an awful shock for you,' said Gracie.

'The doctor said she would have died peacefully in her sleep and he was surprised she had lasted so long, bearing in mind her condition. I didn't know what to say, Grace. She never told me she was dying. Why would she not tell me?' There were tears in his eyes.

Gracie was at a loss. She had never seen a man cry before. If he'd been a woman she would have hugged him... Instead she touched him gently on his shoulder but then he leaned towards her and it seemed the most natural thing in the world to put her arms around him. She held him for a while, until he turned away from her and wiped his eyes.

'I'm sorry, what must you think of me?'

'I think you loved your mother very much and she loved you. Isn't that right?'

'Yes, it is,' he said. 'It's just that there are so many things I should have said to her and now I'll never get the chance.'

'She knows all that you wanted to say, Alan. You looked after her so well,' said Gracie. 'Now, would you like me to make you a brew? And have you eaten anything?'

They sat together in the kitchen drinking tea and eating toast as Alan talked about his mother and how she had brought him up on her own after his father died. 'She did everything for me. Always told me I could be anybody I wanted to be. She was so proud when I went to work at Metrovicks.' Gracie listened to the warmth in his voice and saw the love in his face as he remembered his mother.

It was getting dark when she left the house. Alan wanted to walk her home, but she said she would be fine. On the doorstep he hugged her. 'You're a comfort, Grace. Thank you for being such a good friend.'

Alan had the morning off for his mother's funeral and arrived back in the workshop just as the ear-deafening blast of the air-raid alert sounded. Everyone knew the drill, they'd practised it enough, and more than twenty thousand workers made their way to the concrete underground cellars.

Gracie, Alan and the rest of their workshop went quickly to their allocated cellar. At the entrance a warden checked their passes, but as Gracie flashed hers, he caught hold of her arm. 'Not so fast, young lady. You don't belong in this shelter. You haven't got the right pass.'

'It's all right,' said Alan. 'She's from my section. I'll vouch for her.'

'It's not about vouching for her, pal. She's got to be in the right shelter and this one isn't it.'

'It's probably because she's recently been transferred from anti-aircraft-gun stores – somebody didn't do the paperwork, that's all.'

'Well, that explains it,' said the warden, and Gracie tried to go past him into the shelter. He blocked the entrance with his arm. 'But I still can't let you in. You'll have to go to your previous shelter. If you run fast you might just make it before the Luftwaffe get here.'

'Hang on a minute.' Alan squared up to the warden and his voice grew louder. 'She's not running all the way to that shelter. The bombs could be falling before she gets there!'

'Look, mate, people have to be accounted for and it's up to me to make sure the right people are in this shelter.'

'For God's sake!' Alan was red in the face and looked like he was going to thump the warden.

Gracie spoke up. 'It's all right, Alan, I'll be fine. Now go inside otherwise these people behind us can't get into their shelter. Go on!'

Gracie ran as fast as she could and arrived panting for breath just as the warden was about to close the doors. He directed her to the far end of the cavernous cellar where her erstwhile workmates were gathered. She sat at the end of a bench and was careful to avoid their eyes.

'Hey, you!' It was Sid, one of the men who had called her a German collaborator. 'I don't think you should be allowed in here. For all we know you could have told your boyfriend that we're building bombers here.'

Gracie didn't acknowledge him, but a moment later she heard Trixie's voice: 'For God's sake, Sid, she's helping to build them, isn't she?' The sound of the air-raid warning stopped suddenly and the cellar fell silent as they waited for the bombs to fall. It was as cold as the grave in the cellar, and those who spoke did so in whispers. Half an hour later, with no sound of bombing, the all-clear sounded. As Gracie came out into the fresh air, she was surprised to see Trixie waiting for her. 'How are you, Gracie?' she asked.

'Why would you want to know?'

'Look, I'm sorry for what happened, but you know I have to work with these people. If I'd sided with you they wouldn't be speaking to me either.'

Gracie shook her head in despair.

'I just wanted to ask you if Jacob's all right.'

'You've got a nerve speaking to me. I know what you did!'

'What do you mean?'

'Well, somebody must have told those people about Jacob.'

'What? You don't think I'd do that?'

But Gracie was already walking away when Trixie shouted after her, 'I never said anything, honest I didn't!'

27

Gracie got off the bus at Piccadilly, intending to have a quick look in Lewis's ladies' department before going home for her tea. Clothes rationing had come into force in June and she wanted to see what coupons were needed for a new summer dress. She was waiting at the corner of Moseley Street for a tram to pass when she heard the paper man give his garbled cry. It was a moment before she could pick out a word she understood – 'Torpedoed'.

She turned to read the headline on the board and her blood froze – 'Enemy Aliens' Ship Torpedoed'. She fumbled in her bag for two pennies and stood on the pavement to read the front page while the crowds of workers on their way home wove around her. '*Arandora Star*... Canada... torpedoed...U-boat... hundreds drowned... Italians... Germans.'

She could scarcely breathe and her mind raced. Could Jacob have been on that ship? No, he was in a camp somewhere, wasn't he? Anyway, she'd know if he was dead, she'd feel his loss, but all she felt was bewilderment. Italians, the paper said. Oh, God! Maria. Mr Mancini, a lovely man, making his ice cream, always smiling...

Someone bumped into her, throwing her forward, jolting her brain. She should go and see Maria right away. No, there'd be chaos in her house, the not-knowing, the lurking grief: better to leave her a while to look after her mother.

She stood on the pavement, unable to move. I should go home, she thought, but she couldn't face the empty house. Then it came to her: Mam would finish work soon. She decided to walk the short distance to the Midland. She would know what to do – would know how to calm her down.

Gracie waited at the staff entrance as the workers left, but there was no sign of her mother. She hadn't said she was working overtime, but maybe she'd been asked at the last minute. A woman wearing a chambermaid's uniform came through the door in a hurry and Gracie asked whether Sarah Earnshaw was doing an extra shift. The woman rushed away, calling over her shoulder, 'No, love, she finished early today.'

Gracie dragged herself home, but the house was empty, with no sign that her mother had come in at all. Where could she be? She sat on the back doorstep in the warm July evening and read the paper again and again, gleaning every detail. The liner *Arandora Star*, once a cruise ship, had left Liverpool bound for Canada with more than a thousand souls on board, Italians and other enemy aliens, including Germans, as well as crew. A marauding U-boat had spotted the ship and unleashed a torpedo on the port side inflicting a fatal blow. The ship had sunk within thirty minutes in the cold Atlantic, off the coast of Ireland. A rescue mission was under way.

So there was hope, wasn't there? Jacob might not have been on the ship and, even if he was, he might have been rescued. Then the darkest fears filled her mind. What if he had drowned?

She knew what that felt like. 'Jacob!' she cried. 'Where are you?' Silently she added, Mam, where are you when I need you?

She was still sitting outside as the sun set behind the coal shed leaving a shepherd's delight of a sky. She remembered again that night when Jacob had climbed its walls. '"With love's light wings did I o'erperch these walls,"' he had said then, and in his last message, 'But I will climb them for you.' She clung to his meaning now more than ever – there were obstacles that prevented them being together, but he would overcome them to be with her.

It was almost midnight when her mother crept into the house and tiptoed into the kitchen, carrying her shoes. She switched on the light and let out a surprised cry at the sight of Gracie sitting in the fireside chair. 'For the love of God, Gracie, you frightened the life out of me. Why aren't you in bed?'

'Where have you been?'

'I've been working. There was a dinner dance so they offered me an extra shift waitressing.'

'You're lying,' said Gracie. 'I went there to find you and I was told you left at dinnertime.'

Sarah ignored Gracie's accusation. 'What's happened? Why were you looking for me?'

Well, at least she didn't deny it, thought Gracie, and she took a deep breath to stifle the sob in her throat. 'An enemy-aliens ship on its way to Canada has been sunk and I'm worried that Jacob might have been on it.'

Sarah's face was at once full of concern. 'Oh, Gracie, my love.' She stepped towards her with her arms outstretched.

Gracie moved back, and this time she couldn't fight the sobs. 'No, Mam! Don't touch me. I've been sitting here all this time, wondering where you were. Then I started thinking about the other nights when you said you were working late. Were you lying then too?'

'Honestly, I've been doing plenty of late shifts, you know that. There's been more money coming in.'

'But you've been coming home later and later, and tonight... when I needed you... Where have you been tonight, Mam?' The question hung in the air and Gracie saw the flush on her mother's neck and face, remnants of lipstick, pencilled eyebrows. 'Just tell me the truth.'

Sarah sat down and hid her face with her hands. Gracie waited. Eventually, Sarah put her hands in her lap and looked at her daughter. 'The truth is... I've met a man.'

Gracie's eyes widened in disbelief, but she said nothing.

'I've been meeting him on and off over the past few months. A lot of the time I was working.'

'Who is he? Where did you meet him?' Gracie's tone was sharp.

'There's no need to be angry, Gracie. I'll tell you everything. His name is Martin and I met him at the Midland.'

'How old is he?'

'A year older than me. In fact, we knew each other back in Belfast. You could say we were childhood sweethearts.'

'And what do you do, the pair of you, when you meet up?'

Shock registered on Sarah's face and she quickly looked away.

'Oh, my God!' said Gracie. 'How could you?'

Now it was Sarah's turn to be angry. 'Why shouldn't I?' she shouted. 'You've no idea how lonely it's been for me all these years.'

Gracie paced the room trying to imagine... No, trying not to imagine! 'Why didn't you tell me about him?'

Sarah gave a derisive laugh. 'Because I knew you wouldn't

like it and I'd end up with your disapproval heaped on my head for ever and a day!'

Gracie snapped back, 'What a hypocrite you are! All those warnings you've given me over the years about not getting into trouble, not letting myself down—'

'Gracie, you don't know him. He's a good man.'

'And I don't want to know him. Thank you very much!' Gracie flew out of the room and up the stairs, banging the bedroom door behind her. She needed to be alone, not to go over her mother's deceit but to concentrate on Jacob and to pray that he was safe. That was what mattered and she called out to him: 'Oh, Jacob, where are you? Please be safe.'

Alan met her the following morning and they travelled to work together. He knew about the sinking, he had been listening to the wireless, and after the shock of the first reports he had followed the story right up to the early morning bulletin before he'd left for work.

'Tell me everything,' said Gracie.

'Are you sure?'

'Yes. I need to know.'

Alan explained that heavy casualties were to be expected. Not only had the ship sunk so quickly, but it seemed that there had been insufficient lifeboats on board. The first ship to arrive on the scene had reported many bodies in the water. Gracie closed her eyes and tried to control her erratic breathing. Seeing her distress, Alan took her hand and squeezed it tightly. He went on, 'Most of the casualties were probably Italian. They outnumbered enemy aliens from other countries, like Germany and Austria. The survivors are being brought back to Liverpool.'

'So what should I do now?'

'You'll have to wait, Grace. There's nothing else for it. You don't even know if Jacob was on the ship. So, one of two things will happen: Jacob will be safe in a camp somewhere and you'll get a letter from him when he's allowed to write, or the authorities will notify his next of kin.'

'How long can I wait to hear nothing?' Gracie cried.

'Shush now, be strong.' He held her hand until they arrived at the factory gates.

At the end of the day he was waiting for her. 'You made it through, then,' he said. 'I wondered whether I should have sent you home. It must have been difficult to concentrate.'

'Being occupied is better. It's a pity I have to go home.'

Alan looked at her sideways. 'Is there something else you're not telling me?'

Gracie sighed. 'On top of everything I've got problems with my mother.' She explained about the man-friend.

'Why are you so hard on her? She's found a man and he's even older than she is. What's the harm in it?'

'You don't understand.' Gracie struggled to explain the delicate situation. 'She's... well, they've been out till all hours. You know what I mean?'

Alan gave her a puzzled look, then understanding dawned on his face and he laughed.

'It's not funny!' shouted Gracie.

'I know it isn't. You're upset because she kept it from you, but if she'd told you, you'd still be upset.'

'Stop speaking in riddles,' she said.

'Grace, don't be so naïve. Sometimes people just need physical contact.'

Gracie was shocked by his words, but he was right about physical contact – hadn't she longed to have Jacob's arms around her night after night? But she also realised that she'd been naïve about Alan. His mother had told her he'd had girl-friends in the past and not only that – didn't he regularly go dancing at the Plaza on a Saturday night? Who, she wondered, satisfied Alan's longings?

That night Gracie called at Maria's house to see how the family were coping with the news of the sinking of the *Arandora Star*. 'We're at our wits' end,' said Maria. 'We've been told to expect that a lot of Italian men from the north-west will have died, and the chances are that a fair number of them will be from Ancoats. The church is packed out every minute of the day. That's where Mamma is now. I have to say, after a lot of crying on the day we heard, she's been so strong. There's been a lot of support from our non-Italian neighbours too. But what about you, Gracie? Do you think Jacob might have been on the ship?'

'It's possible. I'll just have to wait like everyone else to find out, but I wanted to ask you a favour. Will you let me know anything that's said at the raincoat factory? If the worst comes to the worst, Jacob's next of kin will be notified, not me.'

'Of course I will, but keep hoping and praying, Gracie. That's all we can do.'

'And what about the baby? You've told your mother?'

'I have.' Maria closed her eyes. When she opened them they were brimming with tears. 'But Tommy wasn't with me and he's not going to marry me.'

'No!' Gracie couldn't believe it. 'But Alan spoke to him and Tommy said he'd stand by you. I was expecting to hear about the wedding.'

'It's not going to happen. He says he wants to join up and as far as I'm concerned he can do what he likes. I was devastated at first, but since Papa was arrested and now this ship's been sunk, I just care about my family. They're all that matters.'

'You're so lucky to have a family who care for each other.'

'You've got your mam, haven't you? She'll support you.'

And Gracie gave a half-hearted nod. She couldn't possibly tell Maria about her mother carrying on: she was far too ashamed.

A week of waiting passed so slowly, each moment stretched to encompass Gracie's worst fears. Every morning she awoke, knowing that Jacob's fate was already sealed: she just didn't know the outcome. One of these days, maybe today, she would know. On the eighth day she came home from work, ate her tea of mackerel and mashed potato, sewed a button on her blouse... There was a rap at the door and her mother went to answer it while Gracie stood waiting in the kitchen. She caught Maria's voice, low and hesitant, her mother's quicker but still a whisper. They came into the kitchen and her mother went to stand next to her and held her hand, even though they hadn't spoken for a week.

'I've got some news for you,' said Maria. Gracie watched her lips shape each word. 'Mr Rosenberg called all the workers together at the end of the day. He had a letter in his hand. It said that Jacob had been on board the SS *Arandora Star* when it was sunk by enemy action and as a consequence he lost his life. I'm so sorry, Gracie. I don't know what to say.'

Gracie fell to her knees and drew a breath so long and so deep that it must have filled her lungs to bursting. Her ears rang with a frightening sound as though the gates of Hell had opened. She rocked back and forth until someone caught her and held her. 'Gracie, Gracie, hush, hush, my lovely girl. Stop screaming, please. You'll hurt yourself.' And Gracie gasped as she realised the deafening noise was coming from her mouth. Slowly, slowly, she brought it to a whimper.

'Try to stand up, love. We'll get you to the chair.' She felt herself half carried, her feet trailing on the floor. 'There now, sit quiet if you can. I'll get you some sweet, strong tea for the shock.'

Gracie looked around her. There was Maria, crying, and her mother with the kettle in her hand. She took it all in and knew Jacob was dead. She'd never see him again. Her tears came softly, steadily, each one adding to the weight of her loss. She drank the tea and let herself be wrapped in the eiderdown from her bed, and all the time she cried and said nothing.

She must have slept a while, and woke to the sound of voices at the front door. It had grown dark in the kitchen, save for the gleam of moonlight through the open curtains. She remembered that Jacob was dead and it hurt so much she wished she was dead too. Maria had gone. A man's voice she didn't recognise cut through her thoughts and she heard her mother answer. With the eiderdown still wrapped round her she went to see who was there. The light of the moon caught the brass buttons on the blue-grey uniform. 'Mam, who is it?'

'It's nobody. Go back inside.'

'Who's that, Sarah?' The man's voice was louder.

Her mother answered him: 'You have to go. I can't speak to you now!'

The man looked over her mother's head straight at her. Then he called, 'Gracie? Are you Gracie?'

'Yes, I am,' she said.

As she watched he pushed past her mother and came towards her. She backed away.

The light came on, and Gracie shaded her eyes as she looked from her mother to the RAF officer and back again.

'This is Martin, the man I told you about,' said Sarah, and she shot a look at him, but he never took his eyes off Gracie's face. She went on, 'I was supposed to have met him this evening, but I didn't go because it wouldn't have been right to leave you when you'd just had such bad news.' Then she turned to Martin. 'I'm asking you to leave because we've just had word of a death and now is not the time to be discussing anything else.'

He looked bewildered. 'But this is Gracie, your daughter, am I right?'

'Martin, please, you need to leave.' Sarah took his arm as if she would push him out.

But Gracie spoke up: 'Yes, I'm Gracie, and this is my mother, but what's that to you?'

He moved towards her, and Gracie stepped back, her eyes wide. 'I can't believe it,' he said, and smiled. 'I'm your father.'

'My father? You're not my father. Tell him, Mam, tell him. He's not my father – make him go away!' she howled.

Sarah put her arm round Gracie and faced him. 'For the love of God, Martin, go! This isn't the time. I told you she's had some terrible news tonight. Can't you see the state she's in?'

He looked at Gracie slumped against her mother, sobbing her heart out, then at Sarah, whose eyes were fierce with defiance. He nodded slowly. 'All right, I'll go. I meant no harm.' And with a shake of his head he turned and walked away.

When he had gone, Sarah tried to hug Gracie, 'Listen to me, love,' but Gracie pushed her away.

'Is it true what he said? Is he my father?'

'It's a long story and maybe I should have—'

'Mam! Just answer the question.'

'Yes, love, he is your father, but you need to know—'

Gracie heard no more. The pounding in her head sent her frantic – first Jacob and now this. She paced the kitchen, shaking and crying, and every time her mother tried to calm her she pushed her away until she could bear it no longer. She threw open the back door, ran across the yard, out into the ginnel, down to Oldham Road and beyond until she could run no more.

She had no idea where she was, hadn't even realised that she was still clutching the eiderdown round her shoulders. On and on she walked, her head full of Jacob's drowning and her mother's deceit. The sky was clear, with just enough moonlight to see the silhouettes of buildings. She crossed a wide bridge, passed a park and saw what looked like a church ahead. Weary and cold, she sought shelter beneath the pillars at the entrance, then wrapped herself in her eiderdown and fell asleep.

The whining siren pierced her brain, growing louder and louder. Even if she knew where the nearest shelter was, she wouldn't go there. She'd rather die right now in an air raid than live with the horrors in her head. The siren stopped. Within moments the ground shook beneath her and she was deafened by what could only be an anti-aircraft gun. She left the church entrance and stood looking up at the tracers smearing the sky red and, in her mind's eye, she saw again Jacob standing next to her as he had done in Heaton Park on that last Sunday of peace. He'd said then that the guns would be fired before long. She'd never dreamed that he wouldn't be here to see them. Nearby there was a heavy thud, then a huge bang, and flames roared into the air, lighting the whole sky. The blast from the explosion reverberated outwards and the force passed through her body throwing her backwards into the air.

She had no idea how long she was unconscious but when she came round she was lying on her back with the all-clear ringing in her ears. Someone was shaking her.

'Eh, lass, what you doin' in't churchyard? Tha shoulda been in't shelter.' Hands helped her to her feet. She blinked the dust out of her eyes and saw a ruddy face beneath a tin helmet. 'Where do you live?' he said.

'Miles Platting.'

'Nay, lass, it were a big bomb right enough, but tha haven't been blown that far.'

'Where am I?' she asked.

'Salford, close by Peel Park where ack-ack gun is. Eh, lass, you're shaking like a leaf. I'll take thee t' ARP post, see if we can get you home.'

'No!' she shouted. 'I'm not going back home, just leave me alone. I'll be all right.'

'I can't do that, lass. You're in shock and you need help.'

Gracie couldn't think straight. All she knew was that Jacob had gone and her mother had lied to her and now she was frightened.

'I think you've had a blow to the head, so I can't let you wander around on your own, but I'll fetch t'ambulance for you.'

'No, I'm not going anywhere.' Then the man's words filtered through to her confused brain. 'Did you say I'm in Salford?'

'Aye, lass, Peel Park.'

'I have a friend who lives in Salford. Could you take me there?' She told him the address.

'Well, it's about twenty minutes' walk. Can you manage that?'

'I think so.'

It might have been twenty minutes, but to Gracie it seemed

endless. Her legs were lead weights and she was barely awake as she walked, but every time she faltered the ARP warden held her upright and told her it wasn't much further. They stopped at last and she registered the sound of a door knocker. Her head drooped as they waited. The door opened and a familiar voice said, 'Who is it?'

'ARP, sir, sorry to bother you. Do you know this young lady? I found her at t' cemetery in middle of the raid, confused like.' He briefly shone his torch on her face and Gracie looked up.

'Oh, my God, Grace, is it you?'

She blinked at the light. 'Alan?' Then her legs gave way.

28

She remembered leaning her head on Alan's shoulder and the brandy burning her throat. Then she told him Jacob was dead – drowned – and she cried till her heart was fit to break. She must have fallen asleep then, because she woke up in a strange bed and a strange room, which she took to be his mother's. She had no recollection of climbing the stairs, but the sensation of being lifted and carried lingered, along with the feeling that she was safe.

She sat up in bed and looked around. There was a note on the bedside table from Alan: *Gone to work. Help yourself to bread and jam. I'll be back at one.* She had missed work – but it didn't matter. Nothing mattered anymore. Besides, she wouldn't have been able to concentrate, weighed down with her constant thoughts of Jacob.

She lay down again and cried softly into the pillow, then sat up and howled in anger at what they had done to Jacob. He was a good man, so clever and caring, and she loved him more than life itself. She thought of him floundering in the icy sea. Drowning wasn't a quick death: there was time to know what was happening. Had he thought of her in his final moments?

She could imagine his terror, for hadn't she nearly died too, drowned in a filthy river? She closed her eyes and felt again the water over her head. She had struggled to live then, but she wouldn't struggle now. She'd just accept it, welcome it even. Her eyes flew open. She had crossed a river last night. Maybe she could find her way back there…

She was out of bed and running down the stairs two at a time to unlock the door and screamed in frustration when it wouldn't open. There was a sound in the hallway behind her and she half turned towards it just as his strong arms closed around her. 'Shush now, Grace.' Alan's voice was soft in her ear. 'You don't need to run anymore. You're here with me.' He turned her round to face him and swept aside the tangled hair that had fallen over her eyes. 'Come into the kitchen,' he said. 'I'm making you some dinner.' And without a word she went with him. 'Aw, Grace, you weren't going out in your bare feet, were you?'

While he made scrambled eggs on toast, Alan talked about the raid the previous night. 'Our first bombing and it looks like the Luftwaffe couldn't hit a barn door with a banjo. Not a single casualty, thank God.'

Gracie ate a little, but the food felt like sawdust in her mouth and she didn't speak at all. When they'd finished Alan suggested she should go into the sitting room and listen to the wireless while he washed the pots. It was *Band Wagon* with Arthur Askey, and he left her to the fun and laughter, but she barely heard it. Thoughts of Jacob came randomly to her mind and she tried to focus on a time when they were together – their first date, when he'd taken her to the Turk's Head. She saw him again as he ran across the road to meet her outside Lewis's, his tie blown over his shoulder, the anxious look in his eyes because he was late. She saw it all, every tiny detail, as though she were watching a film with sound and in Technicolor. It calmed her, soothed her pain, and held back the harsh reality that he was dead until the grief overwhelmed her again.

She was aware of Alan coming to sit next to her, and when he saw her tears he asked, 'How can I help you, Grace?' but she shook her head and retreated again into that ghostly world where Jacob was waiting for her to relive the times they had spent together. The day passed. She ate another meal. It grew dark.

'Do you want to go to sleep now, Grace?' he asked.

She recoiled at the thought of what horrors the night would bring and shook her head.

'You could have a bath,' he said, 'if that would help you to sleep. Do you want me to run a bath for you?'

'All right,' she said.

She lay perfectly still in the warm water with a jazz tune repeating in her head. She was barely aware of the knock at the door and someone calling her name: 'Grace, are you all right in there?'

Jacob was holding her in his arms as they danced and she hummed, 'Dream A Little Dream Of Me'. She relaxed and slipped lower in the water.

'Grace, answer me! Grace! Are you all right?'

She heard the shouting and, startled by the water in her nose and mouth, she screamed in fright, tried to sit up and slipped.

'Oh, Christ, Grace!'

She was lifted by her arms and hauled out of the bath on to the floor. Alan was wrapping her in a towel, then carrying her into his mother's bedroom and laying her on the bed. She felt the rough towel rubbing against her skin. Then it was gone and the bedclothes covered her. He sat on the edge of the bed. 'I'll stay with you awhile until you calm down,' he said. Her whole body was tingling – the sensation relaxed her – and she closed her eyes.

Alan was in the kitchen when she came downstairs and he gave her the lopsided smile she'd seen before when he was unsure of himself. 'You found the dressing-gown I left you. That's good. Did you sleep all right?'

She looked away. 'Yes, thank you.'

'Grace, about what happened last night. I thought that you'd… well, you know. I would never have done such a thing otherwise. I'm so sorry.'

Oddly, she felt no shame. One minute she was dreaming, the next she was sinking, drowning with no hope of rescue, and he had lifted her, held her, and his touch had told her that she was not alone. 'Don't be sorry, Alan. I'm glad you were there.'

'Grace, you know you can stay here for as long as you like, don't you? Or if you want me to take you home I will do.'

'I don't want to go home.'

'What about your mother? She'll be wondering where you are.'

'I don't want to see her.'

'But she'll be worried, won't she?'

'I don't care. I'll never speak to her again.' Her voice was full of anger.

'Do you want to tell me why?' She shook her head. 'Well, if that's how you feel, it's fine, but you're going to need your clothes.'

'I'm sorry, I shouldn't be shouting at you, but I don't want to talk about what happened.' Later when Gracie was calm she said, 'Alan, do you think I could stay here again tonight? I haven't anywhere else to go.'

'You can stay as long as you like, Grace.'

'Thank you. I'll go over to the house this evening and get some things while my mother isn't there. She does an extra shift waitressing at the Midland on Sundays.'

'I'll come with you,' said Alan.

They went along the ginnel at the back of Pearson Street and through the yard door where Gracie retrieved the key from under the bucket next to the step. Inside everything was the same as always, except for the awful memory of hearing Maria say that Jacob 'had lost his life', and the shock of a stranger telling her, 'I'm your father.' She stood awhile in the kitchen, collecting her thoughts, then turned to Alan. 'I'd only just heard that Jacob had died when something else happened. A man came to the door, the one Mam had been seeing, I suppose, and he said he was my father. She didn't deny it and all I could think of was that she'd lied to me all my life. She's not... I'm not who I thought I was.'

Alan gave her his handkerchief to wipe her tears. 'I understand how devastated you are by Jacob's death, but I had no idea that you're trying to cope with your mother's lies as well. I can't believe she'd do that to you. Get your things and I'll take you home.'

She went to her bedroom and packed an old grip bag with some clothes, her washbag and makeup. From the dressing-table drawer she took the Blackpool snow globe, Jacob's letters, the theatre programme from *Romeo and Juliet* and last, from the side of her bed, *Shakespeare's Dramatic Works*.

'Have you got everything?' Alan asked, when she came back to the kitchen.

'Everything I need,' she said and, without a backward glance, they left the way they had come.

Back in Alan's house, Gracie felt better and talked about going to work the next morning.

'Are you sure?' asked Alan. 'I can mark you as sick for a few days at least.'

'No, I have to try,' she told him.

In the evening they listened to some dance music on the radio – Alan said it might cheer her a little – but Gracie's thoughts were as dark as ever. The late news bulletin reported on bombings in London and Portsmouth and, towards the end, there was a brief mention of the confirmed number of casualties and survivors from the *Arandora Star*.

'Why don't you go to bed, Grace, get some sleep?'

She stood up. 'Yes, I think I will.'

Alan stood, too, and put his hands on her shoulders. 'If you need me, if you're frightened, promise me you'll call me and I'll come and sit with you.'

'I promise.' Tears filled her eyes. 'Alan, I don't know how to thank you for helping me like this.'

He kissed her forehead. 'I don't need thanks, Grace. I just want to see you well again.'

The night was bitterly cold and she wrapped the raincoat about her. You couldn't see a hand in front of your face in the blackout, but she had been down this path before. A voice called, 'Be careful, it's slippery underfoot!' It didn't matter – she had to run or she'd lose him. But she caught her foot on something and stumbled. The ground gave way beneath her and she fell into the icy water. Her beautiful coat, heavy as lead on her back, wrapped her tight and dragged her deeper and deeper. She fought to throw it off and cried out for Jacob, but he was gone and she was sinking fast...

Strong arms caught her and held her, and a kiss on her lips gave her breath so she could live.

'Grace... I'm here. Wake up, please.' There was fear in his voice.

She was ice cold and shaking. 'Alan, is it you?'

'Yes.'

'I drowned,' was all she said.

He lay beside her and held her in his arms. 'You're safe now. I'll look after you.' She believed him, closed her eyes and slept the sleep of the dead.

She woke up with a start and reached across the bed. Alan had gone. He had been there with her after her nightmare and was still there much later when she stirred and he whispered, 'Hush now, go back to sleep,' his body next to her and the familiar smell of him.

She reached out to pull aside the blackout curtains. The sun was quite high in the sky – it must be later than she'd thought. On the bedside table there was another note. *You were exhausted. Don't come into work, you're not ready for it yet. See you tonight.*

He was right, of course: she couldn't face it, couldn't even get out of bed. The first tears of the day wetted the pillow and she reached for the comfort of her memories. Jacob on a warm Sunday morning outside Victoria station: how handsome he looked with his dark hair, how tall he was, and she watched again that smile he gave her every time he greeted her. She wiped away her tears and forced herself to get up. Still in her dressing-gown, she managed to unpack her bag and hang up her clothes, then put the snow globe on the bedside table. She took her Shakespeare book downstairs and, without bothering to eat anything, lay on the settee and read for the rest of the day.

When Alan arrived home she was still lying there, still not dressed, her eyes red with crying.

'Ah, Grace, look at you. I know it's hard, but you have to get washed and dressed every day and you have to eat or things will get worse not better.'

'It's all right for you to say that! You don't know how I feel.'

'I don't know what you're feeling, Grace, but I lost my mother not long ago and it knocked me sideways.'

'It's not the same. Jacob was my life. We were going to get married and now he's dead!'

'Don't be angry with me. Jacob's gone and I'm the one trying to help you.'

Gracie took a step back, shocked at his harsh tone. She opened her mouth to scream back at him, but the look on his face stopped her in her tracks and all she could do was weep.

'Listen,' he said. 'I'm going to make us some tea, which you will eat, and while I'm doing that you will go upstairs, have a wash, put on a nice dress and do your hair. Is that clear?'

She nodded.

That evening Alan listened to the radio and Gracie sat with her Shakespeare on her lap, but she wasn't reading. She never turned a page. She just sat there seething with anger. How dare he speak to her like that? She'd thought he cared about her and now, when she needed a friend more than ever, he was shouting at her.

At ten o'clock, Gracie went to bed with a curt 'Goodnight.' Alan said nothing. She tossed and turned but couldn't sleep for thinking about his sharp words, shouting and ordering her about. True, she was the one who had raised her voice, but she had a right to be angry: hadn't she lost the man she was to marry? Maybe she had been wrong to think his grief for his mother was less than she felt for Jacob. She should have thought of his feelings and apologised. Maybe he was still awake: she should ask him to forgive her. No, that would be unseemly, going into a man's bedroom. She tried again to sleep but found herself going over and over the exchanges between them since she had arrived on his doorstep after the air raid. In that short time it felt like the bond between them had strengthened and altered in unexpected ways. He had done everything to support her. His caring had brought her back from the brink and she had to admit that his physical presence had a powerful effect on her. It was as if she was cocooned in his home and sometimes in his arms. She should be ashamed at allowing him to come into her bed to calm and comfort in the night, but at the time she had been so terrified she'd wanted him to stay with her. The more she thought about the growing closeness between them, the more she realised that maybe it was time for her to face up to her grief, thank Alan and go back to the sort of friendship they'd had before. She turned over in bed and closed her eyes. The decision was made. She would leave in the morning.

There was a scream, and she turned just in time to see Eva plunge into the murky water. She reached out and caught her flailing arm, but the current was fast and Eva was heavy. Then she, too, was dragged down and down into the darkness. She woke up in a hospital and in the next bed there was someone covered with a sheet. Poor Eva must have drowned and she went to her and pulled back the sheet. And screamed at the dead face. It was her own, bloodied and pale, her staring eyes as dead as a fish on a slab. Again and again she screamed.

Suddenly she was awake, shaking and sweating, her heart pounding, utterly alone.

29

When the hooter at the raincoat factory sounded at midday, Gracie was waiting at the gate for the workers to come out into the sunshine to sit in the yard and eat their dinner. Maria waved and went over to her. 'Bloomin' 'eck, Gracie, where have you been? Your mam's been round our house twice a day in as many days asking if I know where you are. She said you'd run away.'

'I'll explain in a minute but, first, tell me, is there any word of your father?'

'Nothing for certain, but we don't think he was on the *Arandora Star*. We'd have had a letter by now. The bishop's been speaking to the authorities, and it seems there's a big camp just set up on Melland's Fields in Gorton and a lot of Italian men have been taken there. Mamma's at the church all the time, praying and waiting for news.'

'I hope it's true, Maria. Now, have the Rosenbergs heard anything more about Jacob? Will there be a funeral?'

'I'm so sorry, Gracie, I don't think there'll be a funeral

because there isn't a...' Her voice trailed off, but Gracie understood.

The thought of Jacob being lost in every sense was another blow. She had hoped there would be a grave, somewhere she could visit to be close to him again. Tears filled her eyes and she shook her head. How much more could she take?

'Gracie, I'm so sorry about Jacob. I can see all this is taking such a toll on you. Will you not go home? Your mother's so desperate to find you and I'm sure she'll look after you, whatever it was that happened between you.'

'I'm not going back, Maria. I was devastated when you told me Jacob had died, but what happened between me and my mother after you left made me realise I wanted nothing more to do with her.'

'What could have been so bad? When I left she was comforting you.'

'I can't talk about it, not now, but I'm never going back home.'

'So where have you been staying?'

Gracie bit her lip. She'd already said more than she'd intended.

But Maria had an inkling. 'Oh, no, Gracie, don't tell me you're staying with Alan?'

'I didn't mean it to happen, I just ended up there. Anyway, what's the harm in it? He's a friend.'

'Just be careful, that's all I'm saying.'

'I'll have you know he's been very good to me. Anyway, I'm not staying there any longer. I'm looking for lodgings. I don't suppose there's any chance I could stay with you? I can pay the going rate.'

'I'd like to say yes, Gracie, but I can't help, I'm sorry. We've an elderly neighbour staying with us. Her son was arrested, too, and she couldn't afford the rent on her house without his wage. She'd have been out on the street, if Mamma hadn't taken her in.'

Gracie tried to put a brave face on it, but she had pinned her hopes on Maria and couldn't help wondering whether the story about the elderly neighbour was true. Maybe she just didn't want a grieving lodger when she had enough troubles in her own family. Before she left, she asked about the baby. Maria smiled and patted her slight bump. 'I think everything's going well. I'm not so sick in the mornings now.'

'And Tommy?'

'He finished here on Saturday and he'll have started basic training today. I doubt I'll ever see him again.'

Gracie realised that Maria, too, had suffered the loss of the man she loved and, not only that, she was dealing with his rejection of her and the child. 'Maria, I'm sorry,' she said.

'Don't be. He may be gone, but I have the baby.'

Gracie walked all the way from Cheetham Hill back to Alan's house – she thought it would help her think, but all it did was to churn up the worst emotions imaginable. She was more alone than ever. Jacob was gone and she was finished with her mother. Her friendship with Maria was fading – she had her unborn child to think about and her family – but it was a blow to hear that she couldn't lodge with them. They'd been friends for years, and she would have slept on the floor if Maria had suggested it.

Then there was Alan. He had been her support, even before Jacob died, and he had taken her in and cared for her when she was distraught, but now it was clear he'd had enough. How could he be expected to put up with her weeping and nightmares any longer? She would collect her things and find a lodging house for the night.

He was in the kitchen when she came in. 'Where have you been, Grace? You look exhausted.'

'I went to see Maria at the factory and then I was just walking.'

'What did you go there for?' he demanded.

'I wanted to ask Maria if I could stay at her house.'

'What? I can't believe you'd do that!' he shouted. 'Haven't I told you again and again that you can stay here?'

Gracie couldn't bear to be shouted at. 'It doesn't matter anyway, she said no, but I think she just didn't want me and I know you don't either,' she cried. 'Why would you?' Her voice was rising with every thought. 'Look at me! I can't sleep, I can't stop crying, I'm just a nuisance. I shouldn't have come back here. I can't do this any more!' She rushed to the door and threw it open, but Alan caught her and pulled her back inside.

He shook his head at her. 'You've no idea how far from the truth you are, Grace. I worry about you all the time when I'm at work, in case you do something stupid, and when I came home tonight and you weren't here…'

Gracie slumped into a chair and sobbed. 'I came over the bridge again just now and I looked down at the water. It isn't that high and I knew I could easily climb on the parapet… but I couldn't do it. I was too frightened.'

Alan knelt beside her. 'Oh, my God, Grace. What are we to do?'

'Nothing,' she said. 'I'll just take my things and find lodgings.'

'Please, stay tonight,' he said. 'I don't want you trudging round the streets looking for somewhere to sleep.' And he wiped away her tears. 'Sleep here and we'll see how you feel in the morning.'

She knew he was right and she was grateful to him that he would let her stay even though she was such a burden.

She managed to eat a little of what he had cooked and after that they went into the sitting room, but Alan didn't turn on the wireless. Instead he sat beside her on the settee.

'Grace, I've been thinking, maybe it would help if you talked about Jacob, not about his death but when you were together. I'm a good listener.'

Slowly at first, Gracie began to speak about Jacob, and soon she was weaving the story of their love with scenes and conversations, dramas and misunderstandings, excitement and love. When the story ended she was silent.

'What are you thinking now?' said Alan.

She turned to him and her eyes were dark. 'We had all that and we should have had so much more. Now he's gone and somehow just telling our story has made me so angry. How could he leave me like this? With nothing! He said he loved me, but he's left me alone and I'm just... empty inside.'

'It's not his fault, Grace.'

She sighed. 'But he promised me, and I ache for him... I ache for him.' She closed her eyes and imagined Jacob holding her. Then she caught her breath as she felt arms around her – Alan's arms – pulling her close. She let him do it because there was some comfort in being held and feeling that someone cared.

She didn't know how long he held her, sometimes gently stroking her back, her arms, her cheek. He didn't speak and she had no words. Only the embrace mattered.

When he eventually took his arms away she wanted to say, 'Please don't stop,' but they had sat so long the daylight had faded and the room was in darkness. She couldn't see his face, but his voice was tender. 'Was it all right for me to do that?' he said.

She nodded. 'Yes, thank you.'

'Why don't you go upstairs now, Grace, and get ready for bed? I'll come up and see how you are when I've locked up.'

It was a warm night and she lay on top of the bed in her nightdress. She felt calmer than she had at any time since she'd arrived at Alan's house during the bombing. Maybe tonight she would sleep well.

Her eyes were closed when Alan came into the room. She felt the weight of him lie on the bed and his arms enfolding her. 'Go to sleep now,' he whispered. 'I'll stay with you all night. Don't be frightened, I'll take care of you.'

Her head was on his shoulder and his fingers soothed her temple. In minutes she was sound asleep.

When she awoke in the morning she was in exactly the same position as she had been when she had fallen asleep and Alan was there, smiling at her. 'Well done,' he said. 'You've slept all night and not a nightmare in sight.'

'Is it time to get up?' she asked.

'For me, but not for you. Listen, if you can be as calm as you were last night then you're finding a way to deal with your grief and, who knows, by Monday, if all goes well, you could even go back to work.'

'But I could look for lodgings today and be back at work tomorrow.'

'No, Grace, I want you to stay here. You're not well enough yet to be on your own. Can you not see that?'

And Gracie could see it, because last night she'd realised that one day she might be able to accept Jacob's death, but she couldn't do it on her own. Alan had proved to be the kindest, gentlest and, in fact, her only friend. 'I'll stay until I get back to work,' she said. 'By then you'll have had enough of me for sure.'

For the rest of the week they fell into a routine. Alan would go to work and Gracie would get up and go for a walk, then come back and read for a while before preparing the tea ready for Alan when he came home. In between, she still had the odd attack of anger towards Jacob, but mostly she was just so sad. Her whole life had changed and all her dreams of being married and having children had been shattered. She made a point of doing her hair and makeup before Alan came home, as though she cared what she looked like, because she didn't want him to be annoyed with her again. After tea they would listen to the wireless, Alan liked that, then she'd get ready for bed and he would stay with her all night so she didn't have nightmares.

On Saturday afternoon Alan arrived home from work and they went for a walk in Buile Hill Park in the sunshine. 'You look so much better,' he said, as they strolled along. 'Do you think you could manage to go back to work on Monday?'

'I think so, and then I'll look for lodgings.'

'You know how I feel about that, Grace. We'll need to see how you go on.'

They were sitting on a bench overlooking a flowerbed of brightly coloured dahlias when Alan suddenly said, 'Can I ask you a question?' There was a quality to his tone that made her uneasy.

'Of course you can.'

'Do you like it when I stay with you at night?'

She couldn't lie. 'Yes, it soothes me and I feel safe. I suppose that's why the nightmares have stopped.'

'Did you...' he hesitated '... did you ever lie down with Jacob?'

She was surprised that he would ask her such a thing, but maybe it was because she had already shared with him so much of her relationship with Jacob. 'The night before he left for London he came to see me. We were in my bedroom and we lay together for a while, and that's all it was because... well, we were going to be married and he said we had to wait. Only we couldn't know that we would never get another chance. Sometimes I wish we'd...' She stopped herself.

'What do you wish, Grace?'

She was mortified that she had almost revealed her intimate thoughts. What would he think of her? 'You know I can't answer that... I haven't the words,' she said.

That evening they listened to *In Town Tonight* broadcast from the Ritz Hotel in London. The orchestra played, and Gracie could almost see the people dancing – the women in ballgowns and the men in dinner suits. She smiled to herself.

Alan was watching her. 'That's the first time I've seen you smile since you came here,' he said.

'It's just so lovely to hear the music. We never had a wireless at home.' She tilted her head, studying him. 'Your mother told me you go dancing on Saturday nights at the Plaza. You should have gone tonight. I would've been fine on my own.'

'And why would I do that when I have my best girl here at home?' He smiled. 'Would you like to dance?'

'Don't be silly, there's no room.'

'It's a slow waltz. That doesn't need much room.' And she laughed as he pulled her off the settee.

It felt good to be doing something normal for a change, and when the music stopped, Alan said, 'If I was at the Plaza I'd be wondering whether to ask for a second dance, or just say thank you and leave the floor.'

The dancing had lifted her mood. 'So what's it to be, then?'

'Oh I think I'll...' He pretended to walk away. She hit him playfully on his shoulder and he laughed. 'All right, I'll take a chance on you.'

Later as they sat on the settee and ate some supper, Alan said, 'Aren't you glad you stayed here instead of going off somewhere on your own?'

'I am,' she said. 'I'm better if I have company.'

'Of course you are. Now, it's time we went to bed, I think.'

The night was hot and humid, and when Alan came into the dark bedroom he drew back the curtains and opened the window. He lay beside her and took her in his arms as he had done before, but tonight he had removed his shirt and she breathed in the fresh smell of him and felt his skin against her cheek. He caressed her back as he had done before and she relaxed, but moments later his hand slid across her breasts. She breathed deeply and her eyes closed as he stroked her. She knew what he was doing, but she didn't want to lose the sensation of his hands on her body, even when he eased her nightdress up to her waist and caressed her thighs. His hands moved upwards and she suddenly panicked as the memory of Charlie grabbing at her came flooding back. 'Ah, Grace, don't be frightened,' Alan whispered, and he kissed her. 'You'll be safe with me.' She gave a soft gasp as he touched her then, slowly and gently, as in all the things he did for her, helping her to relax. And when she was ready, he moved on top of her. She caught her breath as she realised he was completely naked. 'Grace… do you want me to do this?'

The ache inside her cried out for him. 'Yes,' she whispered, and gave a soft cry as she felt him deep inside her.

30

Sarah was at her wits' end. It was almost a month since Gracie had left home and she was no nearer finding her. She had been to Maria's house several times in the hope that Gracie would at least be in contact with her friend. Maria admitted she had seen her and that Gracie had talked about getting lodgings, but Sarah was convinced that Maria was hiding something. Assuming that Gracie was still going to work, she had gone to the Metrovicks factory a few days later, in time for the workers leaving at the end of the day. It was chaos. Thousands of people poured through the gates and it was impossible to pick out one girl in a sea of faces.

She worried about her safety too. The Luftwaffe had recently flown over Manchester dropping 'Hitler's Last Appeal to Reason' leaflets. The newspapers ridiculed them because, of course, Britain had no intention of surrendering, but any right-minded person could see this was a sign that they'd soon be dropping bombs instead of propaganda. On the night Gracie had left, the city had been bombed and she had been terrified she might have been caught up in it. It was a relief to hear the next morning that there had been no casualties.

She hadn't seen Martin since the night she'd ordered him out of her house, but she was aware that he would soon be back in the city for his monthly meeting with the other group captains. She was not surprised, therefore, when she came out of the Midland Hotel staff entrance a week later to see him leaning against the railings. She made a point of walking straight past him, but he fell into step beside her.

'Sarah, we have to talk.' He was using his group-captain voice.

'Do we?' She carried on walking.

'You know we do.'

She stopped suddenly. 'I have nothing to say to you. I've lost my daughter because of you. I've no idea where she is and it's your fault!'

'She's my daughter, too. In fact, you wouldn't have a daughter at all if it wasn't for me!'

The slap on his face startled him, but his reactions were razor sharp and he grabbed her wrist. 'Sarah, listen to me.' She pulled away from him, but he wouldn't let go. 'I was rash. I should never have gone to your house that night, but I was desperate to see you again. I couldn't have known that our daughter was there, because you lied to me—'

'I was going to tell you—'

'Were you? If only I could believe that.'

'It all went wrong,' said Sarah. 'I wanted to tell Gracie about you, but it didn't seem fair because she was going through so much heartbreak and worry. I just couldn't burden her with anything else.' Sarah turned away from him to hide the tears welling in her eyes.

He touched her chin and turned her face towards him.

'Sarah, I'm so sorry. I didn't come here to fight with you. God, I was just so carried away that night at seeing Gracie. I wasn't thinking straight and I was insensitive. It was only later that I remembered you said someone had died, but I barely took it in at the time. I was so shocked seeing Gracie standing there – the image of you as a girl – and my only thought was this is my daughter. Please forgive me for being such a fool.'

Sarah could see how upset he was and her heart went out to him. 'I'm to blame just as much as you. I should have told you about Gracie straight way, but I didn't want you to think that I was after money or something from you.'

'I would never have thought that,' he said, and he drew her to him.

She rested her head on his shoulder. 'And now we've lost her, Martin.'

'We'll find her, I promise you,' he said. 'Now dry your eyes and we'll go and find somewhere quiet so you can tell me all about our daughter.'

In the lounge bar of the Grapes public house, Martin bought both of them a glass of Guinness, and after a long drink, he said, 'Now tell me everything about our Gracie.'

Sarah was so pleased to be sharing her pride in their daughter and Martin never stopped smiling.

'So she was good at her lessons, then?' he said.

'Oh, aye, bright as a button, but cheeky sometimes when she knew she was in the right. She's a bit of a mimic – used to take off all the teachers, got into trouble for that. Tells a good story, too, and she's always reading, three or four books a week...' She bit her lip. 'I wonder if she has books now, wherever she is.'

'And you said she had a fiancé?'

'Yes, he's the one who died.' She recounted the story of

their romance, right up to the moment when Martin had arrived on their doorstep.

'I can't believe how crass I was. God, I wouldn't blame Gracie if she never forgives me.'

'She will forgive you, I'm sure of it, but how will we find her?'

By the time they left the Grapes they had a bit of a plan. It would be up to Sarah to carry it out because Martin would be back on his base in Wilmslow for another month. 'But write to me and tell me how you get on,' he said. Outside, he took her hand and they walked in silence awhile. Then he asked. 'What about the man you married? How did that come about?'

'I was very lucky – I could have ended up on the street. You remember Jean, who lived next door to me in Belfast? Well, her aunt owned a boarding house in Manchester and she arranged for me to stay with her till the baby was born. I was so grateful to that woman. David lived next door with his mother and we got friendly. I knew I'd have to give the baby up for adoption, but the nearer the time came the more I wanted to keep it. I knew David had taken a fancy to me, but I never expected him to ask me to marry him. He said he wanted to take care of me and bring up the child as his own. Well, I weighed it all up. He was a kind lad, I liked him, I could keep the baby, and I'd have a roof over my head. His mother died soon after we married, and then I lost David too. He'd been gassed in the Great War and his chest was weak. But I'll always be grateful to him for the five years we had together and for being a good father to Gracie.'

'And Gracie never knew he wasn't her real father?'

'No, so you can understand what a shock she had when she met you.'

'Oh, Sarah, I'm so sorry to have put you and Gracie through

all that. We're going to have to be so careful to bring her round.'

They had arrived at the Victoria Hotel. 'You've taken a room here again, instead of the Midland,' she said.

He smiled. 'I've fond memories of my last stay there.'

Sarah blushed, remembering the night they had spent together, but that had also been the night when Gracie had had word of the *Arandora Star* sinking. She hadn't been there when her daughter had needed her, and she would never forgive herself for that.

'Will you come in for a nightcap?'

'Ach, no, Martin, I can't. I daren't stay out too long just in case Gracie comes back and I'm not there.'

'I understand,' he said, and kissed her tenderly. 'Please God we'll find her soon.'

The following Sunday Sarah went back to Maria. 'I know she's your friend and you don't want to betray a confidence,' she told her, 'but I'm certain you know more than you're saying. Imagine how your mother would feel if you just disappeared and she never heard another word from you. Gracie could be dead for all I know, Maria. Will you not help me?'

Maria didn't meet Sarah's eye. 'I can't be sure where she is.'

'Maybe not, but you've some idea who she's with, haven't you?'

Maria looked even more uneasy. 'All right. I know where she went that night when she left you, but she could be any-where now.'

'Who was she with, Maria?'

'She went to Alan's, but I've no idea where he lives.'

Sarah felt reassured. 'I've met Alan. He came to our house.

He seemed a sensible sort of fella. Lives with his mother, doesn't he?' Maria didn't answer. 'Doesn't he?' said Sarah.

'Actually, his mother died a few months ago.'

'She's not living on her own with a man?' Sarah was appalled. 'I've told her over and over again that a girl's reputation is so easily ruined.' She stopped suddenly, seeing the look on Maria's face, and remembered that she was having a child out of wedlock. 'I'm so sorry, Maria, I shouldn't have said that. I'm so worried about her I don't know what I'm saying any more. I'd better go.' But she had to ask just one more question. 'Is Alan the sort of man who would take advantage of her?'

Maria just shrugged her shoulders.

The next morning Sarah got up very early and was waiting at the gates of Metrovicks as the workers arrived, not in a mad rush as they were at the end of the day, but walking in, talking to friends. She watched Gracie and Alan get off the bus holding hands and walk in her direction. How thin she looks, thought Sarah, and there was a sad weariness in the way she carried herself. They were almost at the gate when Gracie saw her. 'I've nothing to say to you, Mam.'

'Well, I've plenty to say to you.'

Alan looked her up and down. 'Mrs Earnshaw, nothing you can say will persuade Grace to go home. In her eyes, you've been lying to her for years. Why don't you leave us alone?' He took Gracie's arm to lead her away.

Sarah wasn't going to let him dictate to her. 'This is nothing to do with you. I've a right to speak to my daughter.'

'Now look here—' He raised his voice.

'It's all right, Alan,' said Gracie. 'You go on in and I'll be with you in a minute.' He glared at both of them and walked off.

Sarah shook her head in disbelief. 'It's true, isn't it? You're living with him. Oh, for the love of God, Gracie, what have you done?'

'He took me in when I was desperate. You've no idea how lost I was after Jacob's death. The truth is, I'm still not right, but Alan understands. He makes me feel like I can go on living. No one else cared, not even my own mother.'

'Now that's not fair! I've cared for you all your life, and you know it wasn't easy.'

'But where were you when all those terrible things were happening with me? Out with your fancy man, that's where, and when I heard that Jacob was dead you were still more concerned about that man than me!'

'That's not what happened. I told him to leave, remember? But the fact is he's your father, Gracie. Will you not at least meet him? He deserves that, doesn't he?'

'I owe him nothing. I've no intention of meeting him, and while we're at it, I never want to see you again either!'

Sarah watched her daughter walk away and cursed her own stupidity. What right had she to chide her daughter about living in sin, when she herself had conceived and borne a child out of wedlock? By now the crowd of workers had swallowed Gracie and she doubted she would ever see her daughter again.

31

Gracie was glad that Alan had signed up to work overtime on Saturday afternoons: it meant she could have some time to herself. He could get a bit intense. Mam turning up at the crack of dawn at the factory gates had been bad enough, but the way Alan had spoken to her afterwards had really upset her. He was furious, told her she shouldn't have given her the time of day, but the worst of it was his accusation that she had undermined him. 'How dare you tell me to go away while you spoke to her? I'm warning you, Grace, don't ever do anything like that again. Do you understand?' She had apologised and promised to be more respectful in future. She had learned over the past few weeks that it was better not to cross him.

She clocked out, caught the bus into town and was in plenty of time for the matinee at the Opera House. It didn't matter what the show was: two hours in a dark theatre being transported to another world was just what she needed. In the event, the very silly farce she saw cheered her up no end and, after laughing so much, she came out into the bright sunlight, still smiling.

'Looks like you got your money's worth today.' She turned to see Sam, the stage manager, leaning against the wall.

'Hello.' She smiled and went to talk to him. 'I really enjoyed it. Haven't had a good laugh in I don't know how long.'

'I could hear you from the wings – hysterical, snorting, chuckling!'

'No, you didn't! Anyway, I don't snort.'

He raised an eyebrow, as if to say, 'Are you sure about that?'

'I don't know how they do it without collapsing into fits of laughter,' she said.

'Oh, they do plenty of that in rehearsal, but by the time they've said the lines a hundred times they aren't funny to them anymore. Anyway, where have you been? Haven't seen you for a bit.'

Gracie sighed. 'Ah, there's been a lot happening.'

'None of it good, by the sound of it.'

She looked away. 'It's time I was going,' she said.

'You can't go yet. You've not had the special matinee back-stage tour for the person who laughed the most at today's performance.'

She was laughing again. 'You're having me on! There's no such tour.'

He looked affronted at her doubting him. 'Oh yes there is, but it's only available to people called Gracie.'

She feigned surprise. 'Oh, that's me. I'm Gracie and I claim my backstage tour.'

Sam offered her his arm. 'Well, then, let's get started.' They walked back into the theatre together.

They went through the auditorium, up the steps at the side of the stage and into the wings. 'I'll take you to meet some of the cast first.' He led her down a narrow passageway to the dressing rooms, knocked on the first door and went in. Along one wall was a row of mirrors surrounded by light bulbs. She recognised the two men sitting in front of them, taking off their makeup, as the main characters. Sam introduced them. 'This is Paul, hoping to be a matinee idol before he's thirty, and Theo just hopes he can remember his lines. And this is Gracie,' he added. 'She was the one laughing like a drain in the middle of the stalls.'

'Good for you, Gracie. Glad you enjoyed it,' said Paul, while Theo toasted her with a glass of whisky.

The female principals were next door, and Gracie was surprised that they were in the middle of undressing when she and Sam walked in. They didn't seem at all bothered that Sam saw them in their underwear. Up close she could see how thick their makeup was and her eyes widened when one woman pulled off a wig and set it on a stand, revealing her real hair in a tight net.

Back in the corridor, Sam said, 'I'll show you the costume store next.'

The room was lined with rows of rails packed tight with all sorts of dresses, suits and uniforms of different eras, from medieval to Tudor, Victorian, the roaring twenties... At the far end an older woman, with dyed red hair and lipstick to match, was working at a sewing machine.

'Hello, Mrs B,' said Sam. 'I've brought Gracie to see you.'

'How do, cock,' she said. 'I'm Mrs Booth, wardrobe mistress. Come to see where the hard graft happens, have you?'

'There are some beautiful costumes here. Did you make them?'

'Well, in forty years I've made plenty. Here, look at this one.' And she took a crinoline dress of green silk with a bodice of seed pearls from a rail and held it up against Gracie.

'It's beautiful,' said Gracie. 'I can see all the work that's

271

gone into it – the cut on the bias, the stitchwork on the pearls, the little darts to shape the bust.'

'You're a needlewoman yourself?'

'I used to make raincoats,' said Gracie. 'I love clothes.'

'Right, have to rush, Mrs B,' said Sam. 'She's having the whole tour.'

They came round the back of the stage and Sam pointed out the mechanics to raise and lower the curtains and the scenery, then moved on to the stage and the set for the farce.

'I didn't realise the stage was so big,' said Gracie. 'It looked quite cosy from the stalls.'

'That's because it's all about deception,' said Sam, and his eyes seemed to twinkle. 'We can make you believe anything. Come on, you haven't seen what I do yet.' He led her into the corner of the wings close to the edge of the stage. 'This is it.' He sounded excited. She tried to keep the disappointment out of her voice, when all she could see was a tiny space among the black curtains and a lectern with a high stool. 'What is it?' she said.

'The control centre – everything you see and hear in a performance begins here. Sit on the stool. Now look straight ahead through the gap.'

She smiled in delight. 'I can see the whole stage.'

Sam reached across and switched on a shaded light that illuminated the lectern. 'And there's your script. Open it. Here's your headphones. You speak into this piece at the front.' He put the contraption on to her head. 'Now say hello to Brian.' Gracie shook her head. 'Go on, just speak to him.'

'Hello, Brian.'

'Hello, who's this with the sultry voice?'

'It's Gracie.' She suppressed a giggle.

'Now tell him you want lights for the opening scene.'

Gracie repeated the words and first the house lights dimmed, then seconds later she gasped as the entire stage lit up. She turned to see Sam smiling at her reaction. 'It's good when you can do that, isn't it?' he said. 'Now tell him you want a single spot, downstage centre.'

The stage was plunged into darkness, then a pool of light appeared at the front. Gracie was enthralled. Sam took the headphones from her and pointed to the spotlight. 'That's where the magic is. Why don't you go and stand in it?'

'I couldn't,' she said.

'Oh, I think you could.'

Her footsteps seemed so loud and the spotlight much further away than she'd thought. Standing in the light she was surrounded by darkness. The real world had disappeared and left her alone in some other dimension...

Sam called to her, 'Say something.'

'I can't,' she said, and her voice filled the auditorium.

'I think you can,' came the answer.

She collected her thoughts, took a deep breath, then spoke the lines that had reverberated in her head every day since Jacob's death. '"What's here? A cup closed in my true love's hand? Poison I see hath been his untimely end... Let me die."'

When the last word had left her lips she stood a moment, overcome with sadness, until the house lights flickered on and she turned to see Sam clapping as he crossed the stage towards her. 'Well, I didn't see that coming!' He laughed.

She was covered with embarrassment. What had she been thinking of, speaking lines from *Romeo and Juliet*? 'I have to go,' she said. 'Thanks for showing me round. I really loved it.'

'I was just about to ask you if you wanted to come to the pub. We usually go to the Sawyers for an hour before the evening performance.'

'Thank you for asking me, but I can't be late home. I have to go now.' She ran down the steps at the side of the stage and up the aisle.

She heard him shout after her, 'See you next week, Gracie!' but she didn't look back.

The bus was packed and it crawled all the way through Salford. Alan would surely be at home, wondering where she was and why his tea wasn't ready, but she was determined that he wouldn't spoil her good mood.

He was reading the newspaper when she came in and the atmosphere was already charged. 'Where have you been?' he asked.

She had already decided that she wouldn't tell him about going to the theatre. It wasn't the sort of thing he would approve of, so she told him she had been walking around the shops. 'I thought I might buy a new dress,' she said. 'I've got the coupons.'

'Where is it, then?'

'The ones I liked were too dear. I'll have to save up a bit longer.'

He eyed her with suspicion. 'I thought you might have gone to see your mother.'

'I told you, I'm having nothing more to do with her. Why are you going on about it?'

He stood up. 'Because you're weak, Grace. You haven't got the guts to stand up to her. She did a terrible thing to you, lying about your father. I saw how much it hurt you. God, you know how close you were to a nervous breakdown, don't you? If it hadn't been for me you'd have been dead in the river weeks ago!'

'Maybe that was because I'd lost Jacob.'

'Don't get clever with me,' he snapped. 'However you look

at it, I'm the one taking care of you and I keep you calm and stable. You don't want to go back to those terrible thoughts and nightmares, do you?'

All the joy of the afternoon had drained away and she was back on the knife edge. Tears welled in her eyes and the old feeling of emptiness filled her heart. She sank on to the settee and put her head in her hands.

Alan's arm was round her shoulders and he spoke gently to her. 'You see what happens when you get overwrought? You're not well, Grace, but I'll look after you. Now, why don't you have a lie-down and I'll call you when your tea's ready?'

That night she hoped to go straight to sleep, but when Alan got into bed beside her, the tenderness he had shown her during the evening had disappeared and the roughness of his love-making shocked her. He knew he'd hurt her and afterwards he said he was sorry – called her 'my lovely Grace' and said, 'You know how much you mean to me, don't you?'

On the Monday morning the director of Metrovicks called a meeting of all workers involved in aircraft building and anti-aircraft-gun manufacture. He explained that the government expected the two factories to increase productivity. 'The race is on to complete the six Manchester bombers in production by Christmas, and more ack-ack guns are desperately needed,' he said. There would be plenty of overtime for those who wanted it, including all day Saturday and Sunday until pro-duction levels increased. She knew Alan would want to earn extra money, but she would rather have Saturday afternoon and Sunday to herself.

Leaving the meeting, she was caught up in the crowd when

someone tapped her shoulder. She turned to see Trixie at her side.

'I've got something important to tell you,' she said.

'I'm not listening, Trixie.' She tried to move away from her, but it was impossible in the crush.

'You remember I said I wasn't the one who told the foreman about Jacob being German. Well, I knew I hadn't told him, so I set out to find the real culprit. It took me a while, but now I know. Would you like me to tell you who it was?'

'Leave me alone. I'm not speaking to you.'

'I know that, but you're going to have to listen.' Trixie leaned in closer. 'It was your very good friend Alan who gave away your secret.'

Gracie glared at her. 'I don't believe you. Why would he do that?'

'Maybe because he wanted to get you transferred to his workshop. He likes to keep you close, doesn't he?'

Gracie hid her shock. 'That's the most ridiculous thing I've ever heard.'

'That's not all,' said Trixie. 'There was another girl before you.'

But Gracie had seen a gap in the crowd and moved quickly away.

That evening after her tea, Gracie didn't pick up her book as usual. Instead she went over in mind what Trixie had said. She was fairly certain that Trixie had told the foreman about Jacob – the very fact that she had stopped speaking to her was evidence enough – but what worried her was the reason Trixie gave as to why Alan might do such a thing. 'He keeps you close, doesn't he?' she had said, and there was no denying that.

'Are you all right?' Alan had put down his newspaper and was staring at her.

'Yes, I'm fine.' She attempted a smile.

'Don't lie to me, Grace. I know when you're troubled.'

'It's not worth talking about.'

'Out with it,' he said. 'I'll not have you worrying.'

She didn't want to upset him but, on the other hand, he wouldn't be happy if he thought she was keeping something from him. 'Trixie spoke to me today.'

'I hope you sent her packing.' His voice was stern.

'I was stuck next to her while we were waiting to leave the meeting this morning. I told her I didn't want to speak to her. It didn't matter because she carried on anyway.'

Alan moved forward in his chair and said calmly. 'Tell me exactly what she said.'

Gracie swallowed hard and tried desperately to think of a way out of the mess she had got herself into. 'It really doesn't matter. I didn't believe her anyway.'

'What did she say?'

'She said it wasn't her who told the foreman about Jacob. It was you.'

She held her breath, waiting for him to be angry, and then, to her astonishment, he smiled.

'Yes, I told the foreman, but that was on the first day you started work. I wanted him to know that you were vulnerable with Jacob being in the camp and I asked him to look after you. When Dunkirk happened and the foreman's son was killed, it's quite possible he might have told someone else. Who knows? But the thing is, Grace, I don't blame the man. His boy was dead. When I saw how people were treating you, I went straight to him and offered to take you into my workshop. It was the right thing for both of you.'

'But you said it was Trixie who told everyone.'

'No, love, I think you're a bit confused. You weren't taking things in at that time. Now, forget all about it.' And he gave her a hug and kissed her. 'I haven't forgotten that you want a new dress.' Gracie was well aware of what he was doing, with his clumsy change of subject, treating her like a child, offering a distraction. 'I thought we could go to Kendal Milne or Lewis's after work one night and you could choose something you like – my treat. Then on Saturday night we'll go out somewhere nice so you can wear it. Would you like that?'

'Could we go to the theatre?' she said.

'I'm not wasting money on that. No, we'll go out for our tea and on to the Plaza after. I haven't been out dancing for ages.'

32

'Hello, stranger.' Sam was sitting on the theatre steps in the sunshine and his slow smile told her he was glad to see her. 'Where were you last week? I missed you.'

Gracie returned his smile and sat down beside him. 'A friend asked me to go dancing and I couldn't refuse.'

'Did you have a good time?'

'Not really. I'd sooner have been here. Anyway, never mind that, what's the show this week?'

'A very serious drama, dull as ditchwater, with too many scene changes for its own good, but it has one redeeming feature.'

'What's that?' she asked.

'It's quite short, so you'll have time to come for a drink with us afterwards.'

'I don't think I could, really. I won't know anyone.'

'By the time the play's finished you will.' There was that twinkle in his eye again. 'You see, we're short of a stagehand. Eric's gone to a wedding in Didsbury and he won't be back till the evening performance. Thought you could help us out.'

Gracie looked at him as though he was mad. 'I couldn't do that... I wouldn't have a clue.'

'Could you carry a chair or two on stage and off again when you're told to without dropping them or falling into the orchestra pit?

'But I...'

'Come on, Gracie, it's easy. The lads will tell you what to do and when you're to do it.'

Her heart was pounding as she stood with the other stagehands waiting for the curtain to go up. In the low lighting she saw the actors in the wings and Sam at the lectern. In the hushed atmosphere, only his voice could be heard talking to the technicians. She would never have imagined in her wildest dreams that she would be involved in a play and, in her excitement, words came to her mind: 'Jacob, look where I am. I wish you were with me.'

The performance flew by and Gracie, dressed in the black garb of a stagehand, followed the instructions to set and strike all manner of items. At the curtain call the actors were back on stage to take the applause and Gracie, in the wings, was every bit as elated as they were. It was the most exciting thing she had ever done in her life.

After the intense concentration of the play, it was as though everyone involved was suddenly louder and larger than life. The stagehands called, 'Well done!' or patted her on the back. It was as though she was somehow one of them, even though she'd never worked with them before and never would again.

Sam gave her a huge smile. 'Well done! You didn't fall in the orchestra pit. That deserves a pint at the Sawyers.'

'I don't think I can. I need to get home.'

'But it's only early. You've stayed later than this to see a play before.'

Gracie desperately wanted to be in the company of these people with their easy laughter and friendly ways. Maybe she could go for half an hour or so and still get back before Alan got home.

Sam must have read her thoughts. 'One drink, that's all, and then I promise I'll let you go.'

The Sawyers Arms late on a Saturday afternoon was noisy and busy, but they managed to get a few tables pushed together and cadged a few extra chairs. Once inside, Sam made sure she sat beside him. The next thing she knew a pint pot had been set in front of her. 'I can't drink that!' She laughed.

'Course you can,' said Sam. 'You're a full-fledged stagehand now.'

The high spirits and banter, especially about the mishaps on stage and lines fluffed, just kept on coming and she laughed and laughed. With half the pint of bitter drunk, she reluctantly told Sam she would have to go and he came outside with her.

'Why do you always have to rush away?' he asked. 'You're not married, are you? You don't wear a ring.' Gracie shook her head. 'Then it must be a sweetheart,' he said.

'It's not that either... not really.' How could she explain the complicated relationship she had with Alan? Living in sin with a man she didn't love. She was so ashamed just to think it, let alone say it out loud to someone as nice as Sam. 'I have a friend, his name's Alan,' she said. 'He looks after me... I've not been well.'

'You don't look ill to me, Gracie. You look sad.'

'Not today I'm not. I loved helping out backstage and meeting everyone. I'll never forget it.'

'Of course you won't, because you belong with us.' Gracie

marvelled at the excitement in his face and the brightness in his eyes. 'Don't tell me your heart doesn't beat quicker when you come into the theatre,' he said. 'When you watch a play you completely forget where you are. It's as though you're part of it. Am I right?'

Her eyes were brimming with tears. He might have been Jacob, on the front in Blackpool, explaining how wonderful the theatre was. She closed her eyes. 'Yes, you're right. It's like I'm inside the story.' She felt Sam wipe away the tears on her cheeks and, when she opened her eyes, he was smiling at her.

'I know you have to go, but I wish you and I could just meet and talk, and you wouldn't have to run back to somewhere or someone who makes you sad. Will you meet me, Gracie, please? What about tomorrow? There's no performance on a Sunday.'

She liked him and would love to talk to him about the theatre, but she was wary. Alan would be furious if he found out. No, she couldn't risk it.

It was as if he had read her thoughts. 'I understand you don't know me that well, but there's something about you...' He hesitated. 'Look, I'll be outside the theatre at one o'clock tomorrow and I'll stay there till two.'

She thought of Alan leaving work. If she didn't go right now he would be home before her. 'I'm sorry, but I have to go.' She walked quickly away.

For a few weeks Alan had been going on and on about the heavy bombings in London, Birmingham and Coventry and, with the sporadic raids over Manchester in the early hours over the past few nights, he was convinced there would be a heavy raid very soon. 'It's clear the Luftwaffe are getting their bearings,' he told her. 'I wouldn't be surprised if there weren't more bombs tonight. As soon as the alert sounds, we've got to move quickly into the shelter. Make sure you've got ready what you want to take with you. It could be a long night.'

Gracie was dead to the world and slept through the first moments of the siren winding up, but by the time it was screaming, she was out of bed and into her coat and slippers. She grabbed her book from the side of the bed, then she and Alan rushed downstairs, out to the garden and into the Anderson shelter. It was a miserable, damp, corrugated structure, half buried in the ground, with sandbags on the roof, but Alan had done his best to make it habitable. There were short benches along each side, and he had covered them with blankets he had brought from the house. Then there were Tilly lamps to give them light and a Thermos flask of tea. At the far end of the shelter under the bench there was a sizeable tin that had once held loose biscuits in a grocer's shop. Alan pulled it out, and Gracie watched as he opened the lid, then took a small drawstring bag from his pocket and dropped it inside. 'Why do you always go to that biscuit tin every time we have to come into the shelter? What do you keep in there?' Gracie asked.

'Oh, mostly important papers, like the deeds for the house and the insurance policies. I leave them out here as it's the safest place for them in case the house gets bombed or burned by incendiaries. Then I've only to come here, collect my papers and the insurance will pay up.'

'What about that little bag? You don't leave that out here, do you?'

He laughed. 'No, that's my mother's jewellery and a few sovereigns. If I left that here all the time someone might steal it, whereas nobody would want papers from the Pru.'

The raid was long, heavy and close enough to make the

ground tremble. At the height of it, Alan spread the blankets on the floor and the two of them lay down together. He'd done that during other raids and she knew what he wanted. It was as if the danger aroused him, and while the terrifying explosions rang in her ears, he made love to her.

Before he left for his Sunday shift, Alan warned her not to go out on her own. 'Daylight raids are dangerous too. You've to stay here and go quickly to the shelter if there's a raid.'

Gracie had other ideas. It was too nice a day to be stuck inside, and what was the harm in meeting Sam? She put on the dress Alan had bought her – soft pink with sprays of white flowers and a revere collar with a matching belt that emphasised her waist. She did her makeup, brushed her dark hair until it shone, and teased the soft waves to frame her face. She stared at herself in the mirror and watched her smile disappear. 'What are you doing?' she said out loud. She took off the dress and threw it on to the bed.

Downstairs, she made a cup of tea and stood at the window looking out at the garden. There was the Anderson shelter, half buried, where last night Alan had made love to her on the earth floor. Beyond it the roses were blooming, and if she went outside, the air would be filled with their scent.

It was already one o'clock when she caught the bus and then it kept slowing down because of the night's bomb damage. The roads were strewn with rubble, glass and roof slates. In some places the fire brigade were still training their hoses on smouldering buildings. She got off at Chapel Street and ran up Quay Street. From a distance, she couldn't see anyone outside the theatre. He had promised to wait and she wasn't that late…

She needn't have worried. He was there, leaning on the wall, and his slow smile, which began at the corners of his mouth, as though he had heard some good news, spread across his face. 'Well, look at you in your Sunday best,' he said.

'You don't look so bad yourself,' she replied, noting his twill shirt open at the neck, flannels and brogues with a jacket, hooked on his finger, slung over one shoulder.

'I'm glad you managed to get away. Can you stay for a while?'

'Yes, as long as I'm back for five.'

'That's all the time in the world,' he said. 'Come on, then. I'll show you a bit of Manchester I'll bet you don't know.'

The square of fine Georgian townhouses, overshadowed by warehouses and office buildings, was just a few hundred yards from the theatre. In its centre was a garden of mature trees and shrubs. 'It used to be private, surrounded by iron railings, but they've all been melted down for tanks,' Sam explained. 'I come here sometimes when I need to think. '

They sat on a bench in the shade, and Sam said, 'Well, Gracie Earnshaw, you're a mystery and no mistake.' She could hear the teasing in his voice.

'No, I'm not.' She pretended to be cross. 'I'm just a factory girl from Manchester.'

He raised an eyebrow. 'And one who can perform some of the most poignant lines Shakespeare ever wrote.' He shook his head. 'I couldn't believe it when you stood in the spotlight and delivered it like a classically trained actress. Where did you learn to do that?'

She couldn't resist it. 'Rosenberg Raincoats on Cheetham Hill.' Now they were both laughing.

'Seriously, Gracie, you've acted before, haven't you?'

'Not really. I've always loved telling stories when I was at school and later at work. I'd try to bring them to life. That's all.'

'And the Shakespeare?'

The laughter left her eyes.

Sam said gently, 'What about the Shakespeare, Gracie?'

She didn't dare speak in case she cried. Sam waited. The sun passed behind a cloud, and in the tree above them a thrush sang its heart out. Gracie swallowed her tears. 'I had someone once. We were engaged to be married. I'd never been to the theatre before I met him. He loved it so much and I came to love it too.' She paused. 'We saw *Romeo and Juliet* together…'

'Where is he now?'

'He died.'

'Was he in the forces – killed in action?'

'He drowned.' She hadn't spoken about Jacob's incarceration or death in weeks, even though he was always in her thoughts, and not a day passed when she didn't cry about the terrible things he had endured.

'Do you want to tell me about him?' he asked.

She was about to shake her head, but she saw the kindness in his eyes and it seemed such a natural thing to share the story. 'We met at the raincoat factory and fell in love. Jacob was the nephew of the owner – they're a Jewish family and they didn't approve of me. So we decided to get married and move away to London. On the day of our wedding he was arrested because he was born in Germany. They sent him to an internment camp, a horrible place. Then he was shipped out to Canada with a thousand other prisoners.' She took a deep breath and in the tree above them the thrush sang again. 'The ship was torpedoed.'

Sam put his hand over hers and they sat awhile in silence. He was the first to speak. 'I'm so sorry about Jacob,' he said, 'and I'm sorry I've made you sad.'

She shook her head. 'No, you haven't. The sadness is always there, but you made me laugh today as well.'

He looked at his watch. 'Half an hour till last orders, time for a pint before you have to rush away again.'

'I'm not drinking another pint!'

'All right. I'll buy you a sweet sherry – that's what all the Shakespearean actors drink.'

'Hey, I'm a Mancunian, not a southern jessie – make it a Mackie and a bag of whelks!'

33

On her way home from work Sarah decided to brighten up her blue cotton dress so she called into the haberdashery on Tib Lane and bought some pearl buttons and a yard of lace. She hadn't seen Martin for a month and she wanted to look her best tonight.

She was washing her hair in the sink when there was a knock at the door. I could've put money on that happening, she thought. It'll be Doris worrying about something or nothing. She wrapped her head in a towel and went to the door.

A young soldier stood there, looking nervous. He had something wrapped in newspaper under his arm. 'Hello, missus. I'm looking for Gracie Earnshaw.'

Sarah was immediately alarmed. Why would a soldier be asking about Gracie? 'She's not here,' she said. 'I'm her mother. What do you want her for?'

'I've to deliver this to her.' He held up the parcel.

'She's not here,' Sarah repeated. 'I take it you're not from the Royal Mail, so who's asked you to deliver it?'

The soldier looked up and down the street before leaning in towards Sarah and whispering, 'Jacob Rosenberg.'

Sarah's hand flew to her chest as though her heart had stopped. 'You'd better come in,' she said.

They sat at the kitchen table with the parcel between them and the young soldier, more at ease now with a brew in his hand, explained, 'I knew Gracie from her coming to Warth Mills Camp. I were sentry at gate and a couple of times I passed letters from her to Jacob. I were stupid, shouldn'ta done it – that were before I realised I could get court-martialled. Any road, I got to know Jacob a bit and he would ask me to sneak in paper for him, any old bits I could lay me hands on and the odd pencil, and he paid me a few shillin's. Said he wanted to write summat. Then when he knew he were leavin' the camp he asked me to take what he'd wrote. It were like he wanted it kept safe. He told me to take it to Gracie, gave me this address and all he said was, "It's for her. It's a gift."'

'But why are you only bringing it here now?' Sarah asked.

'I were stuck in't camp. I'm only here now 'cause I've been given embarkation leave before I'm sent on active duty. I'm from Manchester meself and, now I've delivered this, I'm off to see me family in Whalley Range.'

When he had gone Sarah examined the untidy parcel, badly wrapped in a piece of newspaper, with frayed string just about holding it together. It didn't look much like a gift. She could easily open it, have a look then tie it up again, but what would Gracie say if she did that? Don't be stupid – sure she wouldn't even know it had been opened. But it's none of your business, she told herself. Ah, but it might be. The soldier said Jacob had been writing something and, judging by the size of it, he'd had plenty to say, but what would that do to Gracie, reading his words from beyond the grave?

*

Martin was waiting for her in the lounge of the Victoria Hotel. He stood up as she came in and kissed her cheek. 'Has something happened? What's that you've got there?'

'You'd better sit down,' she said. 'I've something to show you.'

They sat on a sofa with a low table in front of them and Sarah quickly told him the soldier's story, then unwrapped the parcel.

Martin stared at the thick wad of scavenged bits of paper covered with small pencilled writing. 'What on earth is it?'

'It's something Jacob wrote for Gracie while he was in the camp. I think it might be a play. I was in two minds whether to open it, but in the end I decided I had to, in case it would be too much of a shock for Gracie. But, honestly, Martin, I only had time to read half a dozen pages and I wept buckets. They were so much in love. I think this would break Gracie's heart all over again.'

He took some pages from the top and read them, then some from further on, and all the while Sarah waited, watching the emotions cross his face. He took a deep breath and leaned back in his chair.

'What do you think?' she asked.

'I can picture him in that awful place, with his scraps of paper, taking comfort from his memories, but it's more than that. It's a play, and I'd wager it's well written at that. I've only read parts of it, but it's a beautiful love story.' He sighed. 'It makes me unbearably sad that she lost him.'

'What shall we do with it, Martin? We can't give it to her, we just can't.'

He took her hand. 'Sarah, my darling, we can't deny Gracie

the chance to have this precious gift from Jacob. She will cry her heart out, I know, but as the years go by she will cherish his words and know how much he loved her.'

They discussed the best way to get the play to Gracie and, hopefully, at the same time, talk to her about coming home.

'Maybe, you should go back to the factory, but to the main office this time. Tell them you have a parcel for Gracie left to her by her deceased fiancé and you want to give it to her personally.'

'Why would they fetch her from her work? They'd say I should leave it at her home.'

'Then you'll say she's moved house and you don't know her address.'

'I don't think that would work.'

'It's worth a try, Sarah.'

'Even if it did work, Gracie wouldn't speak to me. I told you how angry she was last time I went to see her. She said she never wanted to see me again.'

'Sarah, don't get upset, please. It's me who's caused the rift between you. I've been thinking, perhaps you should tell her you're not seeing me anymore. That might be enough to get her to come home and we can take the time to bring her round.'

'I can't deceive her again, it's not fair, and I won't ever stop seeing you.' Her voice was full of passion. 'All I want is for her to know you and love you as much as I do. That's the only way we'll be a family.'

His smile was tender. 'I haven't heard you say, "I love you," since we were twenty and stealing kisses in the stockroom at the draper's shop.'

She lowered her eyes. 'I didn't exactly use those words just now.'

'Oh, I think you did.'

She blushed. 'I'd only say that if you'd said it first.'

'I don't mind saying it, but I want you in my arms when I do. Look at me, Sarah, and tell me you'll stay with me tonight?'

This time Sarah went through the gates of Metrovicks and straight to the main office building. She asked at the desk for someone concerned with the welfare of employees, explaining that she was worried about her daughter. She was asked to take a seat, and ten minutes later a well-groomed lady in a navy blue serge suit and a white blouse came towards her. 'I understand you want to talk to me about your daughter's welfare.'

'Yes,' said Sarah. 'It's a delicate matter...'

'Come into my office,' she said. 'We'll speak in private.'

Sarah explained that Gracie's fiancé had died a few months earlier. 'Now it turns out that he left her something very personal.' Sarah put the play, now a proper parcel wrapped in strong brown paper and tied neatly with string, on the desk. 'I'll be honest with you, my daughter and I had a falling-out and she doesn't live with me anymore. But I really want her to have this gift her fiancé left her. It would mean so much to her. Could you send for her so I can give it to her?'

'I'm afraid that isn't possible, but if you give me the parcel I'll see that she gets it.'

Sarah hesitated. What if it didn't reach Gracie?

The woman seemed to sense her worry. 'I promise you I will go straight to her and put it into her hands. Just tell me her name and the department she works in.'

It would have to be enough. 'Her name is Gracie Earnshaw and she works in the aircraft factory. I don't know the department, but the supervisor's name is Alan. I don't know his surname, I'm afraid.'

The woman frowned. 'Oh, yes, I know who he is.' She shook Sarah's hand and picked up the parcel. 'I'll take it along there now.'

Sarah was disappointed not to get the chance to speak to Gracie, but the letter she had written to her and placed in the parcel with the play was a plea to Gracie's good nature that she would forgive her mother.

34

Gracie was surprised to be summoned to Alan's office: he usually avoided any contact with her during the working day. Had she done something wrong? Was her work unsatisfactory? His door was open and she could see a well-dressed woman, involved in some sort of argument with him. She knocked on his door and he beckoned her in.

'This is Mrs Ashworth, in charge of employee welfare. She wants a word with you.' He looked far from pleased.

'You're Gracie Earnshaw?' The woman spoke kindly to her, and when Gracie nodded, she went on, 'I've just been speaking to your mother.'

So that was it, thought Gracie. Mam was trying to involve the factory in their argument about her leaving home. 'I don't want to see my mother, no matter what she's told you.'

'Please listen.' Now the woman sounded stern. 'She tells me your fiancé passed away a few months ago and it seems he left you something.' She pointed at the parcel on Alan's desk. 'She's come all the way to Trafford Park today to make sure you get it.' She shot a glance at Alan. 'I promised her I would put it into your hands and nobody else's.' And she handed the parcel to Gracie.

She couldn't take it in. What could this be? Jacob was dead, lost. Nothing of him had survived. The sound of rushing water in her ears made her gasp. She closed her eyes and waited for the drowning sensation to pass. She couldn't, wouldn't let this awful panic take hold of her again.

'Are you all right?' The woman's voice seemed so far away.

Then Alan was shouting, 'Of course she's not, she's shaking. I told you she wasn't well!' She felt him guide her to a chair. 'Just go. I'll look after her.'

Her racing heart began to slow. The noise had faded. She felt a tug on the parcel in her hand and gripped it tight.

'Give it to me, Grace. I'll not have this upsetting you. Let it go.'

Her eyes flew open. 'No!' she cried, and clasped the parcel to her chest. 'You can't have it!'

Alan barely spoke to her on the way home and it wasn't until after tea when they went into the sitting room that he said, 'Are you going to open that thing?'

Gracie took the parcel from the sideboard where she had left it. 'I am going to open it, but I'll do it upstairs.'

'Is that wise?' he said. 'Look what happened when you were given it. You've no idea what's in it, and I'm worried this business will send you right back to the terrible state you were in when you fetched up on my doorstep.'

Gracie thought about her panic when she was given the parcel. 'All right, I'll open it here.' She sat on the settee, undid the string and removed the brown paper.

On the top was an envelope with her name on it in her

mother's handwriting – so she must have opened the parcel to see what was in it. She quickly shoved it into her pocket. Her eyes widened at the sight of Jacob's handwriting on the page – '*Gracie's Gift* by Jacob Rosenberg'. What was this? On the next page there was a description of a setting, 'Rosenberg Raincoats factory, Cheetham Hill, Manchester, in the shadow of Strangeways Prison...' and the character of Gracie Earnshaw: 'A pretty girl of about twenty years old puts on a green wrap-round overall and covers her dark hair with a headscarf tied in a turban and stands looking out at the blackened perimeter wall and high tower of Strangeways.'

Gracie was amazed. 'It's a play. Jacob wrote a play and it's about me.' She thought her heart would burst with pride and tears ran down her cheeks.

'Grace, my love, you have to stop this. You'll never get better if you keep having these setbacks. He's gone. Let him go. Now, why don't you give that to me and I'll put it somewhere safe until you're stronger?'

'I'm tired,' she said. 'I don't think I can bear to read it now, but I want to keep it with me. I'll go to bed, I think.' She gathered up all the papers, the wrapping and the string.

'That's a good idea,' said Alan. 'You'll feel better in the morning.'

Upstairs Gracie parcelled up the play, including her mother's letter, and tied it with the string. She scanned the room, looking for somewhere to hide it. The top shelf of the wardrobe was packed with musty bedding. She pulled out a pillowcase, put the play inside it, then slipped it into the folds of a blanket with faded pink edging.

She lay in bed thinking about Jacob. Alan was wrong – she would never let Jacob go, and now she had his play she felt him closer than ever.

When she heard Alan coming to bed, she turned her back and pretended to be asleep. He kissed her shoulder, but she didn't respond. 'Grace, what's the matter?'

She was determined to have nothing to do with him, not after the way he had spoken to her today, wanting to take Jacob's play from her. 'I don't want to. It doesn't seem right.'

'What do you mean?'

She knew he was angry, but she didn't care. 'It's as though Jacob has found me somehow and the play is... I don't know how to explain it. It's as if he wants me to know how much he loved me.'

'For God's sake, just listen to yourself talking nonsense. I'm beginning to think you're not right in the head.' He turned away from her.

Later, as she lay awake, she thought about the pattern of her days and nights with Alan and how she had succumbed bit by bit to his will. He had been good to her, had taken her in, looked after her – but, in exchange for kindness, she had given up her spirit and her freedom.

At dinnertime the following day Gracie walked over to the anti-aircraft factory where she used to work. She was quite prepared to be ignored or even abused by her ex-workmates, but she hoped Trixie would speak to her. They were all sitting at the usual table in the canteen when she came in: a few looked awkward, but most of them ignored her.

She went straight to Trixie. 'Can I talk to you for a moment?' she asked.

She nodded. 'We'll go outside – I could do with some fresh air.'

They stood in the shadow of the old water tower, half dismantled, with its ack-ack gun glinting in the late September sun. 'What do you want?' Trixie asked.

'I'm sorry I was so rude to you when you said Alan was the one who told the foreman about Jacob. I know now that you were right about that.' Trixie acknowledged the apology with a nod. Gracie went on: 'You also said something about Alan keeping me close and, I'm not sure about this, but did you say there was another girl who was involved with him before me?'

'She worked in one of the offices.'

'How did you know about her?'

Trixie looked a bit sheepish. 'People gossip. Even before you got transferred to Alan's workshop they were talking about the two of you. It was obvious from the beginning that he had his eye on you, and it wasn't long before someone mentioned his previous girlfriend. He was obsessed with her and jealous too. She couldn't go anywhere without him and there was talk of, you know...'

'Tell me,' said Gracie.

'They'd been sleeping together.'

'What happened? Did they split up?'

'She broke it off with him, but he wouldn't have it, kept pestering her. She made a complaint about him and somebody in the office was supposed to have warned him off, but even then he went round to her house, trying to get her back.'

'How did she get rid of him?'

'She had two brothers – they threatened to break his legs.'

When the Saturday matinee ended Gracie went backstage to find Sam. She had been awake most of the previous night making her plans, going over and over what she wanted to say to him. She found him on stage talking to a bloodied Macbeth. As soon as he saw her he excused himself and came across.

'I didn't expect you to be here today, with it being a longish play.'

'Oh, I couldn't have missed it and, anyway, I wanted to see you.'

He looked as pleased as punch. 'Well, here I am. Can you come for a drink as well?'

'Actually, I wondered if we could talk – just you and me.'

'I'm intrigued,' he said. 'Give me five minutes to get everything shut down and I'll be right with you.'

Gracie sat in the front row of the stalls looking up at the battlements of Macbeth's castle and thought about the fight she had on her hands. She had wandered into a job and a relationship she would never have chosen for herself. It was time to do what she wanted.

She could hear Sam backstage, saying goodbye to the rest of the company. A minute later he appeared from the wings and came down the steps to sit beside her. 'It's good to see you again, Gracie. Did you enjoy the play?'

'I did.' She smiled. 'There's something very satisfying about a tyrant getting his comeuppance, when you consider we've been bombed every night for the past week.'

'That's Shakespeare for you – always relevant. Now, what can I do for you, if it isn't a pint you're after?'

'I've been thinking about the conversation we had in the pub. "You're one of us," you said.'

'You are. The theatre's in your blood. That's why you're drawn to this place.'

Gracie nodded. 'The more I come here, the more I love it. Can I ask you something?'

'Of course,' he said.

'I keep thinking I'd like to work in a theatre, but I'm not sure how to get taken on. I've no experience, but I'd do anything to be a part of it all.'

He laughed. 'You have experience – you were a stagehand once.'

'I don't think one performance would count, would it?'

'It all depends on how desperate the stage manager is.' He winked. 'I mean, if he had two able-bodied men called up in the space of a fortnight, he's likely to drag anyone off the street just to make sure the show goes on.'

'Do you mean—'

'Eric's left already and Dave's going next week. So, to tell you the truth, I'm desperate. I warn you, the money's not great, but if you're sure it's what you want, then you're more than welcome to join us.'

Gracie's face lit up. She couldn't believe her luck. 'Really, you'll give me a job backstage?'

'Bit of scene shifting, props and prompt maybe, and Mrs B could do with some help in the costume department. When can you start?'

'I wish I could say straight away, but I'll have to hand in my notice and I'll need to find somewhere else to live.' The first part of her plan had worked out better than she could have hoped, but the thought of telling Alan she was leaving him and Metrovicks terrified her.

Sam must have read uncertainty in her face. 'Gracie, are you sure about this? Is there something you're not telling me?'

She had no doubts about working in the theatre, she was determined to do that, but she wouldn't put it past Alan to find a way to stop her. 'You remember I told you I have a friend who looks after me?' Sam nodded. 'It started when I lost my job at the raincoat factory and he got me into Metrovicks where he works. Then, after Jacob died, I needed somewhere to stay and he took me in.' She stopped, overcome with embarrassment. Say it, say it, she told herself. Her voice was no more than a whisper: 'I still live with him.'

'And now you want to leave him?'

'Yes. I just need a fresh start.'

'Have you no family you could stay with?'

'Only Mam, but I fell out with her.'

'Well, a lot of the people who work in the theatre live in digs. Eric lodged with Mrs Booth, and so do I. I'm sure she'd let you have his room. Would you want to do that?'

'If I can afford it.'

'Tell you what,' said Sam, 'can you meet me here tomorrow? I'll open up the theatre and we'll have a chat about the sort of work you'll be doing, then go round to Mrs B's to see if you can rent the room. What do you think?'

'Oh, Sam, it's the best thing that's happened to me in months. I can't thank you enough for giving me a chance. I won't let you down, I promise.'

'I know you won't, Gracie, and you don't have to thank me. The smile on your face is thanks enough. Now, what about going down the pub so we can tell the others you're joining us?'

When she arrived home, the house was in darkness. Maybe, with a bit of luck, Alan hadn't yet come home from work and, if so, she wouldn't be questioned about where she had been. Once inside she drew the blackout curtains and switched on the light. He was sitting in the armchair with his coat on.

'Good grief, you frightened the life out of me!' she said.

'Where have you been?' His voice was low and measured.

The last thing she wanted to do was to alert him. Her plan was to get through the next two weeks, then slip away when he was at work. She would just disappear into thin air and he'd never find her again.

She smiled. 'Aw, I went to see Maria. You should see the size of her. I think it's going to be a big baby, probably a boy.' She chattered on. 'Mind you, Tommy's well-built, isn't he? Have you had your tea?' Another smile.

He stood up and took off his coat. 'I've been out looking for you. You should've left me a note. You know I worry about you. For God's sake, Grace, it's not that long since you were going to jump in the river.'

'Oh, I'm fine now. You shouldn't worry.' She switched on the wireless. 'It's nearly time for the news. You can listen to it while I make something to eat. I've got a nice piece of liver for our tea.'

For the rest of the evening Alan sat staring into space and said very little. Gracie lay on the settee reading her book, but every now and again she glanced at his scowling face. At nine o'clock he announced he was going to bed and left her to lock up. She had no intention of following him up. Instead she read several more chapters and it was almost eleven when she went upstairs. She assumed he was asleep and slipped into bed. A minute later he pressed himself against her and ran his hand over her thighs. She didn't move.

'What's wrong with you?' he said.

'I don't feel like it. I'm tired.'

'No, you're not. You deliberately stayed up late. I've been waiting for you.' He pulled her towards him and began kissing her, his hand on her throat, his lips hard and crushing.

She jerked her head away. 'Not tonight, Alan, please,' she begged.

'Come on, you'll enjoy it.' He rolled on top of her – heavy breathing in her face, hands so strong...

She was angry now. 'I don't want to!'

'Ah, but I do, Grace, so don't say no to me – not ever.'

She tried to push him away, but there was no stopping him. 'Please, Alan, please don't.' But there was nothing she could do, except endure the rough way he used her and vow that this would never happen to her again.

He said nothing when he was finished, and within minutes he was asleep, but she lay awake shaking, not only at the shock of it but at the anger raging inside her.

35

Gracie watched the steady rain beating against the bus window. Both she and her belongings would be soaked by the time she reached the theatre. She didn't care: she wouldn't spend another moment in that house.

She had got up as soon as Alan had left for the Sunday shift and packed her clothes in her grip bag along with her keepsakes from Jacob. Then she stood on tiptoe and reached up to get the play hidden in the blanket on the top shelf in the wardrobe. There was nothing there. In a panic she fetched a chair and stood on it, pulled out the blanket and shook it open. Nothing. Then, one by one, she shook out every piece of bedding and threw it on the floor, but the play had gone. She screamed in frustration at her own stupidity. Twice he'd wanted to take it from her – 'To keep it safe until you're stronger,' he had said.

Frantically, she searched the rest of the house, emptying drawers and cupboards, looking under the beds. It had to be there somewhere. By noon she stood in the middle of the sitting room surrounded by the mess she had made and knew it was hopeless. She could have wept, but instead she was more determined than ever to escape. She swore on Jacob's memory that she would find a way to get the play back.

Sam was waiting for her when she arrived at the theatre. He took one look at her heavy bag and said, 'Good heavens, Gracie, have you done a moonlight flit?'

'Bit of a change of plan,' she said, unable to meet his eye.

'Has something happened?' Instinctively, he understood. 'You've left him.'

'Yes, and I'm not going back.'

'Let's get inside out of the rain.' He unlocked the door, took her bag and led the way backstage to his office. 'First up we'll have a brew,' he said.

He lit the paraffin heater to take the chill off the room and they sat drinking tea while he told her a funny story about the fire watchers on the theatre roof who had fallen asleep: it wasn't until an incendiary had burned through one of their boots that they'd woken up. Gracie was content to sit and listen to his voice, watching the expressions on his face as he spun the yarn. She felt she could do anything she wanted now, and she wanted to be in this theatre.

'Gracie, I hope you don't mind me asking, but does he know you've left?'

She shook her head. 'I can't spend another night in that house.'

'Has he done something to you? Because if he has, I'll go there and sort him out!'

She smiled at his sudden anger. 'You don't need to. I've left him. It's finished.'

'And what about your job? Won't you have to work your notice?'

'I'll just go into the office in the morning and tell them I'm leaving. I won't go near the workshop.'

'Good! So, do you want to start straight away?'

'If that's all right?'

All afternoon Sam showed her the sort of jobs she would be doing. There was so much to take in, like the whole new vocabulary for a start: wings and flats; prompt and props; upstage, downstage... 'Don't worry you'll pick it up quick enough,' he told her, then had her practise raising and lowering the different curtains. It took more effort than she'd imagined and he had to help her. 'You'll soon develop the muscles.'

Sam was a good teacher and his love of the theatre was plain to see but the strange thing was that, all the time they worked together, she hadn't once thought about the awful experience of the previous night.

'Well, that's probably enough for today,' he said. 'Why don't we go and get something to eat and then I'll take you to Mrs B's? She's on Great Clowes Street. I'm sure she'll let you have Eric's room. Now all I need is someone to take over his fire-watching duty.'

'Oh, I'll do that as well,' she said. 'I feel bad about leaving the war work, but I'd still like to do my bit.'

The following morning Gracie went to Trafford Park, taking care to arrive later than the workers, and went straight to the office. She asked to speak to Mrs Ashworth, the woman who had given her Jacob's play. She told her she was leaving the job for personal reasons, but what happened next took Gracie by surprise. 'Has this got anything to do with your supervisor?' she asked. 'Only you're not the first girl who has left that workshop suddenly, and I'm concerned that you have been... shall we say involved with him?'

Gracie thought about the girlfriend Trixie had told her about. She must know about her, and maybe there had been others. She was tempted to say something, but she couldn't risk Alan finding out that she had reported him. 'I don't want to talk about him. I just want to leave.'

'I don't like losing skilled workers any more than I like young women being put in awkward situations. So I'll ask you again, will you tell me why you are leaving?'

'I'm leaving because I've got another job,' said Gracie.

The woman shook her head in frustration. 'Very well. You've been paid up to date and there are no monies owing to you. I'll bid you good morning.'

Gracie had never felt happier. Every day there were new things to learn and the other stagehands helped her, teased her and made her laugh. Mrs Booth took her under her wing right away, pleased to have her help in the costume department, and some female company at home. Then there was the weekly fire-watching duty. Sam wasn't convinced that she should be on the rota at all and insisted he would partner her – for no other reason than he wouldn't be able to sleep anyway worrying about her up on the roof – in the blackout fighting fires. 'Have you a warm coat, it's cold up there,' he said.

'Just the coat I always wear.'

'That won't do. Take yourself off to the costume store and ask Mrs B for something that'll keep you warm.'

She returned half an hour later, looking like a Cossack in a greatcoat, complete with gold epaulettes and frogging down the front, and a fur-trimmed hat. At the sight of her coming across the stage the laughter and banter began. 'This is Manchester not Moscow, Gracie!' and 'If the Luftwaffe catch sight of you on the roof they'll think they've bombed Russia.'

Sam came through the side curtain to see what was going on. He took one look at her and shook his head, but he couldn't help smiling. 'I never expected to be on fire duty with a character from *War and Peace*.'

The moon was just a sliver of light in the black sky above them when she and Sam came out on to the roof of the theatre. He switched on his torch – the beam partly covered so as not to show an upward light – and took her hand. 'Don't worry if you can't see, I'll guide you. The best place to sit is along the north wall. It's quite sheltered and we can get a wide view of the sky.' He had brought cushions to sit on and a blanket, and when they were settled he said, 'Mrs B made us a flask of tea and some butties for later.' His voice was no more than a whisper, but it seemed right somehow in the silence and the dark, just like being in the wings waiting for the show to begin. 'The stirrup pumps and buckets of sand are just next to us against the wall,' he said. 'You remember how to use them?'

'Yes, I think so.' She gave a nervous laugh.

'You're all right, aren't you?'

'Yes! It's just that I can't believe I'm here on a roof firewatching, and I've spent the last week working in the theatre.'

'And what do you think about it all?'

She gave a happy sigh. 'It's been wonderful, Sam. I've loved every minute and it's all down to you for giving me a chance.'

'I wanted you on the team when I saw how you coped that day you stepped in for Eric, but I never thought it would all fall into place so quickly. And the thing is, Gracie, because we're a repertory company, there's a chance you could do other things besides backstage, even audition for a part in one of the plays if you wanted to.'

Gracie had dreamed of acting on stage, but that was all it was – a dream. She shook her head. 'I can't quite picture myself going from shifting furniture and setting props on the stage to performing on it.'

'Stranger things have happened,' said Sam. 'It's pantomime season coming up and that's when people not involved in the show rehearse the next play for the end of January. The good thing is that I get to choose and direct the play, while the usual director will be up to his eyes with *Cinderella*. I'm thinking of doing *Hobson's Choice*. It's a Lancashire play – you could try for a part in that.'

'I'm not sure – maybe some day I might. Have you ever acted?'

'A few times, but mostly I've been backstage.'

'How did you come to work in the theatre?'

'Through my dad, really. He worked at the Oldham Coliseum. He was a carpenter by trade so he built the sets, then came back in the evening to do front-of-house at the performances – selling programmes, checking tickets.' He laughed. 'Only man in Glodwick who owned a dinner suit. Anyway, he used to bring me down to the theatre at weekends and school holidays. There was only him and me, you see. Mam died when I was ten.'

'There was just me and Mam. We had no other family. She works in the Midland Hotel, but...' Gracie was about to say that she didn't see her anymore, but her mother's face came to mind and she was surprised to feel a pang of regret that things between them had come to such a sorry pass.

'You said you'd fallen out with her. Why was that?'

Maybe it was the darkness hiding her face that made it

easier to explain what had happened. 'She was a good mam to me, and even when I grew up the two of us rubbed along together well enough. Then when Jacob was interned I was so caught up with my own worries that I hardly noticed she was out a lot and coming home late. It was a shock when I found out she had a man. I felt she'd let both of us down.' Her laugh was mirthless. 'But that wasn't the worst thing. On the night I heard that Jacob had died she was at home with me. I was in a terrible state when someone came to the door. It was the man she'd been seeing. He asked me if I was Gracie. I said I was and he said he was my father. I'd just heard that Jacob was dead and then I found out my mother had kept the secret from me all my life. I couldn't take it in at first. I had to get away from her – away from both of them – so I left and never went back.'

'It must have been so hard for you, especially when Jacob had just died. Do you miss her?' he asked.

'At first I didn't. I know that sounds awful, but so many things were going on with me. Now I think about her life and I realise she didn't have it easy.'

'What would you say to her if you saw her?'

'It's too late for that. Anyway, she'll be happy with her long-lost sweetheart. I'm not a part of her life any more.'

'And after you fell out with her you went to stay with Alan?'

'I had nowhere else to go... Are you shocked at that?'

'No, of course not, I think—' He looked up at the sky. 'Listen,' he said.

Gracie held her breath, trying to catch the sound: a low drone, barely audible, but the noise increased steadily and a minute later the air-raid siren sounded.

'Quick! Get the stirrup pumps ready!' he shouted. The

throbbing sound of the bomber was coming closer. A search-light panned the sky and Gracie caught her breath at the sight of the dark, cigar-shaped planes. There was a sudden crack as the anti-aircraft guns blazed and red tracers streaked the sky. 'They're somewhere over Chorlton way,' shouted Sam. 'We might get away with it.' They watched, as the fires took hold and soon the rooftops were ablaze.

The following day Gracie was asked to help Mrs Booth in the costume department, making mouse costumes for the panto-mime. She was glad to be sewing again and Mrs B was good company, chatting and gossiping. 'I had a girl working with me before the war. She left to join the Wrens, and since then I've had to do everything myself. It's the same all over, especially with the lads being called up one after another. Mark my words, we'll end up with just old men and women, and what kind of plays will we be putting on then?'

'I suppose Sam could be called up soon,' said Gracie.

'No, he'll be here for the duration – medically exempt, they said. The day war broke out he were straight down the recruiting office to enlist. He knew it would be touch and go whether he'd get taken on. He has something wrong with his eyes, don't know what exactly, happened when he had measles as a baby. He come back here in a right strop. He's still a bit touchy about it. You'll see him with his glasses on when he gets tired.' Mrs B looked up from her sewing and said. 'You like him, do you?'

'Sam? Yes, I do. We get on well together.'

'He's a good lad. What you see is what you get.'

36

The end of November brought the final performance of *Hay Fever* and, as usual, Gracie and Sam were the last to leave the theatre after a show. He was responsible for locking up and insisted Gracie should wait for him so she wouldn't have to walk back to the digs on her own in the blackout.

'What a night that was!' Gracie laughed. 'Right in the middle of the most important scene in the play.'

'It was bound to happen sometime.' Sam was grinning from ear to ear. 'But when the air raid siren started all I could think was that we'd have to give them their money back.'

'And when you walked on stage and asked them if they wanted the show to carry on, it was priceless.'

Sam put on a broad Manchester accent. 'Eh-up, lad, we've paid our money, we can't leave wi'out findin' out how it ends.'

'And that woman,' said Gracie. '"If you think I'm goin' in a shelter in me best clothes, you've got another think comin',"' and when you said, "We'll carry on with the show," they all started cheering!'

'That's it now for plays until the end of January. The

pantomime opens in a week's time and we'll shift to the rehearsal room.'

'Have you settled on the play you want to direct?'

'As I said, it'll probably be *Hobson's Choice* – it's always popular.' He stopped and checked his pocket. 'Damn, I've left my script in the office. Wait here while I nip back and get it.'

Gracie went outside and waited under the portico out of the rain. She took her headscarf from her bag, put it over her hair and turned up her collar.

'Hello, Grace.'

Her heart stopped. 'Alan?'

He emerged from the darkness and stood within a foot of her. 'I thought I'd find you here.'

'How did you—'

'It wasn't a good idea to use your theatre tickets as bookmarks. I thought you might be involved in something like this. I've walked past a few times and seen you in the foyer selling programmes.'

'What do you want, Alan?'

'I want you to stop being so silly and come home with me.'

'I'm not going to do that.' She backed away from him, but he stepped forward and now she was cornered.

'You're no good on your own, Grace. I can get you your job back, and you'll want for nothing with me, you know that. I want you back, Grace. Come on now, we'll go home.'

The anger was rising inside her. 'I'm not coming back. I never want to see you again and, while we're at it, what did you do with my play?'

He seemed puzzled, as though her words had no meaning. 'What?'

'Jacob's play. You stole it.'

'Don't be stupid. I didn't steal it. I just put it somewhere safe, because I didn't want you reading it and getting into a state again. It'll be there for you when you come home, I promise.'

'You can't decide what I can and can't do. I want it back.'

He laughed. 'All right. You can have it back. All you have to do is come home with me.'

'Stop treating me like a child! I'm going nowhere with you.'

'Oh, but you are, Grace.' He grabbed her and dragged her into the street. She tried to pull away from him, but he wrapped his arms around her. 'Let me go!' she screamed.

Suddenly there was shouting from the foyer behind her and light was streaming out into the street. Sam grabbed Alan from behind and hauled him away from her. 'Is this him, Gracie? Is this Alan?'

'Yes,' she screamed.

Sam swung his arm and his fist, once, twice, connected with Alan's jaw and he fell backwards, his blood glistening in the light. Sam dragged him to his feet and shook him hard. 'Now bugger off, you bastard, and if I see you near Gracie again, I'll kill you!'

Alan didn't need to be told twice and the sound of his running feet on the cobbles echoed in the empty street.

And then she was in Sam's arms. He held her tight and told her she was safe and that Alan would never bother her again. Gracie was grateful for his help, but Alan had confronted her in the dark and tried to make her feel she was weak, that she needed him. How was he to know that the opposite was true? She wasn't frightened of him at all.

'Gracie, are you all right?'

'Yes, Sam.'

'Shall I let you go?'

'Yes, Sam.'

'So that was the bastard Alan.'

She smiled. 'You made mincemeat of him. Where did you learn to fight like that?'

'Oldham Coliseum, stage-fighting lessons.'

'I might have known!'

They were still laughing when there was a shout: 'Turn that bloody light out!'

They set off back to their digs through the deserted streets, and Sam asked, 'What did he want?'

'He wanted me to go home with him. I told him no, but he has something belonging to me – something Jacob left me. I searched the house for it before I left, but I couldn't find it. He said tonight I could have it, if I went back to him.'

'God, Gracie, you wouldn't do that, would you?'

'It means so much to me and I desperately want to have it, but I could never go back to Alan... He drains the life out of me.'

'What is it he has?'

'A play.'

'Really? What play is it? We might have it at the theatre. '

'You won't. It's a play Jacob wrote about how we met and fell in love. Well, I think it is. I never read it. I know that's an awful thing to say, but everything about his death was so raw, and it was such a shock suddenly to be given Jacob's story of our romance. I put it away for a few days, thinking I would read it when I was calmer and stronger, but then everything came to a head and I had to leave because—' She stopped. Had she already said too much?

'What happened between you and Alan that made you leave in such a hurry?'

If she had been sitting somewhere just talking to Sam, she probably wouldn't have told him. But they were walking in the dark, her face hidden, and something about the empty streets with just the sound of their footsteps on the cobbles made it easier for her to unburden herself. She spoke softly. 'At first Alan was so kind and I was lonely without Jacob and my mother, but it was more than that. I was so distressed and he looked after me, comforted me...' She paused, finding the words to explain. 'He touched me and it soothed my mind and my body... and I let him... I let him. But as time went on... the way he used me... I couldn't bear it.' She was determined not to cry, not to fall back into that awful weakness and self-pity. 'In the end I said no to him, but it didn't matter.' She swallowed her tears. 'Because he did whatever he wanted anyway.'

They walked on. 'I don't know what to say, Gracie. Was there no one you could tell?'

'Not really. There was a woman who looked after the workers' welfare at the factory and she hinted that he'd been in trouble before for harassing at least one girl, but I didn't want to tell her. By that time I'd packed my bags and left him.' She smiled. 'That's when I came to you.'

'I wish you'd told me what was going on. I'd have done something about him.'

'But you did do something – you gave me the courage to walk away from him. You gave me a job in the theatre.'

'But he's still got your play. You have to get it back. It sounds like it's somewhere in his house.'

'I searched everywhere before I left – but you know what the worst thing is? I've let Jacob down. After all the work he put into it, I lost it.'

'Don't blame yourself. You didn't lose it – it was stolen from you. There must be a way to get it back.'

'I'm sure there is,' said Gracie, 'but I haven't thought of it yet.'

'I could always get a couple of the lads and go round to his house – do our gangster act and put the fear of God into him again.' He pretended to be a boxer delivering a few punches.

She smiled. 'I'll keep you in mind for the part, but I think it might be easier if I went back to his house and had another search for it.'

Sam's eyes widened. 'You have a key?'

'No, but he keeps a spare under a plant pot in the garden.'

'Why don't I come with you?' he said.

'I don't think it would be right for you to go in the house. If anything went wrong I could always say I came back for something, but you could be arrested.'

'I could be a lookout, watching the street and that. We could go tomorrow – he works Sundays, doesn't he?'

'Yes, but I need to think about this, Sam. I don't want to risk something going wrong. I thought I might go and visit my friend Maria in the morning, I haven't seen her for ages, but we could talk when I get back.'

That night in bed Gracie lay awake, thinking about the play, and in her mind's eye she walked through Alan's house from top to bottom searching for a hiding place she might have missed, but she couldn't think of one. In the early hours of the morning she dreamed she was standing at his kitchen window, looking out on the garden at the Anderson shelter and the roses. For a split second she almost thought she had it. Caught between sleep and waking, she racked her brain to remember, but it had gone. 'Damn you, Alan, where is it?'

Ancoats, so close to the centre of the city, had not entirely escaped the bombing. At the corner of Maria's street, the gable end of a house had gone, exposing the interior: the wallpaper;

a smashed picture hanging skew-whiff; a wardrobe with the doors hanging off. The ice-cream parlour window was boarded up, but otherwise Maria's home looked intact. Gracie knocked on the door and waited nervously for her friend to appear, not knowing whether she would greet her kindly.

When Maria hadn't been able to take her in after Jacob's death, she had felt snubbed, and all the time she had been living with Alan she hadn't contacted her. She needn't have worried. The door opened and Maria screamed with excitement. They hugged each other, just like the best friends they had always been.

'Oh, Maria, look at you – huge and blooming!'

And Maria smiled. 'I've another six weeks to go. Come upstairs, I'm dying to hear what you've been doing.'

In the sitting room there was an old woman dressed completely in black. 'This is our neighbour. She's living with us now. Remember I told you her son was interned?'

Gracie shook her hand and the old lady smiled, then shuffled out of the room. So, Maria had been telling the truth when she'd said there was no room for her to lodge with them.

'Now, tell me everything, Gracie, the whole story since I last saw you.'

'Well, I'm not living with Alan—'

'Thank goodness for that.'

'I'm not working at Metrovicks either.'

'Really? How did that happen?'

Gracie had made up her mind that she wouldn't tell Maria what had happened with Alan. She had told Sam the night before, but afterwards she had lain in bed regretting it. What had she been thinking of, speaking to a man about such intimate things, and how would she face him today?

'I'd had enough of him at work and at home,' she told

Maria. 'All the time he kept telling me I was ill or weak and I needed him to look after me. In the end I walked away from him and the job and I'm never going back.'

'Good for you. I never liked him. So where are you living and did you get another job?'

Gracie talked about the theatre, how much she loved it, and her digs on Great Clowes Street.

'And is there a handsome actor there who might take a fancy to you?'

'Even if there was I wouldn't be interested. Sam the stage manager is nice, but I'm not getting involved with anybody. Now tell me about your father and Tony.'

'Papa was sent to the Isle of Man with hundreds of enemy aliens. I know he misses us, but the conditions are very good. He can write to us, he's well fed and he likes the company. So we don't worry about him, just want him back. We don't know where Tony is, but he said in his last letter that he'd been promoted to corporal. Oh, and you'll be glad to know that Charlie was called up. He tried to get out of it by saying he was engaged in war work, but it turned out making water-proofs didn't exempt him.'

Gracie laughed. 'Well, let's hope he gets taken down a peg or two in the forces. And Tommy, do you hear from him?'

Maria shook her head. 'I don't care. He didn't want the baby and I don't want him. But, Gracie, I have to tell you I saw your mother a couple of weeks ago. She asked me for news of you, but I couldn't tell her anything.' Maria stroked her swelling belly. 'I felt so sorry for her. She's lost you and I don't think she'll ever get over it.'

'You don't know the full story, Maria.'

'I know that whatever happened between you two couldn't be so bad that you had to cut her out of your life.'

Gracie sighed. 'She lied to me and I don't think I can forgive her.' Maria opened her mouth to argue, but Gracie went on, 'It turns out the man she married wasn't my father and she never told me. I only found out when my real father turned up that night when you came to tell me Jacob had died. She'd been seeing him for months and never a word to me about any of it.'

'Oh, Gracie, look at me. I'm not married to my child's father, but I'll tell you something. This baby is the most precious thing in my life and I'll never stop loving it till the day I die. Just like your mother. Tommy wanted me to have it adopted but I'm keeping my child, just like your mother did. But I thank God for my family. They'll look after me and my child. Your mother didn't have family around her – how much more difficult was it for her? And now, with all the bombings, you should just go and see her and tell her you're all right. Will you not do that?'

'I don't know – and I can't think about that now.' She stood up. 'It's been lovely to see you and I wish I could stay longer, but I need to go because I'm meeting someone later.'

Maria looked surprised. 'Is it someone special?'

'No, it's the stage manager. We're... em... going to talk about a play.'

'That sounds very important.'

'Not really,' she said, and gave Maria a hug. 'I'm sorry I lost touch with you, but I'll come and see you again soon.'

Sam was waiting for her in the kitchen with a smile so wide that Gracie couldn't help but laugh. 'You look pleased with yourself,' she said.

'Close your eyes and put your hands out.'

'What for?'

'Just do it!'

She sighed, held out her hands and waited.

'Open them!'

She laughed in delight at the sight of an orange. 'Where did you get it? I haven't seen one of these for months.'

'It's not what you know, it's who you know.'

'Shall we eat it now?' she said.

'Save it for later. I'm hoping we're going to find your play. Do you want to do that?'

She felt nervous about the whole thing but, seeing Sam's confidence, she was tempted to think it might be possible. She should be strong and take back what was hers. 'Yes,' she said. 'Let's do it!'

At the end of Alan's street they stopped. 'It's on the right, number twenty, the one with the holly tree in the garden,' Gracie explained. 'We'll walk up together, then I'll nip round the back and get into the house. Best if you stay outside to keep an eye open, but I'm sure Alan won't be home for a few hours yet.'

She went to the back of the house and there was the plant pot. She tilted it and felt underneath for the key. It wasn't there. She tried the other pots, then under the mat and the bucket, but there was no key. She stood on the back step, wondering what to do and looking at the rose bushes, no flowers now, just thorns, and the Anderson shelter. She shuddered at the memory of the nights she had spent in there with Alan. When she'd complained about how uncomfortable it was, he would say, 'It's a safe place. It'll still be intact when the house has been destroyed.'

In a rush of memory last night's dream came back to her. She had been standing in front of the shelter sensing that she was tantalisingly close to knowing where the play had been hidden. Then Alan's words outside the theatre came back to her: 'I've put it somewhere safe.' The shelter… the safe place… That was what he had said about the insurance policies!

She ran across the garden and pulled open the shelter door. It was dark inside but she knew exactly what she was looking for. She hauled out the biscuit tin from under the bench and pulled off the lid. There was the parcel tied with string – Jacob's play. 'Thank God,' she whispered. Clutching it, she hurried out of the shelter, only to stumble on the step and graze her knee.

'I'll bet that hurts.'

It was Alan, looking like he'd just got out of bed.

She stared at him, not knowing what to do. 'I thought you were at work,' she said.

'Did you, now? Well, if you were still employed at Metrovicks you'd know that they've introduced night shifts and I'm about to go to work.' Then he smiled. 'Why don't you come in and we'll talk?' He waved his hand towards the open door. His voice had the soft, kind tone that had soothed her so many times before. She hesitated. 'Come on, Grace, let's talk. You owe me that at least. We can sort something out. You've always said you're no good on your own.'

Anger rose inside her. She owed him nothing. He had won her trust when she was alone and grieving, but instead of helping her he had stripped away her confidence until she was a fragment of herself.

'I don't need you at all,' she shouted. 'I've finished with you for ever.' She backed away from him towards the path at the side of the house. It took him only a second to catch hold of her and crush her in his embrace.

'Let her go!' It was Sam's voice, loud and forceful.

Alan held her fast. 'Oh, it's you, is it? And what if I don't let her go? You'll kill me, wasn't that what you said?' He laughed.

'There's no need for that,' said Sam. 'You see, I know that Gracie isn't the first girl you've taken advantage of. There've been others at work, haven't there? You've even been warned by the management.'

'You don't know that. You're bluffing.'

'Am I? Well, let's just agree that you'll stay away from Gracie, because if you don't, I'll go with her to your work and sit with her while she explains why she had to leave her job to get away from you.'

Alan's grip loosened. Gracie saw her chance and ran to Sam.

Then he was all bravado. 'You can have her,' he shouted. 'I've had my fill of her anyway, with her plays and books and her precious Jacob.'

Sam would have gone for him again, but Gracie held him back. 'Leave it, Sam, we've got what we came for and we're rid of him. That's all that matters.'

They left, with Alan's shouts ringing in their ears about what he would do if they trespassed on his property again, and ran to the end of the road where they stopped. 'We did it!' said Gracie, as Sam lifted her off her feet and swung her around. 'I can't believe I'm rid of him, but the best of it all is that we have the play!'

37

They came into Mrs Booth's kitchen laughing and joking. 'Goodness me,' she said. 'What's to do?'

'We've slain the dragon and found buried treasure!' said Sam, and he danced her round the table.

'So, you'll be ready for your tea, then?'

'I could eat a horse, Mrs B, if there's one goin'.'

Mrs Booth played along. 'The butcher were sold out of horse meat so you'll have to make do wi' Lancashire hotpot.'

'With bread to dip in?'

'What else?'

Over tea, Gracie and Sam told her the story of rescuing Jacob's play with plenty of embellishments.

'Maybe you could put it on at the Opera House,' said Mrs Booth.

'It's worth thinking about it, seeing as I'm directing the next play,' said Sam. 'I'm not that keen on *Hobson's Choice*, really. It's been done too many times. I'd rather have something more modern – a tale of today, something to do with the war. I've got two weeks before I have to cast a play, so maybe you and I could work on Jacob's script, Gracie, see how it sounds when it's acted out.'

Gracie was surprised at his suggestion. 'But you haven't even read it – it might not be suitable.'

But Sam was confident. 'It sounds to me like something Manchester people would enjoy – a love story set in their city.'

'I'd pay to see it,' said Mrs Booth. 'Now, help me clear the table and, when I've washed the pots, I'll leave you to your play reading.'

Gracie sat at the table with the parcel in front of her. The very sight of it threatened to overwhelm her. She pictured Jacob in that filthy mill secretly writing a play – his last gift to her.

'Gracie, I understand that the play is personal to you and I wouldn't blame you if you don't want to share it.'

'It is personal but Jacob dreamed of writing a play. He said he just needed to find the right story. He deserves at least to have it seen by someone who works in the theatre and I can think of no one better than you.'

Sam smiled. 'It would be an honour to read Jacob's play with you.'

She took a deep breath and opened the parcel. On the top was the envelope addressed to her in her mother's hand. She set it to one side.

'Are you not going to open that?' asked Sam.

'It's from my mother and I don't want to read it. Only the play matters.' Then she read out loud, '*Gracie's Gift* by Jacob Rosenberg.' She touched the page that he had touched and smelt again the smell of the mill on the paper.

'Are you all right?' asked Sam.

'Yes, let's get started.'

They read the opening scene and Gracie was transported

back to the raincoat factory, with its sounds and smells, and she remembered the first stirrings of her attraction to Jacob.

Sam was smiling. 'You're good fun, aren't you?'

'I suppose I was.'

'You still are. And I think it's a great opening.'

The evening wore on and they pored over the writing, scene after scene, with Sam commenting and asking questions, until they came to the wedding that had never happened. For the first time since they'd started to read, Gracie stopped and sat back in her chair.

'Gracie, maybe we should put it away now and read the rest another day.'

She wasn't listening. She was thinking, that was the day our story changed from romance to tragedy. It was as though she was sitting in the stalls watching herself in that dingy register office and the tears rolled silently down her face.

'Gracie, don't cry. I can't bear to see you so sad,' said Sam. He reached out as though he would comfort her, but she stood up and wiped her tears.

'I'll be fine,' she said. 'We'll take a break.' She managed a smile. 'And guess what? I've got an orange I might share with you.'

By midnight they were in Warth Mills and Sam described what the stage set would look like and how the scene would be lit. 'I'm wondering if it might be a good idea to have some scenes showing what was happening to you when you weren't with Jacob. It would add an extra dimension for the audience.'

Gracie wasn't convinced. 'But that's not in Jacob's play. We can't go adding things.'

'Well, it could be done,' said Sam, 'but we don't need to talk about that now.'

By two in the morning they were almost at the end. Rumours

were circulating in the camp that they were to be shipped out the next morning with nothing more than they stood up in. They turned the last page. For a moment they were confused: there was no more script. Instead there was a letter from Jacob, his final words to her.

Liebling

I write this letter in Warth Mills, but by tomorrow I will be gone from here. They told us today we are going by ship to Canada. That is all I know, but I suspect we will be held in a camp somewhere there until the war is over. The thought of not seeing you, maybe for years, breaks my heart, but I will endure it and so must you, Gracie.

Do you remember when we were in Blackpool and we talked about the theatre? You made me tell you about my dream that I might one day write a play. I think I said I would do it if I could find a story full of drama, tragedy and love. Well, I found my story – it was there all the time – the story of our love and the tragedy of being parted was the stuff of drama. Now, if our young soldier friend has done what he promised, you have our play in your hands. It's my gift of love to you, Gracie, and with every word I wrote I saw you, as if on a stage.

I often think about when we saw Romeo *and* Juliet. *You were mesmerised by the acting. You said, 'I wish I could do that,' and I told you that you could... if you wanted to. Gracie, don't give up on your dreams.*

I don't know how the play ends, maybe I'll never know, but if the worst happens, Gracie, don't be sad. Follow your heart and you'll find your happy ending. I love you more than life itself.

Jacob

They sat in silence.

For Gracie, the excitement of reading the play gave way to a deep sorrow. For a few hours Jacob had come alive again through his words and actions, and she had felt him with her as she watched their story unfold. But the sudden end of the play had shocked her. Of course Jacob was dead, but she had hoped that somehow, as for Romeo and Juliet, the story of their love would transcend the awful truth. Instead there was no ending, just despair.

She felt a touch on her hand and turned to see Sam looking at her with concern in his eyes. She had forgotten he was there.

'What are you thinking?' he said.

'I'm just so sad,' She gave a soft sigh. 'There is no ending, except death.' She needed to be alone. 'I'm going to bed now.'

'But, Gracie, can't you see? We can easily fix this. Yes, it's a tragedy, but sometimes they're the most powerful plays.'

'I can't talk about it now, Sam, I'm so tired.'

'Would it be all right if I looked through it again?'

'Of course you can, and thank you for helping me get it back. I'll see you in the morning.'

'Goodnight, Gracie.'

When she came down to breakfast, Sam was still sitting at the table with the play. 'Have you been up all night?' she asked.

'Not quite, I slept for a couple of hours. I made a lot of notes about how we can stage the play. I can see it all in my mind. As soon as you're ready, we'll go to the rehearsal rooms and start work on the script. I want to see what it sounds like – we'll act it out together.'

'Are you sure you want to do this?'

'Absolutely.'

'But there's no ending.'

'Gracie, that's not a problem. We'll find one, don't worry. We've got a fortnight to get the script ready before we cast it. There's no time to waste.'

The rehearsal rooms were round the corner from the Opera House in Wood Street. On the ground floor there was an insurance office, but Sam had the keys to a side door, beyond which there was a flight of stairs and a glazed door that led into a large function room, with a stage, a small office and a kitchen.

'After you went to bed last night I made two copies of the first scene in the raincoat factory so we could get cracking first thing. I asked Mrs B to take the whole script into the theatre office to have it typed up in duplicate.' Sam gave her a handwritten copy. 'You're playing yourself, of course, and I'll do Jacob's part and the others as they come up. We're going to work our way through the scene just getting a feel for the lines.'

'Sam, I've never been in a play. You need to get a proper actress to do it.'

'No. We need to do this together. You're the one who's lived this story and I'm only asking you to be yourself. Anyway, there's nobody watching. It's just you and me.'

She took the script from him and they began. After the first run-through they started again, and this time Sam gave her some direction: an expression; a gesture; where to walk. And, bit by bit, she began to enjoy it, and the memory of how she had felt in the factory that morning came flooding back to her.

They took a break and Sam asked how she was.

'I never imagined it would be like this.' Her face was flushed with excitement and concentration. 'How do you think it's going?'

'Oh, it's working really well. Now, if you're ready, we'll go over the scene again and this time I want you to add some of the bits where you're not with Jacob. Just make it up and we'll decide whether or not to put them in.'

Gracie was more at home with telling the story without a script and she was able to add other conversations. After each one Sam would stop her and scribble down what she had said.

They forgot about dinner, but around two o'clock Mrs Booth arrived with corned beef sandwiches and Vimto. 'Don't forget to eat them – I know you of old, Sam. And these are from the office, the next scene in Heaton Park.' She handed Sam some papers and chuckled. 'They said it were right good and just like the real Gracie. Any road, I'd better get back – these pantomime costumes are a bugger.'

By the time they had finished that scene, Sam had notes in pencil all over his script and Gracie was in her element. 'I like the way you tease Jacob,' he said. 'He's not quite sure what to make of you, but it's clear he's falling in love.'

Gracie was taken aback. 'Is it? I didn't see that at the time.'

'No, you didn't, and that's part of the charm. Gracie, the women in the audience will love the romance of it, and the men, well, they'll just fall in love.'

Gracie blushed. 'I don't think that'll happen.'

'Oh, it will, but don't worry about it. You've done really well. I think it's time to call it a day here, and tonight we'll look at those extra scenes you came up with.'

They had walked the length of Deansgate when the heavens opened. 'Come on,' said Sam. 'Let's get inside. The Shambles is nearby, and I'm sure you could murder a pint.'

The Old Wellington Inn was a black-and-white Tudor build-ing. From the outside it appeared to lean over the Shambles area as though the upper floor was curious to see who was coming through the door downstairs. Inside, it was dark oak, cured by centuries of pipe smoke, and a counter that was several inches lower than usual, having been made for shorter men, now centuries dead. They sat next to the roaring fire in winged armchairs with pints of beer and discussed the day. 'I think those little scenes you added should stay in,' said Sam. 'They develop your character, especially when you and your mother are together.'

Gracie shrugged her shoulders. 'I'm not so sure. Mam was a bit wary about Jacob to begin with.'

'But that's good – the audience can see the romance through someone else's eyes.' Gracie didn't answer.

'Is it difficult for you because you've fallen out with her?'

Gracie swirled the beer in her glass, not knowing what to say. Yes, Mam had deceived her for all those years, and she was still angry about that, but lately there had been times when she'd missed her home-spun common sense and advice, and sometimes she wondered if it was her grief at losing Jacob that had caused her to cut Mam out of her life.

Sam was still talking. 'I was thinking about a scene in the register office. It's so poignant with your mother there, looking after you.'

It had been a long day, concentrating so hard trying to please Sam. She really wasn't at ease putting her mother in the play, and he shouldn't have asked if that was because she had fallen out with her. It was none of his business. 'I don't want to talk about it,' she said. 'I'm going home now.' He stood to go with her. 'No, you stop here and finish your beer. I want to be on my own.' She left the pub and went out into the rain beating off the streets, but she hardly noticed it.

She hadn't gone very far before Sam caught up with her.

'Gracie, I'm so sorry. I didn't mean to upset you. I'd never do that.' She ignored him, but he kept pace beside her, pleading with her to stop. They passed the cathedral and he said, 'Let's stand in out of the rain. You're soaked to the skin.'

She stopped and looked at him. It was strange to see him without a smile. He seemed breathless, and when he spoke, his words were broken. 'I… never meant to… upset you, Gracie. Come back to the pub… or take shelter till it eases.'

'No, just leave me!' She hurried on.

Back at the digs she had a bath to take the chill from her bones and washed her hair, then lay in the warm water thinking about Sam. She shouldn't have upset him: he didn't deserve that. She wrapped her head in a towel, put on her dressing-gown and went down to the kitchen to dry her hair. She listened at the door for the sound of his voice, hoping he wasn't there. Everything was quiet – Mrs Booth must be alone. She opened the door slowly and peeped into the room. Sam was staring into the fire. Just as carefully she backed away closing the door…

'I know you're there, Gracie. Why don't you just come in?'

She clutched the collar of her dressing-gown under her chin and stepped into the room, her eyes lowered. 'Sam, I'm very sorry about before. I shouldn't have behaved like that.'

He sighed. 'It wasn't your fault. I pushed you too hard in rehearsal. I've been sitting here thinking how brave you are. You lost the man you loved and I'm asking you to live through the happiness and the pain all over again. It must be more than you can bear.'

She lifted her head. 'No, I want to do it. I have to do it for Jacob.'

'Are you sure?'

'Yes. I can't let him down, and I won't let you down either. We've worked on this together and I want to see it through.'

'All right, but you have to tell me if it's too much.'

'I will, don't worry.'

'Anyway, you'll want to dry your hair,' he said, 'so I'll leave you to it.'

'You don't have to go. I'm only going to sit in front of the fire. We can talk about tomorrow's rehearsal.' She sat on the rug, took a comb from her dressing-gown and began to coax out the tangles.

After a moment Sam said, 'Does that hurt?'

She smiled. 'No, but it's tiring on the arms, especially when I do the back.'

'Here,' he said, holding out his hand for the comb. 'I'll do it for you.' He knelt on the rug, took a tress of her hair and gently teased it until it was smooth, then moved on to the next section, and all the while he talked about the play. 'I think by the end of the week we'll have worked through the whole lot. Then this weekend I thought you and I could work on those extra Gracie scenes and I'll edit them into the text.' He suddenly stopped combing. 'Am I doing this right?'

'I take it you mean the hair, not the play. If you ever get tired of the theatre, you'd make a very good hairdresser.'

He pretended to be annoyed. 'Don't get cheeky with me.'

Gracie laughed. 'Once you've started you have to finish the job.'

When her hair was sleek and straight he handed the comb back to her and sat in the chair, watching her as she finished drying it in front of the fire. After a while she said, 'You were right what you said in the pub about it being difficult for me to have my mother as a character in the play.'

'Is that because you're still angry with her or because you miss her?'

'Hmm... Both, I suppose. More and more I wonder how she is and how she's getting on without me.'

'That letter she put inside the play, why don't you just read it? Then you'll know how she is.'

It was a good question, but too complicated to answer.

'I'm sure she's desperate to hear from you and she's probably very sorry for what she did. Why don't you go and get the letter and read it?'

Gracie twirled her hair round her finger. She'd been thinking exactly the same thing, but she knew whatever her mother had said would upset her. 'Maybe I'll read it later.'

'Gracie, look at me,' said Sam. 'Go and get the letter now, please.'

She sighed. 'All right, but she'd better not be asking me to meet that man!'

She returned with it and sat on the chair opposite Sam, but she made no attempt to open the envelope.

'Gracie...'

'I'll do it. I'll do it.' And she ripped it open. There was one sheet of paper with writing on both sides. When she had finished reading she covered her face with her hands, fingertips pressing on her eyes to hold back the tears. Stop it! Stop it! she told herself, refusing to remember the awful night when she'd run away from home.

First one hand was taken from her face, then the other. Her eyes were tightly closed. Then she was pulled gently to her feet and Sam's arms enfolded her. She clung to him. Her breathing slowed and her head cleared. This sadness was a realisation of the hurt she had brought on herself and, most upsetting of all, the hurt she had inflicted on her mother. She had no idea how long Sam held her in his arms, her head against his chest listening to his heart beat, while he ran his fingers through her hair.

'Gracie,' he whispered.

'Yes, Sam?'

'Shall I let you go?'

'Yes, Sam.' She stepped away from him and saw the sadness in his eyes. 'Thank you,' she said.

'You don't have to thank me.'

'Yes, I do, because you made me read the letter and I'm glad I did.' She watched the familiar smile spread across his face.

'Will you go and see your mother?'

'I'll think about it.'

Later, as she lay in bed, she read again her mother's letter and was surprised at how much her words echoed Maria's thoughts about her unborn child. The bond, already so strong when the child had not yet been born, must strengthen over the years, invisible but indestructible. Yet it wasn't that simple. A man had come between them and she had no room in her heart for the father who had never wanted her.

Into the following week they worked on the register-office scene. Gracie found it difficult to go through it all again, but Sam guided her as she remembered her joy at the thought that she would soon be married, and her despair as the minutes ticked by with no sign of Jacob. Sam read the part of her mother, and she found herself thinking of how difficult that day had been for her as well. How had she not seen that before? The scene afterwards with the news that Jacob had been arrested drained her, and Sam said, 'We'll finish there. You've done enough today, Gracie. I'm amazed by what you can do. Sometimes I find myself mesmerised by your performance, and I completely forget that I'm meant to be directing you.'

She hugged him in delight. 'Thank you, Sam. I can't tell you how much that's means to me.' When she stepped back, he wasn't smiling. Had she said something wrong?

'Em... why don't you go back to the digs and have a rest? I need to talk to the carpenters about the set.'

'All right,' she said. 'Shall I see you back there, then?'

He was looking again at his script. 'Yes... yes, I'll see you later.'

38

Sarah finished her shift at the Midland and made her way through Albert Square to Wood Street. She had memorised the details: number twenty, side door, up to the function room. At the top of the stairs she stopped to get her breath and, through the glass panel in the door, she saw her.

Gracie was on her feet, speaking, and she knew at once that she was telling one of her stories. How beautiful she looked, and when she suddenly laughed, Sarah thought, Thank God she's happy. The young man, Sam, appeared and she watched the two of them together and couldn't help smiling. She had taken to him as soon as they'd met. She had just come off her shift at the hotel and he had been waiting outside. 'Mrs Earnshaw? Could I have a word with you?' It was a miracle, so it was. In the space of a minute her life had changed.

When she walked into the room, Gracie looked puzzled and turned to Sam, frowning, but he was already coming towards her. 'Hello, Mrs Earnshaw,' he said. 'Thanks for coming.'

She gave him a nervous smile and turned to Gracie. 'It's good to see you, love.'

'Hello, Mam.'

They stared at each other, both wondering how to begin a conversation. It was Sam who eventually spoke: 'I'm going to the theatre to see how they're getting on with the props. I'll be back in an hour.'

When he had gone Sarah said, 'How are you?'

'I'm all right.'

'You look well.' She might have said, 'Better than the last time I saw you,' but she didn't. 'And you're working in the Opera House?'

'Yes.'

'Did you read my letter?'

Gracie nodded. 'Not right away. I read it last week.'

Sarah wondered why she hadn't bothered to read it before. 'All day I've been thinking about what to say to you. Never got beyond "I'm sorry". I just kept thinking about the day you were born.'

Gracie stared at her hands, interlaced her fingers…

'You were a beautiful baby, lots of black hair and blue eyes. I was so proud that you were mine. They let me keep you a couple of days, then brought the papers for me to sign to have you adopted.' She closed her eyes for moment. 'I wouldn't sign them. Oh, they were angry, said they had a good home for you to go to and I was a troublemaker. But I stood my ground and I brought you back to the house where I was lodging, without any notion of how I would manage. I knew David from next door, a nice lad, quiet, you know? I couldn't believe it when he came round and asked me to marry him. I was desperate to keep you and he said he'd bring you up as his own. Gracie, you might not believe me, but I grew to love David and I was devastated when he died.'

Gracie cleared her throat. 'I understand all that, but why

didn't you tell me he wasn't my father? Maybe not as a child, but when I was older.'

'I could say that I didn't think there was any point or I didn't want to upset you, and that would be true enough, but the real reason was David. He doted on you. I can still see him on his hands and knees with you on his back romping round the kitchen giving you thrupenny rides like the donkeys at Blackpool.'

'I don't understand.'

'I didn't tell you because I thought it would be a betrayal of David and everything he did for us. I worried that if I told you he wasn't your father you would be so disappointed that the love you had for him might have been spoiled. And, if I'm being honest, that you'd think less of me too.'

'You should have told me, Mam. You had no right to assume I'd stop loving him. He was a good father to me, and I don't think you understand that it was my real father barging into my life that sent me running out the door.'

'That should never have happened. I wanted to tell you about him, but how could I when you were waiting to hear whether Jacob was alive or dead? I hoped in time I could tell you and you'd get to know him, but it all went wrong.'

'We don't need him, Mam. We were always happy, just the two of us.'

Sarah closed her eyes for a moment, and when she opened them they were brimming with tears. 'But I need him, Gracie. I've fallen in love with him all over again. Yes, I loved David, but I've learned that you can fall in love more than once in a lifetime. Look at you – you loved Jacob, but you'll fall in love again.'

'I can't see that happening.'

'What about you and Sam? It looked like—'

'We're good friends, that's all.'

'And what about you and me? I've missed you so much.'

'Don't cry, Mam, please. I'm sorry I put you through all that. I wasn't myself, but since I've been working with Sam, I've been doing a lot of thinking and I know life wasn't easy for you, bringing up a daughter on your own. I owe you so much.'

'You won't disappear again, will you? I couldn't bear that.'

'No, I won't. I'll keep in touch and we'll see each other, but I'm not coming back home.'

'Do you think maybe some time in the future you might like to meet Martin? He's a good man – you'd like him.'

'Don't ask me that, Mam, I don't know.'

Sarah left the building glad that they were back on speaking terms – it was a start – and she hoped, in time, that they could mend their relationship. Gracie would be busy with the play rehearsals for a while, but she had promised to meet up over Christmas.

Gracie was ready for Sam when he came back and she'd have given him a piece of her mind if he hadn't looked so sheepish, putting his head round the door and asking, 'Is it safe for me to come in?'

'You'd better have a decent apology rehearsed!'

'Ah, Gracie, you knew you were going to make it up with her sooner or later. I just hurried it along a bit. Anyway, how did you get on?'

'Hmm... Well, you can't hold a grudge against your mam, when you think back to all she did for you, but I'm not going to meet Martin.' She shook a finger at him. 'No more med- dling, Mr Maguire!'

'Oh, I'll be far too busy for that once we get the cast in here on Monday.' He took a sheet of paper from his jacket pocket. 'I've been working on the cast list – tell me what you think.' He slid it across the table.

Her eyes widened. 'You've got me down to play Gracie! Sam, we talked about this before. I can't do it, I'm not an actress. I didn't even audition.'

'You've had the longest audition ever. Two weeks, the whole play, all in front of the director.'

'I can't believe this. We agreed I'd help you with the script, and I thought maybe I'd get a walk-on part. Sam, I can't be a main character when I've never been on the stage in my life!'

'You must have known I would cast you. Didn't I keep telling you how good you were?'

'I thought you were just being nice.'

Sam threw back his head and laughed. 'I was being nice, but that's because you were so good. I tell you, nobody could play this part as well as you. For goodness' sake, you know every thought in the character's head because she's you, and I've seen the way you can convey what's going on in her mind to anyone watching. I'm telling you, Gracie, that's a gift that only the best actresses possess.'

'So if I'm playing Gracie, why aren't you playing Jacob, like you did when we worked on it together?'

'I can't direct and act as well. It wouldn't work. Anyway, Paul's great – you're a good match.'

'I don't know, Sam. What if I can't—'

'You have to do it. Didn't Jacob say in his letter that you could act and you should follow your dream? He'd want you to do this. And I'm telling you, you must do it.'

39

The Sunday before Christmas was a crisp, clear day. Sam and Gracie had spent the morning finding the biggest tree they could fit into Mrs Booth's house. In the afternoon they decorated it, then hung paper chains to criss-cross the parlour and a paper bell from the lampshade. They left for their weekly fire-watching duty around five o'clock, just as the full moon was rising. On the theatre roof they went through their preparations: stirrup pumps full of water; sand in buckets; flask and butties. Then they settled down with their cushions and blankets. Gracie looked forward to the nights when she and Sam scanned the skies for German bombers dropping incendiaries. They had been lucky so far that nothing much had fallen on the theatre roof, but occasionally they had to act fast to make sure fires didn't take hold. Most of the time they sat and talked through the night, discussing the play, putting the world to rights and laughing more often than not. Sometimes Sam told her to put her head on his shoulder and go to sleep while he kept watch.

'You know what Mrs Booth told me?' said Gracie. 'That

traitor Lord Haw-Haw said on the radio from Germany that the Manchester people have bought their turkeys for Christmas, but they wouldn't be cooking them.'

'I can't believe that,' said Sam. 'There's not a turkey to be had in Manchester.'

'You shouldn't joke. He meant we'll be bombed before Christmas.'

'Well, it's a good night for it. That's a bomber's moon if ever I saw one.'

Just after six thirty the sirens sounded, and shortly before seven Gracie spotted the first of the enemy planes – Heinkels and Junkers, dropping incendiaries. They took up their positions and watched the first flames take hold on the roofs, setting them ablaze.

'From the look of it they're dropping over towards the cathedral and up near Piccadilly,' said Sam. But as they watched, a plane flew just above a barrage balloon and roared over their heads. Suddenly the roof was littered with incandescent flames, crackling and spitting like fireworks. They grabbed their buckets of water and stirrup pumps and went from one small fire to another, pumping water over the spreading flames. But the unattended ones were gaining a hold. 'Use the sand bucket to smother them, while I get more water,' Sam shouted.

She picked up the bucket and shovel and ran towards an incendiary close to the parapet wall. The bucket was heavy and she had her eyes on the blaze. She screamed as she tripped over something, tried to get her balance and, with no hands free to break her fall, she fell against the wall and darkness enveloped her...

★

'Oh, God! Gracie, please wake up, please.'

It was Sam's voice... She blinked at the torch light. 'I'm all right,' she said, and tried to sit up, but her head was throbbing and she fell back again. 'Where am I?'

'You're on the landing inside the roof door.'

Her head was spinning, but she struggled to her knees. 'We have to put the fires out!'

'Not you, Gracie. Stay here where you're safe. I'll do it.'

'No! I'm all right. Just help me up and we'll do it together.'

When they had extinguished the fires on the roof, they stood watching the flames that no one could put out, a beacon that would light the way to the heart of the city for the next wave of bombers carrying the high explosives to flatten Manchester. Sam put his arm round her shoulders. 'Come on, you daft apeth. It's time for us to take shelter, and don't you dare frighten me like that again.'

With his torch he led the way down through the theatre and on into the space beneath the stage. He turned on the light. 'We'll be safe here.'

They sat on a big sofa in the middle of the room and Gracie looked round in wonder. The ceiling was low and there were higgledy-piggledy piles of mismatched furniture and all manner of props. She peered up at the stage floor above her. 'Just think, in a month from now I'll be acting on that stage. I can't believe it. Sometimes I wonder what I'm doing in a play, or if somebody's going to realise I'm an imposter.'

Sam shook his head. 'Nobody will ever think that about you. You're going to be a huge success.'

'I can't think about that. What's important is Jacob's play. I want to do it justice.'

'Gracie, the play is wonderful because you are wonderful.' The look in his eyes was so intense that, for a moment, she thought he was going to kiss her. Her eyes closed and she held her breath... There was the merest touch of his lips on her forehead and when she opened her eyes again he looked so sad. 'Gracie, I—'

Suddenly there were heavy thuds, followed by explosions so powerful that the shock reverberated up through the ground and into their bodies. 'Come on,' he shouted. 'Help me turn over the sofa so we can shelter under it. The bombs shouldn't penetrate down here, but there might be some debris.'

They crawled under it, Sam at one end, her at the other. Neither spoke.

Gracie wondered whether she should ask him what he'd been going to say when the bombs started falling. Maybe, like her, he was going over in his mind what had just happened between them. To hear Sam say she was wonderful had warmed her heart, and when he looked at her there was such tenderness in his eyes... Then when she'd thought he was going to kiss her, she'd longed to feel his lips on hers and his arms around her. Those few seconds had left her stunned. Sam was her friend. She had been with him every day for the last month, working on the play, and she had to admit that she had found herself at odd moments watching him with fondness: when he smiled or threw back his head and laughed, when he was excited at an idea and talked so quickly she had to ask him to slow down. She remembered, too, the days when he would take off his jacket and she would find her eyes lingering on his broad shoulders, imagining him without his shirt.

'Penny for them,' he said.

She was tempted to say, 'Wouldn't you like to know?' but she pretended she was still thinking about the play. 'It would be lovely if we could send the audience away with their spirits raised.'

'A happy ending, you mean?'

'Well, I don't see how that could be, but Jacob's last words in his letter were positive.'

'We don't need to worry about it now. It'll be right in the end,' said Sam. 'The strangest things can happen in the theatre.'

By midnight there had been no all-clear, but there was a lull in the bombing and Sam said, 'Stay here. I'm going up on the roof to see what's happening.'

'Where you go, I go,' said Gracie.

'Well, you'd better keep close to me.'

They came out on the roof to an orange sky and, as far as the eye could see, there were buildings ablaze.

'Dear God,' said Sam. 'There'll be nothing left.'

'Look at the Royal Exchange. You can just see the dome and the flames around it. What about Oldham Road? We can't see it from here, can we? I hope to God Mam's safe in the pub cellar.'

There was a loud detonation not far away that set their ears ringing. 'That's down at Knott Mill,' said Sam. 'Come on, time to get back inside.'

The electricity had gone off when they returned, and in the pitch black Gracie's fears for her mother grew. 'Sam, what if something happens to Mam? I couldn't bear it.'

'She'll be in a shelter, and I promise you, when the all-clear sounds, we'll go straight to your house and I'm sure she'll be all right. I know it's upsetting, but try to sleep. It's going to be a long night. Here, lean on me,' and he switched off the torch to save the battery.

Gracie slept on and off, waking to the sound of explosions or shock waves that shook the building, until the all-clear sounded at six thirty in the morning, exactly twelve hours after the first alert. Sam switched on his torch and Gracie woke to f ind herself lying full length on the floor with her head on Sam's lap. 'Good morning,' he said. 'At least we're still in one piece.'

She sat up and yawned. 'Can we go and find Mam now?' Outside, the air was thick with dust and the smell of burning. They picked their way along Deansgate, what was left of it. Hotels and shops were gutted, several buildings were still ablaze and the gas mains had ruptured, forcing them to make detours. On Oldham Road there was debris everywhere, but fewer fires. As they came nearer to Pearson Street, Gracie could bear it no longer and grabbed Sam's hand. 'Let's run!'

The pub on the corner was still intact, but she could see piles of rubble strewn over the road, with smoke rising from them. 'There's bombed houses!' she shouted, and set off again, jumping over roof slates and glass, Sam behind her. Her heart stopped. She let out a shout, 'It's still here!' and then she was banging on the door. 'Mam, are you there?' she screamed.

The door opened and there she was. They hugged each other and cried and laughed at the relief. Sarah told them she had been in the pub cellar all night. They knew the bombs had been very close, and when they'd come out after the all-clear, they'd seen that the end of the street had gone. 'We were two houses away from it,' she said. 'Thank goodness you've come – I'm still shaking. Now, tell me, did you come past the Victoria Hotel? Is it still standing?'

'We did, but it's all gone. It must've taken a direct hit.' Gracie saw the panic on her mother's face. 'What is it?'

'Martin was staying there last night after his meeting. He was coming to see me today. Oh, God, if something's happened to him...'

Her words sent a shiver up Gracie's spine. It was happening again, only this time it was her mother who was terrified that she had lost someone she loved. She hugged her and tried to comfort her. 'There are plenty of shelters near the hotel. He'll be in one of those, I'm sure.'

But Sarah wasn't listening. 'I'll get my coat and go and look for him.'

'No, Mam, it's chaos in the town. Better to wait here.' Hadn't her mother given her the same advice when Jacob didn't arrive at the register office? 'Why don't I make us some breakfast while we wait for him?'

They ate the bread and jam and drank strong tea and Sarah, calmer now with Gracie beside her, talked about Martin. 'I knew it was too good to be true, finding him after all those years. I couldn't believe it when I met him again. It was the strangest thing – it didn't feel like twenty years, it was as if we'd seen each other just the other day. We loved each other long ago and we still loved each other.' She shook her head at the wonder of it. 'He helped me when I lost you, Gracie. He kept saying, "We'll find her, don't worry," and now I can't bear to think that he might not get the chance to know you.' She put her head in her hands, a picture of despair, and Gracie's heart went out to her. She would give anything to have Martin come through the door and spare her mother's pain.

There was a pounding at the door and the sound of people shouting. Sarah was out of her chair, racing to open it, Gracie and Sam behind her. It was Ted in his ARP uniform, grey with ash. 'We've a kiddie trapped in one of the bombed houses. We need help to remove the rubble.'

They joined the people already in the chain while Ted and another ARP warden climbed over the pile of debris and began carefully to remove the rubble. The work was slow and Sam called, 'We need to work in two teams, the strongest people for the heavier stuff and another for the lighter. I'll come up and help you.'

There was a shout further down the street. 'I'll shift the heavy stuff too.'

Gracie heard her mother scream and turned to see her run towards the airman who had offered to help. He caught her in his arms and kissed her. It was Martin, her father.

The rescue operation went on apace, and an hour later there was a call for silence. Everyone held their breath.

'We can hear her crying!' Ted shouted. They waited as Sam, Martin and Ted discussed what to do. Then Gracie held her breath as Martin lowered Sam through a gap into the remains of the house. The minutes ticked by, until she heard Martin shout, 'We've got her!' The child emerged and was handed down the chain. There was cheering all around her, but Gracie didn't take her eyes off Martin as he leaned over the gap, his hand outstretched. She could see it was taking all his strength to haul Sam out. He slipped, righted himself and pulled again. Now Ted was there too reaching out... Sam's head emerged and seconds later he was lying on top of the rubble. Gracie breathed again.

The four of them came into the kitchen, elated at the rescue of the little girl. Gracie took it all in: Martin and Sam shaking hands; her mother gazing up at Martin, and the casual way he put his arm round her; Sam, covered with dust, grinning at her, and her sudden urge to kiss him.

It was a moment before she realised her mother was speaking. 'Gracie, this is Martin.' He held out his hand. She went to shake it, then hugged him instead. They sat round the table and Martin explained that the Victoria Hotel had been evacuated when the incendiaries had taken hold. 'We were directed to the Grosvenor Hotel on the other side of Deansgate – it had a shelter in the basement – and when the all-clear sounded we went up to the dining room for breakfast. All very civilised,' he said.

Martin had a four-day pass – his last recruits had finished their training and the next batch weren't due until Boxing Day – and Sarah asked Gracie and Sam to join them on Christmas Day.

On the way back to their digs Sam asked, 'What did you think about Martin?'

'He makes Mam happy and, yes, I liked him. I'm not saying having a father again after all these years isn't strange.' She smiled. 'But I think I could get used to it.'

Manchester suffered two more nights of heavy bombing and on Christmas Day, as they walked to her mother's house, Gracie and Sam were devastated by the terrible destruction: buildings still burning, others stark black shells, homes and factories destroyed.

'How will this ever be put right?' she asked.

'I don't know,' said Sam, 'but it will, because Manchester people are awkward buggers and they never give up.'

When they arrived, Sarah and Martin were waiting for them with glasses of sherry, clearly excited. 'We have an announcement,' said Martin. 'I've asked Sarah to marry me and she said yes.'

Gracie was stunned, but one look at her mother's smiling face and she hugged and kissed them both. Sometimes happy endings do happen.

Sarah had done her best with the Christmas dinner: a piece of ham, roast potatoes, carrots and Brussel sprouts with plenty of gravy. But the best thing was the company, what

Martin called 'the craic', the four of them round the table, her family and Sam.

That night, she lay in bed thinking about the day – the devastation in the streets, the joy of her mam and Martin – and on the way home, with Sam at her side, her sudden realisation that she was falling in love with him.

After Christmas the rehearsals for *Gracie's Gift* resumed with a sense of urgency and, at times, blind panic. With each day that passed Gracie looked for any sign that Sam might be attracted to her, but all she could say for sure was that they were best friends and he liked being with her.

In the final week of rehearsals, everyone involved knew that the play had become more and more powerful, and Gracie was sure it was something to do with the Christmas bombings: the ruined city; the mounting death toll in the newspapers; the fear that it could happen again at any time. Even the hardened stagehands could be seen in the wings wiping their eyes, but she was still worried about the ending.

'Jacob is dead and Gracie is grief-stricken. Where's the hope in that, Sam? Now more than ever we need to lift people's spirits.'

'There must be something we could do,' he said. 'We'll look through Jacob's original manuscript tonight – see if it sparks an idea.'

They sat together at the table and began to read but there was something about seeing Jacob's handwriting again and the smell of the paper that evoked memories of the last time they had been together. She hadn't cried for him in many weeks, but in her mind's eye she saw him in the mill, still smiling as they took him away. Her eyes blurred and she wiped away the tears before they could fall, but Sam didn't miss anything. 'I haven't seen you cry in a while. I thought maybe—' He stopped himself. 'We won't do this, now.'

'Yes, we will,' she said fiercely. 'I'm fine.'

It was midnight when they finished reading, and they had found no obvious solution to the missing ending.

'I'll go to bed now.' Her voice was full of disappointment. 'Maybe if I sleep on it something will come.'

'I'll take another quick look, you never know,' said Sam.

Alone in her room, she wondered what Jacob would make of his play now that it was about to go on stage at the Opera House. 'I hope you like it,' she whispered.

There was a soft knock on her bedroom door and Sam said, 'Are you awake?'

She sat up in bed. 'Yes, come in.'

He had the play in his hand and she could see at once that he had found something. 'I read Jacob's letter again and it came to me. The play's the thing, you see. So we start the play with the soldier coming to your door and giving you the parcel. You open it up and the idea is, as you begin to read it, the play comes to life on the stage. Then at the end we see you again, as though you've just finished reading it, but now the audience hears Jacob's voice, and he says, "I don't know how the play ends, maybe I'll never know, but if the worst happens, Gracie, don't be sad. Follow your heart and you'll find your happy ending." What do you think?' Sam's eyes were bright with excitement.

'It's good,' she said. 'It's like what's happening in Manchester right now. The worst has happened, and now we have to believe that everything will come right in the end.' She laughed at his cleverness.

'We'll try it out in rehearsal tomorrow,' said Sam. 'Now you need to get some sleep.'

On the Saturday night after the dress rehearsal most of the cast and stagehands went to the Sawyers Arms for a few drinks. Everyone was in good humour, the new ending was more hopeful about the future, and they were looking forward to the opening night on Monday. Gracie, against her better judgement, drank two pints too quickly, and when someone decided to play some boogie-woogie music on the piano, one of the stagehands asked her to dance. When the music switched to a slow smooch he pulled her close, but just then Sam tapped him on his shoulder and stepped in. She was in his arms, where she had longed to be, and it felt like Heaven.

When the music stopped, she looked up to see him smiling at her. 'Shall I let you go, Gracie?'

She smiled. 'No, Sam... not this time.'

He bent his head and kissed her full on the lips, then kissed her and kissed her again. Her heart was racing. Her best friend, her love... When she opened her eyes, he took her hand and led her out into the cold January night. 'Gracie, I'm so sorry. I never meant that to happen, even though I've wanted to kiss you for so long.'

She was confused. 'What's the matter, Sam?'

'I want you to know that if things had been different and I'd met you before you fell in love with Jacob, I'd have loved you just as much as he did. And maybe you'd have loved me too. But every day on the stage I see how much you love him, how loyal you are to him, and what I did just now was so thoughtless. Forgive me, Gracie.' He turned to walk away.

She caught his arm. 'But you don't understand, listen—'

'Let me go, Gracie, I can't say any more. I need to think. Ask one of the lads to see you home.'

She didn't sleep a wink. Twice she got up and went to his bedroom door, but each time she lost her nerve. What would he think of her, coming to him in the middle of the night?

In a way, what Sam had said was right. She did love Jacob and always would, but she loved Sam too, of that was she was certain. The simple truth was that love wasn't rationed – it didn't run out. She had enough love for both of them. She just had to make Sam realise that.

In the early morning, she got out of bed and retrieved Jacob's play from her dressing-table to read again his final letter: *Gracie, don't be sad. Follow your heart and you'll find your happy ending.* She smiled. 'Thank you, my love.'

She got dressed quickly, and left Sam a note: *I'm at the theatre, come quick.*

The morning was cold and bright, just what she needed to clear her head, when so much depended on getting this right. She was leaning against a pillar next to the *Gracie's Gift* poster when he arrived. 'Best play ever or your money back,' she said.

Well, at least she had made him smile.

'Why did you want me to meet you here?'

'You'll see, let's go in.'

Sam switched on the lights and they went on to the stage. 'Now what?' he said.

Gracie explained: 'We've already added the bit at the end when Gracie finishes reading the play and we hear Jacob's words that send the audience away full of hope. But I want more than that – I want a happy ending.'

'But the story doesn't have one.'

'Not yet, but Gracie's story isn't over, Sam. You see, I want her to fall in love again.'

He frowned, not understanding at first, but then a slow smile, beginning at the corners of his mouth, crossed his face and melted her heart. 'Really?' he said.

'We need to write it together, you and me.' She took up her position on the stage. 'I'll start,' she said. 'This new character, we'll call him Sam, is very handsome, kind, great fun.'

'Clever, you've missed out clever.' Sam played along. 'He's been Gracie's friend for a while, looks after her, and wants her to be happy. Oh, and he thinks she's beautiful. At the end of the play he comes to see if she's all right, because sometimes she gets upset.'

Sam crossed the stage and they stood facing each other. 'Gracie, I know how much Jacob means to you and he'll be with you always. But the world is such a sad place and we have to find a way to be happy again.' He took her in his arms. 'I've loved you from the moment we met, but I hid it, my love, because you were grieving. I was happy just to be with you.'

'And I needed you, Sam, but I didn't know that all the while love was waiting in the wings. Lately, I sensed it there, but I was scared to love again until I remembered Jacob's words – find your happy ending, he said, and that's what I've done. I've found you.'

'Are you telling me you love me, Gracie?'

'Yes, Sam, with all my heart.'

'And this is the moment when I kiss you and the lights go out, isn't it?'

She nodded. 'But after that we'll be together for the rest of our lives.'

★

Gracie stood in the wings, closed her eyes and took a deep breath. The story was waiting to be told. Mam and Martin would be in their seats in the front stalls alongside Doris, Albert and their other neighbours from Pearson Street. Maria would have left her baby girl with her mother to be there with their friends from the raincoat factory. She felt an arm round her waist and there was Sam. He kissed her neck. 'You'll be wonderful, my darling. I love you.'

The house lights dimmed and the audience fell silent. Now there was just her and Jacob. 'Thank you for my gift,' she whispered, crossed the stage and walked into the spotlight.

Acknowledgements

My heartfelt thanks go to Judith Murdoch my agent, Rosie de Courcy, Sophie Robinson and the team at Head of Zeus, and Anne Doughty for her support and friendship. I'm also indebted to Graham Phythian for his comprehensive book *Blitz Britain: Manchester and Salford* and to Denise and Errol Gross for their contributions. Above all, thanks to my family for their love and support.